Janessa

Enjoy!

[illegible]

12/2014

[illegible]

12/2014

A Monumental Journey 2

In search of the First Tribe

By

Richard L Cederberg

authorHOUSE™
1663 Liberty Drive, Suite 200
Bloomington, Indiana 47403
(800) 839-8640
www.AuthorHouse.com

This book is a work of fiction. People, places, events, and situations are the product of the author's imagination. Any resemblence to actual persons, living or dead, or historical events, is purely coincidental.

First published by AuthorHouse 03/28/05

ISBN: 1-4208-2199-7 (e)
ISBN: 1-4208-3132-1 (sc)
ISBN: 1-4208-2197-0 (dj)

Library of Congress Control Number: 2004195547

Printed in the United States of America
Bloomington, Indiana

This book is printed on acid-free paper.

Dedications

First and Foremost

I'd like to dedicate my second novel, *A Monumental Journey 2, In search of the First Tribe,* and those yet unwritten, to **my blessed and gifted wife Michele Elizabeth Cederberg**, and also **my very talented and inspirational son Garrett.** Your life Garrett, how you have expressed yourself and your strong spiritual convictions, has inspired me to create one of my favorite characters in the Monumental Journey series. Each day I am grateful for the wisdom, encouragement, inspiration, and love you both have bestowed unselfishly to me.

Secondly

My father Lloyd William Cederberg, I praise God for the long awaited reconciliation between us in 2004, and I am thankful for the ineffable encouragement you have offered me. Because of this refreshing amendment, I proffer this poem by the **Norwegian poet and novelist *Bjornst Jerne Bjornson*** (1832-1910)

Lo, this land that lifts around it
Threatening peaks, while stern seas bound it,
With cold winters, summers bleak
Curtly smiling, never meek,

Tis the giant we must master,

Till he work our will the faster.

He shall carry through the clamor,

He shall haul and saw and hammer,

Turn to light the tumbling torrent,

All his din and rage abhorrent

Shall, if we but do our duty

Win for us a realm of beauty

Thirdly

My daughter Crista Michele, Good things come to those that diligently press forward and hope. Don't ever let go of your dreams!

Special thanks to:

1. *Michele E. Cederberg*

Photos, illustrations, art direction, and author picture

Sweeterberg@aol.com

Featured in chapters one, three, thirteen, fifteen, twenty-two b, twenty-four, twenty-five, twenty-seven, twenty-nine, thirty-six, thirty-nine, forty-one, and forty-four a

2. *Dave E. Bunnell*

www.goodearthgraphics.com/under_earth

dave@goodearthgraphics.com

Featured in chapters fourteen, sixteen, and forty-four b

3. *Photos by Russell*

Stockholm Sweden

rgc717@earthlink.net

Featured in chapters twenty-two a, thirty-five, and forty-five

4. *Christine Shaw*

Foxhill BathUK

Thanks so much for the exceptional picture of you and a very special dolphin friend. Featured in chapter five

Prologue

After departing Flores Island, in the Azorean Archipelagoes, the 21st of April, we bid farewell to the European continents westernmost waters. Thankfully the weather conditions had been exceedingly complimentary on our crossing, allowing us to navigate tremendous distances swiftly and safely. Not once had we been exposed to the magnetic drought bands ravaging various areas on the planets surface. The journey had been changing my life in profound ways, and was also demanding from me a mental discipline, and physical fortitude, I never knew I possessed. My life in Aberdeen Scotland as an intellect, with a doctorate in English literature, Scandinavian Mythology, and the Ancient Northern languages, had been child's play compared to the demanding life God had prearranged for me along with these steadfast Christian people aboard the schooner *Heimdall*. We had pledged before the Most High God, to retrace the Rognvald Vikings ancient route to the western coasts of America, in our search for the First Tribe.

In the early 1470's, fifteen ninety-five foot wooden vessels, sanctioned by the beloved King Agar, and designed and constructed by the metallurgist, inventor, craftsman, Gamelin, departed the vast northern Scottish mainland, a small island in the Pentland Firth, and many of the southern Orkney Islands, to find new lands to raise their families in. They were eager to be detached from the rampaging and bloodthirsty Baaldurian's. These were a wicked tribe separated from the original Viking nation by their choice to follow the antediluvian blood witchcrafts instead of Jesus Christ.

Part of our journey would require us presenting the First Tribe with the greatest symbol of Viking faith in the Holy Risen Christ ever created, the Tempest, a sword we had miraculously discovered diving at the Shallows of Three Rocks, north of Concello de Carino, in the Bay of Biscay. The presentation had to be accomplished before the day of many collisions, a foretold battle between the Rognvald and Baaldurian Viking tribes. According to the etchings on the Tempest, and innumerable ancient writings, this epoch confrontation was destined to occur on an island somewhere in southern Alaska. The inspiring inscription on the Tempest sword said it all, *"Christ before all else"*, and we had all made this ancient Viking mandate our daily proclamation as well. I never wondered anymore what I would do with my days; I was now part of a dedicated team, dependant on one another and the Holy Spirit to survive. Together we'd been given an extraordinary vision, and daily we prayerfully struggled to accomplish it.

Brisk salty air, the wind snugly held by large white sails, sunburned, bizarre circumstances, extraordinary people, bone tired, having our lives threatened, and confined for weeks at a time on a beautifully constructed, three masted, one hundred and twenty foot computerized schooner, was now my life as well as my crewmates, and we were living it with passion. Our adventures thus far had challenged us well beyond our personal capabilities, and at times we all struggled piteously with hopelessness and fear. Still though we were resolute, and our faith was strong in what Christ was doing in our lives. We all understood that being together and prayerfully focused, that we would continue unraveling, and solving, many ancient and remarkable mysteries.

"Together and wretched we sail the raging unknown to find destinies embrace and complete the vision in honor to our great king."

An unknown Rognvald scribe

One

Isla Socorro

"Captain Olaf," John's imperturbable voice crackled over the radios. "Sorry to bother you this time of morning, the radar is showing Isla Socorro twenty miles off our port bow sir; we've finally made it."

A few moments passed silently.

"Copy that John," the Captain groaned, reluctantly swinging his feet off the side of the bunk. Glancing over at the 4:47am on the digital clock staring back benignly in a reddish glow, he yawned deeply and rubbed his face.

"I'm on my way, give me a few minutes."

June 26th

It had been sixty-seven days since we'd departed the Isle of Flowers in the Azorean Archipelagoes, and the memory of the decisive victory over the two Mortiken vessels still humbled everyone when we discussed it. Thankfully, Garrett, Helga, and Rorek were able to locate the problem with the "Chameleon Surface Adapting Technology", and had repaired it within minutes.

"It was just an oversight," Rorek reiterated more than a few times during the repair. "One of the modular boards wasn't locked into place when we installed the main unit on deck. I suppose the earthquake must have loosened it and the contacts were lost."

Simply locking the board into place had brought our new laser defense system back on line, and we felt delighted because of it. The professor in Rabat, Jonah and Roxanne communicated with regularly, had sent another encrypted e-mail on April 25th; in it he'd confirmed that Amalek Baaldur and Krystal Blackeyes were not on the two vessels we'd destroyed off Northern Flores. Divine intervention had kept them both hidden on the third vessel anchored off the island of Pico. Considering this unfortunate news, I assumed that God still had plans for these two, and had a strong suspicion they would both be involved in our lives in the upcoming weeks and months. Fifty plus Mortiken had been destroyed on the two vessels, and 600,000 Euro was lost. Apparently the devilish duo were planning on rendezvousing with the two Mortiken vessels we'd destroyed on the 22nd to transfer the large sum of money aboard their vessel. Rumor had it that after transferring the Euros they would be making the long journey to Panama to use these proceeds to help finance the colossal Mortiken military installation being constructed in the Chagres National Park outside of Portobello. Fortunately though, their plans had been thwarted by the courageous crew of the *Heimdall,* and for this encouraging incident, we certainly praised God.

Panama was autocratic now, and the Mortiken were its rulers. Having been granted absolute autonomy, they were now in control of one of the most critical transitional points on the planet, the Panama Canal. The endeavor was being financed, in part, by untraceable Middle Eastern drug cartels, and this disturbing association was affecting canal levies, local governments and had begun creating havoc. Everything was being radically restructured to accommodate the emerging Mortiken agenda, this ostensibly being the attempt to control the worldwide flow of commodities and people in the most strategic places on planet earth.

It now appeared that all sea going traffic, tankers, freighters, pleasure cruises etc., opposed to the Mortiken agenda was being re-routed around the tip of South America. All these vessels were being strongly compelled to buy their fuel from several Middle Eastern controlled fuel depots in the city of Montevideo in the Rio de la Plata inlet, and near the Isla de Coiba, offshore western Panama. Because of the insalubrious political changes in Panama, many of the locals were relocating down to Colombia in expectation of violently unstable scenarios erupting in the near future; it certainly didn't look promising for the Panamanian people. The professor also confirmed that the last report he'd intercepted, showed Amalek

Baaldur and Krystal Blackeyes heading back into the Mediterranean for a high-level meeting in the Aegean Sea, either on the island of Serifos or Kithnos. Those present at this summit would be representing several geographic areas. Middle Eastern financiers would be there, along with someone high up in the Russian military, and also several governmental, and military dignitaries from Sonora & Sinaloa Mexico. Why Mexico was involved was baffling the professor. He promised, that in the weeks to come he'd inform us immediately when anything new or relevant came across his, or any of his associate's desks. The professor also wished us well in our endeavors, and hoped that someday he might be able to visit us, or we could visit him in Rabat. We were now a part of his Virtual Informational Network, and we all felt exceptionally thankful for our association with him.

Jonah stayed aboard the *Heimdall* until we'd reached Salvador in the Brazilian state of Bahia, on the morning of April 29th. Located on the southeastern promontory of Todos os Santos, this welcomed pause offered us a breather from our grueling non-stop journey. We stayed two nights on the tip of the Salvador peninsula, several blocks from the Barra lighthouse, in the Hotel Albergue Barra. Before Jonah departed, on the afternoon of April 30th, we all had dinner together and saw some of the beautiful sites in the Cidade Baixa (the lower city). Jonah booked his flight from Salvador to Mexico City on-line aboard the *Heimdall* on April 25th, and after a stay of two days in Mexico City Jonah would then be intercepting a flight that would take him to San Diego California where a friend would be picking him up at Lindbergh field and taking him to their log home in Pine Valley. Jonah's previously planned archeological expedition would take himself, and twenty-one others, to the mysterious Lake Powell in south-central Utah. This new expedition would begin on the 11th of May, and require forty-four days to conclude.

The *Heimdall* set sail again on the 1st of May in the early am. We would require a minimum of four refueling/restocking stops before reaching our destination in San Diego. The first one, after we'd left Salvador, was the city of Stanley in the Falkland Islands also known as the Islas Malvinas, and we arrived there on May 16th. The areas around Stanley were large windswept terrains, mostly devoid of trees, ugly and desolate really, and we could hardly wait to leave. On the 19th of May we thankfully left the Falklands and sailed non-stop until we'd reached Callao Peru on the 7th of June. On the 10th of June we left Callao and headed for San Cristobal in the Galapagos Islands. We arrived there safely on June 14th and stayed until the 19th resting, writing, photographing, scuba-diving, and partaking of Betsy's superb gastronomy. In this extraordinary place, also known as the Colon Archipelagoes we all experienced another wonderful respite from our personal responsibilities and rigorous traveling agenda.

Captain Olaf and Rorek were especially fond of these reclusive islands. Having been here twice in the last twelve years; they had acquired artifacts and several framed photos that were strewn throughout the *Heimdall,* depicting in colorful detail the islands of Genovesa, San Salvador, Pinter, and Isabela. In the Captain and Rorek's berth they also had three (in a series of ten) of Herman Melville's beautifully descriptive sketches of the Galapagos entitled the "Encantadas".

The Galapagos Islands are all volcanic in nature, having vast smooth beaches, and mountainous interiors that culminate in the centers with high craters.

Helga and Betsy loved these vast expanses of beaches and soon after we'd arrived, several mornings were spent exploring them. Rolf the Wolfhound also loved these long expanses of sandy beach and for several afternoons, along with me, Garrett, and Betsy, he ran and played fetch for many hours, chasing and barking at every animal he came into contact with. One afternoon Rolf accidentally stumbled upon a herd of burrowing land lizards sunning themselves. When he deposited himself unexpectedly into their midst, barking and acting crazy, they all immediately let out a loud screeching sound, scrambled to their feet, and began furiously digging down into the soft sand of the hillsides to escape. Well, not to be outdone, our impulsive Rolf followed suit and began digging along with the grunting lizards. It was obvious that he was not going to be outdone; Rolf's fervent digging was producing a blizzard of sand flying in every direction, much of it falling on the lizards. Absolutely frustrated with his boisterous barking and the sand showers, the huge lizards all stopped digging, herded together, and with a piteous opus of snorting sounds, took off running as fast as they could into the sand dunes to escape Rolf's rambunctious temperament. When Rolf finally realized that he'd been snubbed, and his new friends weren't going to play with him, he sat down with a flustered wuff, looked around with a questioning expression, sneezed several times, barked indignantly in the direction of the fleeing lizards, and then slowly trotted out towards the ocean and grabbed a piece of driftwood to begin another game of fetch. Such was the incessant impulsiveness of our new wolfhound, and without uncertainty, we were all entertained daily by his endearing and unpredictable behavior.

The Galapagos Islands are also a profuse volcanic sanctuary, teeming with hundreds of varieties of wildlife. Everywhere we went we saw an astonishing amount of birds, including beautifully colorful flamingos, flightless cormorants, finches, and even penguins in several of the secluded costal areas. On several of our scuba dives we encountered a number of species of giant tortoise which we all successfully hitched rides on and played with for hours. Also, on one of those memorable days, an unusually playful marine lizard in the iguana family swam underwater with us for thirty minutes and thoroughly entertained us.

After we'd left the Galapagos, the afternoon of the 19th, we began sailing non-stop towards the Revillagigedo Archipelagoes. Our first stop would be the Isla Socorro where all of us would be exploring the celebrated cave inland from the Cabo Pearce peninsula. We would be attempting to understand the runic petraglyphs and pictographs in abundance there and hopefully find more clues and information to guide us in our search for the First Tribe.

During the extent of the journey, we'd faithfully struggled to understand the Tempest swords mystifyingly etched maps, and unique design. The metallurgist Gamelin had created something almost unfathomable, and it was stretching our combined efforts to comprehend the complexities of his exquisite craftsmanship. Somewhere between the Falklands and Callao Peru Roxanne had haphazardly placed the sword down on the highly reflective research table between two mirrors, and what we beheld after that stunned us. Sunlight on the swords etchings reflected into the first mirror and then back into the second seemed to boil right up off the table in an unfathomable holographic image. Similar to standing in a room with mirrors on both walls, and seeing an image reflected into infinity, this combination of rudiments, and the concentrated reflective angle of the sun, created an intensely three dimensional effect around us. As far as we could tell, it appeared that two different geography's, in two different locations, one on each side of the sword, were hovering mysteriously around us. After carefully photographing the anomaly, from several different angles, Roxanne and I carefully scanned the images and uploaded the files to Jonah.

Over the last several years Jonah had established a friendship with someone inside the MODIS project, a very intelligent, but eccentric older man who had gone on several of Jonah's archaeological expeditions to Utah. The MODIS Company utilized MRIS, "moderate resolution imaging spectroradiometry" to procure super high resolution pictures of planet earth from the Terra/Aqua (EOS-AM) satellites. This information/data was processed in thirty-six spectral bands, and mid-wavelength infra-red, in a geometric instantaneous field of view. After this data was cross referenced with a program of global geographical grids, and virtually laid over a map of earth's latitudes and longitudes, two possible locations came back. One of them appeared to be the Revillagigedo Archipelagoes and the other was below the Coast Ranges somewhere in Alaska on the Revillagigedo Island, two entirely different geographies with the same name. It was obvious that this discovery was something far more than mere happenstance. How could Gamelin have known about these two different places, having never been to either one? What did these maps mean?

Two

Morning mischief and preparing to disembark

"John thanks for the wakeup call," the Captain murmured, stumbling up the wheelhouse stairs. Yawning deeply and rubbing his eyes, he glanced over John's night-time logs, quietly nodded in approval, and then stretched.

"Man, I'm ready for another week off, how bout you?"

"I'm with you there Olaf; it has been a long journey, really bloody long. What do you wanna do now sir?"

"Let's get the crew up, strike sails, and wait for sunrise, I'll tell them myself," the Captain said with a mischievous chuckle.

Impulsively rubbing the still painful scar on his cheek, he reached for the radio.

"Looks like another long day for the *Heimdall* crew," John continued, "do you want to turn off the spotlight now?"

The Captain nodded he did, yawning and stretching several times as he keyed on the radio. Acting as if he was looking around for something, Olaf impulsively took a long gulp from John's steaming coffee cup; after he'd realized what he'd done he looked up at John, smiled sheepishly, and shrugged his shoulders.

"Crew, this is your beloved Captain. Sorry bout the hour folks, but I just had to tell somebody that we'd arrived! Yes . . . you heard me right, after sixty-seven days of sailing; we've finally arrived! Let's get motivated ya lackey riff-raff! Hop to it, I want the sails down in thirty minutes ya slimy scum or someone's not getting their ration a rum! YO HO . . . let's go we've got work to do! Rise and shine and greet another glorious day ya lazy swab's!" The Captain laughed raucously as he put down the radio. "I always wanted to be Captain Bligh for a day, it feels GOOD!" Everyone mumbled sleepily on the radios, confirming they were getting up.

"The weather reports are good," John informed, chuckling at the Captains antics and flicking off the Navtex receiver. "I haven't heard a bad report for this area all night." John turned and grinned when Olaf began mumbling under his breath.

"Is something wrong sir?" John queried.

"Uh . . . no, it's nothing my friend, nothing really, I was just reminiscing. It's hard to believe what we've been through since we left Aberdeen with Gabriel. I can't ever remember cramming so much life and adventure into so short a period of time."

"Oh . . . you're right about that Olaf," John shook his head. "When Gabriel joined up, everything changed for us that's a fact! He's a very gifted and intelligent young man, and his involvement with the mission has changed all our lives for the better."

"Hey . . . thanks for that big John," I said, having just reached the wheelhouse stairs. "I love you too, thanks for the compliment brother. Looks like another long day for us huh?"

"Looks that way son and good morning to you." the Captain nodded.

"Morning to you too Captain, what can I do to help?" With a yawn and a stretch I reached out and shook the Captain and John's hands. Before the Captain could answer though, a sudden boisterous youthful intrusion rowdily interrupted us.

"WUZZUP most pusillanimous dudes," Garrett bellowed with a hearty laugh.

Bounding up the stairs he had appeared suddenly in the wash of light flooding outside the wheelhouse door. A wild mass of disheveled hair stuck up everywhere on his head, and hung down over one eye. The only thing he had on this morning was what he'd slept in, an enormous pair of baggy red shorts.

"Hey . . . can you dig that word Dr. Gabriel, I learned that hand-grenade last night when I was e-mailin my pop." I smiled, and gave Garrett a nod, but couldn't help but feel puzzled with his choice, especially in the present company.

"Hey . . . it's a real good one little brother, but I didn't think any of us were lily-livered or cowardly dude." Garrett's jovial demeanor quickly changed and he grunted with indignance.

"Whatever man, I was just messin around. Why can't you just flow sometimes Dr. Nerdoid?" Garrett was right, and I felt a warm flush of embarrassment beginning to fill my face.

"I cut some serious zees last night dudes," Garrett continued, changing the subject, "probably cuz I didn't have to listen to big John sawin logs all night."

Now Garrett's impulsive humor had turned into gut-wrenching guffaws, and when I saw him reach in and irreverently pull open one of John's shoestrings, I knew something was about to happen. Jumping back out of the doorway he began taunting John and then he openly challenged him to a boxing match. Captain Olaf quickly grabbed the big wheel when John let go, it was apparent that he'd finally had enough of Garrett's shenanigans. Posturing aggressively for a moment, John roared fiercely.

"YOU SCRAWNY RUNT, I'm gonna thrash your crème puff butt!" Quickly moving out of the way I gasped as John literally flew out of the wheelhouse door and tackled Garrett, immediately he put him into a firm headlock.

"Owwww . . . dude you wanna mess with me you dilapidated old Navy fart, I'm gonna pound on you till you beg fur mercy," Garrett croaked, groaning under the increasing pressure. Suddenly awakened by the uproar, Rolf crawled out from underneath the raft barking and shaking vigorously. John and Garrett were passionately involved in a wild exhibition now, and both started laughing raucously when Rolf began nipping at John's open shoelace and running in circles around them. Rolf, Garrett and John's exuberance was clearly defining the moment, thankfully another leg of our journey was coming to an end and we were all relieved.

"Good morning children, and you too Captain Olaf," Betsy shouted, giggling from the cabin door. "Is anyone hungry yet?"

"YES MOTHER," we all roared at the same time.

"Ok then . . . Helga, Lizzy, Roxanne and I are going to start breakfast, OK, CAN ANYBODY HEAR ME?"

"Sounds excellent lass," the Captain shouted over the high spirits still locked in combat on the deck.

"Perchance . . . have you seen Rorek?"

"He's in the engine room Captain; he'll be up in a jiffy. He looks good. He told me just a few minutes ago that he feels much better since he started drinking Lizzy's herb tea, and the flu appears to be gone now." Olaf nodded, smiled, and waved.

After Betsy departed, and John and Garrett had finally had enough of their wild shenanigans, everyone jumped to the task of getting the sails down, and began preparations for our approach to Socorro. Thirty minutes later we were floating motionless in the calm Pacific Ocean and off our starboard bow a faint glow had begun demarcating the horizon, another beautiful day was dawning.

During breakfast we discussed the utter uniqueness of the Revillagigedo Islands. Being somewhat similar to their southern sisters, the Galapagos Islands, their isolation in the Pacific Ocean had made them an extraordinary place of endemism. Largely uninhabited by man, these desolate islands were also a major gathering location for a variety of large pelagic species, including tropical fish, black tip reef sharks, hammerheads, Galapagos reef sharks, giant Pacific manta rays, and arguably the most majestic creature in the sea, the enormous whale shark. Somewhere between one-fourth and one-half of the flora, as well as most of the birds and invertebrates existing on the islands, were found nowhere else in the world, making these mysterious archipelagoes a very unique place indeed. The four islands, Socorro, Clarion, San Benedicto, and Roca Partida were generally a dry environment, receiving an annual rainfall of twenty-four inches, and were little more than enormous volcanic rocks covered by dry forests with rocky or sandy beaches around the perimeters.

After we'd departed the Galapagos Islands, Captain Olaf and Rorek, being curious about where we were headed, had discovered that the Mexican Navy was maintaining a small presence on Isla Socorro and had been since 1957. In that same year the government had graciously consented to construct a permanent base with a small airstrip attached on one of the higher ridges, and also a harbor to assist the military's mission. There was also a small civilian village on the southern tip of the island with perhaps three thousand inhabitants. Through dissipating mists, as we approached the jagged southeastern shores, we began distinguishing vague shapes of large and small buildings in the distance. The stretch of concrete delineating the airstrip looked like a discarded cigarette on top of the ridge, and just distant, also emerging from the morning mists, was the peak of the 3,707 ft Evermann Volcano.

Apparently, at the beginning of the century, Dr. Barton Warren Evermann's scientific explorations on Isla Socorro had resulted in the most comprehensive biological collections ever obtained there, and his findings were taught in most college curriculums internationally. Because of these extraordinary achievements, the volcano had been named in his honor.

About half a mile out, Captain Olaf tried contacting the base commander to inform him of the *Heimdall's* approach; oddly though, all he got was a recorded message. The message informed him that because of a prolonged exposure to the dreadful drought the previous year, the base would be closed for an indefinite period. Apparently the Navy had been relocated to the city of Manzanillo in Colima, along with all the civilian villagers, and because of this the island was now completely deserted. Thankfully our work would be unhindered by foreign politics for the duration of our stay. I could see from the Captains jubilant expression that he was pleased with this news.

The closer we got to the island the more bewildered we became, not only was it uninhabited, but it also appeared completely devastated. The rolling hills were totally devoid of anything green and because of this; the deep canyons and valleys, descending down the sides of the Evermann volcano, appeared like ugly blackened gashes. I was sure that the drought had encouraged this denudation process; everywhere we looked the plant life was gone. From all over the island we saw the irrefutable evidence of vast sediment runoff, there was no plant life to hold it in place anymore and this of course had led to the formation of hundreds of deep erosion gullies. As we got closer we also sensed a foreboding hovering over the island, and it made me shudder with uneasiness.

Captain Olaf anchored the Heimdall two hundred yards offshore Cabo Pearce peninsula in twenty-five fathoms of dark blue water. While John, Garrett, and Rorek prepared the raft for departure, Roxanne began organizing for her work in the cave. Having retrieved all the information she'd received from her contemporaries earlier in the year, she was shuffling all those papers and discs into folders and stuffing them into her backpack. Hopefully there would be another significant discovery today to help further our search for the First Tribe.

Three

Another disquieting discovery

9:00am

The bow of the eighteen foot raft ground to a halt on the fine grained black sand of Socorro's eastern beach, and after we'd disembarked, preparations for the day began. Lizzy and Rorek had stayed aboard the *Heimdall* this morning to begin repairs, Lizzy on the sails, and Rorek replacing brushes and bearings on the secondary electrical generator. On the southern side of Cabo Pearce peninsula, from the shoreline out several hundred yards, the water was a brownish color from rain runoff during the last storm. Shortly after we'd disembarked Roxanne set up a small canopy she thought she might need. Rolf and Garrett, overwhelmed with a strange energy, took off running towards one of the large ravines down the beach and swiftly disappeared. Captain Olaf's shouts fell on deaf ears though, so he radioed the ever impulsive Garrett and reminded him that we had a lot of work to accomplish today and it was essential that he stay in touch regularly, Garrett assured the Captain that he would.

John had extended the large telescope now and was beginning a preliminary scan in the general direction Roxanne was pointing; somewhere up on that 3700 ft mountainside was the cave the Viking tribe had occupied centuries before. I quickly anticipated that scrutinizing the terrain would be a tedious process, the mountainside was vast, and there appeared to be several dozen possibilities that matched the description of what we were looking for.

<u>10:45am</u>

"Hey guys, I think I've found it," John chortled, quickly handing the telescope to Roxanne.

"Take a look up towards the top," he pointed, "about two hundred feet below that uneven precipice . . . see it? Roxanne took the telescope and focused it where John had pointed.

"I can't see John, where is it?" Roxanne whined.

"Right next to that large twisted tree and that huge boulder, there's an opening with a large flat area on top of it." John continued moving the telescope slightly for her.

"Oh gosh, I see it now, it's our cave," she gasped in excitement. "I can even see the table and chairs the university left behind next to the entrance. Yippee! Captain Olaf, how are we going to get up there?" Olaf shrugged and reached for the telescope.

<u>11:50am</u>

Captain Olaf was thoroughly befuddled; he'd been searching for over an hour and his efforts had revealed no evidence of a path anywhere on the precarious boulder strewn mountainside. Although we knew the USC researchers had established access earlier this year, just how they'd done it was eluding him. About the time the Captain was contemplating getting an up-date from Garrett, the impetuous teenager radioed in with unexpected news.

"Garrett to expedition, Garrett to the bloody land lubing expedition, do you copy you lazy bums? What are you dudes doing down there . . . sleepin?"

"We copy you Garrett, thanks for checking in and no, we're not sleeping," Captain Olaf scowled.

"Watch out with that lazy bum stuff you little midget," John added with a chuckle.

"Hey . . . guess what," Garrett continued, "me and Rolfy are big time down and comfy at the cave. I can see the canopy and you dudes look like little bugs. Hey Roxy this place is way cool, you're gonna dig it. There's a letter with your name on it, I think it's from one of the other researchers. It's addressed to the high princess of old Viking stuff; no not really I'm just spoofin Rox."

"I know you are honey," Roxanne answered. "Garrett, would you open up the letter and tell me if it's from Maryanne." A few moments passed.

"It is Roxy, and she sends her love," Garrett answered.

"Thanks sweetie."

While Garrett and the Captain continued talking, we faintly heard Rolf's energetic barking echoing ethereally down the mountainside and through the ravines.

"Garrett, how did you get up there so quickly?" the Captain stammered. "I've been scanning the mountainside for an hour and I didn't see anything that resembles a path."

"It was a cinch for me boss, that's because I'm the bomb and you dudes can't touch that. I know you guys are helpless without me, so I'll tell ya what, for twenty bucks each, I'll let ya come up here and stay with me and the mutt."

"Garrett . . ." the Captain said sternly.

"Sorry boss! Well . . . just go the same direction me and Rolfy did, up that nasty ravine, the one with burnt trees and split boulders. At the end, maybe three hundred yards, you can go right or left . . . go right. Another hundred yards you'll see a wooden sign, it says: "USC research team" with an arrow pointin upwards, follow the path, it'll take ya right to where we're standing."

"Copy that son, thank you so much, you've helped us resolve a big problem. We're on our way up Garrett; you stay put until we reach your position. Do you copy?"

"Copy that and no problema boss; we'll just hang till y'all get here. The view is the bomb awesome; this island's so cool dudes, it's so bloody beautiful here and it's huge, kinda cold up here too. Betsy I'm gettin hungry and thirsty, I forgot to bring my backpack, could you bring it for me? Rolf's hungry too; he's been sniffin round the cave and lickin rocks. He took a big stinkin dump on the way up, its still on the path so be careful, I don't want nobody stepping in that monster turd, sucker looks like a baseball bat, ya can't miss it! Be cool on the way up, it's not an easy path, there's a lotta loose rock and its steep . . . see ya!"

"Garrett . . . Betsy gave John your backpack, he's going to bring it up for you. He also said that you and he have some unfinished business from this morning. He said don't worry though; he'll be gentle on your brittle bones. See you soon, and thanks again son, I'm really proud of you, Captain Olaf out!"

"Hey thanks Cap! By the way," Garrett laughed, "tell that old dilapidated navy fart I'll kick his butt any day of the week."

Fifteen minutes later, Garrett radioed in again to say that he had climbed the highest peak and was now sitting on top of the world looking out at the ocean.

<u>12:15pm</u>

Garrett's directions were exceptional. We easily found the wooden sign and began climbing up what appeared to be a natural walkway carved right into the mountainside. In several places the path did narrow considerably, becoming treacherous and somewhat difficult to trek over, so we were all compelled to walk in single file. Like Garrett had forewarned, the path was also filled with loose lava fragments, so we decided to use our hiking sticks as judiciously as possible and tie a nylon rope between us.

The higher we got, the more the island opened up visually, it was breathtaking and picturesque. Just north of us we viewed an enormous stand of trees, and it appeared that they'd weathered the magnetic drought bands unharmed. Just before this vividly green forest, the lava flow turned back towards the mountain and had abruptly stopped in clumpy mountainous ridges. Through the binoculars, we observed an enormous outcropping of tightly packed basalt columns; perhaps fifty feet high, and possibly eighteen inches in diameter that had formed an enormous dam like structure. John laughingly decided to nickname the formation “the horizontal ladders” because they bore such a striking resemblance to an enormous ladder lying on its side. After an hour and a half of hiking we all decided that stopping for fifteen minutes was in our best interest. When we had, Roxanne started taking photos, Betsy handed out snacks, and I began contemplating how desolate and magnificent this island appeared, and what a blessing it was to be standing in a place like this. While we talked and ate, and waited for Roxanne to finish her shoot, I took the opportunity to share an ancient Scottish legend about giants crossing the North Sea on basalt bridges so they wouldn’t get their feet wet. After I’d finished with the colorful tale; the crew stared at me benignly and began chuckling.

“Yah right Gabriel, that’s the biggest tale we’ve heard you tell yet,” John laughed.

“Yep, you’re one heck of a yarn spinner boy,” Captain Olaf remarked.

“Did you really get a college degree for studying that weird stuff?” Helga asked with a grin.

“Its Nordic mythology,” I snapped defensively, “it’s supposed to be fun, and embraced in light of its moral lessons about good and bad. What’s wrong with you guys, have a little fun with me here, they’re delightful stories.” With an air of indifference everyone shrugged.

While we hiked on I found myself dealing with a strange euphoria because of how absolutely stunning it was here. The irregular volcanic terrain, and dazzling visual panoramas reminded me of a quote from a terrific science fiction, adventure story I'd read in my third year of college entitled, "A Journey to the Centre of the Earth".

"My curiosity was aroused to fever-pitch, and my uncle tried in vain to restrain me. When he saw that my impatience was likely to do me more harm than the satisfaction of my curiosity, he gave way."

In the story Professor Hardwigg, his young nephew Harry, and Hans the eider down hunter, decided that they were going to enter the earth, and travel to its center by way of Mount Sneffel's, an ancient extinct volcano outside of Reykjavik in Iceland. I just loved Harry in the story; he was a character that I had found myself emulating often in my life. Incessantly impatient and always curious about the unknown and at times even somewhat self deprecating, Harry was always compelled to understand and learn about everything and always struggled with peculiar fears the way I did.

I loved Jules Verne; he was one of my favorite authors, and also a man that I truly admired. He was a Frenchman, born in Nantes France, and lived from 1828-1905. After rebelling against his parents and running away to sea at the age of eleven, and then being sent back home shortly thereafter as a failure, Verne pledged that for the rest of his life he would travel only in his imagination, and in this promise he found extraordinary literary success. Writing more than fifty works that combined scientific fantasy, and exciting adventure, Verne has been considered by most to be the father of science fiction literature. Many of Verne's novels accurately predicted some of the technology seen in the modern world today, including spacecraft, guided missiles, aircraft, and submarines.

2:30pm

After a two hour and fifteen minute trek we safely reached the cave and found Garrett napping just inside the cave entrance; Rolf was nowhere to be found. After waking him, John handed Garrett his backpack and he immediately pulled out an apple and a candy bar and wolfed it down with a bottle of water. After fifteen minutes of calling and whistling, Rolf suddenly bounded up the path, from the direction of the horizontal ladders, and eagerly greeted everyone with several short barks and sloppy licks. Inside the cave there was still furniture and belongings the USC research team had left behind, including two large work tables with chairs, several unused ledgers, five propane lanterns with ten full gallons of fuel, four cots with blankets, a portable pantry filled with canned goods, a rusted 30/30 rifle, and a broken portable radio with leaking batteries.

After a satisfying lunch of tuna sandwiches, apples, and herb tea, Roxanne began her study of the cave, and we all willingly offered ourselves as her provisional assistants. She noted, on the flat rock directly above the cave entrance, that the Rognvald symbol was prominently carved into the weathered rock, the familiar sword and helmet over a shield announced the past occupants. This cave appeared several hundred feet deep; long expanses of perfectly flat surface, perfect for the runic petraglyphs and paintings were found in abundance along the first thirty feet on each side. In the forward third of the cave we found ten carved out depressions in the walls, perhaps fifteen feet in depth. Inside six of them we found several roped off areas where the researchers had toiled several months previous. Considering the scant remnants of decayed blankets, articles of clothes, and mundane artifacts left behind, it appeared these deep depressions had once been private living chambers for the Viking families. Thirty feet back from the entrance was a large circle of rocks, perhaps eight feet in diameter and three feet high. Directly above the circle of rocks was a blackened vent for the smoke of the fire to exit out through. Encircled around the fire pit were several, cleverly built, flat hatched wooden benches interwoven together. This was obviously a gathering place where the clan solved problems and had eaten their meals together. After four hours of studying the petraglyphs and paintings, and forty-five minutes were spent researching something on the computer, Roxanne summoned everyone together to share her findings.

"According to these carvings, the Rognvald's ran into more difficulties when they reached this island," Roxanne began with a deep sigh.

"Thirteen vessels arrived, and several months' later, eleven vessels departed, but it doesn't reveal the exact reasons why. It appears over fifty people stayed behind. From the way the sun and earth are portrayed in this section, they remained on Socorro for decades, right here in this cave, and then for some reason both vessels set sail north. Now here's where it gets interesting, apparently one of the two vessels came back to this very island three days after they'd departed. According to this series of carvings, the second vessel sunk off another island northeast, a day's journey from here. A terrible commotion on the seas surface sank one of the vessels and everyone died. It was carrying thirty unfortunate souls. They all have the same insignia over their heads, but it's a symbol I don't recognize. The image of this sizeable chest on the sea floor, filled with these little asymmetrical shapes, seems to indicate that there was another treasure, perhaps gems or gold coins, it's hard to differentiate. The petraglyphs show large winged underwater creatures trying to save the poor unfortunates from drowning after the vessel went down. It also shows that eighteen men on the first vessel dove down to try and save their clansmen. Those men described an enormous underwater tower surrounded by creatures that had heads that looked like hammers."

The skeptical looks on everyone's faces quickly flustered Roxanne, so she stopped talking. Even I was becoming doubtful about her colorfully interpretive recount and didn't know what to think. After a few disgruntled moments she finally picked up a piece of paper and started sharing some of the notes she'd accumulated earlier on the computer.

"I know this sounds absurd, it even seemed that way to me at first, but it's not, so let me appeal to your intellects with some hard facts," she sneered sarcastically. "I went on-line earlier to rediscover something I'd remembered reading last year. I believe they're describing an island just northeast of us, in these very same archipelagoes, it's called San Benedicto. Apparently this place has one of the most spectacular diving destinations in the world, another one being right here off the shores of Socorro Island. I personally believe the formation they're describing is called the "Boiler", by modern divers, and it's just off the northwestern tip of San Benedicto Island. The article says the pinnacle is twenty-five ft under the surface and goes down one hundred and twenty feet, again I believe that this is the enormous tower they've carved here. Also, according to the pictures, this tragedy happened when the sun was directly overhead, and visibility underwater was the greatest, that's why they were able to illustrate these creatures in so much detail. I believe the large winged creatures they're describing are the giant Pacific manta rays that make that northern part of San Benedicto famous. The creatures with heads like hammers are obviously Hammerhead sharks. As far as I can tell, all the creatures they've drawn here have been living in this same geographical vicinity for centuries. Captain, do you think it might be wise to go to San Benedicto, I think it might be worth exploring?"

Four

The unexpected storm

There was a flurry of dialogue when Roxanne finished, most of it centering on the fantastic possibilities being suggested by her. It was obvious that no one, from the Rognvald tribe, had occupied this cave for centuries and the paintings and petraglyphs we'd studied thus far hadn't given any explanation that could substantiate any other premise.

The burning question now was where did the Viking families go?

"Olaf do you copy," Rorek's question over the radio startled us.

"Go ahead Rorek, what's up?" the Captain replied.

"Can you see directly west of your location Olaf?"

"No we can't brother, the mountain is blocking our view . . . why?"

"A huge weather system is heading in; it's almost over us. The reports are saying three inches of rain tonight Olaf, and then confirm it moving south early tomorrow morning. From where Lizzy and I are standing, the western skies look threatening brother, they're black as tar and swirling."

"Goodness me hold on a moment Rorek, I'll get back with you," the Captain replied, suddenly distraught.

Several minutes after Rorek radioed, dark clouds indeed billowed over the mountainous ledges two hundred feet above us and powerful flashes from the bowels of the approaching storm rumbled with an odd foreboding. The rain soon began splatting down in the pulverized pumice around us, and with an ever increasing frequency the wind picked up and began surging in powerful sporadic gusts. The temperature must have dropped twenty degrees while we were huddled together on the six foot ledge just outside the caves entrance, and during several unusually strong gusts, bits of loosened rock began falling haphazardly around the entrance and down onto our heads. Because of these suddenly dangerous conditions, Captain Olaf motioned for all of us to get into the cave where it was safer, and considerably warmer.

"Olaf, I'd plan on staying in the cave till it passes, this one's gonna be a humdinger, do you copy?"

"I copy and agree with you Rorek, hold on" the Captain groaned. With the Captains despondent expression we all shrugged yes and glumly accepted this unexpected change of plans.

"Rorek we're all in agreement, we'll stay here for the duration. Can you see the raft, is it secured?"

"Affirmative Olaf . . . John lashed it properly, and it's well protected in that small cove. I don't think the canopy's gonna make it though, it's already down and underwater."

"Copy that brother, thankyou, keep us posted. Also Rorek, go ahead and drop the aft anchor, let's be safe . . . Olaf out."

"Copy that brother, good idea . . . Rorek out."

The more I thought about it, the more it became evident that it wouldn't be that inconvenient staying here for the night. There were four cots and twice that number in heavy thick blankets. There were five excellent Coleman lanterns and plenty of fuel. There was the water and snacks we'd brought along, and the portable pantry left behind had various canned meats, fruits and vegetables. There was a large stack of dry firewood the USC researchers hadn't used, and we also had Rolf to keep watch over us. After we'd taken stock of our provisions, and realized that God had provided us with everything that we required for this unexpected stay, we then joined hands and gave thanks. Somehow though, after we'd prayed, I kept feeling that perhaps we should have given thanks before we knew that God had provided these necessities.

The rain became torrential, and was accompanied occasionally with hail the size of marbles; I wondered how Lizzy and Rorek were weathering this, it must have been dreadfully noisy on the schooner and we all hoped that no damage would be sustained. The cave was quite remarkable and the roar of the storm outside was considerably lessened. Thankfully we'd been provided a safe, impermeable abode on this gigantic rock out in the middle of nowhere. Nevertheless, aside from the relentless weather and seeming inconvenience, the ladies prepared a wonderful makeshift dinner of canned meat, canned vegetables, canned fruit, and also the apples we'd brought along from the *Heimdall.* After the repast, while we were sitting around the roaring fire, contented, sipping coffee, and contemplating our next move, Garrett unexpectedly startled us from where he'd been exploring at the rear of the cave.

"ROXY . . . ," he yelled, his stentorian voice booming louder than usual over the smooth rock walls. "There's a bunch more pictures at the back here; you gotta see this stuff, it's totally creepy!"

"Coming honey, give me a minute," Roxy shouted back as we all got up.

Rolf, having fallen asleep on his back next to the fire with all four legs sticking straight up, awoke with a grunt while we were shuffling about. Jumping up awkwardly he stumbled back with us to where Garrett was holding a lantern and began barking excitedly upon reaching his side. Several moments later, after everyone had congregated at the rear of the cave, we watched and listened while Garrett pointed out what he'd found. The find was exciting and everyone began discussing how uniquely different these paintings were compared to the ones at the front of the cave. For ten minutes, while Garrett held the lantern close, Roxanne quietly studied the carvings and pictures. Afterwards she turned towards us with a look of disbelief and shrugged her shoulders.

"Wow . . ." she exclaimed, "I really don't know what to make of this. I'm puzzled why they're so detached from the other petraglyphs towards the front of the cave. They must have been done at a different time by someone else."

"What are we looking at here Roxy?" Helga asked, as everyone gathered close in the dismal light.

"Wait a minute guys, I'll fetch some more lanterns," Betsy offered, and ran back towards the fire with Rolf in noisy pursuit. After Betsy returned, and three lanterns were strategically placed for optimum viewing, Roxanne began telling a remarkable story.

"These carvings are depicting a settlement having been built somewhere north of us. Do you remember where we saw those basalt columns on the way up?" Everyone shook their heads yes.

"Well, according to what's drawn here, it appears that someone established a more permanent village on the other side of John's vertical ladders, somewhere in the middle of that distant forest. Captain Olaf, perhaps it might be constructive to stay here another day or so, and explore that forest. You know the USC research team made no mention of this in the note they left me and that leads me to believe that they might not have even been aware of it. There's nothing here for us, everything useful was removed by the researchers when they departed in March. These few artifacts lying around are very common; I'm assuming that's why they left them all behind. I'll photograph the walls in the morning before we leave, at least we'll have something visual for the *Heimdall's* records. Captain would it be OK to stay another day?"

"I have no problem staying awhile longer lass, as long as everyone's in agreement," the Captain answered motioning for a vote of hands. Everyone agreed except Rolf who was once again on his back by the fire with all four legs sticking straight up, sound asleep.

"Perhaps we should contact Rorek Captain," Helga suggested, moving directly into the light of the lanterns, "and have him use the Virtual Earth Watch tomorrow morning. That way he could determine whether or not there's anything in the forest that resembles a village, and if not we won't have to waste our time looking."

"Oh that's a great idea Helga; but it's mine Captain, I suggested the same thing to her this afternoon, she stole it from me!" Garrett blurted.

"I did not Garrett!" Helga screeched defensively.

"Yes you did you stinkin thief," Garrett shot back angrily.

"Garrett, you're a little rat, why don't you leave me alone?" Garrett smirked cheekily at Helga, and then after Helga quickly shot the same look back at Garrett, he balked indignantly and turned away.

"Alright children end it now!" the Captain ordered sternly. "I don't give a rat's patoot whose idea it was, it doesn't matter. John radio my brother and tell him about this idea, if the weather permits I think it would be to our advantage to proceed with it."

"I have the same opinion Olaf; it would save us a lot of time," John agreed as he turned back towards the waning campfire to get the radio.

"Its 11:00pm people," the Captain murmured, looking at his watch, "perhaps it's time we call it a day."

As the rest of us headed back towards the fire I began remembering my own immature conduct in the past, and it made me chuckle. When these crew members got cantankerous and belligerent with one another it always seemed to amuse me, but it also reminded me about how I'd behaved when I was younger, with my parents and older friends, and I was grateful that I'd finally gotten past it. Hopefully Helga and Garrett would do the same someday.

The rain was still torrential after we'd all snuggled in and pulled the blankets over us. After prayers, we all murmured goodnights and quickly drifted off.

Five

Moving the *Heimdall* to Cabo Middleton peninsula

June 27th 6:00am

I realized when my eyes finally fluttered open, just how desolate and bleak our environs were. How the Rognvald's had ever survived in a place like this, for so many years, was beyond my ability to comprehend. An impenetrable and profound stillness hung in the air this morning, similar to the stillness we'd experienced at the primary campsite in the Pontevedra Province, and the distinction between the stillness at this moment, and the storms thunderous din the night before was quite remarkable. It seemed everything in life had opposites, light and dark, faith and unbelief, sound and silence, start and stop, obeying and disobeying, awake and asleep, alive and dead, love and hate, and the marking out between the two was either a simple choice, or the passage of time. While I was pondering these heady thoughts an unexpected whispering startled me, and I perceived a mighty hand resting on me and a voice like the sound of rushing waters saying: *"Be still and know that I am God, I will be exalted among the nations I will be exalted in the earth."* Somehow I'd heard one of my favorite verses from the Bible, Psalm 46:10, but how could this be?

I shuddered at my smallness in this vast universe; did the Most High God love me personally, and communicate just with me? Why did God love me so much? Why would He ever take the time to speak with me personally? What a grand responsibility our lives were, and how very little we knew about Gods profound mysteries.

After standing up and removing the warm blanket, I was irreverently accosted by the cold damp environment and shivered deeply. A loud rustling from the rear of the cave startled me so I spun around to defend myself; squinting into the gloom, and without any second thoughts, I was at once convinced it must be vampire bats! Oh how I hated bats, rats with wings and fangs must surely be God's sense of humor. Was God angry at me for some reason this morning? No, how could He be, He just spoke to me. Confused and frightened, I prepared myself for the death swarm I knew was forthcoming. Oh Lord, what a way to start the new day, all my vital juices sucked dry and thoroughly emaciated by a swarm of raging bloodsuckers.

I somehow knew that when they'd finally overwhelmed me, that dozens would get stuck in my hair, I could see them flopping about erratically while thrusting their sucking razor fangs into my scalp over and over again. I wanted to scream and warn the others but somehow my voice froze. Now there was a bewildering lump in my throat and I feared that I may have accidentally swallowed one of the creatures unsuspecting, so impulsively I stuck my finger down my throat and tried to vomit it out. Kneeling down, still trying to dislodge the beast, I covered my head to protect myself from the ensuing nightmare, and began fervently praying for the others, hoping their lives wouldn't soon be sacrificed like mine. What would my mother and father think, having come so far just to be killed by blood sucking rats? What would they think, seeing me in the casket emaciated and shriveled up like a crumpled old brown bag? Oh Lord God, please have mercy on my wretched soul, please save me from these despicable beasts; it just can't be my time yet.

Thankfully the assault never came, and when I realized what a demented idiot I'd been, a wave of embarrassment flooded over me and I felt like crawling into a hole. Suddenly logical, I construed that it must have been small rocks, loosened by the rain last night, but of course there was no way that I was going to stroll back there and confirm this.

Slowly stretching out the stiffness from a night spent sleeping on solid rock, I began observing bright sunlight quietly beckoning through the caves entrance with elongated yellow fingers. Moving outside and sitting down just beyond the opening, I sighed in contentment as the warm rays caressed me. All I needed now was a hot mug of frothy steaming coffee, and I would never ask for anything ever again. Sudden movement in the cave, accompanied with groans, alerted me that everyone was beginning to awaken. Now I was even more hopeful that Betsy would sense my increasingly profound need and brew some of the life giving elixir. Taking in the immeasurable expanse of ocean in front of me, I realized that not one remnant of the storm remained in the morning skies; they were deeply azure and crystal clear. Today was going to be nothing short of exceptional, and I was glad to be alive.

"Olaf, do you copy?" the radios crackled noisily in the morning stillness. Rorek sounded excited.

"Go ahead Rorek," the Captain groaned several moments later, "what's up?"

"I have the island on VEW. Roxanne's symbol interpretation was correct; I do see the remains of another village on the north side of the forest. From what I can see though it's been uninhabited for a very long time."

After hearing Rorek's message, everyone got up abruptly and began folding their blankets. This was inspiring news, and once again our desire to explore was challenging us to move forward.

"Copy that Rorek, give us a moment here brother, I'll be back shortly." The Captain keyed off the radio and motioned for everyone to gather round.

"Looks like we have another opportunity, are we all in agreement to pursue this new find?" Everyone, especially Roxanne, confirmed a sincere desire to explore this unexpected discovery. The Captain nodded in approval, and then keyed on the radio.

"Rorek, we'll be down as soon as we're packed. Tell me brother, what do you think . . . should we sail the Heimdall to the other side of the island or should we hike over, what would save us time?"

"I believe taking the Heimdall over would be the best way Olaf. It would probably take five or six hours from your location, coming down to the Heimdall would take you about two hours, and then dieseling over will take about an hour, we'll save some time that way for sure. The forest extends all the way down within twenty yards of the shoreline at Cabo Middleton; the access looks easier there, more so than trying to traverse the lava fields north of your position. Once we're ashore, it should only be a ten minute walk to the village."

"Copy that brother, sounds like sound advice; we would need additional supplies anyway. We'll be there shortly, Olaf out."

It looked like coffee was going to have to wait this morning and I sighed miserably. Just before we left the cave, Betsy handed out the remainder of the apples she'd brought, two slices of bread each, and one bottle of water for our meager breakfast. The Captain decided to bring along the five Coleman lanterns and fuel that'd been left behind in the cave, they were all in excellent condition, and he strongly felt that they might prove invaluable to our efforts in the future.

Rolf was quite energetic as we began the trek down, and his enthusiastic barking echoed starkly against the austere mountainside rising threateningly on our right. Rolf was always excited to get underway, but as always, after a few minutes, he settled down and quietly moved in beside someone for the rest of the journey, today he'd chosen Betsy and me.

Upon our return to the Heimdall I don't think I ever enjoyed steaming hot frothy coffee more than I did this morning. Being thoroughly disgusted with my incessant whining on the way down, Betsy quickly showed me how to brew it for myself. After several failed attempts, Garrett's merciless joking, and the crew's unsuppressed fits of laughter, I finally made a pot that was somewhat satisfactory, and I gulped it greedily. Knowing we'd be pressed for time, Lizzy had begun preparing breakfast after she'd heard us discussing our intentions of moving the schooner to Cabo Middleton, she also had a special gift in the culinary arts, and the savory warm breakfast was superb.

The night spent in the cave, and my curious obsession with coffee this morning, had unearthed something deep inside my heart. Most of the morning was spent preoccupied with a puzzling thought process, and because of it, I felt somehow that I was being irrevocably changed. An overwhelming thankfulness for my close friends, our journey, and the simple things welled up from deep inside me. Unlike the wealth and snootiness I'd been born into, the honesty of my present life now embraced me with simpler things, the love of the crew, health, sharing, and the comforting arms of

Gods Holy Spirit. I began to understand that it wasn't what you took from people or situations that defined the quintessence of your life; it was what you gave of yourself that mattered most. This had been a difficult lesson to grasp, and had been for the majority of my self-centered life. I'd always been taught that taking everything you can get, in any way you can get it was everyone's responsibility in this world, otherwise someone would beat you to the punch and take what was intended for you. I was learning that *"seeking first the kingdom of God and His righteousness"* was the primary mandate for all followers of Christ Jesus, and when you did it Gods way, he would then give you what you needed to accomplish what He wanted for His glory. I remembered the verse that Jonah had shared with me numerous times in our early e-mails from *Jeremiah 29:13. "Ye shall seek me, and find me, when ye shall search for me with all your heart."* I knew now that God had put me on this earth for a special reason, and had given me my gifts and abilities to use for His glory not mine, and it was my responsibility to find what He'd given me and minister to it. It almost felt like this was basic training for the next life, and I had an overwhelmingly important responsibility to fulfill Gods plan for me on earth, as well as every other person involved in our journey.

As we approached the northern end of the Isla Socorro, the Captain began encountering rocks protruding from the surface of the sea. Lizzy had made excellent use of her free time after she'd repaired the sails the day before. From the research she'd accomplished on-line, about the geography of Isla Socorro, she was able to confirm that these treacherous rocks were also surrounded by innumerable boulders fifteen metres below the surface and home to several schools of the Eastern Pacific's most unique species. From up in the crows nest, John and Helga reported seeing bright orange Clarion angelfish maneuvering together in perfect symmetry, and even though we never saw them, Lizzy informed us there were also red-tailed, and crosshatched Triggerfish found also in the Galapagos and Hawaii, native to this area. Apparently the bottom here was a diver's paradise. At a depth of thirty feet the underwater volcanic terrain resembled a moonscape with bizarre structures that you could actually swim through. There were also irregular pockets in the rock, and peculiar little caves where shy moray eels, sea urchins, Socorro lobsters, and octopus, made their year round habitation.

Where the Captain anchored three hundred yards off the peninsula, the water was a stunning transparent blue and had no murky brown runoff from the storm the evening before. While preparations were being accomplished for departure, one lone dolphin suddenly appeared next to the stern diving platform where Roxanne was washing out some buckets to use.

With no uncertainty the dolphin swam up close to Roxanne and nuzzled her face for several moments. It was a poignant moment, and I was thankful that my camera had been in hand. Moments after the dolphin had swum away, the raft was lowered and everyone got aboard for the short trip in. This beach was very similar in appearance to the one at Cabo Pearce, and fine-grained blackish sand embraced the rafts bow as it softly ground to a halt on the shoreline.

“Let’s get the raft out of the water entirely crew,” the Captain ordered. “Let’s tie it off on these rocks here; I think it will be safer.”

“Aye sir,” several of us murmured. After John had lashed it securely, and the equipment was off-loaded, we all joined hands and prayed, asking God for his guidance and blessings on our endeavors today. These moments in prayerful unity helped reinforce the awesome responsibility God had given us on our voyage thus far, and we always came away from our meditations focused in one accord and eager to continue our work.

Today was very special; since we’d departed Aberdeen, it was the first time the whole crew had disembarked together for an escapade, and I anticipated something very special happening because of it. It was evident that Rolf and Betsy were on a mission together today, as soon as they’d jumped out of the raft they both took off running inland. Within moments Rolf inadvertently stumbled upon an enormous tree lizard scavenging under the peripheral ferns, quite startled the lizard took off running, and then with an excited bark Rolf followed in hot pursuit.

For a few moments I felt compelled to pause and take note of these northern surroundings, it was entirely different here than where we'd been earlier in the day. The trees appeared vigorous with an abundance of healthy foliage; they were also filled with hundreds of green parakeets noisily flitting about in a frenzied ballet. Establishing the genus of what I was observing was proving difficult though, the flora and fauna were fairly dissimilar from the sparse few trees and plants I'd observed yesterday and I found myself quite perplexed trying to understand why the drought bands hadn't ravaged this part of the island. The air here had an enveloping sweetness, thoroughly refreshing, probably from the abundance of negative ions being produced by the thousands of trees and ferns on the northern shores. I found great pleasure this morning in just breathing deeply.

"I found a trail," Betsy cried out excitedly, a short distance away, "and I can see some structures about three hundred yards inland.

"Alright lass," the Captain acknowledged, "let's head that way crew. Everybody turn their radios on please!"

The short trek brought us to a weed infested clearing hidden amongst the trees. It was filled with the decaying remnants of wooden huts, and two well built, undamaged rock crannogs of medium dimension. Most of the constructions were amateur in scope though, and the once developed area appeared three acres in size. It was obvious also, as soon as we had entered the settlement, that this place had long been abandoned. The village appeared squalid, not only in its abandonment, but also in the way that these wretched Viking descendants appeared to have lived daily. Having been built in a haphazard fashion, the village exhibited none of the architectural or engineering acumen the settlement in the Pontevedra Province had. There was no logic to these constructions; they were just strewn about randomly as if no one had cared.

Twenty minutes after we'd entered the clearing, our enthusiastic canine suddenly burst through the dense ferns and trotted up to us; clutched tightly in his mouth was an unwelcome surprise. Dropping the limp body in front of him, he sat down with a grunt, and began howling mightily into the sky. After pushing the poor creature towards us with his nose, he stared at us silently with his head cocked while we all groaned in disappointment. Apparently, in his zeal this morning, Rolf had overtaken and grabbed that large tree lizard and shaken it so hard that he'd killed the poor creature.

Six

Rolf's discovery in the burial grounds

After burying the ill-fated lizard, we spent several exhausting hours poking in and around the ramshackle gathering of huts. After we'd finished, Roxanne was convinced there was nothing of value in this old village; there weren't any vestiges of artifact, art, or implement bearing the Rognvald insignia anywhere. Consequently a feeling of disenchantment began creeping into all of our hearts, and a dismal sense of failure fell upon us.

"There's nothing at all for us here," Roxanne moaned, "perhaps it's time to move on, this site is useless. This is the first time we haven't found something of value in our explorations Captain. I wonder what happened here; it seems strange there's nothing left except these structures. I'm certainly glad I went to Flores back in February instead of this worthless dump."

"It's funny Roxanne," Lizzy mused quietly, "since we left Aberdeen, the Lord has never led us anywhere that didn't connect us to the next phase of our journey, or somehow benefit our endeavors. Honey it's hard for me to believe that this time it would be any different."

"I know everyone's unhappy about this, and that includes me!" Rorek interposed. "We must pray and get some wisdom before we make any rash decisions lass. We're here, we've found nothing of value yet, and we must accept that and move on!" Although Rorek was making a lot of sense, Roxanne still kicked the dirt and walked away sulking. I'd never seen her like this before, something was wrong.

"It's not like us to loose our focus lass," Rorek continued, speaking directly at Roxanne. "Remember the Mortiken attack? We could have died in that fight. Remember my sickness? I could have died in that hospital. Remember the Wormwood people? Remember the Shallows? Remember the fatman? Remember the Maelstrom lass? Goodness me, the list has gotten long since we left Aberdeen." As Rorek spoke, an evangelist's passion had bubbled up from deep inside him and he was gesticulating with his fists to further emphasize the conviction he had in his heart about what he was saying.

"Those were challenging circumstances that required faith and a unified team effort," he continued, "and with Gods guidance we made it through each one of those seemingly impossible situations. Surely we've learned more about ourselves than we're exhibiting here; remember how we've been called. Even if nothing comes of our endeavors on Socorro, we're still in Gods will, so let's get focused again!"

"Maybe there's something obvious we're missin," Garrett mused, shrugging his shoulders, deeply affected by Lizzy and Rorek's comments.

"You're probably right little brother," John agreed pensively. Helga nodded quietly with John and then added.

"Perhaps we should relax awhile, eat something, and discuss our options, Captain, what do you think?"

"Well now, hmmm, I don't know about you guys but I think I'm hungry enough to eat that nasty lizard Rolf brought back," Captain Olaf laughed heartily. "Betsy, can you girls throw something together?"

"Oh sure Captain, give us a few minutes." Betsy replied motioning towards Lizzy and Helga.

With the newfound prospects of nourishment, and Rorek and Lizzy's solid encouragement, everyone's spirits began perking up. After devouring the excellent sandwiches and then washing them down with Lizzy's potent herb tea, we all felt focused again and began eagerly discussing what we should do next. Suddenly alert, Rolf sprang up with a disconcerted whimpering; he began sniffing the inland air in the direction of the lava flow. Barking nervously he began pacing back and forth restlessly in an effort to satisfy something that had gripped him.

The northwestern wind had changed direction dramatically while we were eating; now it was blowing briskly from the south and the air actually smelled different than when we'd arrived earlier, had Rolf caught a scent of something? Several moments later, totally focused, the wolfhound trotted off towards the basalt columns with his head down. Sniffing the ground furiously; he began moving in slowly increasing circles. Jumping up impulsively we all followed the wolfhound, intrigued as he maneuvered his way deeper into the trees. Eventually it became harder to follow because of his pace, he was moving faster and the circles were getting larger and larger; soon we lost sight of him altogether. Thirty minutes later Rolf's loud barking alerted us to the fact that he'd found something.

The burial grounds encompassed an area more than four times the size of the village; it was perhaps fifteen acres. There were hundreds of stone and wooden markers haphazardly placed everywhere, it appeared that many generations had been buried here in this desolate location. Rolf was in the southwestern quadrant barking loudly and pawing at the ground in one location. When we all finally arrived he got very still and stared intently at the Captain with large dark eyes, almost as if he were waiting for permission to do something.

"Gabriel, what do you think the hound wants?" the Captain pondered.

"Can I try something sir?" The Captain nodded to go ahead.

"Rolf," I asked, kneeling down and looking him straight in the eyes, "is there something here you want to show us, is there something here boy?" Rolf's only response was one short airy wuff.

"OK boy, go ahead and fetch it then!"

As soon as I'd given the command Rolf began digging furiously over one of the grave markers, while we all watched in eager anticipation. About one foot underground a scratchy metallic sound alerted us that Rolf had found something.

"Good boy Rolfy," we all shouted. "Can we do it now boy, can we?"

Rolf stopped short, watching us intently he howled for a moment and then sat down. Not having brought along any tools, we searched around the immediate area for something to dig with and fortunately found several stubby flat branches that were suitable to the task. Ten minutes later we pulled out a rusted chest, and after removing the dirt still moist from last nights storm Rolf stood up on his back legs and danced around like a circus dog.

On the cover of the chest was the sword and helmet over a shield, the familiar insignia of the Rognvald's. After several moments John broke the encrusted lock, and as we slowly opened the lid, the old hinges produced a grating sound reminiscent of fingernails on a chalkboard. Inside were several worthless trinkets and a tarnished copper cylinder five inches in diameter and twenty-two inches long, with tightly fitted caps on each end. Roxanne was perplexed and turned the tube over and over, scrutinizing the craftsmanship, and several peculiar markings; finally she shrugged her shoulders and handed it to John.

"Perhaps you can figure out a way to open this thing John, I don't know what it is; I've never seen anything like it before."

John took the tube and shook it slightly, there was something inside. After a few moments he also shrugged and handed it to Rorek, who in turn handed it to the Captain, and it proceeded in similar fashion around the whole circle until it ended up back in John's hands. Everyone shrugged and shook their heads; no one knew what to think or do.

"Alright then . . . I'm going to try something that just came to me," John said, getting down on one knee. Grabbing the tube in both of his strong hands, he took several deep breaths and squeezed as hard as he could. There was a loud pop, and both ends blew off in opposite directions.

"Whoa dude that was awesome," Garrett marveled, "that's exactly what I woulda done ya know." Chuckling and flashing a large toothy smile, he impetuously dove at Rolf and they began tumbling in one big blurred ball.

There were two scrolls inside the copper tube and also a wooden talisman etched with the Rognvald insignia. I could see that Roxanne had been deeply affected by this find because several large tears began welling up in her eyes; shortly thereafter she turned to all of us and said glumly.

"I'm sorry that I was such a baby back there. It was out of character for me, I don't know what's wrong with me. I just really miss my Jonah." Looking up awkwardly she began sobbing, so Betsy, Helga, and Lizzy immediately began ministering to her. Within minutes she wiped her nose and tears, stood up straight, and then she and I began deciphering the crudely written runic symbols.

<u>The oldest scroll read</u>:

Embracing visions of King Agar to honor First Tribe

The Most High God smiles on those willing to pursue the unknown in faith

Visions of noble Agar and mysterious Gamelin remind us of our legacy

In far-away places, times beckon towards us daily

A son not yet born, and distant warriors, will help redeem a far land

We have spent too many sun cycles waiting, crying for news from the northlands, the soul fire is waning; our desolation consumes us with continual grief

Children cry unceasingly, in aimless wanderings they die

We have little hope in ever finding our long departed families now

With choking hands, and foul Loki's persistent whisperings

We find no expectation, or joy in tomorrow's sunrise.

<u>The first part of the newer scroll read</u>:

We sail distant beyond blackened beaches,

Great upheaval met us a day's journey north and

In defeat we were embraced by the gentle winged Leviathan,

Rivers of mourning fall from eyes dismayed

On wings of giant water birds amongst hammer fish

We watch in sorrow as families descend lifeless to oceans bottom

We will die here now, alone in shadows of the Fire Mountain

Our hope is gone; we are defeated, like families on Shallows of Three Rocks

Our eternal hope now is in the anointed ones mercy, Christ before all else!

<u>2nd part, apparently written many decades later</u>

With mighty clan Vildarsen our hope now sings anew

Together the chosen family pursues First Tribe in strongest vessel

The son not yet born, a mighty warrior foretold in vision

Will help many in the season of his coming

In day's future he will unite with ghost warriors on voyage to northlands

On water birds Vildarsen's seek fallen warriors beneath the Fire Mountain

Rulers of the water kingdom, clan Vildarsen search for lost blood rocks, and wait for Ghost warriors and chosen one to take mighty son, yet unborn, to First Tribe for day of many collisions

Of course we were all stunned, this was bloody incredible, and the information on these scrolls was overwhelming. Roxanne quickly sat down on an old stump, next to an adjoining grave marker, and began weeping again. While the crew stared blankly in disbelief, I once again read the incredible messages aloud.

Were we the Ghost warriors these ancient words were talking about?"

Did this have something to do with the CSAT? After all we were now being touted in Europe as the "Ghost Vessel".

Why would they bury this incredible information in a graveyard?

Was God trying to show us something about trusting Him in all things?

Did God even use animals to bring about, and fulfill his will?

It seemed that Rolf was now as much a part of our endeavors as we were. The chance that anyone could have ever found these messages was remote; what had happened for us here today seemed preposterous, inconceivable, and so far fetched as to boggle the imagination, but here they were! Clutched in my two hands were two pieces of ancient parchment, prophetic in nature, and written centuries before, and the information contained on these pages was priceless, informative, and unreservedly timely.

Upon leaving the graveyard we slowly made our way back to the raft. Amidst the late afternoon commotion from hundreds of foraging green parakeets, we all hiked silently, rapt in mystifying feelings about the incredible discovery we'd just made. The skies were filling with reddened clouds, a foreshadowing of good weather ahead, and were also beginning to obscure the suns western decline in an undulating luminosity. Deeply affected as a poet and writer this afternoon, I'd somehow discovered peace and inspiration in my soul that was beyond any pitiful narrative I might compose. As we walked, and while the soft reddish afternoon hues soothed my eyes, my soul began quietly singing praises, and I gave thanks to the Lord God for this incredible journey that I was part of.

Seven

What the ancient scrolls meant to us

June 28th

After Betsy's magnificent breakfast and prayer, we all decided to stay one more day because our yearning to understand the mysterious scrolls was foremost in all our minds. There were numerous things we understood from what we'd read.

1. It was Gods will that we'd found these scrolls, here in this forsaken place. Finding this inscrutable information buried in a place of death was thought provoking. There was so much to think

about concerning our stay on this Isle, what we'd experienced, what we'd found, and the temporary but perplexing malfunction of our faith and patience.

2. The Rognvald's and the Vildarsen's were on Isla Socorro together.

3. The Vildarsen's had been given a vision to accomplish.

After the tragedy north of here, the last boat returned apparently with the intention of staying on Socorro forever. Years later, the Vildarsen's were given their vision, and this vision confirmed what King Agar and Gamelin had apparently foreseen centuries before. Ghost warriors would pick up one of the Vildarsen descendants, someone not yet born, and this man would continue with those people until the First Tribe had been found. It was incredible, and evident that we were the Ghost warriors written about here.

4. Vildarsen's had returned to the place where they'd lost their brethren, and had become skilled in swimming with the giant Pacific Manta Rays.

Apparently, their mission was to search out where the other vessel had sunk to find some treasure that was lost, and always be prepared for the Ghost warriors.

5. Again there was mention of the chosen one being with the Ghost warriors.

I found myself often dealing with an irrational fear that crept into my thoughts at the most inopportune times. Why had God chosen me for this station? What was it about me that made me worthy? Was it because of my middle name Baaldur? Once before, on the leather scroll, it had been intimated that I was the chosen one, and then it had been substantiated to me personally by Floki Vildarsen just before his death. Floki had even transferred his mantle to me, some arcane and unfathomable responsibility that I was supposed to continue on with.

6. We were apparently going to meet a descendant from the clan Vildarsen, a warrior who'd been given the responsibility of joining forces with us in our search for the First Tribe, and one skilled with the giant Pacific manta rays.

Where would we be encountering this man? What did he look like? Was he an inhabitant of San Benedicto Island? Like Socorro this island was also volcanic in nature, approximately three miles long in a north-south direction, and three quarters of a mile in width. For years though the Mexican government had closed all the Revillagigedo Archipelagoes to sport-fishing, or squatting of any kind, because of environmental abuse, so the question now was how anyone could have survived there in these modern times, complying with those laws?

Eight

The Magdalena's Captain shares an extraordinary story

June 29th 8:00am

After prayer we'd all agreed that sailing to San Benedicto Island was compulsory to begin our search for this descendant from clan Vildarsen. There was an irony in what the scrolls communicated though, while we were searching for him, he was ostensibly waiting for us to find him. It was evident that he was someone many generations removed from the original voyage, so if he wasn't on San Benedicto or dead, then he might possibly be part of a more modern society on one of the mainland's, and if he was, where could we possibly start our search for him? The more I thought about finding this person, the more it seemed impossible. Roxanne and Captain Olaf decided to e-mail Jonah with all the details of our last two days on Socorro, it was their intention to ask his advice about our present dilemma. We were awaiting his reply.

11am

On the voyage over Garrett and Helga brought the VEW on-line to get a look at our next destination. After they'd achieved a stable view Garrett informed us there were two vessels visible on the northern shores, an enormous yellow schooner that was anchored, and a much smaller vessel detached from the schooner that was motoring about. When the Captain examined the images he let out a chuckle, and soon afterwards began rolling with laughter.

"I know that schooner," he blurted, "I recognize their colors, and that string of colorful ensigns she carries. Rorek and I met them years ago while we were vacationing in the Galapagos, it's the Magdalena; they're a sport-fishing/diving charter based out of Manzanillo in Colima." The Captain fetched his radio and keyed on.

"Rorek guess who's anchored off San Benedicto brother?"

"Don't have a clue," Rorek shouted amidst a deafening clamor inside the engine room.

"It's the schooner Magdalena brother, we met them in the Galapagos, must be fifteen years now. Remember Captain Janus, the one with the long ponytail, and that crazy half-legged first mate, the guy who thought he was a descendant of Viking warriors, I think he called himself Utgard . . . do you remember?"

"Aye brother I do remember those screwballs. Weren't they the ones that chartered diving and fishing tours to the Islas Maria's?"

"Yep the very same ones brother, when you're done Rorek please try to raise them on the radio, I want to talk to that guy."

Twenty minutes later Rorek had successfully contacted the Magdalena and sure enough, Captain Janus was still in charge of the schooners endeavors. Olaf and he began reminiscing fondly, and in the conversation he was informed that the Magdalena still chartered fishing and diving tours to the Islas Maria's, but now they'd expanded their tours as far south as the Gulf of Tehuantepec and as far north as Santa Catalina Island offshore Los Angeles.

Captain Janus informed Olaf that Utgard had been murdered in a drunken brawl several years ago in an El Bedito pub on the southern Baja peninsula, and he'd since replaced him with another first mate. He said that they missed Utgard terribly; apparently he'd known all the best diving locales in the Archipelagoes and had mastered the art of swimming with the giant Pacific manta rays, something that fetched his business top dollars from the tourists. In his recollections Captain Janus remembered Utgard had always claimed he'd been born on the Isla San Benedicto, and was raised by a clan of people that had journeyed there from Isla Socorro, and that he'd lost his leg, from the knee down, in a shark attack looking for a treasure on the underwater pinnacle known as the boiler. It was remarkable, what

Captain Janus was now sharing had begun to corroborate some of what we'd just found written on the ancient scrolls.

Apparently after the volcanic eruption in 1952 the island became increasingly inhospitable, and the small Viking clan was forced to leave, Captain Janus guessed Utgard was twelve years of age when they had. After sailing northeast on a large wooden vessel, that Utgard claimed his family ancestry had preserved for hundreds of years in a cave on the western side of the isle, they ended up in Cabo San Lucas. There the family found work in the fishing industry and it was also there that Captain Janus had met the mysterious Utgard years later when he was forty-two. Two years after Captain Janus had hired him, Utgard and his wife gave birth to a son, a son Utgard regretted they'd had; he was different than anyone in the family and was a constant challenge in his upbringing. Still though, out of respect for his ancestors, and holding true to their sacrosanct family tradition, Utgard faithfully taught his son the ancient language passed down for centuries through each generation, and also the art of riding the giant Pacific manta rays. His wild son soon became the focal point of continuous jokes in San Lucas; his ability to communicate with and ride the giant mantas had unfortunately made him a target for relentless heckling from all the kids, and also some adults. His strict routine of lifting weights and body surfing daily, the way he dressed, and his extremely long brown hair were also targets of constant ridicule. When he carved his first sword at the age of ten and pretended he was a Viking warrior, the son found himself fighting many times a week to defend himself and his family honor. In his late teens the son had become extremely powerful physically, and also an uncanny fighter. It was rumored he could easily take on four big men at the same time and defeat them, this done quite often to defend his poor mescal addicted father from those bent on doing him harm. At nineteen years of age the son found himself enamored with something new, seemingly overnight he'd developed an insatiable curiosity about his family's history, finding out where the family had come from, what they'd done, and who his distant relatives were. He was also compelled to continue his father's legendary quest to find the lost family treasure on Isla San Benedicto. Nothing Utgard or his wife tried could dissuade their rowdy son from his zealous pursuits; he had a singularity of purpose that defied all the family's attempts to transform.

One night, after an unusually long binge on mescal, Utgard was murdered by a gang of thugs outside a bar. The family was devastated with this unfortunate event, consequently Utgard's distraught wife, her sisters, and several other family's quickly made plans to relocate to a small costal township outside the Laguna Caimanero in Sinaloa. The defiant son however refused to leave with them; he'd decided to stay in San Lucas with the sole intention of exacting a revenge for his father's death. With tears and pleading the whole family could not convince him otherwise, he was unshakeable in his decision. He had dearly loved and respected his tormented father and had made all the families swear an oath to an honorable lifelong secrecy about his intentions, and also what they would soon read about and see in the news. With much disinclination they all agreed to his demands.

Shortly thereafter the family left San Lucas heartbroken, and never spoke a word of it again.

To this day the bizarre deaths of those six gang members remain an unsolved mystery in Southern Baja. They were all found drowned one morning, outside the bar where Utgard had been murdered, without any mark on them. With their stomachs full of mescal, they'd been hung upside down on the edge of a pier with only their heads in the water. For months the incident had been thoroughly investigated but not one shred of evidence had ever been found that could even remotely incriminate the son. It was said, that after the bizarre deaths, the son quickly gained a deep respect from even the most cutthroat of the population in San Lucas, and that he'd inherited a nickname. People began calling him "The Norse", and most began treating him with a respect that he'd never known when his father was alive.

Several months after the incident, the wild son started a fishing/ diving business, which over several years became extremely profitable. He was well known for his extensive underwater knowledge of numerous areas around Lands End, the Revillagigedo Archipelagoes, and the Sea of Cortez, and he had more dives than any other human being alive on San Benedicto's boiler. After those many years of ridicule in his youth, he was now recognized world-wide for his incredible ability to communicate with and ride the giant Pacific manta rays, just like his beloved father had been. According to what Captain Janus had heard, the son was being considered for the "Guinness World Book of Records" for two thousand dives on the famous site. While he'd been interviewed, he was asked numerous times what had motivated his peculiar passion, and he would always shrug and say, *"I'm just pursuing an old family legend to honor my beloved father and my family ancestry."*

"Captain Olaf . . . Utgard's son will be here tomorrow morning early," Captain Janus nodded with a smile. "He motors over from San Lucas every other weekend, and spends two or three days diving on the boiler. He once told me that he does it to pray over the graves of his ancestors; I have no idea what he means sir."

While our Captain was conversing with Captain Janus, everyone had made their way outside the wheelhouse door and was listening to their astonishing radio conversation.

"Captain Janus, have there been any reports about Mortiken in this area?" The Captain asked curiously.

"As far as I know Olaf they seem to be focused on Panama right now and several European countries. I admit though, I don't follow the news about that scum too often; it seems to far removed from what we do here. I've heard rumors though; from a military commander I'm acquainted with in San Diego, that there are sightings of the Mortiken around the Imperial dam in Colorado. The Air Force Colonel concludes that the Mortiken are interested in controlling the flow of the Colorado River. No one really knows why yet, and I have no other knowledge on the subject Captain. Oh by the way Captain, I've also read that someone discovered a secret entrance to a massive Underground River in the northern Sea of

Cortez, somewhere up around the city of Campo. I don't know why I told you that Olaf, I just thought that you might be interested."

"Thankyou for that sir, I don't know why you did either, but maybe someday we will. Did Utgard ever mention anything about the Rognvald's in your conversations with him?"

"No sir he didn't, but I know for a fact that his son was very interested in the history of the Rognvald/Baaldur religious split in the late 1460s. He was consumed by it in his late teens, especially the far-fetched legends about that bizarre sword some magician made. He became very scholarly in the subject and spent hundreds of hours researching everything about it online; he talked incessantly about it with everyone. I remember him saying once that he was very impressed with what the University of Southern California, and the University of Porto was accomplishing with Rognvald and Baaldurian history, he also mentioned someone else's work he'd admired, I think I remember the name Roxanne."

Roxanne gasped when she heard her name mentioned. Captain Janus's story was far-fetched to say the least, but logically, why would he be making something up like this? Was it possible that Utgard's son was the man the writers of the scrolls had foretold? Had God just opened up a door that would have been impossible for us to find otherwise?

"Captain Janus," Captain Olaf asked, finally relenting to the bewildered expressions on all our faces, "would you happen to know what the sons name is sir?"

"Yes sir I do, he was on my payroll for three weeks several years back. His name is Anders. He's also known in Cabo San Lucas, and Sinaloa, as Anders the Norse, the wild son of Utgard and Bethelynn Vildarsen."

Nine

News from Jonah

June 30th 4:52am

A clamoring bell in the computer room sounded. Awakened abruptly from a magnificent dream I sat up with an unwelcome start, disoriented, and thoroughly disgruntled from having been snatched so ignominiously by such a harsh sound, apparently an e-mail had come through.

It certainly seemed plausible that Ander's the Norse was the man written about in the scrolls we'd found, now the *Heimdall* was going to rendezvous with this enigmatic man and quite frankly, I was astonished at Gods timing. If the storm had never happened and we hadn't been forced to stay overnight in the cave, we may have simply departed these archipelagoes unawares and never have contacted Captain Janus, and if we hadn't done this we'd never been given the opportunity to cross paths with Anders. If any part of our journey had taken longer or shorter than it had, since we'd started, would we have missed this rendezvous with him? I was beginning to understand that Gods timing was absolutely flawless to the second, perhaps a powerfully predestined alliance was about to take place, and our journey was going to open up in ways we could never have imagined. Were we really going to meet the man spoken about in the scrolls today, Ander's the Norse, the wild son of Utgard and Bethelynn Vildarsen? Was it possible that this man might be joining us?

Unfortunately we weren't able to get together with Captain Janus, or physically see the Magdalena, he was pressed for time, late as usual he'd laughed, and they had to weigh anchor and sail back to San Lucas before we would arrive. He offered his regrets, and said he'd hopefully see us soon. Captain Olaf told him that our next major destination was San Diego, and they both promised to stay in touch.

After an in-depth discussion with the Captain and John, Rorek informed us that we were now safely enshrouded in the CSAT. Basing this decision on what Captain Janus had shared yesterday about this unique man, they'd decided it might be wise to view him from a distance to substantiate, or refute, what the Magdalena's Captain had said about him. Although this invisibility safeguard seemed a bit dramatic to me, I could certainly appreciate the logical implications that had prompted their decision. I was sure though, that Anders was very accustomed to encountering various vessels, here on San Benedicto, and interfacing with many "out of the ordinary" personalities and difficult situations. From what I'd heard, I was sure that Anders was fearless and unwavering in all of his endeavors and I shuddered, remembering the story about the six gang members. Still, if it was Gods will that this meeting with Anders the Norse was predestined to develop into an alliance, then this precaution seemed somewhat superfluous to me. Time would tell though, whether or not this decision had been a substantiated safeguard or what, if any, consequence would result from it.

Jonah had finally responded to Roxanne's e-mails in two parts, and what he'd written was sobering. After breakfast, and morning prayers, Helga got up and read his correspondences.

Howdy Heimdall,

Your news about the archipelagoes is incredible. Sorry about the night in the cave, but God works in mysterious ways, time will tell what that is. The two pieces of parchment seem too good to be true, the information is incredible, praise God for this discovery, also tell Rolfy, "atta boy". I guess time will tell whether or not you'll find this man spoken about in the scrolls. Perhaps we won't have to do anything people, perhaps the Lord has already done it for us, time will tell. I'll get a hold of our contacts Roxanne to see if they have anymore info about this.

Don't the last four months seem like a dream guys? So much has happened for us in our journey. Hey guess what, I don't have another expedition until January of next year. That means we could possibly be together, as a complete family, for the rest of the year, I'm really excited about this. I have an odd feeling our journey is going to get increasingly perilous from here on out people. I think we need to prepare ourselves on every level.

I'm home now, praise God! I returned to Pine Valley on June 26th, three days later than I anticipated. It sure feels good to be in the cabin again, I can hardly wait till all you guys get here. I miss you too honey, an awful lot, too much time has passed since we were with each other in Salvador. I really miss all the rest of you guys too. I've been down with a cold for the last few days, and have also developed some problems with the upper vertebrae in my neck. The chiropractor said it was muscle strain from the strenuous hiking, carrying a heavy backpack, and flying around Lake Powell. He said I'd be back to normal someday, I didn't think that would ever be possible, Ha Ha Ha! Anyway, Lake Powell was awesome, and the archeologists were overwhelmed with what I'd discovered last year, they must have taken a thousand pictures. We were able to make it into Navajo Creek, the Glen Canyon Dam, a little town called Wahweap, Padre Canyon, the San Juan arm, and all the way up to the little township of Hite. We also flew over to Needles in Canyonlands National Park and stayed several days in Peekaboo springs. It was really great, wish you all were there. (-:

Now for some news of a serious nature, the Mortiken have gained some control in the Gulf of California, and a small contingent of them have infiltrated up the Colorado River, just past the city of Campo. Apparently they're trying to manipulate the Imperial Dam policies. Don't know much more than this though, the Air Force are heavily involved, and have a black out on all this information. Rumor has it two large vessels came through the Panama Canal, and successfully made covert passage up through the Gulf of California with assistance from a radical faction of the Mexican government in Sinaloa & Sonora. Somebody was bought off I think. I've learned from the professor in Rabat that the "Isla Tiburon" and "Angel de la Guarda" are now under Mortiken and Middle Eastern control, and being heavily funded from somewhere north of the Mediterranean. Personally I think they're being funded by the Russians, because there's been a huge weapons transaction to the Mortiken of Russian AK-47s. Try pulling down on the location with the VEW when you have a chance, I really want to confirm this, let me know. Three weeks ago they captured the airport at the fishing resort near Bahia Kino Norte in Sonora. Since then, unscheduled flights are arriving six times nightly with goods, military equipment, and get this; apparently there are giants on the flights. The professor e-mailed me an encrypted satellite photo to substantiate this. I was a little suspicious when he told me, but sure enough they are certainly giant's people, all of them. From what I saw, they dress like the Mortiken you fought on March 11th. The professor also told me there'd been large pontoon planes flying in and out of the Northern

Orkney Islands, and the outer Shetland Islands. Some flights have even gone in and out of two of the smaller northern islands in the Faroes . . . Fugloy and Vidoy. Things are changing fast, really fast, please be careful on your journey north, can't wait to see y'all.

Stay in touch, in Christ's love, Jonah

2nd e-mail

Hey Roxy . . . just a follow-up to your request about Utgard Vildarsen. There was a small business in San Lucas called ***"Vildarsen Fishing & Diving",*** *they operated from 1965-1987, after that, Utgard did join forces with the schooner Magdalena. Apparently the schooners business quadrupled within a year. He was married to a woman named Bethelynn, and yes, they did have a son several years after Utgard joined the Magdalena crew. I can't find anything else though.*

There is another ***"Vildarsen Oceanic Tours"*** *based in El Castillo in Sinaloa. I couldn't find any start date for that business though. This is all I could come across sugarplum, see you soon, love you, Jonah*

P.S. By the way, the two men that were killed in the Vigo prison, remember? The professor informed me that they were the tattooed fatman and his son.

Someone got into the prison and murdered them, thought you should know.

Love J

The news about the fatman and his son was distressing, but it seemed to reinforce something that everyone already had known about the loathsome duo, they were both cursed in their choices. I wondered who'd murdered them. Thirty minutes after we'd finished with Jonah's e-mails Garrett began yelling excitedly on the radios.

"Hey boss, there's a big beefy brown and white speedboat approaching our position with a long haired dude drivin it."

Ten

Ander's the Norse, son of Utgard & Bethelynn Vildarsen

The speedboat was one of the great muscle boats with the engine under a wooden shroud towards the rear gunwale. It was a beautifully sleek vessel with an open bow, seats all around, and sunken cabins in the middle. It appeared to be constructed of some kind of dark wood, and we could feel the engines low throated rumbling in our bones as it approached. There was only one man aboard, visible from our present position. He was perhaps late twenty's, Scandinavian in appearance, suntanned, smooth shaven, with very long wind blown brown hair. He was at least 6'4", and had a powerful musculature very similar to John and Garrett's.

As soon as he'd brought the rumbling boat to a halt, seventy-five yards from our anchorage, he heaved out his bow anchor. Walking back to the stern, he effortlessly hoisted a hinged diving platform over the rear gunwale, and locked it into place. Already in swimming trunks, he pulled off his short sleeved shirt, put on a single diving tank and mask, grabbed two fins, and stepped out onto the diving platform. Reaching back over the gunwale he grabbed something long and wooden, resembling a narrow curving megaphone, perhaps four feet in length. Kneeling down on the diving platform, he put most of the peculiar object into the water and after taking several deep breathes, began blowing bursts every two seconds. A hollow resonance radiated up from underneath the water, and the peculiar sound reminded me of the bellowing of a distant elephant. Within minutes, an enormous Pacific manta ray quietly surfaced next to the platform, and the man began stroking the top of it. After putting the horn back inside the boat, he jumped into the water, adjusted his face mask, put in his mouthpiece, situated himself on the back of the motionless creature, and then quietly they disappeared underwater.

Five minutes later, still clinging to the back of the manta, he resurfaced in close proximity to the *Heimdall.* Circumspectly we watched as he slid off the creature and swim up against the schooners hull; without any compunction he began hitting it forcefully with one of his fists. How could he have known we were here?

"Hey . . . I can see your stupid anchor chain people. You might be able to hide your vessel topside, but you can't fool the mantas. The hull is visible underwater too you idiots, come on . . . show yourself."

The Captain shrugged; somewhat offended by the man's comments he looked up at the sky chewing his lip. Several moments later, with a gesture of disappointment he quickly motioned for Rorek to disengage the CSAT. No we can't do this I thought; impulsively holding up my hand I motioned for Rorek to stop, I'd gotten an idea. Whispering my plan into the Captains ear he smiled and motioned for Rorek to wait, and then motioned for me to go ahead. Leaning over the *Heimdall's* railings, and purposely using the same old Orknean dialect the scribes had used on the scrolls, I asked my first question.

"Hello friend, is your name Ander's Vildarsen?"

The man looked shocked; he swam back a few more yards and responded in the same dialect. "Who wants to know . . . friend?" He answered cynically.

"My name is Gabriel, and I'm from Aberdeen Scotland. I'm aboard the schooner Heimdall along with eight other people, and an Irish wolfhound named Rolf."

"How do you know my name?" Ander's blurted. "Are you the "ghost vessel" from Europe that I've read about?"

As soon as Ander's asked this question, Captain Olaf gave Rorek the order to disengage the CSAT. The Heimdall suddenly appearing startled Ander's, and he swam back another twenty yards to scrutinize us from a distance. Promptly he spoke something to the manta ray, and the creature quickly sank out of sight. Turning back towards us he pulled his face mask up on top of his head and with a bewildered look, he finished answering the first question.

"I am Ander's . . . Ander's Vildarsen, son of Utgard and Bethelynn," he stammered in quite adequate English. "Who are you people?"

"Come aboard friend, and we'll tell you. My name is Olaf son; I'm from Norway and the Captain aboard this schooner."

Having approached the rear starboard rails, the Captain motioned Ander's towards the stern of the vessel, but he seemed reluctant. Pensively Ander's side-stroked around the entire hull of the *Heimdall,* and then five minutes later he swam back to his speedboat, removed his diving equipment, pulled up the anchor, started the engine, and slowly motored over to our anchorage. When he was close enough he threw a line to John, who was now standing on the stern diving platform ready to receive him. After securing the boat, John extended a hand, and Ander's came aboard and calmly shook everyone's hands. There was something about this moment that reminded me of that late afternoon in Aberdeen on the docks earlier this year, when I'd been invited aboard the Heimdall for the first time. That day had certainly changed my life, and I wondered if it would do the same for Anders today.

For the next six hours we shared what our journey was about. We also shared about our discoveries since arriving in the Revillagigedo's and told him about our dear brother Jonah and his wife Roxanne. We also admitted that we were the ghost vessel, the very same one that had been discussed in the news and on the internet for the last several months.

Ander's sat quietly on the edge of his chair, eyes blazing at times, listening to the adventures we'd had in Europe. Numerous times during the discussion he'd expressed appreciation for our fortitude and skills, and also praised God that we'd found each other. Our narrative about the confrontation with the Mortiken brought tears to his eyes, and he mentioned that he'd seen two of the scallywag's vessel's heading north up into the gulf about a month ago in the early evening. He also knew there was something amiss at the Bahia Kino Norte airport; his mother had called two weeks prior and told him the family couldn't book business flights through that area anymore. The rumor that the airport was being turned into a military installation had been substantiated by his mother, after she'd flown over the site in a private plane.

"I have some crazy buddies that live in Guerrero Negro on the western side of the peninsula," Anders shared, "that's were they produce salt for the whole state, big business there. They take diving tours out to Guadalupe and Cedros Island in the Pacific. They also have two very cool bright red bi-planes, and fly regularly overland east to the gulf for business, well . . . twice a month anyway. I've gone along with them four times in the past, it's really an enjoyable trip, there's this little restaurant over there in Bay Town that makes the best carne asada tacos. Anyway . . . after flying over four weekends ago, they called and told me they'd seen a lot of construction on the eastern side of Angel de la Guarda Island. When they flew in closer, they saw a big airstrip being built and a lot of people, really big people, dressed in weird garments with hoods. When they flew over they said all of them began shaking their fists and screaming.

After they circled around again, they started shooting at the plane, so they figured it was someplace they weren't supposed to be and they split. They did get some good pictures though, I've got um all at home, maybe you guys can sail over and have a look before you head north. Whataya think? My wife Angelina makes the best "Pescado en salsa" in Baja, she learned from her mother. Hey, it would be my honor to have all of you over to my humble cottage for dinner. Have you guys ever been to Lands End?"

Captain Olaf shook his head in a temporary affirmation to the invitation and said, "We'll see . . . we'll see. No son, none of us have ever been to Lands End."

After reading the two scrolls Anders seemed flabbergasted and shared that ever since he'd been a very small boy he was somehow aware that God had chosen him for something special because of his peculiar interests. The gifts he'd been given, and the passionate desire to pursue the truth, about the Rognvald's and the Baaldur's, was something he'd never lost interest in over the years. He'd also known that he'd be leaving someday and heading north with strangers, and that the ancient Rognvald sword and a vast treasure would somehow be part of the equation.

"I've had dreams since I was a little boy about leaving with distant warriors on a mysterious quest. Gosh, I guess you guys really are the ghost warriors they wrote about in the scrolls, it's really amazing they were given that insight, praise God, it's really happening for us," Anders said, shaking his head.

"You know, my family thought I was crazy, even my wife did, especially when I told them our ancestors were someday going to be involved in a great battle in a far-a-way land. I tried telling them many times about the extreme differences between the two tribes, and that the Mortiken were the ancient Baaldurian Viking tribe, but they thought I was crazy. My aunt in El Castillo still thinks the Mortiken are from another planet because of how they look, some of my family's really weird. I remembered my father saying, when I was young, that if the Christ loved us so much why did He put us on this forsaken rock in the middle of nowhere. My whole family was really soured by it all, and most left Christianity and became Roman Catholic, or rejoined the assemblies of the elder Troth. I think that's why my father started drinking mescal, he was devastated when the family embraced the old ways, and because of my poor father's transgression, I certainly grew up prejudiced towards God. Father told me it was a real tough life on the island, a daily struggle for food, and everyone always argued. You know something, my father would never have made all those dives on the boiler or learned how to ride and communicate with the mantas if they hadn't been stuck on that island for all those years. Somehow the diving kept my father focused and rational, even after he'd lost part of his leg, so in that aspect it was a good thing. I know now that it was Gods plan for them to be there, and because of it I learned about the mantas and the Rognvald treasure too. So really, in hind sight, it was all good, and I'm a better man because of all their suffering."

A year and a half after his father's violent demise, still overwhelmed and trying to rationalize the event, Ander's continued to fight and drink, and had also established a reputation in San Lucas as someone you just didn't look at wrong. His heart had ultimately softened though, and had miraculously opened to his wife's continually loving message about relationship with Jesus Christ and the healing and wisdom it brought; Anders finally abandoned the ancient religion and drinking, and made a decision for Christ.

"It was the best thing I've ever done, and it changed me in profound ways. Unfortunately the family saw my acceptance of Jesus Christ as Lord and Savior as an act of rebellion, but you know something, I really never cared what they thought anyway, I knew that I'd made the right decision." After Anders shared this fact he stopped, shook his head, and wiped away some tears that had begun running down his cheeks.

"Some people just don't get it," Ander's murmured softly. "My family doesn't understand Christianity, or what having relationship with the Creator is all about. It sure has made all the difference in the world for my wife and me. It brought us so much closer together.

Now she trusts me when I travel and work." Suddenly cheerful, Anders laughed heartily along with the rest of us, and asked Betsy for another cup of coffee; after she handed it to him he nodded politely and gulped it all down. After putting down the cup he stood up, apparently ready to depart.

"Anders wait, lets pray before you leave," Captain Olaf suggested, motioning with his hand for him to join in a circle with the others.

"Alright sir, that would be wise," He agreed. After we'd all joined in a circle we each took turns praying for Gods wisdom about what we should be doing at this mysterious juncture in our journey.

"I believe that God put us in each others paths today Anders," the Captain began contemplatively after we'd finished, "do you agree with that son?"

"Yes sir I do!" Anders replied without hesitation.

"I also believe that you're supposed to join the Heimdall crew son and help us in our search for the First Tribe."

The whole crew shook their heads agreeing with the Captain. Pensive again, Anders walked over to one of the portholes and quietly gazed out at the sea. For several minutes he stood unmoved, and then suddenly, with a decisive snort, he spun back around and walked over to the Captain.

"I believe you're right sir, permission to come aboard the Heimdall as a new crew member sir."

"Excellent son, welcome aboard the *Heimdall,*" the Captain laughed while everyone applauded. "What can we do to make your transition easier?"

"Well sir, I believe that I can take care of most things myself, I'll have to make arrangements for my business though, and inform my beloved wife. Funny thing, we were talking just last week that this was going to happen someday, I guess that someday has finally arrived." Anders looked puzzled for a moment, and then asked, "Would you guys like to swim with the manta's before we leave Benedicto?"

"Dude . . . that'd be way cool!" Garrett shouted enthusiastically. "Yah baby, let's do it brother! How bout it Cap, can we, can we, can we?"

Anders smiled at Garrett; they faced off at each other, flexed, growled, and slapped high fives while the Captain looked around at the rest of the crew for opinions. While I shrugged indifferently, and most nodded half-heartedly, he saw only John, Helga, and Garrett eagerly shaking their heads.

"I can't think of any reason why not then," the Captain conceded, "how about tomorrow morning son?" Anders shook his head eagerly.

"Captain . . . I haven't ever said anything about this," Anders began hesitantly, pulling at his long hair, "but my father found something on the boiler years ago. After the volcano blew in 1952, everything got rearranged on the bottom, and he found a whole load of stuff from the old vessel that went down. Perhaps, when we get to my home I can show it to you? I've kept it hidden for years, no one knows about it, not even my wife, father swore me to absolute secrecy. Father also confirmed that I would know when the time was right, I think the time is right now sir."

Eleven

Swimming with the giant Pacific Manta Rays

July 1st

The day dawned glorious and a balmy zephyr was gusting sweetly from the south. Garrett was so excited to get started that he'd dove off the side of the *Heimdall* and swam over to the speedboat to find Anders, but no one was aboard. Taped over the stern diving platform was a note that Anders had left: *Will return by 7am, have your diving equipment ready.*

Garrett swam back and informed Captain Olaf about the note, and the Captain instructed John and Rorek to bring up the scuba equipment and get things organized. John, Helga, Garrett, Captain Olaf, and I would be diving with Anders this morning, and my poor stomach was flopping about like a fish on the floor. There were bloody hammerhead sharks in the water here, and no one seemed bothered about that trifling fact except me. I'd struggled with fears about the unknown all my life, and never fully understood where the basis of those fears had originated. Sitting here in the galley, I was beginning to feel that old recurring flush of panic oozing over me again, and all I could do with my breakfast this morning was turn it over and over and over, I knew that if I swallowed anything I would probably vomit.

"Don't worry bout nothing little bother Gabriel," John laughed, hungrily wolfing down his omelet. "It'll be cool man. Anders knows these waters really well, and he wouldn't ask us along if he thought it would be dangerous. Hey, I've been in the water with sharks before. All you have to do is keep an eye on them and if they get near, just bonk um on the nose." With a gasp, I looked at John incredulously and shook my head.

"John, Anders father got his leg bit off," I argued, squirming on my chair and finally pushing away my plate. "He got his bloody leg bit off!" Before I could continue whining, Rorek announced that Anders had resurfaced and was coming aboard.

"Let's get topside people," the Captain ordered on the radio, "we need to get suited up and ready to go NOW! Let's hustle!"

Trudging up the stairs grumbling, I began remembering the stories I'd heard in my past about divers swimming up close and personal with sharks. Those stories had always made me shudder at the potential for danger, irregardless of how safe the divers thought they were. Logically though, from what Anders had shared yesterday, swimming with the gentle Pacific manta rays seemed a lot safer, and infinitely more seductive than swimming with sharks. According to him, the creatures were perfectly harmless to humans; maybe I'd be OK then, but I still couldn't help but wonder what the next few hours held in store for all of us. After we'd reached the deck, and cursory "good mornings" were exchanged, we began suiting up for the day's adventure.

"Hey Anders," I inquired, struggling with the straps on my air tank, "dude why is this place called the Boiler?"

"Gabriel . . . look at the sea around the island this morning, it's flat, calm, except for the occasional swell coming through right?

"Yah . . . it's nice and smooth out there, that's a fact," I nodded.

"Well . . . the pinnacle is about twenty-five feet under the surface right over there," he pointed, "now watch what happens when the next set of waves passes over."

A few moments later, a large set came rolling into the area and what happened then really impressed me. While the first swell was passing over the seamount, a strange churning erupted on the surface; it actually looked like a giant pot of water boiling on the stove. It rumbled and hissed violently for a few moments, and then shortly after the swell passed over, the surface of the water became calm again. I knew now why the nickname "boiler" illustrated this place clearly.

"Dude that was awesome, looks like a giant jacuzzi," Garrett shouted excitedly from the diving platform. "Hey . . . let's get goin molasses butts, what's takin you slowpokes?"

Anders and Garrett slapped high fives and began laughing. They'd begun joking, and occasionally punching each other on the shoulders while suiting up. It appeared Anders possessed many traits in his personality like Garrett had, and it was becoming painfully apparent that they also shared a similar sense of humor, arcane, guttural, and thoroughly frivolous. This morning Garrett was as excited as I'd ever seen him, and based on their rowdy deportment together, it seemed Anders and he had already begun developing a solid relationship. I pondered the ramifications of Garrett and Anders being siblings, and how this would impact the chemistry of daily life aboard the *Heimdall.* I found myself thankful that they were just friends. Still, Garrett had a remarkable way with people, he had this ability to reach down inside your heart and leave you feeling genuinely special, but then conversely, he had this perplexing capacity to take you on a rollercoaster ride of emotional changes and exasperate you for reasons known only to him. He was often pigheaded, and seemed to know exactly what he wanted to do, getting loud, brusque, and sometimes even confrontational to make his points known. Afterwards though, he would always resolve any negative circumstances he'd instigated with a kind of love and wisdom that amazed and confounded everyone. He was truly blessed with an eclectic intermingling of personality traits that would invariably, at some point in time, leave you very charmed with the gifted young man that he'd become. In his expressions of love, and intense audaciousness, I found my greatest camaraderie with him and I was very proud to call him my friend and brother.

"Ok . . . here's what to expect below this morning," Anders began after everyone was suited up and ready. "There's a lot of activity down there today. The conditions are excellent though, the clearest I've seen in months, so we're blessed. There's a school of Clarion Angelfish around the pinnacle, I'm sure you've already seen them over at Socorro, and I counted three hammerheads in the distance. I also counted seven rays this morning, along with Maybelle; she's been my personal buddy for five years. The hammerheads won't bother us though, not unless you aggravate them, they're real shy, and they will stay away." Anders glanced over at me and nodded.

"That's a real relief," I muttered suspiciously.

"When we get into the water," Anders continued with a chuckle, "follow me and do exactly what I do. I've already told Maybelle you're coming down, she'll alert the others, OK . . . you guys ready to go?" Anders glanced over at the Captain when he'd finished and then Olaf began.

"Thanks Anders! Alright people, this will be quite an experience for us I'm sure. Let's follow Anders instructions precisely. Gabriel, if you have any problems, I want you to return to the surface immediately, let's not take any chances today son. As a matter of fact people, I want all of us to keep an eye out for each other this morning, OK? John, you and Gabriel stay close."

"Aye sir . . . no problem," John replied with a puckish grin. "Hey . . . Gabriel's gonna do just fine Captain; he didn't eat any breakfast this morning, so at least he won't puke down there." John winked irreverently at me, and then winced when Helga punched his arm.

Well, that did it; I was really embarrassed now, and began to feel frustration, anger, and a host of other junk boiling up from somewhere deep inside my bowels. Glancing around surreptitiously I found myself wanting to throw something at John, but couldn't find anything in the immediate area. Oh how rude people could be, why did everybody always pick on me? Struggling to preserve my integrity and cool; I grimaced, and bit my tongue. Everyone, including Anders, began chuckling after that crack, and within seconds the chuckling had become waves of gut-wrenching laughter. This was going on far too long. I was a Doctor of English Literature, and I wasn't going to take this crap anymore. I decided right then and there that I was going to quit the Heimdall as soon as we'd reached San Diego, I could get a job at the University of Southern California. There at least I'd find some respect.

"Hey you guys . . ." I began stammering, but right at the very moment I'd have stuck my foot firmly in my mouth, Betsy mysteriously appeared at my side, gently grabbing my arm she moved in close and whispered.

"Honey, they're just playing with you. They're not serious, they love and respect you Gabriel, and so do I."

Betsy kissed my cheek, and when I saw her reassuring smile, my heart melted, and my head fell in shame. Betsy's gentle wisdom had once again quelled that gigantic ego of mine. The monster I thought I'd put to rest in the Bay of Biscay months ago had once again reared its ugly head, and now right in plain view of our new friend Anders. Thankfully though there was something in Betsy's heart that came out in her words and it very effectively soothed that temperamental beast inside me. Oh how I wished I could put that thing to rest permanently. Looking up awkwardly, I shrugged my shoulders and mumbled, "Sorry guys, I'm still a nutch."

Everyone smiled, patted my back, and reminded me that I was loved. Now it was time to swallow my pride, control my perplexing fears, and get down to business. Each in turn, we all walked off the stern diving platform and disappeared under the dark blue water.

It was truly breathtaking, a thespian production featuring thousands of exotic fish whose interface was truly an astonishing sight. Floating motionless for several minutes, my eyes beheld a flawlessly proportioned interaction rivaling the greatest ballet or symphony I'd ever seen or heard. Mysteriously though, our presence caused only a momentary inquisitiveness, and within minutes we'd been completely accepted into this aquatic domain and soon ignored. As we followed Anders down, I noticed that the sun, reflecting down from the surface above, had become a yellowish circle with feathery edges, a golden medallion hovering and undulating with each passing wave. It was mesmerizing in this place, and while the delightful glow of sapphire water embraced us in a slowly increasing chill, we all sank deeper into the yawning cerulean gloom.

Shortly after we'd begun our descent, a wonderfully unexpected peace infused my whole being, the churning inside my stomach finally ended, and I felt strong and focused again. Captain Olaf and Anders swam side by side, while Garrett, Helga, John, and I, swam huddled together several yards above them. I couldn't prove it, but I think they were protecting me.

The pinnacle was awesome! Covered with fuzzy brownish/green seaweed, and similar in appearance to one of the formations at the shallows of three rocks, it descended mysteriously into the gloom below. Somewhere around sixty feet deep, Garrett, Helga, and John began gesticulating at me and pointing, a huge shape had come to a lazy halt directly over me and stalled. The female Manta was enormous. With a wing span of six meters, (at least twenty feet) the creamy white, exceptionally rough underbelly of this cartilaginous fish hovered above me like a small floating island. Some of the exhaled bubbles from my tank, slowly meandering towards the surface, floated up underneath her and each time the bubbles touched her, she seemed to quiver. There were two cephalic lobes, resembling two huge horns, extending out from the front of the creature; I knew now why sailors had been of a mind to call this creature a "devilfish" in years past. On the outside of the lobes, closer to the main body were the eyes, and when I swam up next to her, she seemed to smile back with a gentleness that certainly contradicted her size. It was exhilarating, and almost overwhelming, to be in the presence of such an immense yet non-threatening creature.

Anders appeared next to me suddenly and motioned for me to follow him. As we approached the top of the manta he tapped my shoulder and pointed down farther, twenty-five feet below I saw Captain Olaf moving through the water in a beautifully symbiotic ballet on the top of another manta. I was thoroughly overwhelmed in a blanket of goose pimples; it was an incredible sight. There were hundreds of brightly colored Clarion angelfish around another manta parallel to us, cleaning her gills. Apparently one of the reasons the manta rays came to this area was to be cleaned regularly and groomed by these gorgeous fish, how incredible Gods creation was. It appeared Garrett, John, and Helga were already riding their mantas; I could see all of them moving lazily through the water in the distance with glowing faces resembling bright beacons. Anders quickly showed me were to grab a hold of the manta on top, and when I had, he gently touched her, and the giant creature began moving with slow powerful strokes . . . I was beside myself and my stomach was in my mouth in an instant. Oh how I wished mother and father and all my old friends could have seen me now, this was mind-boggling, it was even better than being in the Hebrides by myself. The manta slowly arched up and down, once coming within three feet of the surface. Next it moved towards the pinnacle, and with a sharp sliding turn took me all the way to the bottom. What a rush! I didn't like it though; the pressure on the bottom was much too great, and quickly began bothering me. Somehow I think the manta knew this, because afterwards she never went that deep with me again.

The time passed quickly, and before I knew it, Anders and Captain Olaf were motioning for all of us to resurface. Because we'd all gone so deep, Anders had us stop at the forty foot level and wait for twenty minutes before ascending; he'd said it was very important to the well-being of our blood chemistry, something that I really didn't understand. It ended so very differently than it had started, and although I felt like a new man after the days adventurous exploits, I found myself once again flushed with embarrassment about my immaturity earlier and sat at the farthest end of the table because of it. When Betsy came up and embraced me with a firm hug, she reminded me about how proud she was with what I'd accomplished today. My heart once again melted, and the anger that I was holding onto towards John, and the circumstances, vanished.

"The most dangerous source of lies is what our own minds try to convince us of Gabriel." Betsy shared.

During her short talk Betsy helped me recognize that there was always a battle that ensued, inside our minds, when we purpose to obey Christ and walk in obedience. What we all struggle with sometimes convinces us to respond in ways that disparage the glory of God, simply because we respond in the sin nature instead of the Christ nature. With her sobering, and judicious lexis, I rapidly began understanding how I'd failed innumerable times in my own responses to others who challenged me in the areas where my self-image was the weakest. Because of my foolish choices I was often downgraded to wallowing in, and sifting through, the ashes of my own inanity. Although my emotions were an important part of my makeup, and also an element of who I was as a human being, they could oftentimes, left unguarded, become an enemy to God's will for my life. Betsy also told me that the most important stewardship we have in life is the stewardship of our own hearts, and if our hearts become embittered or corrupted in any way, God cannot use us because we become incapable of ministering to others in His love. She also reminded me that my life had changed dramatically in the last five months and that I had adapted well to challenging circumstances, from her perspective I was growing more than she could have ever imagined. I sighed deeply when Betsy finished with her loving encouragements; she was so very wise in areas that I didn't have a clue about. What did this wonderful woman see in me, and why did my heart hurt so when she was near?

Captain Olaf invited Anders to eat with us, and everyone stood up and applauded when he arrived. Because of his graciousness and skills, our day had become a magical experience we would never forget. While we ate, the wonderful meal Betsy, Roxanne, and Lizzy had graciously prepared, we eagerly shared our impressions of what we'd individually experienced, and discussed plans for tomorrow's departure. To end Garrett's niggling persistence, Captain Olaf finally decided to let him, Betsy, and I go on ahead with Anders to San Lucas in the speedboat. There Anders would make arrangements for us to dock the *Heimdall* for an indeterminate period while he made preparations for his departure with us to San Diego.

After dinner, I took the opportunity to e-mail father and mother about what I'd experienced today. I was once again proud to be part of such a distinguished team and fervently promised myself that I'd never consider quitting an option again.

Twelve

The Four Families

July 2nd 8:00am

Once again Garrett was beside himself, he wanted to get aboard the muscle boat and leave. Captain Olaf had instructed us to take along two way radios, and one of the cell phones so we could stay in touch. He realized the radios could possibly be ineffective at such a great distance, but promised he would continue calling every four hours until we'd made contact. We also took along backpacks with several changes of clothes, two small hand weapons, my laptop in a waterproof case, and food and water for several days, just in case. Anders told us the trip in would probably require six hours of continual high-speed travel. Barring any foul weather, or sudden swells; it was entirely possible we'd be back together early morning on July 3rd. Once we'd arrived in Cabo San Lucas, Anders would stop and make arrangements concerning his departure, and then if all went as planned, we'd be heading north along the East Cape to his secluded home just north of Los Barilles. When we'd arrived, one of Betsy's responsibilities would be booking hotel rooms, or cabanas, for the entire crew. Anders suggested the Hotel Punta Pescadero, three miles north of his home; he knew the owner and could get us good discount rates. Betsy and Captain Olaf, as well as the rest of the crew, embraced his idea and agreed with it. We also considered it wise to e-mail Jonah and inform him about these new plans, and tell him our arrival in San Diego would most likely be delayed.

There was something peculiar with what Anders father had discovered after the 1952 volcanic eruption, on San Benedicto. Considering that the emergence of this discovery would probably change our plans, Roxanne suggested that Jonah meet us in San Lucas and then voyage with us to San Diego aboard the *Heimdall;* everyone agreed her idea was logical. After an hour was spent sorting out many details, we joined hands and prayed for safety and Gods will while we were apart. Anders seized another opportunity to pray with us, and afterwards we all knew without any doubt, that our new friend was very thankful we'd found each other and was now part of the team.

The engine on the speedboat roared into life, and then idled in a deep throated rumbling. With all his teeth showing Garrett smiled gleefully, and began rubbing his hands together in eager anticipation of becoming one with the power and speed of the Raptor. After we'd come aboard and stowed our gear in the cabin amidships, Anders deftly maneuvered away from the *Heimdall.* When we were clear, the speedboat literally exploded into life and all of us grabbed the safety rails and held on for dear life. Wow, what a rush! Within seconds we were flying over the water at seventy-five miles per hour, this vessel was certainly impressive, incredibly smooth, and unusually powerful. Waving enthusiastically until the *Heimdall* became a tiny spot on the distant horizon, we then quickly settled in for the two hundred and sixty mile journey towards the mainland.

The muscle boat was a "Carrera performance craft," the "300 Raptor." With an open bow and a cabin in the middle; it could comfortably accommodate four people. It had a small kitchen with two refrigerators, a four burner propane stove, and an adequate chemical toilet. Anders had designed the Raptor especially for his needs, and also had a special diving platform installed that dropped over the rear gunwale and locked into place. He'd needed this special feature for diving purposes. Surprisingly, the hull wasn't wood at all; it was a brown fiberglass composite that looked exactly like wood. On each side of the bow, detailed beautifully in red and white paint, were Viking swords similar in appearance to the Tempest, it was truly impressive looking. What we found attached to the middle of the instrumentation panel really astounded us though, there was a sixteen inch brass plaque engraved with a sword and helmet over a shield.

"Anders . . ." I yelled over the deep throated roar of the engine, "do you know what this symbol means?" Vigorously he shook his head that he did and unexpectedly brought the boat to a swift stop.

"It's the symbol of the Rognvald's Gabriel, hold on a minute." Anders stepped down into the cabin, and when he'd returned several moments later, I was given a skillfully crafted gold medallion; it was beautifully etched with the same Rognvald symbol we'd seen several times since departing Aberdeen.

"Where'd you get this big dude?" Garrett asked his face quickly contorting in bewilderment.

"From my father little dude, and he got it from his father, hand to hand, you know what I mean? It's been passed down since the original voyage in the 1470's. Rumor has it Gamelin himself made these medallions; I think there were fifteen of them, one for each vessel." Anders shook his head with a sly grin, and then put the medallion back inside the cabin.

"So you're originally a Rognvald?" Betsy queried, nodding curiously.

"No Betsy I'm from the Vildarsen clan; the Rognvald's were the First Tribe, the leaders of the whole nation. King Agar and Gamelin were literally from the clan of Rognvald's. There were hundreds of different clan names involved with the first tribe; the Rognvald's were the ones God chose to introduce Christianity into the realm, and they were the ones that the Baaldur clan hated specifically. The Baaldur's didn't care what any other clan did unless they'd sided with the Rognvald's; they wanted to kill anyone who'd joined forces with the Rognvald's. Christianity seriously threatened their wicked belief system, they were dedicated to destroying Christianity in anyway they could."

"So . . ." Betsy pondered, "back when this all started, the Vildarsen's were another clan/family that sided with the Rognvald's in their spiritual choices."

"Yes that's correct! But not only did the Vildarsen's side with the Rognvald's in their choices, they were also called by God to fulfill something else Betsy. They were empowered by King Agar from a vision he'd been given after months of intercessory prayer to actually teach Christianity to all the clans, and also prepare young warriors to do physical battle against the Baaldurian's. Christ before all else was the mandate that the Vildarsen's personally received in prayer for the whole Viking nation. This was an undeniable mandate, a battle standard of sorts which would forever pit them against the wicked Baaldurian ethos. Consequently, with King Agar's permission, Gamelin was given permission to etch that very phrase, along with a picture of a sword being plunged into a wicked dragons head, on the original symbolic Tempest sword."

Curiously, after he'd mentioned the Tempest sword, Anders demeanor changed unexpectedly, and his mood became visibly darkened. Grumbling under his breath, he turned abruptly towards the stern of the vessel and began fiddling with one of the running lights. Knowing that something was wrong, I hastily took the opportunity to change the subject. Captain Olaf had strictly instructed us, before we'd left the *Heimdall,* not to say a word about our discovery of the

Tempest, or the rubies, to anyone, including Anders, not until he'd deemed the time was right, and we'd all promised to hold fast to his wishes.

"Were all the people on Isla Socorro Vildarsen's then Anders?"

"No Gabriel," Anders answered softly with a deep sigh, "there were four chosen families, including the Vildarsen's, that decided to stay when they'd reached Isla Socorro, the Bjornson's, the Undset's and the Amundsen's."

"But the Vildarsen's were the only ones who survived?" Garrett interjected.

"No little brother, not at all. Part of the Amundsen and Bjornson clans are still working with my mother and her sisters over in El Castillo, in Sinaloa Mexico. Years ago, maybe forty people from the three clans relocated there because none of them cared for the corrupt community in San Lucas; as a matter of fact they hated everything about that settlement. There are still a great number of Vildarsens, Bjornson's, and Amundsen's scattered all over. My mother told me several years ago, after searching the internet for months, that she'd discovered descendants from all three families living in enormous settlements, pretty much concealed from modern society, spread out all over the Yukon Territories, Alaska, and apparently several rebellious clans were hidden in underground settlements, but no one knows where. Unfortunately though, the other family's bloodline tragically ended, because the entire Undset clan perished on the boiler in that bloody storm. For awhile it really freaked everyone, loosing an entire clan was perceived as a severe failure on Gods part, it was truly a catastrophe that took years for everyone to recover from, and in the process most lost their faith in Jesus Christ. I really believe though, that the death of all the Undset's was what turned so many away from the old ways of Christianity and into the arms of dead legalism and the Troth, not the suffering they endured on the island. It was the Undset's that were given the wisdom to head north to find the First Tribe, and the other clans decided to follow their lead after weeks of prayer together. Being the only ones wiped out following their own vision had a real negative effect on everyone. Talk about suffering and tragedy becoming a precursor for change, well, I've already told you guys what happened after that."

"Primarily then," I postulated, after agreeing with Anders provocative point, "most of the original Orknean, and Shetland Viking clans were then of Norwegian descent?"

"That's something that all the scholars argue about Gabriel, but according to my own personal studies, and what I read passed down through my family's generational records, it's in my opinion that yes, a great part of the Northern Viking nation migrated to Northern Scotland, the Orkney Islands and the Shetland islands from all the costal areas between Bergen and Stavanger on Norway's western coast. Of course some scattered tribes also migrated from parts of Sweden and southern Scotland, but yah; I strongly believe that the majority of the original Viking nation came from the western coasts of Norway."

"DUDE . . . WOW," Garrett exclaimed. Suddenly looking as if a bolt of lightening had struck his brain, he jumped up with a wild look.

"That's where Captain Olaf and Rorek are from! They're last name is Amundsen man!"

"They're both Amundsen's, you're kidding!" Anders was startled. Garrett shook his head no and laughed.

"It really is their name Anders." Betsy added, shaking her head in agreement.

"Where are they from Garrett?" Anders asked, looking puzzled.

"Dude they're both from Stavanger Norway! That's where they were born, and that's where the bloody *Heimdall* was constructed."

I was amazed with this information; we'd never talked about this before. I suddenly realized that I didn't know anybodies last name on this crew, except Captain Olaf and Rorek's now. Olaf and Rorek Amundsen, WOW, cool! Stavanger Norway was only three hundred and ten miles from my hometown of Aberdeen, and I'd been there several times with father in my late preteens. Being the hub of Norway's petroleum industry, Stavanger was one of the first ports my father had successfully negotiated an oil contract with when he'd started Proudmore Oil Inc.

"You know something, that means that Olaf and Rorek's lineage was one of the original families under the First Tribe," I stammered. "They're bloody related with the original Viking nation!"

Anders looked shocked. Twisting his long brown hair, he stood quietly absorbed in a thought process for several minutes.

"Hey guys," he cried out suddenly, "this conversation is really incredible, but we've got to get going if we're going to make it to San Lucas before dark. We'll talk more when we get there, OK? Something very cool is happening dudes."

Everyone agreed.

After we'd gotten underway, Garrett's persistent curiosity about the boats engine, and the control panel was foremost in his mind, so Anders told him he'd put in the powerful Mercury HP550 EFI 502ci 490 HP Bravo I-xz engine. It had a ninety gallon fuel tank, full instrumentation with radar and bezels, and every bell and whistle you could think of. Garrett was very impressed, as were the rest of us. About an hour later, Anders brought the boat to a stop again and asked Garrett if he wanted to captain it.

To this very day I can't help but laugh when I reminisce about what transpired between Garrett and Anders in the next few moments, it was utterly enchanting. I've always wished that my camera had been in my hands though, because the expression on my little brother Garrett's face lit up the boat like a burst of brilliant sunlight, I swear we got sunburned from it. Garrett was suddenly in heaven. Within seconds he had that boat up to seventy-five miles an hour, and for fifteen minutes after that he couldn't stop screaming in excitement. Anders showed him and me the compass heading to maintain, and twenty minutes later went below and fell asleep. It wasn't until 4:30pm that Betsy and I finally awakened Anders, Cabo San Lucas was looming on the horizon right off the bow.

Thirteen

Cabo San Lucas

Cabo San Lucas now is a very celebrated resort town, named after the small cape extending eastward from Baja's southernmost tip. In the 1930's San Lucas was a small fishing village with one cannery, and a population of just around four hundred resilient souls. In the 40's and early 50's Cabo San Lucas got her first taste of modern development when millionaires built vacation homes along the expanse of cliffs overlooking the bays and coves.

The region experienced a sport fishing explosion in the 50's and 60's, and because of an abundance of billfishing off the tip of the peninsula, it earned the nickname "Marlin Alley". Understandably, the area brought in hundreds of curious anglers and wealthy boat owners, being that the magnificently wild stories being spun up in the Northlands had created so much inquisitiveness.

In the early days, one story teller reported that the place was rich in gold and pearls, ruled by the Amazonian queen "Calafia" and populated by beautiful Amazon women. It was hard for me to accept how some people could believe a story like that, and then relocate to see if it was true.

Construction of the Transpeninsular Highway was completed in 1973, and fueled the population growth to all time high of fifteen hundred. The Highway allowed anyone in automobiles, or RV's, the opportunity to make the six day round trip. With a permanent population now around forty thousand people, mostly retired, the main source of San Lucas' income is still the tourist industry, sport fishing, and diving.

On the tip, referred to as "Lands end", sits the world famous rock arch formation known as "El Arco", where the Pacific Ocean meets the warm water of the Sea of Cortez, also known as the Gulf of California. Two primary towns, small and very different from one another inhabit the southern peninsula, San Jose del Cabo, and Cabo San Lucas. The twenty mile stretch between the towns is known as the seacoast "Corridor" and home to many elegant hotels and world famous golf courses. Apparently farther north, up the East Cape, was where Anders secluded cottage, and the Hotel Punta Pescadero was. Eventually, and hopefully, we'd be anchoring the *Heimdall* there and taking some time off.

After he'd come up from his nap, Anders took the wheel from Garrett and began maneuvering us into the Bahia de Cabo San Lucas. Suddenly cognizant of her responsibilities, Betsy seized the opportunity to call Captain Olaf to inform him that we'd arrived. He and the crew were overjoyed to hear from us, and said the *Heimdall* would probably be in around 6am in the morning. They'd decided to make the crossing on the diesel, considering that without Garrett and me aboard, they were unfortunately short-handed for sailing. The Captain was concerned about where we'd meet after they'd arrived, so Anders suggested we rendezvous out beyond the surf line east of Lands End, and then head north along the East Cape towards Punta Pescadero together. The Captain and Rorek agreed with the suggestion, afterwhich we all exchanged well wishes and hung up.

It seemed everyone was acquainted with Anders in the harbor; all waved enthusiastically and most greeted him with "Que pasa Norseman." Anders took us through a narrow opening past the Marinas de Baja and then towards the main dock off our starboard.

Instead of accessing the main dock though, Anders veered past a grouping of boat ramps, and several dozen vessels. A new sandblasted sign hung above the pier, clearly announcing that this spot belonged to, **Norse diving & fishing-Anders Vildarsen-proprietor.**

"Should we take our backpacks dude?" Garrett shouted as we all jumped off the side of the Raptor. Anders shook his head no, and motioned for us to follow.

"Hey Gabriel," Anders shouted back over his shoulder, "Please lock the cabin doors and take the ignition key with you dude!"

I nodded and waved that I would. When we caught up with him, we walked one hundred and fifty yards up a cracked blacktop street, past the flea market plaza, to a well maintained single story wooden building with a red fiberglass tile roof. Behind the front counter, sitting at an ornately carved oak desk, working on a computer, was a striking woman in her late twenties with waist length dark hair.

"Hey precious," Anders greeted her as he launched himself over the front counter. "Didja miss me?"

"Anders," the woman's face glowed like the sun and they embraced and kissed. With a huge smile he turned and introduced us; it was Angelina, his most exquisite wife.

"So very nice to meet all of you, welcome to San Lucas, are you hungry? Would you like some dinner?" she asked, smiling radiantly while shaking all our hands.

"Dude . . ." Garrett turned, scrunching up his nose, "don't you live up the coast a ways? What was the name of that place again man?"

"Punta Pescadero little brother," Anders smiled. "Yes we do, but tonight we're eating over at the Hotel Fininsterra, they owe me several favors and we'll use them to get us all some comida mas fina in substantial amounts. We won't be heading up the coast until tomorrow morning, is that alright with you guys?"

"Cool dude, but where we gonna crash tonight?" Garrett inquired. Anders brow puckered and he looked over at his wife, she shrugged her shoulders.

"What do you mean little brother?"

"Sleep dude . . . where are we going to sleep tonight?" Garrett reiterated his question.

"I'll get us rooms at the hotel we're eating at," Betsy interjected, "how bout that guys?"

Anders and his wife looked uncomfortable for a moment, and began talking feverishly in Spanish with one another. After several moments though Anders politely accepted Betsy's proposal, and Angelina began closing down the computer and preparing to leave.

Dinner was superb, the service was splendid, and Betsy was impressed beyond words with the sauces that were used in the main courses, they were silky smooth and fantastically palatable. Everyone seemed to know Anders and his wife in the restaurant, so Betsy finally mustered the courage and asked if it would be acceptable to introduce her to the chef so she could pick his brain.

"No problem," they both agreed. "Angelina will introduce you; the executive chef is her mother."

Betsy chuckled, and glanced at Angelina shyly, "I guess the chef is a lady then huh? Sorry bout that."

When they came back, about an hour later, Betsy was beaming; she'd been able to procure at least twenty new recipes, and was eager to try them all. While she talked with Angelina, Garrett and I looked at each other and began rubbing our stomachs and sighing. The tempting voice of Betsy's culinary bliss was calling us in the days ahead, and our mouths and stomachs were eagerly awaiting her wondrous creations.

Later, around 11pm, after we'd all retired, I heard the cell phone ring in Betsy's room several doors down. Five minutes later my room phone rang, it was Betsy. She informed me Captain Olaf had called, and she needed to talk to everyone ASAP.

"Should I call Anders?"

"Already did Gabriel, he'll be up in a few minutes, please hurry,"

"Should I go fetch Garrett?" Before Betsy could answer though, I was startled by a sharp rapping on my door.

"Hold on a minute Betsy . . . who is it?"

"It's the King a Scotland dummy, who dya think it is? Let's go, Betsy is waitin for us."

"Garrett's here now Betsy; we'll be down shortly OK . . . bye bye."

After letting Garrett in and getting punched in the shoulder because I took too long, I quickly brushed my teeth, and then we both raced down the hall to Betsy's room where Anders was already waiting.

"The Captain called," she began, "Jonah's flying down, and he'll be at the Los Cabos International airport 9am tomorrow morning."

"Very cool," Garrett chimed as we both slapped high fives. "I miss that guy a lot. Hey Anders you gonna dig Jonah man, that dudes the bomb. Dude that guy knows so much about the Bible it'll blow you away, he's our really good friend."

Anders eyes lit up and he eagerly shook his head. "I'm looking forward to meeting him little brother."

"The Captain wants to know if we should rent a car to pick Jonah up in," Betsy continued, "they're docking in San Lucas for supplies and to fuel up the *Heimdall,* they won't be able to help us. I don't know exactly how we're going to do this though, any suggestions?"

"Betsy . . . I have an idea," Anders began, "and this will work out perfectly for all of us actually. Angelina and I have to get our truck up the coast; it's parked over by the business . . ."

"I saw that ride man," Garrett interrupted, "its old but its bomb. I love those big honkin chrome splits on the back." Anders shook his head and agreed.

"Since I have to take the Raptor up the coast," Anders continued, "Angelina was going to drive the truck, but she hates driving alone. How about this Betsy, you, Gabriel, and Garrett take the truck and pick up Jonah at the airport, then continue on up to Pescadero. We'll rendezvous with the *Heimdall,* and get them into the main dock so they can get what they need. After that we'll head north and meet up with you. Getting there is a cinch, just take highway #1 all the way to Los Barriles and then take the dirt road towards Pescadero, we're three miles south, can't miss it. What dya think?"

"I don't see any problem with the idea," I answered. "Sounds excellent, I like it, how far is it Anders?"

"Twenty-nine miles northeast to the airport, and after that you head north exactly forty-five miles to get to our cottage, so the whole trip is just under seventy-five miles."

"Sounds good to me how about you guys?" I said looking around at the others. Everyone agreed.

"Dude . . . I'm drivin your bomb truck!" Garrett grinned at Anders and shook his head slyly; standing up they faced off, flexed, growled like warriors, and then punched each others shoulders and stomped the ground.

"I don't have any problem little brother, as long as Captain Olaf says it's cool."

"I'll call him and ask," Betsy offered. "He was concerned about all the details the last time I talked to him."

"Everyone sends their love guys," the Captain began, overjoyed with the plan we'd made. "Hey . . . Rolf's been searching high and low for you guys, I guess he misses you a lot. I'm really glad you taught him how to do his business in that big old oil pan Gabriel, good grief that dog is full of it! He drops bigger turds than I've ever seen before; it took three of us to hoist up that oil pan and drop that monstrous mess overboard." Captain Olaf laughed as raucously as I'd ever heard him. He seemed in exceptionally high spirits, and just before hanging up he prayed with us and said that they'd be contacting us early in the morning.

Fourteen

Jonah arrives at *Los Cabos* International

July 3rd 5:30am

The *Heimdall* anchored an eighth mile south/east of Lands End, and everyone aboard was anxious to get underway.

"Gabriel, you guys get up and get motivated," Captain Olaf ordered, "there's a lot to accomplish today. Jonah called a few minutes ago, his flight was just about ready to leave Lindbergh Field in San Diego. He'll arrive at Los Cabos International around 9:30am; the flight has a stopover in Mexico City for thirty minutes. Betsy, if you're hearing me make sure that sometime today you make reservations at the Hotel and talk to Anders about that discount he mentioned. Reserve nine rooms for seven days, and include the meals OK? Put it on Gabriel's card. Make sure we get one room on ground level that Rolf can stay in with someone."

"I will, promise." Betsy murmured sleepily.

"We'll have time to rest when we get to the hotel folks. Please keep your radios on, and Garrett, give the spare radio to Anders this morning, Captain Olaf out."

"Aye Aye sir," I murmured groggily. "Garrett, did you copy that?"

"Yah dude I'm not deaf, I heard him, I got a radio too dweeb," Garrett grumped. "I'm gonna get me a quick shower, gimme twenty minutes. Betsy I'm hungry, when we gonna eat?"

"I'm gonna shower too Garrett," Betsy groaned as she stretched, "It'll help me wake up. We'll eat when we get down to the docks honey; I saw a little café there yesterday afternoon."

"Cool Betsy, thanks." Just as I keyed off the radio, Anders announced himself and came in.

"Gabriel . . . Angelina and I are going down to the docks now," he began, "she needs to back up some files and let city hall know we're closing down the business for awhile. I'm going to fuel the Raptor and check the truck, I'll make sure the tire pressure and all the fluid levels are good for the trip."

"Sounds wise brother," I agreed. A question welled up in my spirit as I was offering Anders a cup of coffee. I felt hesitant to ask though and thought I might be prying, but I took a deep breath and asked anyway.

"How did your wife react when you told her you were leaving with us Anders?"

"She cried man, what can I say." Anders answered immediately. "She knew this day was coming. I've known it for years myself, course it doesn't make it any easier when it gets here, she's got peace with it though." Out of the blue Anders began quoting scripture in the ancient dialect.

"This is the plan determined for the whole world; this is the hand stretched out over all nations. For the Lord Almighty has purposed, and who can thwart him? His hand is stretched out, and who can turn it back?"

Tears began welling up in my eyes after Anders finished, and when he saw me brushing away tears he quickly hung his head because tears had begun rolling down his cheeks also.

"We're part of Gods master plan Gabriel," Anders said softly, standing straight and wiping his eyes, "a marvelous master plan that will bring us to the day when all things are given back to Christ. My wife knows this, and she's willing to make any sacrifice necessary to fulfill her part in this great plan."

"Brother, I feel so privileged that you're part of the *Heimdall* team now, and I feel so honored that God put us together, just finding each other was a miracle." Anders smiled and reached out to shake my hand, instead though we both hugged. This was assuredly a man God had put with us to help complete the journey we'd been given.

"Where was that scripture you quoted?" I asked inquisitively.

"Isaiah brother . . . Isaiah 14: 26-27. It's one of my favorite books, that prophet was awesome dude. Hey Gabriel, make sure you pick up your backpacks on the Raptor before you guys take off, and leave the key behind the wheel by the plaque, I'll see ya later." Anders waved over his shoulder as he jogged the hall, and then disappeared down the stairs.

Forty-five minutes later Betsy, Garrett and I checked out of the Hotel Fininstera and walked up Avenue Solmar towards the bay. While we walked, I shared the discussion I'd had with Anders earlier. Betsy and Garrett also agreed that something very powerful was happening with the *Heimdall* crew. After we'd eaten breakfast at the little café, Betsy and I began to load the truck for the drive up to the airport. Anders and Angelina were no where to be found though, and right after breakfast Garrett had also disappeared. Betsy radioed Captain Olaf, after we'd finished loading, and inquired about any last minute instructions there might be before we departed.

"Everything's good on our end guys," the Captain began. "This place is just bloody awesome; that Arch is really something, WOW, and there's a bloody huge cave up about two hundred yards from the point that goes back inland underground like a river about a quarter mile.

John and Rorek took two small utility rafts and explored the cave for about an hour. When they got back John radioed Anders, he confirmed that he'd rendezvous with us around 10:00am at our anchorage and escort us in. It should take three hours to refuel and stock up, and then we'll head north around 2pm and meet up with you. Is there anything else we need that you can think of lass?"

"Yah there is Captain; we're almost out of that heavy duty white thread we use for sail repairs. I think we have one spool left. We also need more batteries for the CSAT packs; you know the little modules we wear. John knows what kind they are, I can't remember. I remember Helga saying we needed some 3.5 floppies and a couple stacks of CD-R's, and we should probably stock up on Lizzy's special herbs and coffee too, we're very low."

"Copy that . . . I'll remove a battery from one of the packs and get the numbers, and I'll let Lizzy take care of the herbs. Thanks lass, you guys take care; keep your radios on. By the way, are the batteries still charged?"

"We charged the backup batteries last night boss, everything's cool. Should we keep the cell phone on also?"

Garrett had unexpectedly answered Captain Olaf, and Betsy and I could see him walking up the road with a package under his arm.

"Absolutely son, Jonah will be contacting you on that phone. By the way, he called Roxanne just a few minutes ago; his flight arrived safely in Mexico City. He also confirmed he'd be calling you on that cell number when he lands at Los Cabos. He'll be on the south concourse at gate B-11."

"Copy that Cap, Betsy just wrote it down. Hey, I got the package from Anders boss, thanks. We're ready to split now, see y'all up the coast . . . Garrett out."

"10/4 Garrett, you guys be careful, use wisdom in your choices. Gabriel, you're in charge until you pick up Jonah OK?"

"Copy that Captain, I'll do my best."

"I love you guys; see you soon . . . Captain Olaf out."

The trip north took about thirty minutes, and when we'd reached the airport it had just turned 9:00am. After finding a parking place the three of us jogged out to gate B-11. The attendant there told us flight #717 from San Diego was on time, and should be arriving at 9:30am as planned; we thanked her and sat down to wait. Jonah's phone call came immediately after his flight touched down. We told him we were already here and he seemed delighted. As soon as he'd entered the waiting area though, we all knew something was amiss; he appeared disgruntled and lost in thought.

"Gabriel, did you bring along your laptop?" Jonah asked tersely after brief hellos and hugs.

"Yes I did Jonah, is there something wrong?"

"I have to retrieve an encrypted e-mail from the professor in Rabat." Jonah began as we moved briskly across the concourse. "He phoned me while I was in Mexico City; we couldn't talk freely over an open line so he told me, in code, to pickup the message as soon as I'd landed. It looks like something significant is happening in the Sea of Cortez."

"Dude sounds serious, computers in the truck Jonah," Garrett shouted after we'd cleared the doors. Without any hesitation we all began running across the parking lot.

"It's ready to go Jonah; we put a full charge on it last night." I yelled over my shoulder. Jonah nodded, and we ran even faster towards the truck. After I'd gotten into the menus, Jonah quickly accessed his account and retrieved the professor's e-mail. After releasing it from the encryption he motioned for us to gather around, and then somberly shared the contents with us.

Jonah – Mortiken have made it through the Panama Canal -stop- satellite surveillance shows four vessels, 48 hours ago, anchored off the island of Nayarit in the Islas Maria's -stop- be very careful in the Gulf while you and the crew are there -stop- Intelligence puts Amalek

Baaldur and Krystal Blackeyes aboard one of the four vessels -stop- Situation is extremely dangerous now -stop- $1,500,000 bounty on "Ghost Vessel"-stop- Intelligence positive they're heading north into Sea of Cortez, destination, Angel de la Guarda Island -stop- Satellite photos show airstrip now completed -stop- according to intercepted transmissions, fleet will be traveling tonight west of Ceralvo and San Jose islands, reason undetermined -stop- Angel de la Guarda is purported base of operations for invasion into the USA and Alaska -stop- town of Campo is now under Mortiken control -stop- something must be done to stop them there in Sea of Cortez -stop- Entrance to huge underground river near Campo confirmed, do not have exact coordinates as yet, will confirm later - stop - Gods speed. Profrabat/morrocco@earthnet.net

"We have got to do something while we're here," Jonah asserted, rubbing his forehead and sighing, "We've got to slow those bums down somehow. I'm not sure how though, I'm just not sure what we could do. Betsy please get a hold of Olaf on the phone, I need to discuss this with him and Rorek. Can I contact the professor through this laptop Gabriel?"

I nodded yes and made the adjustments. Exceptionally preoccupied with this precarious new development I wondered what we'd be doing now. This was the second time we'd heard about an Underground River in the northernmost parts of the Sea of Cortez, Captain Janus had mentioned it to Captain Olaf also. I wondered what significance this fact had and why we'd become privy to it, could this have something to do with why the Mortiken had captured Campo? After Garrett skidded back onto highway #1 and roared north, I began sorting out what I was feeling and wrote the thoughts in my journal.

I felt really uneasy about being a marked man, with a bounty of a million and a half dollars on our heads. It seemed preposterous, ludicrous, outrageous, and ridiculously absurd that the Mortiken would consider us such a threat that they'd be offering that amount of money for our capture or destruction. Where had all that money come from?

Amalek Baaldur and Krystal Blackeyes were in the Sea of Cortez at the very same time the *Heimdall* was, and that bothered me. Did they somehow know we were here, and if they did, had they purposely followed us? Did they know about Anders? If we intercepted the four vessels, would there be an opportunity for us to inflict more damage on this malevolent tribe as we'd done off the island of Flores? We certainly needed to pray together and ask for Gods wisdom and direction in this. I wondered if Anders friends, in Guerrero Negro, would somehow be instrumental in our situation. I wondered if they'd be willing to help if we needed it, maybe they were already involved in the battle and we didn't know it. Were they somehow related to Anders?

There's no way we could travel up inside the Sea of Cortez now, especially in the *Heimdall,* we'd be openly vulnerable, unless it was cloaked in the CSAT, and even then it would be too dangerous.

Perhaps we could anchor off Guerrero Negro to keep the vessel hidden. Was a week of down time at Hotel Punta Pescadero a good idea now? Considering the unfolding circumstances, it might be better to move the *Heimdall* north to San Diego. Perhaps the Raptor might accomplish what the *Heimdall* couldn't. The speed and maneuverability of the craft would make it extremely difficult to intercept or track, but it was very loud, and this would surely be a detriment to safely accomplishing a clandestine mission. If it was Gods will for us to deal another blow to the Mortiken, how in the world could we accomplish it?

"Do we have any weapons with us?" Jonah's question interrupted my thoughts about ten minutes after we'd gotten underway.

"We've got two hand weapons with fifty rounds," Garrett began looking over his shoulder, "also John's night-vision binoculars, three combat knives, a half dozen hand grenades and four of those CSAT modules."

"What . . . how did we get those modules?" Betsy asked.

"Hand grenades?" I looked at Garrett puzzled.

"John brought everything ashore this morning, before him and Rorek took the rafts into the cave, and he gave um to Anders; after breakfast Anders gave um to me before he went out to the *Heimdall.* I guess they had a powwow aboard the *Heimdall* last night and after prayer they figured we might need hand grenades and the modules," Garrett shrugged. "I didn't ask any questions . . . it was totally cool with me."

Fifteen

Driving north past the Sierra de la Laguna

After I'd finished writing and we'd passed the sign for Las Casitas, I accessed the internet to find out more about this beautifully rugged terrain we were traveling through.

Here at the southern end of Baja California Sur, a remnant of the Rocky Mountain chain remained – the Sierra de la Laguna. Most of the trees and shrubs in this habitat were deciduous and would loose their leaves at the onset of the extended dry season, and for this reason they were also known as "tropical deciduous forests". The rugged range ran true north/south for more than fifty miles and we'd begun seeing it just north of the city of San Jose del Cabo, and would be viewing it now for most of our drive up to Punta Pescadero. The highest peaks in the range reached seven thousand feet in elevation, with the steepest slopes being on the western side of the range. The Sierra de la Laguna had often been called an "island in the sky" because the topography effectively isolated it from all the surrounding deserts. With forty inches of rain per year on the peaks, the mountains supported very unique eco-systems. Rare mixes of desert, sub-tropical, tropical, and sub-alpine species grew here, and were found nowhere else in North America. Many species featured thick waxy skins, or stored moisture in fleshy leaves and stems. The gargantuan columnar cacti, agaves, and other succulents mingled with plants and trees, and certain other tropical genus. I found it strange that . . .

"Gabriel," Jonah's voice bit with an unexpected urgency, "can we access the VEW from your laptop?"

"Sure Jonah, I'll contact Helga and she'll get us tied into the satellite dish through the main computer on the *Heimdall.*"

"Garrett, would you stop the truck son, we need to be at a standstill for this."

"No problem boss, what's yur idea?" Garrett asked in the rear view mirror.

Jonah held up a finger while Garrett pulled the truck onto the gravel shoulder. After the truck had come to a stop we all piled out and stretched, while Betsy handed out snacks and water I put the laptop on the tailgate and began my setup. Outside the air was warm and perfectly still, and it seemed we were a thousand miles away from any kind of civilization, it was very desolate here. Apparently sensing what I was thinking, Betsy handed me the binoculars and whispered, "It's beautiful isn't it Gabriel, look at those mountains out there, it reminds me of the high desert in the Anza Borrego and Arizona here."

Indeed, it was ruggedly beautiful.

The mountains rose imposingly in the distance, and I could see a smattering of snow in the higher elevations. Before Jonah had interrupted me, I was reading that two hundred and twenty-five species of plants made this habitat their home, with as much as ten percent of the flora being endemic.

"OK . . . here's my theory," Jonah began suddenly, rubbing his nose. All of us gathered around as he began speaking.

"Something the professor wrote piqued my curiosity; he said the Mortiken would be traveling tonight west of Cerralvo and San Jose islands, and no one knew why. That means from Nayarit they'd have to sail northwest towards the East Cape right?" We all shook our heads affirmative.

"Alright . . . their route would then have to take them towards the southwestern tip of Cerralvo, right past Los Barriles."

"I see where you're going with this Jonah," I interjected. "If we pull down with a wide view on the VEW, we'll be able to find the vessels and track where they're headed."

"Exactly son . . . let's bring the program up!" Jonah smiled, rubbing his hands together gleefully. "Where are we now Garrett?"

"Jonah, we're still on Highway #1, we passed the sign for Santiago maybe ten miles back." Garrett pulled out the map Anders had given him, and after a minute of scrutinizing he looked up.

"According to this map boss, we're still about twelve miles from Los Barriles."

"Alright son thanks, good job. Betsy did you get a hold of Helga?"

"Yes Jonah, she's linking us up as we speak, maybe five more minutes and we'll be ready."

"Jonah if we can establish that the Mortiken vessels are headed towards those two islands shouldn't the *Heimdall* stay put?" Jonah looked perplexed and began pulling his goatee thoughtfully.

“What are you thinking Gabriel?” he asked.

“Well . . . considering the professor informed us they’d be passing by Cerralvo and San Jose tonight, wouldn’t it be logical to assume that they’re now enroute, or possibly at a standstill somewhere in the gulf? They could very well be on a southern parallel with us as we speak; the gulf is not that far from here. Jonah, the Captain said the *Heimdall* and the Raptor would probably leave San Lucas at 2pm this afternoon, its 4pm now. It’s very possible they could intersect the Mortiken vessels unawares if they continue north.”

“Oh Lord, let me look at that map Garrett,” Jonah muttered. Sweat had begun beading up on his forehead, and I could feel him churning inside with concern. After Jonah and I located our present position, in conjunction with the coast, and calculated how far the Mortiken could have come overnight from Nayarit, I suggested where the four vessels might be anchored in the Sea of Cortez, and with my finger circled an area about fifty square miles in circumference. Jonah agreed that my calculations were accurate.

“Jonah . . . Helga just called, the VEW’s hot,” Betsy shouted excitedly from inside the truck.

“Outstanding . . . lets see if we can establish some hard facts about this, Gabriel get us a view please.”

I could see Jonah was excited, and at the same time anxious, I knew he was concerned about the welfare of the crew and the *Heimdall.* He wanted some hard facts before he’d put out a distress call to Captain Olaf. It was a shrewd decision he’d made, to use the VEW to quantify the enemies position and I had agreed with it wholeheartedly. After establishing a strong link with the satellite, I fed in the geographical coordinates, and within seconds we'd established a clear view of the East Cape.

"Oh Lord . . ." I said, choking up with emotion, it had suddenly become all too clear. "Jonah, those four vessels are less than ten miles away!"

"What!" Jonah exclaimed. "Let me see!" Garrett, Betsy, and Jonah crowded around me, staring at the computer.

"Where are they dude?" Garrett asked, squinting into the screen.

"They're right there," I pointed, "slightly north, off the coast of Los Barriles."

"Betsy, I need the cell phone now please." Betsy handed the phone to Jonah and after he'd dialed, he continued conversing with us.

"The *Heimdall* has got to get into shore now, its critical, you were absolutely right Gabriel. You and Garrett look at the map and figure out where the *Heimdall* might be now and let me know." Jonah had kept his hand over the receiver while he was talking to us, but quickly removed it when the connection was made.

"Helga . . . hi this is Jonah, I'm fine, thank you, yourself? Excellent! Hey is Captain Olaf there, I need to talk to him ASAP! You guys are moving right? Good! When did you leave San Lucas? Twelve noon? Wow . . . early huh? Refueling and restocking went well? Everything we needed . . . excellent! OK thanks Helga, see you soon. Hello Olaf, nice to hear your voice my good friend, bad news though, I'll explain the details later, just listen. There is four Mortiken vessels anchored . . . hold on a second Olaf."

While Jonah was talking I'd put the map down in front of him and pointed out that the Mortiken were positively anchored three hundred yards north of Los Barilles, and less than ten miles from our present position.

"Olaf . . . Gabriel and Garrett have just confirmed that four Mortiken vessels are anchored three hundred yards north of Los Barriles. Captain where is the *Heimdall* now?" Right at that moment the radios squawked noisily, it was Anders.

"Truck, this is Anders copy?"

"Olaf, please hold a moment! Anders, this is Jonah, nice to make your acquaintance brother, what's up?"

"Same here Jonah. Hey look, we're ahead of the *Heimdall* about twenty miles; we're stationary in the water and parallel to Buena Vista. I can see four Mortiken vessels anchored north of Los Barriles and the decks are crawling with the Baaldur scumbags. What's your position?"

"Jonah, I'm on the radio now so we can all talk," Captain Olaf interrupted. "Anders I heard what you said about the Mortiken, what do you suggest we do son?"

"Sir, respectfully . . . you've got to get the *Heimdall* out of the gulf. If you continue on your present course you'll become a target for the scum in less than thirty minutes. There's a small secluded bay coming up on your port, a lot of trees, nice beaches, and lots of flowers. I suggest that you pull in and engage your CSAT as soon as you're anchored. Nowhere in the inlet is less than forty feet deep, the schooner will be safe there sir."

"I agree with Anders Olaf," Jonah exclaimed, "you've got to disappear; they might have scout boats out to guard themselves."

"Copy that Jonah, excellent idea Anders, thanks for the advice. John is maneuvering the *Heimdall* towards the cove as we speak; curious, it was directly off our port when you suggested it Anders. I want you and Angelina to get back as soon as you can, copy?"

"Copy that, good idea sir, we can anchor on the shore side of the vessel, and no one will see us. We're on our way back now, Anders out."

"Jonah, are you still on?"

"Go ahead Olaf."

"Alright Jonah . . . I want you to continue to Los Barriles. I know this is unexpected, but there's a reason God gave us that wisdom last night to get the CSAT modules to you. When you arrive, hide the truck somewhere. Use the VEW on close proximity and find a place to access the beaches safely."

"Captain Olaf," Anders interjected, "sorry to butt in, but that area is filled with big rock formations and cactus so hiding the truck will be no problem. They can get in and out very safely."

"Copy that Anders, thank you. Jonah you, Garrett, and Gabriel use the CSAT modules after you leave the truck, Betsy stays inside with a module on also, and a radio. Take along the night-vision and the hand weapons, the grenades are your call, depending on the circumstances you may need them. I want the three of you to get in as close as you can without being seen; photograph all four vessels and anything else that might help us."

"Copy that Olaf, I think you're right. We might be able to track the origin of the four vessels; perhaps we can upload some of the shots to Rabat and the professor can establish some facts that we don't already know."

"That's a possibility Jonah, did someone bring along the earpieces for the radios?"

"I did Captain," Betsy confirmed, "I've got them in my backpack."

"Excellent lass, get those installed immediately, I want everything as quiet as possible from here on. Communicate only when it's necessary. Call me back when it's done, everyone copy."

"Copy that sir," we all chorused. "We're on our way!"

"Jonah, my watch says 4:47pm, what does yours say?"

"Captain, we're adjusting ours the same . . . Anders?"

"Copy that Jonah, I'm in sync with you now too, be careful brother . . . Anders out."

Sixteen

Unresolved mysteries

"Jonah, why do you think that Amalek Baaldur and the witch Krystal Blackeyes are here in the Sea of Cortez? Jonah shrugged. Several moments of silence passed while he contemplated an answer.

"Maybe it's as far as they could travel from Nayarit before daylight Gabriel, apparently they don't move about during the day. I don't have a clue why those two are here; something big must be in the offing. But what it is . . . who knows. I guess we're going to find out real soon though huh, why do you ask Gabriel?"

Garrett and Betsy's attention suddenly shifted towards our conversation, so I decided to take advantage of their apparent interest, perhaps together we could extrapolate some answers to several unresolved mysteries.

"There are things that still seem unresolved to me since we left Flores Jonah."

"Go ahead son, Betsy, Garrett can you hear Gabriel?" They both motioned that they were listening.

"Jonah . . . while we were underwater at the Shallows of three rocks Helga told us that three vessels were headed in our direction, two in our general direction, and one directly towards us, I don't recollect her exact words, but you guys remember that right?" Both Betsy, and Jonah nodded they did.

"I remember that too dude," Garrett added over his shoulder, "so what?"

"Well . . . the peevish spy told us the Mortiken were in that part of the Bay of Biscay and that they were looking for us, I remember exactly what the spy said Jonah, he said, *"they've been watching you in Carino sir, and three ships were sent out to box you in."* According to what he said Jonah, the three vessels in Carino harbor were watching what we were doing. Why? Where did they come from? Why in the world would they be interested in us? For all intents and purposes we're just a research vessel. Remember the peevish spy also told us that while they were searching for us, all three vessels engines stopped at once. I remember him saying it was the strangest thing he'd ever heard, all three stopping at the same time. Actually, he really looked surprised, as if he didn't know anything about it. Jonah, I believe it's possible that the Captain of each vessel stopped their vessels at precisely the same moment, but I'm still not entirely clear on the reasons why. He wasn't lying about the vessels being there though; Helga picked them up on radar. I also remember the spy saying, quote: *"when they knew you were going to dock here, (in La Coruna), they hired me to follow you and get as much information as I could."* Remember him saying that guys?" Betsy and Garrett agreed.

"The spy said whoever hired him would call when they needed a job done, and afterwards a courier would pay him off, but he never saw the courier, the Euros were apparently left in an envelope. For some reason I think he was lying about being hired all the time too, I think this was his first job, remember how impressed he was with the five hundred euros? It really wasn't that much money. The peevish spy said the one that hired him said they thought we might have the sword, remember that? I think his exact words were: *"they want what they think you've found."* He had to be talking about the sword, who knew we were looking for the sword except you, Roxanne, and . . ."

"Oh good Lord," Jonah interrupted, "You don't think . . ."

"We never told anyone Jonah. We've never told anyone anything about the Tempest, gosh, Anders still doesn't know. I know it looks like Regan Pendleton sold us out but I just can't convince myself to believe it, Regan's much too instrumental in transporting the Rognvald tribes on that freighter his churches renovated. Let's unravel this some more; I've got a hunch about something, see if you agree."

As I was talking I could see Jonah shaking his head in agreement to my thoughts about Regan Pendleton. I think he knew that Regan wasn't working against us and that he had our best interests at heart. Betsy poured coffee for everyone and after taking several long gulps, I continued.

"Guys, how did they even know we were in La Coruna? That information must have been generated somehow in Concello de Carino, but from whom? Would it be logical to assume that the Wormwood was one of the three vessels following us south along the Spanish coast towards La Coruna? Having been alerted by the three vessels, or someone else, the Wormwood could have been prepared beforehand for the deception, but I just can't figure out why. I don't remember seeing the Wormwood at Carino, do you? Heck, I couldn't describe any vessel that was anchored there if I had too. Could any of you guys?" Garrett and Betsy shook there heads and murmured no.

"OK . . . why was there such a stink in the harbor the day after we sunk that vessel, it got worldwide news coverage . . . but why? Remember the view Garrett got on the VEW Betsy, the harbor was crawling with hundreds of people, five different news crews, the police force; I even think the military was there weren't they Garrett?"

"Yah I remember the military dude, there was a big Navy vessel anchored right outside the harbor entrance. What was so important about sinking the Wormwood anyway Jonah?"

"I really don't know Garrett," Jonah answered. "Roxanne and I weren't there."

"Dude I remember that day real clear," Garrett began reminiscing, "it did seem like a lot of hubbub for just a stupid boat gettin sunk. Remember Roxanne's colleague, the one stayin in the hotel there Jonah?"

"Yah Garrett, I do remember Roxanne saying something about her," Jonah concurred, pulling vigorously at his white goatee, "why son?"

"She told Roxanne she'd been watching the scene for hours; she also thought it was way too much activity for just a boat sinkin. Man what's up with that?"

"Didn't sinking the Wormwood seem a little too easy?" I mused. "Hey, don't get me wrong, John did an excellent job, but the bloody harbor was empty, the vessel was two hundred yards off in a corner by itself, no lights were on, and no one was aboard. Looking back, it all seemed a little too convenient don't you think? If it had been a Mortiken vessel, why didn't they follow us down to the docks after the spy had been killed and try to stop us before we left La Coruna? I think the Mortiken were somewhere near La Coruna, but not in the city, I personally think their main objective was Porto Portugal. Remember when we rescued Roxanne that night, the Mortiken were all over that city. The Campanha train station and the main airport were filled with the scumbags. That many people infiltrating a city the size of Porto just doesn't happen overnight, they'd been building up troops for several weeks there. Another thing, do we know for sure that the guy Garrett and John saw dead was really the peevish spy?

"Hey dude," Garrett snapped defensively, "me and John didn't get up close and personal with that corpus delecti, it was disgusting man! The poor shmuck had on the same clothes and the same ugly sharkskin loafers as the spy did. Truth be told, we never saw his face, most of it was pulp, so yur right Gabriel von Einstein, I couldn't say for absolutely positive if it was him or not."

"Do you mean that his face was crushed Garrett?"

"Yah Gab, his face was whacked badly, bloody pulp dude; you couldn't even recognize who he was," Garrett grimaced.

"Then it stands to reason that he might have been confronted by whoever killed him, maybe someone he knew, otherwise the back of his head would have been crushed, not his face."

"Hmmm, you're probably right Gab," Garrett sighed. "Dude, all I know is the poor schmuck looked like an elephant stepped on him, and homey, I'm positive he didn't feel squat when he croaked, he was blotto in a micro-second."

Garrett's descriptions had been raw, but the power in what he'd said made me shudder. I suddenly felt compassion for whomever it might have been that night, and sympathy for Garrett and John's discovery of the brutalized body.

"Good point Gabriel," Jonah agreed. "You know, if it wasn't our spy that got killed then leaving the hard disc recorder behind was done purposely because someone wanted us to have it. Considering the gravity of the situation, especially after we'd found the corpse, we'd be forced to leave the area with the recorder still in our possession. What if it's a bugging device and what if they were listening to your whole conversation when the spy was with you at the cafe."

"I never thought of that," Garrett said in amazement. "Jonah, me and Helga need to open that thing up and check it out huh?"

"I believe so Garrett; we need to find out for sure. I'll put in a call; Helga can get it done while we're busy here."

"Cool . . . is it possible that pink panther wannabe is still alive Jonah? Do you think the dude could have been playing us?"

"I don't think so son, I really don't think the guy was smart enough, I'm inclined to believe that he was just a pawn someone was using."

"Another thing," I continued, "why did the taxi service come off strike at exactly the time we needed to escape? That was weird and it seemed too convenient. Remember the spy said the people who called him engineered the taxi strike so he could get in close and record us, and also remember they told him they thought we'd get drunk and brag?"

"Yah, now that you mention it, I do remember him saying that," Betsy mused. "That taxi strike also seemed a bit convenient to me and just as we were leaving the café. Hey it couldn't be Regan Pendleton Jonah, those people told the spy we'd be getting drunk and bragging, presumably about the sword. Even the spy realized we weren't drunks or braggarts, and after he did, his demeanor changed towards us. He even told Gabriel that he was chosen for something powerful remember that Gabriel?"

"Yah I do Betsy, it was peculiar that he'd say something like that, how could he have known anything about us, why would he say something like that?"

"I'm having dreadful thoughts," Jonah said softly, "could Regan be in cahoots with the Mortiken and not even know it, possibly someone close to him, or someone inside the Rognvald clan? I wonder if he had any assistants, or employees; do you remember seeing anyone else close to him Betsy?"

"No," Betsy replied, "but I didn't see all that much when I was up there, the main gate was closed most of the time. You know, I remember thinking it was strange that the big gate opened again just as I was preparing to leave, I'd never have gotten those photographs you wanted otherwise. I betcha whoever heard the radio transmissions opened the gate so I could take the pictures, but why? Hey, here's another thing, how did the Fatman know exactly where to find us in the Ria de Vigo?

"Yah, now that I think about it, it almost seemed like that fat puke knew we were going to be there," Garrett added, "how would they know that? Besides, that skanky book Helga found had the Wormwood's name written in it. There's something else bout that entry that always puzzled me Jonah, the ink looked fresh."

"That's right Garrett . . . Helga noticed the very same thing, the entry had been made recently, like within the week." Betsy agreed.

"Didn't you guys say that nothing worthwhile was in that book except the names of several vessels?" Jonah asked.

"Yah," Garrett answered, "we looked at it twice, but never found anything worthwhile. Do you think the Wormwood entry was done for our sakes, because someone knew we'd find it?"

"Possibly," Jonah shook his head. "Perhaps there's some code in the text we haven't discovered."

"Guys . . ." I continued, "doesn't it seem strange that shortly after we encountered the Fatman and his son they ended up dead? How long did the police chief say they were looting on the Ria de Vigo, two years, maybe more, and they were never caught? You know, someone snuck into the Vigo prison and killed them both, does that sound as suspicious to you guys as it does to me? It's like they had this job to do and when they got done they . . ."

"Yah dude . . . they got whacked," Garrett exclaimed, hitting the dashboard, "Somethins really fishy here man!"

"Guys, there's only one conclusion I can come to, someone that knows about our mission is working against us from behind the scenes, someone that's very clever, and they're using someone we've met personally but they don't know it. Jonah I have this hunch. There's a way we can clear this up, well at least we can clear up part of this mystery anyway."

"What is it son?"

"Remember when we met you and Roxanne on the jetty in Carino?"

"Yah I do, it was the first time we saw each other," Jonah nodded.

"That's right, but there was something else Jonah, did you know that Helga was taking pictures the whole time everyone was talking?

"I don't remember seeing her doing that son."

"Jonah, she took pictures of the boardwalk and all the vessels in the harbor. We have a photographic record we could use to determine whether or not the Wormwood was there when we arrived, and if the other vessels were there too, we might be able to identify them. We could match the names in that book Helga found with the names on the bows."

I knew that I'd touched a nerve because everyone gasped at the very same moment. Thankfully, after months of fighting with these thoughts, and all the other feelings churning around inside me, I'd finally gotten this burden off my chest and everyone seemed to be running with it. There was still one thing that I hadn't shared however, something that'd been bugging me for quite a few weeks.

I'd been having this recurring dream about someone standing on rocky underground shores, near an enormously wide river, staring up at a heavenly light descending through a hole. What this dream meant was eluding me though; all I could figure was that perhaps it might be a harbinger of some future situation we were all going to be involved in, but who could ever tell about dreams. Betsy was exceptionally proud of the excellent conversation I'd instigated this afternoon, she hugged me and kissed my cheek, and then without the slightest compunction, for the first time since we'd met, I eagerly reciprocated. While Jonah grinned and winked at Garrett in the

rearview mirror, Garrett simpered under his breath, "Coupla bloody lovebirds."

Seventeen

The Mortiken ravage Vildarsens cottage

As we approached Los Barilles I watched the sun dip below the mountainous summits west of us and in less than a minute the temperature dropped at least twenty-five degrees. After finding a suitable area, Garrett parked the truck under a rocky overhang facing west away from the shore. In this location we were fully encircled by large trees and hundreds of smaller Agave cacti, and completely hidden from the coastline and the Mortiken vessels. It was a terrific place to hide the truck. Betsy was still uneasy though, and she suggested we join hands and pray. Afterwards, infused with peace and a lot more focused, we attached the CSAT modules securely to our belts and ran a preliminary test. When we disappeared, Betsy's flabbergasted reaction made me laugh.

"Gosh guys," she cried out in astonishment, "I can't see you at all!" After squinting and peering from every possible direction and walking around where she thought we might be, she finally admitted, "You look exactly like what you're around, this is so cool."

The shoreline was perhaps four hundred yards away, and as it got darker we began discerning orange glowing undulations in the distance, it was becoming obvious that the stories we'd heard about the Mortiken dancing around raging fires on the bows of their vessels could very well be true. We decided to take along the two hand weapons, hunting knives, night-vision binoculars, nighttime flashlights, one backpack with snack food and water, and also the digital camera with telephoto and special shutter time delay attachments for clear nighttime photos. After praying one more time and making sure Betsy was secure, we informed the *Heimdall* of our intentions and quietly departed.

Cautiously moving towards the shoreline, the sounds of the Mortiken nighttime fire rituals filled us all with a spine-chilling apprehension. The repetitive chanting was similar to what we'd heard during our first encounter back in March when the Mortiken had approached us on their smacks near the Roscoff barges. Hearing these sounds again was a somber reminder of that violent evening and once again I thanked God that we'd made it through that battle unharmed. As we moved closer I was gripped in my stomach with a dreadful foreboding about what we'd be seeing and encountering tonight.

"Dude, it feels funky here," Garrett whispered in the radios. "Those stinkin vessels are filled with evil." Jonah and I both nodded in agreement.

The more that I thought about it the more I felt grateful for the distant clamor coming from the four vessels; it was helping obscure the crunching sounds our boots were making. Walking over these extremely coarse granite granules would have surely alerted anyone to our surreptitious movement if it had been quiet. Being constantly watchful, Jonah was purposely maintaining a space of thirty feet in front of Garrett and me, unexpectedly he held up his hand with a clenched fist and we both stopped breathlessly, what had he seen?

"Garrett, Gabriel," Jonah whispered in the radios, "make your way up towards me, we've got troubles ahead."

After reaching his side, Jonah held a finger up to his lips, and then he pointed north. As Garrett and I peered through the ever thickening gloom our eyes slowly began focusing on a wooden cottage with two large adjacent buildings, perhaps fifty yards from our present position. We could see a group of Mortiken inside the home wildly gesticulating, breaking windows, smashing furniture, and throwing out all they could get their hands on, sounds of destruction, accompanied with abundant blasphemy was saturating the nighttime air. The scene was stirring fears up in me, and I'd begun dealing with unfamiliar anxieties as we inched closer. Beached on the shoreline, in front of the cottage, were five small boats with numerous guards stationed around them, each was clutching a semi-automatic weapon, the old AK47's used in Vietnam and Afghanistan. I remembered what the professor had written Jonah about the tribe being supplied with Russian weapons, it was accurate information.

A sudden shuffling close to our feet startled us, and we spun around to defend ourselves. Jonah fumbled for the red flashlight in the backpack Garrett was carrying, and after finding it he quickly illuminated the ground below. I almost laughed out loud as my eyes focused on the reason for our sudden anxiety; apparently we'd disturbed hundreds of foraging kangaroo rats, now franticly dispersing because of our clumsy infringement into their feeding grounds. Relieved it wasn't snakes; we all sighed and watched the nocturnal creatures haphazardly scurry inland to less intimidating hunting grounds.

"Phew, that was weird . . . nasty little boogers," Garrett muttered, while Jonah turned off the flashlight and returned it to Garrett's backpack.

"Anders . . . do you copy?" Jonah whispered as we continued inching forward.

"I copy you Jonah."

"Anders, what does your home look like?"

"It's a large wooden cottage, white with tan trim, white fiberglass shingles. We have two outer buildings towards the rear of the property; one of them is really long, same colors, and a narrow pier out forty feet into the gulf where we tie up the Raptor. There's also a big tower between the two buildings where I store water from the well I dug."

"Anders, is your home in the vicinity we're in now?"

"It is Jonah, four hundred yards north of Los Barriles, why do you ask?"

What we were looking at was exactly what Anders had described; their home was less than fifty yards ahead of us now, but why were the Mortiken there? As we approached the clearing we all stopped behind a large columnar cactus, easily over thirty feet in height, and quietly watched.

"Jonah, why did you ask about our home," Anders reiterated softly. Jonah groaned and rubbed his forehead, I could see he was having trouble trying to formulate an answer; finally he sighed and shrugged his shoulders.

"Anders, the Mortiken are destroying your home, what could they possibly want from you?"

We heard Angelina let out a startled shriek and the radios went silent. Several minutes later, Anders whispered. "Jonah, they're probably after what my father found on the boiler. One of the outlying buildings is over a hundred feet long, are they around that?"

"No, they're in the main cottage; it doesn't appear that they're even aware of the outer buildings," Jonah replied, "why?"

"Jonah, please try to protect that building! The last Rognvald vessel is stored there, the one my parents came to San Lucas on."

A stunned silence ensued; it was hard grasping what Anders had just said. One of the fifteen original Rognvald Viking longboats was stored in Anders shed?

"Do you think they're after the vessel Anders?" Jonah gasped. I could hear the crew excitedly discussing what Anders had just divulged and Rolf was barking fervently, also caught up in the spirit of the moment.

"I don't think so Jonah, I don't think anyone knows about it, I've never told a soul. After my father quit working on it I took up the task; it's in perfect condition now, completely seaworthy. No it's not the vessel Jonah, I'm sure they're after the rubies my father found. The vessel that sank on the boiler had a chest with three hundred and thirty-three stones inside, a bloody fortune."

Before we had any time to assimilate what else we'd just heard, there was a thunderous commotion off to our right and our attention was instantly diverted away from the conversation. A group of Mortiken had unexpectedly appeared only yards away from us, and there was someone else, further back in the shadows, bellowing orders in a cruel stentorian voice.

"Captain, the Mortiken are right next to us," Jonah whispered, "maintain radio silence until I contact you."

"Copy that Jonah, be very careful men, we'll be praying here."

A calculated thumping was getting louder by the second and the ground shook with an exaggerated intensity, the description of boulders being dropped at regular intervals came to mind. It would be very difficult to adequately make clear the spectacle we witnessed in the following moments, but let the reader appreciate this, that what we saw lumbering by made us cower together in an awful dread. I felt helplessly overwhelmed and quickly began experiencing difficulty drawing regular breaths. In the next few moments my life, and what I understood as normal, would change forever.

I'd read about giants in folklore and mythology, and I'd listened with great excitement to all the stories I'd heard in my youth, about the creatures that bush pilots had seen in the northern Orkneys, but nothing I'd ever heard before could have prepared me for the reality of this moment. Jonah and Garrett's eyes opened wide in utter astonishment as we gazed up at the largest, most brutally evil looking human being we'd ever seen, it was Amalek Baaldur, the supreme Mortiken leader.

Eighteen

Amalek Baaldur & the witch, Krystal Blackeyes

He was massive . . . a colossal Titan with epic physical proportions, a Herculean Goliath, an evil doppelganger Jack must have encountered at the top of the infamous beanstalk and catapulted down to earth to save the heavens. Time seemed to stand still as I gazed up at this gigantean ogre, and every fear I'd ever struggled with was again intimidating me with niggling lies. Wickedness dripped from his snarling, twisted features, and I feared Pandora's Box had been opened, and with the opening, a monster savage of temper had emerged. As I gazed upon his abhorrent countenance a ghastly apprehension gripped my bowels, I foresaw an ancient evil ensconced on a black throne, surrounded by vile angels attempting to leave the earth wet with the slaughter of their malicious pursuits. Edgar Allen Poe's words in the first stanza of "The Doomed City" whispered in my mind:

Lo . . . death has reared himself a throne
In a strange city lying alone
Far down within the dim west
Where the good and the bad and the worst and the best
Have gone to their eternal rest
There shrines and palaces and towers
Time eaten towers that tremble not
Resemble nothing that is ours
Around, by lifting words forgot
Resignedly beneath the sky, the melancholy waters lie.

I was simultaneously enamored and horror-stricken by this man, and it seemed at this moment in time that my sagacity had utterly deceived me. An ancient wickedness had been deposited in this man/creature, and irrefutably, we had now been exposed to it. We were entirely dependant on our Holy Lord God for everything needed to endure the moments ahead.

Amalek had eyes similar to a shark, black and dead, and at no time during the next two hours did I see anyone, subservient to this frightening man/creature, ever make eye contact with him. Everyone that came near kept their heads bowed and spoke in respectful tones.

All the Mortiken were dressed in ankle length hooded djellabahs, and each had a foul and rancorous deportment. In the exterior lights, around Anders cottage, I could see that some had their hoods down and some didn't, Amalek's hood was down. Fully exposed in the moonlight, his hideously gray skin and lumpy bald skull made us all tremble in revulsion. The five bodyguards around him were also imposing, seven to eight feet in height and four to five hundred pounds in weight they appeared as fleshly war machines, malevolent, hideous, sycophantic, but restlessly obedient to their aberrant leader. The creature that Captain Olaf and I defeated in March must have been one of these, the similarities were striking. Next to Amalek though, at eleven feet in height and over nine hundred pounds, they appeared as children, mere flies he could flick away with an impulsive finger.

The giant roared as he approached the clearing near Anders cottage and everyone cowered, all bowing in a ritualistic subservience at the sound of his stentorian verbalizing. Amalek was communicating in an amalgam of peripheral Orknean and Shetland Scottish, in a parlance that I understood.

"FIND BLOOD ROCKS OR SOMEONE DIES, I ROAST HIM MYSELF" In a renewed effort to satisfy their leader they began hitting one another and cursing blasphemously, it appeared no one wanted to be roasted tonight.

As they were slowly passing by the columnar cactus we were hidden behind, one Mortiken suddenly broke rank and began walking directly towards us. I was petrified! Putting a finger up to his lips, Jonah motioned for us to follow. Quietly we moved several yards to our left and waited breathlessly. When Amalek noticed one of his guards had moved away, he swore blasphemously, bent over, picked up a large rock, and then threw it at him. The rock narrowly missed the man, now standing six feet away from us, and hit the cactus so violently that it caused one of the long thick stems to break off and crash down at our feet. Within seconds a foul stream of dark urine began splashing down right where Garrett had been crouched several moments earlier, and we all shuddered in revulsion as it pooled up next to where we were standing and slowly seeped into the porous ground. The stench was overwhelming and I began to gag, quickly laying hands on me, Jonah prayed silently and thankfully the gagging stopped. Garrett put a finger down his throat and shook his head grimacing.

The giant and his followers finally made it into the clearing around Anders home, and in a mounting frustration Amalek began hitting several unfortunates on the heads and shoulders. One man crumpled in a heap after being hit, and with a bloodcurdling scream Amalek stomped his head and killed him after he'd refused to get up.

"FIND BLOOD ROCKS," he screamed again, "OR ALL BURN TONIGHT."

The cursing steadily intensified while they franticly searched, Anders had hidden the rubies well, but unfortunately his home was being destroyed while they searched. The possibility of failure was clearly infuriating Amalek and while he paced back and forth, roaring at his subordinates, they scurried about in abject fear and frustration. After ten minutes, and now completely at wits end, Amalek roared viciously at the heavens, and then turned towards the largest vessel. In a booming voice he commanded: "BRING ME THE WITCH!" After this order was given a profound silence fell around Anders home and everyone standing along the shore. Within seconds we heard the creaking hinges of a metal door opening in the distance, and a curious murmuring gradually began to influence the deafening stillness.

Anders startled us on the radios. "Jonah you've got to get the chest of rubies secured," he whispered.

"Jonah this is Olaf . . . can you do it?"

"At this point I can't say Olaf, you have no idea what we're confronted with here. I've never seen anything like this, this tribe is horrifying, we really could use some help. If we're caught Olaf, they'll kill us without a second thought. Amalek has already killed one of his own."

"Jonah, how many do you count?"

"I've counted twenty-seven in the immediate area Olaf, but there must be over a hundred on all four vessels." Both Garrett and I quickly agreed on this number. There was several seconds of silence and then . . .

"Boss, we can do it, we can get those stinkin rubies"

Suddenly level-headed, Garrett stood up and squared his shoulders. Grabbing Jonah's hand with a warrior's fortitude, he began to instill confidence in both of us.

"I'm not afraid of those scumbags," he whispered, "we can do this together Jonah, in Gods strength, we can do this!"

Garrett, Jonah, and I looked at each other, and after several moments of dithering, and struggling with a flood of tenuous thoughts, we finally decided to proceed.

"We can do all things through Christ Jesus that strengthens us," Jonah confirmed in a whisper as we all grabbed hands and quickly prayed for wisdom and fortitude. "Thanks Garrett, you are amazing . . . alright let's do this men!"

"The chest weighs thirty-five pounds," Anders began softly after Jonah carefully and quietly confirmed our intentions, "it won't make any noise when you carry it, years ago I packed all the stones in foam. Go around the back of the long shed Jonah, the one where the old vessel is stored. Pace twenty strides directly off the rear door, when you stop you should be right in the middle of my wife's cactus garden. There's a bird bath there, it looks like a big pile of rocks, about four feet in height with a pool on the top, don't worry though its one solid piece. On the right side, as you approach, there's an indentation in the rocks that a hand fits into perfectly, put your hand into that and pull back, the whole pile will move towards you about three feet and stop. Walk around the back, the chest is in a rock lined hole under the pile of rocks."

"Jonah, take your time," Captain Olaf continued, "remember they cannot see you while you're cloaked in the CSAT."

A look of astonishment appeared suddenly on Garrett's face as he listened to the Captains instructions and encouragement. For some reason, while I was watching my little brother's reaction, I had my own burst of cerebral clarity, and I understood the meaning of Garrett's amazed expression. We could walk through their midst and remain completely invisible, they couldn't see us at all, they could only hear us if we made noise. This was a great advantage, and the only reason we wouldn't do this would be our own fear.

"Jonah, it looks like you and the boys are going to have some company. John and Anders just left in the raft; they've brought along shotguns, bats, and two magnetic mines, and they've also brought scuba gear for two people."

"Jonah . . . sorry to interrupt Captain . . . Jonah its John, we're moving towards you now, ETA thirty minutes. If it's possible, please try and retrieve the rubies before we arrive."

"Captain Olaf, this is Betsy, what am I supposed to do?"

"Betsy," Anders interrupted, "Can you make your way towards my home and rendezvous with the fellas?"

"Captain, is this alright with you?" Betsy asked.

"Yes lass, this is our present plan. Do you want Gabriel to come back and escort you?"

"No . . . I think I can make it. What should I do with the truck sir? The laptop is still here and also the other backpacks."

"Betsy, can you carry everything with you?"

"I think so sir; I can put everything into one backpack, and then carry the computer by hand. When should I leave, and where should I go?"

"Betsy, John here . . . when you get within sight of the cottage, radio in, we'll have better information for you by then, copy?"

"Alright John I copy, I'll see you guys soon, please be careful, I really want to get home to my berth tonight."

"All right Jonah," John continued, "Anders and I are heading in your direction; we'll be beaching the raft a hundred yards south of Anders home. Jonah we need you to establish what vessels we're going to destroy, how far from shore they are, and how they're positioned in conjunction with the rest of the fleet. Don't target Amalek's vessel, we'll wait on him. We've prayed about this and felt led to leave him alone for the time being. We'll deal with that scum later. Anders and I are going to attach mines, like we did off Flores, and then wait till they're several miles away to detonate. Actually, with this RCFM (radio controlled firing mechanism) we can detonate from as far away as ten miles, copy?"

"Copy that John. Gabriel, Garrett, and I are maneuvering towards the rear of the shed as we speak. Contact us when you arrive . . . Jonah out."

The murmuring, from the Mortiken offshore had increased in intensity now, so we all stopped and watched. From the largest of the four vessels a boat had been lowered into the water with three figures aboard and was now moving in our direction. We could discern the shape of a petite white female sitting in the center, and while the two huge rowers pulled mechanically, her wispy long hair floated ghostlike around her as if she were surrounded by hundreds of thumb fairies. Periodically tossing some kind of a powder to her right and left, she began chanting in a guttural rhythm. Soon, the low throated sound was pulsing over the surrounding area as more Mortiken joined in, it was spine-chilling. I began experiencing waves of goose pimples as the sound became more unified; surely this woman was summoning demonic spirits. Slowly she made her way towards the shoreline. In the occasional splashes of light, which illuminated her face, I caught glimpses of yet another slave to the Baaldurian blood witchcraft deception, and from what I was seeing tonight, she looked as depraved as Amalek. Quite suddenly beleaguered, by the wicked Mortiken ethos, I impulsively prayed and thanked God for the life and friends that He'd given me. This must be the female the European media narrative had christened Krystal Blackeyes, the wicked companion of Amalek Baaldur. There was a dreadful feeling that preceded this woman, and as I capitulated to a revulsion grinding in my gut, I heard a slight rustling to my left; Jonah was pulling the night vision binoculars out of the backpack. There was a dazed expression on his face, and I could see sweat beading up on his forehead.

"Jonah, what's wrong?" I whispered.

With a look of concern Garrett moved over and put his hand on Jonah's shoulder. Instead of saying anything though he put a finger up to his lips and shook his head. After that he moved towards a waist high boulder, crouched down, and began focusing the binoculars on the small boat just now making a landfall. Moving away several yards, Garrett and I also crouched down and continued watching the unfolding scene.

Within moments Jonah spun around horrified and collapsed in a heap; he rolled over on his side and began convulsing in deep sobs. I was thankful that the decibel level of the Mortiken chanting had covered up the sound of Jonah's fall; otherwise we may have been discovered.

"What's wrong Jonah, are you hurt?" Garrett pleaded softly, after we'd rushed to his side and knelt down. Jonah turned his (now completely pallid) face towards us, and in-between chocking sobs he whispered.

"That woman on the boat, oh Lord God . . . SHE'S MY SISTER!"

Nineteen

Garrett and Gabriel safely retrieve the hidden rubies

There was absolutely nothing Garrett and I could do to help Jonah with this horrendous realization. I found it extremely difficult watching my dear friend in the grips of such anguish, but sadly this abhorrent woman had turned out to be his younger sister. While the three of us crouched next to the rock and waited, I couldn't help but recall several past conversations I'd had with Jonah, earlier this year, about his younger sister.

She was the little girl he'd played with on the swing-set in their parents suburban back yard, the little girl that used to grasp his hand in fear when they uncovered sand crabs at the beach, the little girl he used to fly kites with in the city park, the little girl that used to go to Sunday school dressed in pink, the little girl he'd shared hotdogs with on Sunday afternoon barbeques, and the little girl he'd defended from bullies. These memories of their childhood together had brought tears to my eyes; it was hard to believe how her personal choices, through the years, had changed her life so terribly.

Jonah's family had been destroyed by the arrant indiscretions of a Mother and Father with no spiritual discernment, and who were too proud to communicate about, or reconcile, their cosmic differences. The loveless environment Jonah, Eloise, and the middle brother had grown up in created three entirely different personalities; consequently the children were forced to find their own paths, devoid of parental supervision, spiritual guidance, or a close knit sibling bond. The relationships were filled with jealousy, envy, apathy, drug use, and contentions, and the dissimilarity between the children now, in their adult years, was beyond comprehension. It seemed impossible that these three could have come from the same seed, and out of the same womb. It was beyond any power of reasoning I had understanding that Jonah and this woman were brother and sister. I could feel Jonah's heart wracked with pain and confusion, and I began searching inside myself to find words worthy of allaying the ghastly discovery he'd made. An overwhelming inadequacy descended upon me as I struggled though, and I realized that for all the schooling and abilities God had given me, that I was utterly helpless to affect any positive change in Jonah whatsoever at this juncture, it was completely in Gods hands. For some reason, when this revelation took root in my heart, I was flooded with a peace that I'd rarely experienced before, and my faith in what God was doing in my life, and the lives of my precious friends, increased profoundly. I knew from experience that there were some things in our lives that we were powerless to affect in any way, they had to be given to God, daily prayed about, and walked in faith with.

"Garrett, Gabriel," Jonah gasped as he struggled to regain his composure, "you boys are going to have to get the rubies on your own. Follow Anders instructions, and get back as soon as you can, do whatever it takes, and please be safe."

"Jonah, what are you going to do?"

"I'll head back towards the truck Garrett and find Betsy; I don't want her near any of this horrible, filthy wickedness. Oh Lord God I can't believe this. When I locate her we'll go south and try to locate John and Anders. We'll rendezvous at the raft later, stay in touch on the radios." I eagerly nodded my head in agreement and shook Jonah's hand firmly.

"I love you brother, we're with you in this. It's hard to understand now, but something good will come out of this some day Jonah, you'll see."

Garrett handed Jonah a hand weapon and reminded him to target the two vessels John and Anders were going to destroy, and also he needed to determine how far from shore they were, and then radio that information in. As we were about to leave, Jonah grabbed both our hands and whispered.

"Look fellas don't worry about me! You're right Gabriel; we'll get through this someday. My sister Eloise is in a horrible mess, I hope she hasn't gone too far, I pray for Gods mercy on her. She's had problems for many years, but I just never realized how far she was going to take that fascination she had with witchcraft and drugs. How she ever ended up with the Mortiken is beyond me. I'm going to trust Christ Jesus for her future, there's absolutely nothing that I can do for her. She's become Gods enemy now and unfortunately ours also, we have to do what's necessary to accomplish the job God has given us. Let's pray that something good happens from this someday."

After praying, Garrett and I waved and then we began cautiously maneuvering towards the rear of the long shed. The chanting was depressing, a grinding guttural sound over and over again, it never seemed to end. Did they ever take a breath? While the intensity of the sound grew, an otherworldly creepiness oozed through the nighttime air like a rank mist and made us both shudder. Garrett and I were still filled with a strange trepidation as we walked amongst the grotesque Mortiken soldiers. At one point Garrett got within three feet of one brute. Seemingly to bolster his courage, he just stared and made faces at him while the Mortiken fervently picked his nose and wiped it on the breast of his filthy djellabah. After moving past, Garrett picked up a small rock and threw it at him. Being camouflaged by the CSAT, the rock disappeared when Garrett picked it up and remained invisible until it had left Garrett's hand. When he'd been hit, the Mortiken spun around in rage and roared at the one he thought had hit him, who in turn roared back, and within moments a fight broke out. Obviously amused, Garrett picked up another rock and threw it at one of the Mortiken guards escorting the witch. After he'd been hit, he also spun around and roared at the Mortiken closest to him, and once again another fight developed. These people were idiots. The whole time we were moving stealthily through Anders property I'd been watching Krystal Blackeyes staring silently out towards the enormous columnar cactus we'd hidden ourselves behind earlier. While her cadaverous black eyes darted around the area, she'd begun throwing powder all around herself and scowling, it appeared she was searching for something. It reminded me of an animal that had developed a scent, but still couldn't decide what direction to go in. At one point Garrett and I heard her say something in a low growl that shocked us both.

"I can feel you Jonah, where are you?"

When Amalek had reached her side the chanting stopped completely and a deathly stillness prevailed over the entire area. Garrett and I stopped, barely breathing, and quietly watched the drama unfold. I was shocked at the disparity in their physical sizes; Jonah's sister barely reached the middle of Amalek's thigh, she was waiflike next to him. The giant knelt down and whispered something into the witch's ear, and then with an ethereal smile she sprinkled powder on his head and kissed his cheek. With a twitching sneer, the giant got back up and stood quietly while the witch danced in circles around him and began screaming. Her voice made my blood curdle; the sound was disproportionate to her diminutive size, and possessed a demented fervency that would make any rock vocalist envious. All the Mortiken froze when she began shrieking, even the ones that were visible on the four vessels stopped dead; like zombies they all turned towards her and bowed in reverence. She was also speaking in an amalgam of peripheral Orknean and Shetland Scottish dialects, but her fluency in the language was woefully lacking. I distinctly heard her say though, *"You have only power I give you."*

As Garrett and I quietly watched several lines from a poem entitled "Adonais" by Shelley, bubbled up in my brain, which seemed to embody the unfolding scene around Krystal Blackeyes.

"Midst others of less note came one frail form,

A phantom among men, companionless

As the last cloud of an expiring storm whose thunder, is its knell."

Having followed Anders instructions to the letter, Garrett and I easily found the place where he'd hidden the chest. Without prior knowledge, no one would have ever found this hiding place Anders had constructed, what a resourceful and creative man he was. After retrieving the vast fortune, we cautiously made our way south toward the rendezvous point which had earlier been established. Our progress took us right through the middle of the Mortiken throngs and kept us on our toes at all times, being discovered now would have been disastrous, and also a guaranteed death sentence. The setting was one of utter disarray and made us both quiver with fear and apprehension. Thank God for the CSAT, without it we would have never been able to accomplish this mission tonight. Everywhere around us the ground was strewn with linen, towels, glass, furniture, clothes, pots and pans, pictures, books, and also three men were lying dead in bloody heaps, recipients of Amalek's brutally uncontrolled fury. For some inscrutable reason the Mortiken never searched the two outlying buildings. It certainly seemed as if an invisible barrier had kept them from even seeing the structures, and I thanked God for His obvious intervention.

Amalek and his soldiers were preparing to leave now and we watched as he calmly ordered everyone towards the vessels. At one point earlier, while Garrett and I had stopped and watched for several moments, I distinctly overheard one of Amalek's lieutenants suggesting that the bloodrocks may be farther north, and Amalek, never being predictable, had acquiesced to his subordinate's suggestion after conferring briefly with Krystal Blackeyes. The mood amongst the Mortiken was subdued now and it almost felt like we were walking through a graveyard at midnight. The blasphemies had ended and there was no fighting or grumbling between the Mortiken as they all boarded and secured the smacks.

Fifteen minutes later all four vessels moved out into the gulf and headed north. The chugging drone of diesel engines was the only sound now that disturbed the tranquility of the early evening air, and while Garrett and I watched, Amalek's vessels faded slowly into the distant gloom.

Twenty

Back together

John radioed and informed us it was safe to uncloak, and gave us the coordinates where the raft was located. Thankfully they'd been triumphant in their mission; the mines were now securely attached underneath the vessels and ready to detonate. It seemed though that there was a small controversy brewing between John and Anders; they'd begun arguing about when to detonate the mines. After we'd reached the raft, Garrett, Anders, John, Betsy, Jonah, and I joined hands and thanked God for getting us safely through the evening thus far, it was good to be back together. Everyone offered Jonah greetings, and also regrets and sympathy's about his sister. Jonah's appearance was becoming increasingly troubled, his complexion was still pallid and it was apparent that something demoralizing had gripped his heart and mind.

The controversy between John and Anders was quickly coming to a head, John wanted to detonate right away, but Anders didn't. Knowing John was in charge and had seniority, Anders was maintaining polite judiciousness in his arguments, but I could see the two warriors struggling, trying to find their place with one another. Anders strongly suggested that we wait until the Mortiken had reached the southwestern tip of Cerralvo Island. There was a submarine canyon forty-five hundred feet deep between the island and the mainland there, and he contended that if we sunk them there it would be impossible for the Mortiken to retrieve anything of the two vessels after they'd gone down.

Only after twenty minutes of heated discussion, with Captain Olaf and Rorek acting as adjudicators on the radio, did John begin seeing the indisputable logic in Anders arguments. He finally acquiesced and we all sighed in relief when they'd established a common ground. Although the arguments on each side had been insightful, it became obvious to me early in the disagreement that Anders had an understanding about the Sea of Cortez that was incontestable. Living on its shores and exploring the terrain for many years, he was knowledgeable about things here that we never would be. I certainly understood how easy it was to feel threatened by someone new, especially someone with the skills that Anders possessed, and it was also easy to let our individual opinions interfere with what

God wanted us to accomplish together. We couldn't let a spirit of pride destroy us! With Anders, and Angelina, now an integral part of the *Heimdall* team, it was imperative that we amend our interpersonal chemistry and find equitable balances with all of our combined skills for Gods glory, and not our own. Anders was an intelligent, finely gifted, powerful warrior that up to this point in time had made his own way in life; he really didn't need anyone helping him make decisions, especially in his own backyard. All of us needed to take these facts into consideration as the days went by and our relationships grew.

Rorek suggested we get back to the schooner and let Anders and John take the Raptor in pursuit of the Mortiken. With night vision they could stay a mile or more away from the other vessels, that way the sound of the Raptors rumbling engine would be less of a factor in giving them away. Rorek's idea was eagerly accepted by everyone, and helped dispel the lingering tension from the disagreement; shortly thereafter we all loaded into the raft and headed south.

Somehow Garrett had convinced Captain Olaf and Rorek to let him and I go along with John and Anders on the mission. They'd both finally agreed, as long as we were sensitive to the gravity of the situation and followed John's orders explicitly, he was the mission leader. Anders informed us the trip north to Cerralvo would take less than thirty minutes, and while he was talking he also remembered there was muffler inserts stowed aboard the Raptor in his tool chest.

He recalled the manufacturer telling him that they would cut down a large percentage of the engine noise and, with this being so, it would allow us to get as close as an eighth of a mile without being detected. After a quick meal and prayer, we boarded the Raptor and slowly pulled away. Waving vigorously the four of us headed north in the same direction as the enemy vessels had earlier.

Twenty-one

Mayhem in the Sea of Cortez

Anders quickly located the vessels on the Raptors radar; they were four miles northeast of the Salinas peninsula, and half a mile southwest of Cerralvo Island right over the submarine canyon. All the vessels were now stationary in the water. Anders opened the Raptor up and within seconds we were flying over the dark smooth waters under a moon soaked, star crammed, July sky. In less than twenty minutes John spotted the southern tip of the island and Anders slowed the boat down. After we'd gotten closer he held up a fist and Anders brought the Raptor to a stop. In the distance, through the night vision binoculars, he could discern five vessels;

oddly it appeared that a Mexican Navy frigate had rendezvoused with Amalek Baaldurs fleet.

"What's the stinkin Mexican Navy doin there?" Garrett whispered, peering into the darkness. "You know something big John, that vessel looks just like the one I saw outside the La Coruna harbor after you whacked the Wormwood."

"You're right Garrett, it is similar. I remember the pictures on the VEW, that's weird. Let's find out what they're doing here little brother," John suggested.

"Anders, do you have a telescope?"

"Yah I do, hold on." Anders went down into the cabins and came back with a long brass telescope.

"Let's see what's goin on with these bums." John muttered, extending the telescope to its fullest and squinting through.

"Anders . . . can you get us a little closer?" John inquired after a minute of surveillance.

"Sure no problem . . ." Anders whispered, slowly creeping the boat forward, "let me know when we're close enough John."

"Hold on . . ." John exclaimed several minutes later, "I can't believe this, what the heck is going on here."

"What is it?" I asked kneeling next to him on the bow.

"The Mexican Navy is supplying the Mortiken with weapons and ordinance; there must be fifty crates aboard already. They've got a crane rigged on the frigate to pass them over. Gabriel, please radio Captain Olaf and Rorek, I should talk to them ASAP. Is that one of the vessels we mined Anders, do you recognize any of those ensigns on the military vessel?" John asked, handing the telescope to him.

"John, that's the Sinaloa colors," Anders answered after focusing the telescope on the vessel, "they're probably from the Navy base in Topolobampo Bay. A ferry runs between La Paz, Mazatlan, and Topolobampo four times a week, and lately I've heard it's been making trips up around Angel de la Guarda Island regularly with a military escort. You know something else brother, I can also see the colors for Sonora flying below the Sinaloan colors."

"Is the vessel they're loading the one we mined," John reiterated excitedly.

"It is John; I recognize the large discoloration on the bow under the anchor just above the waterline."

"Do you know what this means guys," John whispered enthusiastically, "we have an opportunity . . . .

"John, I'm sorry to interrupt you, but Captain Olaf's on the radio."

"Thanks Gab."

John took several minutes informing the Captain and Rorek what was happening, and towards the end of the conversation he made a suggestion that stunned all of us. He asked the Captains permission to detonate while the military frigate was off-loading the weapons. The explosion could easily be construed as an accident while moving the ordinance and weapons from one ship to another, and would almost assuredly be covered up by the Mexican government. The destruction would be extensive; because the vast amount of ammunition on deck would amplify the explosion as much as ten fold. We could accomplish what we'd intended to do, and also disrupt one of the supply lines the Mortiken had obviously established on the Mexican mainland, we could also possibly sink a Navy frigate in the process. The Captain gave his permission as long as Amalek's vessel was a safe distance from the others.

There was a grouping of fifteen rocks slightly northwest of our position that Anders was familiar with, deftly he maneuvered the Raptor behind them. This extrusion protruded no more than four feet above the water line, still though; it offered an excellent place to hide behind. Through the night vision it appeared the Mexican Frigate still had several dozen crates to move over to the Mortiken vessel. The first vessel had reached its limit and was preparing to let the second vessel in to accept the remainder of the ordinance. Unfortunately the second vessel hadn't been mined so John abruptly made a decision to detonate while the first was still in proximity to the frigate.

The night was balmy, and resplendent moonlight was being reflected on the waters unperturbed glassy surface without hindrance. A dull industrial clamor, along with the subdued shouts of men, drifted unseen over the surface of the water from the direction of the five vessels. The sky above was profuse with millions of twinkling stars and reminded me of Gods promise to Abraham. We hadn't seen our dolphin friends for many weeks; I missed them and wondered when they'd be making their next appearance. In Europe they'd been so instrumental in what we'd accomplished thus far. Here, hidden behind these rocks, the pungent smell of bird droppings and rotting fish offended my sensibilities and also struck me as a foreshadowing of what soon might be coming for those who had pitted themselves, not only against the ancient Rognvald's, but also against all of humanity and against the Most High God. While diesels roared on the distant vessels John took the RCFM out of his backpack and flicked the cover up; an anomalous peace fell on all of us, the time to take care of business was at hand.

"Anders . . . would you like the honors brother?" John asked handing the switch to him. Anders turned with a humorless glint in his eyes; slowly he shook his head and answered.

"Yes I would . . . thankyou John. This is for every ugly thing the Baaldurians have ever done, and also for the destruction of our home." Anders suddenly lowered the switch and asked what time it was.

"12:05am brother," Garrett answered.

"Alright scumbags," Anders murmured without emotion, "Happy 4th of July, compliments of the *Heimdall* crew."

There was a low thunderous WHOMP when Anders flicked up the switch, instantly the surface of the sea vibrated like water in a small plastic pool after the sides had been kicked.

"SHEESH . . . it's just like Flores," Garrett screamed as he hunched down and covered his ears. "Whoaaaa dude . . . IT"S LOUD!"

Within seconds of the initial detonations the night sky was stained with huge billowing fire balls. Explosions began repeating continually as the ordinance spontaneously ignited, ripping through the night air with deafeningly erratic sounds. Quickly the two mined Mortiken vessels broke in two and began sinking. Within minutes the Military frigate was burning in several places on its deck, and moments after that the conflagration had gotten below decks and began igniting the frigates fuel stores. The resultant explosions came in a deafening succession of staccato bursts. They were astounding, more so than anything I'd ever seen or heard in my lifetime, what a 4th of July exhibition this was. The stern deck on the frigate came apart in jagged pieces and began filling the nighttime sky with hundreds of fiery missiles arching up, and then like meteorites plummeting back down and disappearing with an exaggerated sizzling in the dark waters. Through the night vision John clearly saw lifeboats being lowered from the frigate and men had begun jumping off the sides, there was chaos. Strangely, several men on the Mexican frigate were firing weapons towards Amalek's vessel, now rapidly escaping north. Quite a few small fires were raging on the stern of the second vessel, right behind Amalek's vessel, and the Mortiken appeared horrified as they scurried about like confused rats in an effort to put them out.

"LOOK AT THAT," Anders screamed, pointing in the direction of Amalek's vessel, "there on top of the wheelhouse."

What I saw through the night-vision made me shudder; Krystal Blackeyes was on the main cabin roof, a waif-like silhouette dancing in circles, her long hair floating like fairies in the luminous moonlight. With her right hand she was mysteriously throwing powder all around her, and we could actually hear her screaming bitterly at the fiery incident they were leaving behind. Once again I was reminded of verse by Shelley in his "Ode to Naples."

Gaze on oppression, till at that dread risk,

Aghast she passes from the earth's disc.

Fear not but gaze - for freemen mightier grow and slaves more feeble, gazing on their foe.

Clutched in her left hand, by wisps of hair on the back of the skull, was the decapitated head of one of the Mortiken soldiers Amalek had murdered earlier in the evening.

Part 2
"In search of the First Tribe"

For Jonah's sister Eloise

Life, imitating water, flowing inexorably
Here, then gone
Temporal experience slowly blended
Into the unyielding river of endless seconds
Hidden constructs of joys and sorrows like
Drops of water languishing in stifling summer sun
Piteously we all surrender in times unyielding grip

Everyone capitulates, choosing life, choosing death,
Times inexorable assault whispers continually
Still, just like you Eloise, many choose speciously
And slowly dissipate in loveless indifference
Beyond the pale, confused and repulsive,
Many end up embracing evils honeyed dark pretext
And die the second death.

From the poetic journals of Gabriel Proudmore

Twenty-two

Later that month

It was now July 13th, the air was insufferably muggy, and the likelihood of another miserable summer filled me with a particular loathing. Rolf was restless this morning; he'd awakened early with a head of steam and was charging around the deck, his rapid fire barking rippled through the morning stillness with discordant persistence. Obviously eager to eat, he was doing the only thing he knew how to get my attention, make a lot of noise.

Rolf hated confinement. Considering his original home had been the enormous valley in the Pontevedra Province, the schooner must have felt like a jail cell at times. As soon as I'd gotten topside, Rolf charged at me full throttle. Springing up on his rear legs, he deposited his front paws squarely on my shoulders and began licking my face with great jubilation. It was obvious the poor guy needed attention, so I quickly poured out his breakfast and then promised we'd go ashore later to play, on Anders dinghy, right after we'd both eaten. Eyes fixed on me unblinkingly, and listening quietly while I talked, he offered me a short obligatory "wuff" when I'd finished, licked my hand, and then commenced to wolf his kibbles with complete abandon.

Garrett and Betsy opted to stay aboard the *Heimdall* for the last six days, they too wanted to putz around, write, and take care of Rolf's needs; Rorek also stayed aboard to finish repairs on several pieces of troublesome machinery. The rest of the crew decided to stay full-time at the Hotel Punta Pescadero, and after Anders and Angelina had departed for San Diego the morning of the 8th everyone finally checked in.

From the *Heimdall*'s stern port deck we could clearly see the grass lined stone staircase that led up to the Hotel Pescadero. The crew would often walk down and wave at us from the beach or from the rear balconies of their suites, occasionally calling to inform us about how delightful the diversion was, and suggesting we join them. We declined. The Captain was the only one who came out to the schooner for a few hours each day to accomplish charting with Rorek. Later, he would return to the Hotel for dinner, some TV, and a soft bed. After the recent incident with the Mortiken, and the exasperation caused by discovering the horrible truth about Krystal Blackeyes, this time of peace was certainly well appreciated, and also proving beneficial to our health and emotional well-being.

Nine days had passed since the *Heimdall*'s early morning, July 4th mission, which destroyed two Mortiken vessels and a Mexican navy frigate in the Sea of Cortez. During that time, a re-shuffling of priorities had begun for the *Heimdall* crew, and also for Anders and Angelina. On the 5th of July, Helga and Garrett had made a startling discovery in several of the photos she'd taken of the Concello de Carino, & La Coruna harbors. This photographic evidence corroborated what Jonah, Betsy, Garrett and I had discussed on the road trip up to Los Barriles.

The whole premise that a spy was working against us, through someone we knew who was unaware of the ill-intentioned relationship, was beginning to make a lot more sense.

Helga's digital photographs proved, with no uncertainty, that the Wormwood had been anchored in the Concello de Carino harbor when we'd arrived, along with three other vessels whose names had been discovered notated in the ledger she'd found on the Fatman's vessel. In one photo, Helga had captured a lone person on the deck of the Wormwood who appeared to be a high-ranking officer in the Mexican Navy, suggesting that the Wormwood might be the recreational vessel for this person, but who was he? Several of Helga's other photos revealed a disheveled young man in both harbors with a bicycle, it appeared that he was watching our every move and communicating a great deal on a portable two-way radio. The day Regan Pendleton had conversed with us, aboard the *Heimdall,* this same sinister young man had also been photographed by Helga. He'd been standing at the start of the jetty, by the bait stand, with a radio, and he was wielding what appeared to be a listening device pointed in our direction. Could this be the real spy, and was he affiliated with Regan Pendleton?

We'd found out that the Extremis was a diving vessel and the smallest of the three vessels. The Red Dragon was the largest and surely the most unique of the three, a very functional showpiece resembling something pirates might use. For all intents and purposes, the Dolphin looked like it did business as a long range fishing charter. All three had been confirmed, with satellite reconnaissance photos, as being the three vessels that had attempted to rendezvous with us while we were diving on the Shallows of Three Rocks. Although the names on the bows had not been confirmed in the photos, the physical shapes of each vessel had been conclusively corroborated by marine experts, affiliated with the professor in Rabat, as being the vessels that had converged on us in the Bay of Biscay. It appeared that these same three vessels had also been used in the elaborate scheme to seemingly coerce the *Heimdall* into La Coruna allegedly to get the listening device into our hands.

Captain Olaf openly admitted, during past lengthy discussions on the subject, that his reasoning for not staying another night anchored on the Shallows of Three Rocks, after we'd finished the dive, had been motivated by the threat the three vessels presented to our safety. Even after we'd thought this out more objectively, it was still difficult to ascertain whether the threat the Captain perceived was real, or just transitory anxiety based on unfolding circumstances. Irregardless though, there were still several loose ends that none of us felt at all conclusive about.

1. <u>*Why did all three vessels stop at the same time?*</u>

We all felt a logical explanation could have been the huge waves generated by the 6.6 earthquake, three hundred kilometers off the western coast of Brittany France; this might have caused the vessels to falter simultaneously. Considering they would have all been inundated at the very same moment, this possibility seemed tangible, but then again, it could have just been an elaborate ruse coordinated between the three vessels to get us to leave that day.

2. *Where were those three vessels now?*

They hadn't followed us down to La Coruna and none of Helga's pictures had revealed them in the harbor while we were there. The professor's investigative assistant in Rabat was researching satellite survey photos from that time period, and several weeks after, to see if they might be able to track their movements. There was also a possibility that those three vessels could have been part of the fleet that had transported the Mortiken through the Bay of Biscay for the Porto Portugal incursion.

3. *Was the peevish spy really dead?*

Helga was researching the newscasts and articles generated from this incident to try and understand its relevance, and why we ostensibly thought we'd been set up to destroy the Wormwood. According to our one bit of photographic evidence, all the Wormwoods ensigns had been flying in La Coruna; curiously one of those small flags was Sinaloan. The vessel may have belonged to the same Mexican Naval officer we'd seen in Carino, it was possible that he was visiting La Coruna on business, and had just been another pawn in the elaborate game. Considering that the Navy frigate, we'd just recently sunk, was also flying a Sinaloan ensign, the notion that a representative from the Mexican military in secret negotiations with the Mortiken was also provocative, but alas we had no conclusive proof. Perhaps, if Helga could find some news articles from that day, we might have a much better understanding about the significance of the whole matter.

After disassembling the hard-disc recorder, on the 6th, Garrett and Helga made another surprising discovery during their non-stop squabbling. It was indeed an expensive hard-disc recorder, but there was also a very sophisticated listening device hidden inside, just like Jonah had suggested. Whoever had been monitoring the transmissions through this device had heard everything the *Heimdall* crew had discussed since the recorder came into our possession at the Maria Pita Café in La Coruna, Portugal. Captain Olaf ordered Garrett to disable the listening device, burn the chip and dispose of it in the ocean. Thankfully we'd never discussed the Tempest sword on the radios or cell phones, but we all wondered if any of Anders transmissions on the radios that evening or any of our outright verbal discussions about the sword had been intercepted.

According to the professor in Rabat, all the European factions opposed to the Mortiken up-rising were thrilled with our July 4th victory. The clandestine mission was being touted as extraordinary. He also told us that one of the very few reputable European newspapers that chose to print anything about the story had stated:

"The infamous "Ghost Vessel" has quickly acquired a reputation unsurpassed, in their personal crusade against this ancient tribe of evil Viking outcasts. We salute whoever they might be, and consider their clandestine agenda honorable and also compulsory to the eventual defeat of the Mortiken, and their malevolent worldwide agenda."

Aside from a handful of upbeat newspaper articles, nothing at all was ever seen on CNN or the internet concerning the loss; it appeared the cover-up had been far reaching.

The military base and airport on the island of Angel de la Guarda was still closed. The Mortiken had been set back several weeks with their weapons and ordinance losses, and the Sinaloan weapons connection had been temporarily shut down by a governmental/ military affiliation that had been quite embarrassed with the bizarre and unexplainable loss. No one had any rational explanation about how it had happened, other than the transference of weapons and ordinance had been ill-fated. We knew though, that a group of determined Ghost Vessel people had once again been triumphant.

Something dreadful had happened to Jonah that evening on July 3rd when he'd realized that the witch Krystal Blackeyes was his younger sister Eloise; it seemed he'd given up on his personal involvement with the *Heimdall*'s journey. While he lay groaning next to the rock that night, I'd witnessed something bizarre rise up in Jonah's eyes. He appeared defeated, and the warrior spirit had been snatched away from him. Darkness began shrouding his temperament, and he became saturnine as the next few days passed, you could almost physically see a black cloud descending upon his whole being. Jonah was involved in a terrible spiritual war. He wasn't eating regularly, his sleep habits had become erratic, he'd withdrawn from everyone, and every morning he'd grumble to Roxanne about being pummeled by frightful dreams. Complaining of intense headaches, he'd begun to bemoan a life that seemed derisory to him; his successes seemed shallow, pathetic, and certainly ineffectual in changing anything or anyone for the better. He'd worked all his life and had never seen any real fruit from his labors.

"Who have I really affected for Gods kingdom?" He muttered many times shaking his head. "My family . . . oh Lord God . . . did you know that Eloise has a son? He's my nephew and a drunkard living on the streets, he sells his body to women for money, and brags that his mother is the best thing in his life. He swears that everything wrong with him is because of a father he never knew, a father that abandoned him before he was even born. Eloise brought him up, not the father; he's who he is because of his mother's appalling influence; his father had nothing at all to do with who he's become. Look at what they've both become, LOOK AT WHAT MY SISTER HAS BECOME, she's a witch, the high priestess of that filthy Baaldurian evil!"

Roxanne could only shake her head despairingly; she'd never seen Jonah so completely wounded in their seventeen years of marriage. Sobbing, she suggested they go home as soon as possible so he could convalesce and she could get herself back into a workable frame of mind. Captain Olaf tearfully agreed that her suggestion was the only thing that could be done at the present. Jonah needed time to pray, he needed time to hike the mountains and beaches with his wife, and they wanted to take his boat out in the ocean to quietly reflect. He required time alone to again find meaning in what

God had called him to do, and he needed a healing touch from the Holy Spirit. Roxanne also extended a helping hand to Angelina and offered to board her in the guest home until she and Anders could establish what they wanted to do.

Jonah and Roxanne flew back to San Diego from Los Cabos International on the 7th and were now recuperating at their log home in Pine Valley California.

Anders and Angelina spent several days rummaging through the devastated remains of their property trying to figure out what their next move might be. They were very quiet during the extent of their search, and very non-communicative in their personal introspections. We all respected this silence however, considering the anguish they were suffering, from the destruction and loss, was monumental. Remorsefully, after many tears, they both agreed it was time to close down Norse diving and fishing and move on with the *Heimdall.* A new season was incontrovertibly emerging for both of them, and the wind of change was filling both their hearts with a new wonder. Both prayerfully decided to accept Roxanne's gracious proposal to board them in the guest home in Pine Valley, with the understanding that they would help out with the financial burdens, and the maintenance of the property. They'd also decided to make the journey north on the "Raptor" so they could transport some of their personal belongings to their temporary home. Anders would berth the "Raptor" with Jonah's boat, the "Sea Pro" in San Diego harbor, and then fly back down to Los Cabo's International to continue his involvement with the *Heimdall* mission.

After shutting down the business and saying goodbye to Angelina's mother, and many lifelong friends in Cabo San Lucas, Anders and Angelina departed for San Diego on the 8th of July in the very early morning. The journey was approximately eleven hundred miles, and with a half day stopover at Guerrero Negro to inform his buddies about their new plans; Anders was planning on returning to us on July 15th.

Twenty-three

Regan Pendleton's up-date

The ancient Viking vessel, Anders and Utgard had spent painstaking years restoring had to be relocated. On the 5th of July none of us had a clue about how that was going to be done, or where it was going to be taken. Oftentimes though, as I'd come to realize about our journey, God moves in mysterious ways for His people. Before they'd departed for Pine Valley on the 6th, Jonah and Roxanne had received an incredibly informative e-mail from Regan Pendleton, and Roxanne shared the contents with the crew at lunch. In detail she had informed us that the newly renovated freighter, the assembly of churches had purchased from the shipyards in Stavanger Norway, was now enroute; they'd been traveling for four and a half weeks and were now refueling in eastern Argentina. Instead of leaving in late June, as was previously planned, they'd been able to depart early the first week of June. The weather had been excellent thus far, and was successfully facilitating their swift safe passage; the relocation was going as planned and everyone on the ship was anticipating something compelling happening in the very near future.

There were over three thousand aboard the freighter from the widely scattered Rognvald's. There were tribes from Jan Mayen Island in the Norwegian Sea, from Karmoy Island on the western Norwegian coast, from Suduroy the southernmost Faroe Island, also from Muckle Roe in the Foula Islands around the Sneug in the Shetlands, also Shapinsay & Stronsay Islands in the Orkneys, and from South Georgia around the Royal Bay in the South Sandwich Islands. Unfortunately the tribe located in the southern Shetlands on Elephant Island had mysteriously disappeared, and there were no clues whatsoever about where they'd relocated to. I remember Jonah mentioning, in one of his most recent e-mails, that Mortiken hordes were also being removed by plane from the Northern Faroes, and from the smaller islands of Fugloy & Vidoy. I wondered how the Rognvald descendants, living on the southernmost Faroe Island of Suduroy and the Mortiken, living in the northern Faroe Islands had remained so close to one another for so long without conflict. Could it be that they'd lived for hundreds of years in such close proximity and had never known it? Regan's letter revealed that the freighter was headed towards Prince William Sound in Alaska. Lord willing their safe arrival was anticipated the second or third week of August.

The tribes would be living on the fifty mile long, three hundred and fifteen square mile, Montague Island, located at Latitude 60 degrees 05' N, and Longitude 147 degrees 23' W.

In my research I'd found out that the assembly of churches, Regan Pendleton belonged to, had purchased the island for a mere twenty-five thousand dollars after the cataclysmic earthquake on March 28th 1964. That monster had been centered in the Prince William Sound, and had registered 9.2 on the Richter scale. This earthquake was the second largest in recorded history, the largest being the 9.5 quake in Chile in 1960. The damage had been so dreadful in the area that it ended up lifting the seafloor, at Cape Cleare on southern Montague Island, over twelve feet and created the greatest tectonic uplift on land in history, thirty-three vertical feet. The results from the quake could only stagger the imagination; local waves in the Valdez arm reached an astonishing seventy meters, or 229.658 feet in height. The thought of being confronted with a two hundred and thirty foot wall of water made me light-headed, and I shuddered at the sheer power of such an occurrence. Long period seismic waves had traveled around the globe for several weeks afterwards, and apparently the entire earth vibrated like a church bell during that time. Fishing boats were sunk at their moorings from as far away as Louisiana, and oscillations in well water height were reported from as far away as South Africa.

Upon arrival, the freighter would be anchoring between the Montague and Green Islands; there it would be protected from the sudden and fierce storms in the Gulf of Alaska. As far as the majority of scholars were concerned, (their opinions having been derived from the ancient scrolls, photos, and parchments already published) it was now anticipated that after the First Tribe had been located, that all the tribes living on Montague, the Yukon and Canada, would be relocating two hundred miles southeast to Kodiak Island for the feted Rognvald reunion in the near future. According to what Roxanne and I had discovered from the etchings on the Tempest, the First Tribe could very well be hidden on the Revillagigedo Island, around the Tongass National Forest in Southeast Alaska, time would tell though. It was now our responsibility to locate them and present them with the Tempest, the newly acquired ancient vessel, and also three hundred and ninety-nine rubies, valued at close to half a billion dollars. It was at times sobering to realize that the legendary Tempest sword, and the fortune of Rognvald rubies, was now aboard the *Heimdall.*

The churches had prepared everything in advance on Montague Island. Construction for the Viking relocation had begun in the late 80's and had taken over twenty-five years to complete. Hundreds of crannog type shelters, wooden and stone, were built in five different locations in rustically fenced communities, twelve windmills with electrical generators, and one large paddle wheel (in the local river) were built to provide power. Mills were installed for grain preparation, drainage canals were dug and lined, septic systems with vertical pits were installed, twenty-two fresh water wells had been drilled, and great wooden gravity reservoirs towered, in various places over each one of the five villages, allowing each home the luxury of running water. There was thankfully a diverse abundance of Flora and Fauna on the northern end of the island, in the Chugach National Forest, that the builders and hunters from all the tribes could use for their constructions and food needs. It appeared, aside from four freighter deliveries per year, that the relocated tribes on Montague Island would be entirely self contained, self sufficient, and somewhat modernized from how they'd lived before.

Regan Pendleton was jubilant when we'd called him back on the 7th, as were the clan leaders aboard the freighter. They all knew it was a miracle discovering this ancient vessel intact, and all considered its appearance would have considerable impact against the Baaldurian scum, especially if the elders of the first tribe were aboard wielding the legendary Tempest sword. We'd prayerfully decided to store the ancient vessel inside the harbor at Cape Cleare on the southern tip of Montague Island. There in a specially designed floating garage the vessel would be hidden and safe until it was needed. The board of directors, from all the churches, immediately authorized the money necessary for the building, and Regan promised that physical construction would begin within one week; they anticipated it being completed in early to middle August. Regan was terribly grieved about Jonah's dark night of the soul, and reminisced about a time he'd crashed himself. He promised to notify all the churches, via the internet, to begin praying non-stop for our beloved brother and also promised to stay in touch with him personally to keep him up-dated. He also assured us he would let us know what he knew about the photographs of the juvenile miscreant we'd sent him. Now, the biggest problem facing the crew of the *Heimdall* was how we were going to safely transport the ancient Viking vessel three thousand miles north to Cape Cleare on the Montague Island.

Twenty-four

Jonah's dark night of the soul

July 14th

Disgruntled, stomach churning, and sweat soaked, oh how I hated waking up in this despondent condition, and like seditious dominoes; I anticipated the day collapsing around me. The evening before, after gorging myself on one of Betsy's culinary marvels, I'd returned to my berth and reclined for several minutes to let the food slide into a more comfortable position. The soft pillow embraced me in such a way that I ended up drifting off hopelessly and did not awaken again until early morning. I was beleaguered, and quite harassed by ghastly visions concerning poor Jonah, his sister Eloise, her son, Amalek Baaldur, and the depraved Mortiken ethos. The last dream I remembered was quite histrionic and left me with a lingering chill.

In that small window

Disturbingly shaken from my dreams I bolted upright
A random knocking was rattling the old wooden door
A silhouette squinted scornfully
His djellabah clung to him wet and foul,
Wet strings of hair danced in the wind
A new storm was raging
"Sanctuary," he growled in ominous tones
The knocking intensified
"A moment please" I cried out
"Sanctuary," he roared vehemently
Unevenly beating, my heart improvised with my racing imagination
While I fumbled for my slippers
The fading fire cast eerie shadows
On gnarled features now grimacing in rage
In that small window
Bony hands repeatedly pounded the door
The old hinges groaned in protest
"What do you want?" I cried out impassioned
Staring in dread hopelessness I sat motionless and waited
Finally cursing, he turned and disappeared into the darkness

I needed to write Father and Mother an up-date, to inform them about the progress of our journey, and explicate the details of what had been happening recently. It was also my intention to ask Fathers opinion about how we might transport the ancient Viking vessel to Montague Island. As I was writing though, an unexpected e-mail from Roxanne arrived, and it was addressed to me personally.

Gabriel, our very dear and trusted friend,

Greetings, Jonah sends his love, and has requested that I send you this segment from his early journals before we were married. The day that Eloise snapped is reflected in this entry Jonah wrote over twenty years ago. When we read it, he was reminded about what God had promised him during that time regarding his family and his lack of involvement with them. From that point on, he began to noticeably recover. He thought you might be interested in reading it, he also said you would understand his reasons for sending it, being the gifted writer and poet that you are dear friend.

Jonah is doing well, he's been walking often on the beach to sort things out. Regan Pendleton has called several times; his encouragements are helping Jonah a lot. Apparently the whole church is praying for Jonah's healing, praise God, this is a real blessing. News about the freighter, the tribes, and Montague Island are just incredible. God is moving mightily isn't he? The hikes we're taking in the mountains are rejuvenating Jonah physically, emotionally, and spiritually. He really looks forward to seeing you Gabriel, and also he misses the crew very much. He wants to take you out to the islands, on his boat, if there's time when the Heimdall arrives. Be careful dear brother, we both love you dearly.

In Christ's unfathomable love,

Roxanne and Jonah

With caprice impulsiveness, the shadow puppets troubled dark mind exploded that afternoon. Out of one snarling mouth, hells foul fury flowed in fierce words. Like curdled milk, in a fleeting moment of confusion, I drank in the acrimonious onslaught of savage words from this embittered woman, grimacing while my stomach slowly turned sour. My mood darkened, as if a fierce storm had suddenly inundated a small island. It took every ounce of my faith and self-control to keep myself from retaliating to her verbal viciousness, and descending to the level of such an implacable adversary.

I had choices to make. I could respond with a sacrosanct mélange of Christianeze, or I could wag my tongue and defend myself with an obstreperous out-flowing of my own verbal viciousness. I could also shrug my shoulders and use sycophantic cynicism to understate the seriousness of what was happening, or I could turn on heel and walk away. What was the right approach?

Oh the extensiveness of the anger that burned in me. My eyes flared uncontrollably, and air escaped from between my teeth in short gasps as I fervently tried to stabilize my deteriorating emotions. I wanted retribution for the vile disembogue of hateful words, and coming from someone I thought was so close made it even more difficult to understand or accept. In that quagmire of stormy moments I realized that I'd passed the point of no return, and I felt myself undeniably being released from one of the most exasperatingly contradictive humans I'd ever known. My efforts were no longer needed.

IT WAS OVER BETWEEN HER AND ME!

I capitulated to a brief rancorous battle deep inside, and while my heart, mind, and emotions collided with a fury that rivaled a gigantean tsunami, I grimaced silently and bit my tongue. The depths of struggling the emotions, the heart, and the mind can achieve together are stunning. It's epically incongruous how one can be embraced as a friend for so long, and then suddenly, at one unfortunate juncture, be turned against with the fury of leviathan.

I felt stifled; it was like being trapped in a death struggle.

I believe now, that it's in these hyper-charged moments of emotional and spiritual conflict with others, that we as human beings can chart new territories in lovingly intelligent or violent responses. I had personally failed miserably many times in the past. Verbal retaliations to predatory malice had always left me feeling very ugly; people can really be hurtful and mean at times, and afterwards they can give you the impression that they've done nothing at all. On occasion though, I had responded to brutal verbal attacks from others in such a lovingly intelligent way that I even shocked myself. I certainly preferred this way to all the other options, but unfortunately I didn't often feel so magnanimous in my responses.

I sighed as I realized that my many years of trying and responsibility, for this malignant woman, had come to a dreadful end. Something permanent happened between the shadow puppet and me on that calamitous afternoon, the relationship, in one hour's time, had become wholly untenable. I felt as though I'd stepped into a stargate and quite suddenly been thrust into an alien land, and there was forced, quite against my wishes, to endure a vile language unknown to me. It was not a place I belonged or had any intention of staying; it was stifling in that spiritually dead place she dwelt. How do people survive without Christ Jesus living in the midst of such mental, emotional, and spiritual oppression in this world?

Lasciviously played out with vicious aplomb and tempered with a dark wisdom, the shadows attack against me ultimately failed. I was extremely thankful though, that by not descending to those perverse depths she had agreed to dwell in, I was given the perspective, and perspicuity necessary to challenge the situation from a far more intelligent and Godly direction. Alas another season has ended in my life with an ugly abruptness. I can't help but feel that I've failed again. Thankfully though, I do have an overwhelming peace with the whole situation. So now, dearest Eloise, you're entirely in Gods hands, because there's nothing else that I can do for you.

Your brother Jonah

Twenty-five

Billy Quoybarray

Regan Pendleton's response, to the pictures of the peculiar young man we'd sent, came back in a fax six days after they'd been sent.

Heimdall crew, greetings:

It was written once that "the cruelest lies are often told in silence", I believe that it was Robert Lewis Stevenson who wrote this, and in our regrettable situation brothers and sisters, I find myself agreeing with his ageless wise assertion. Forgive me for the amount of time that it's taken to respond to your inquiry. The photos you sent really shocked me, of-course then I found myself enduring several days of denial and grieving. After many tears I finally accepted the sad reality that this devious betrayal had really been carried out against me, the Rognvald's, and now the illustrious crew of the *Heimdall.* It wasn't until yesterday that God concluded giving me the wisdom I deemed essential to respond to your inquiry, so let me begin.

The young mans name is Billy Quoyburray. He arrived shortly after I received my solar powered computer, and he worked with me personally for three years; right up until the day the tribe and I left Concello de Carino in early June. For some reason he didn't want to go with us, a choice I found frustrating, especially since he knew so much about my churches mission with the Rognvalds. He helped me with paperwork, and many of the mundane daily chores there wasn't enough time for me to accomplish. He also led me to believe he was a on a training sabbatical to become a Christian missionary, and based on this information I employed him. He was somewhat knowledgeable about the Bible, and continually walked humbly as a servant. To this day I find it difficult to believe that he's a Mortiken spy involved in murderous exploits and deception. How could I have been taken so?

Billy was supposed to accompany me the day that I met you on the jetty, but he told me he felt sick and needed to stay behind. When I'd returned to the clan, after our initial meeting, I was informed that he'd caught the afternoon mail flight down to La Coruna to see a doctor about his nagging physical problem. I really didn't think anything about it, he'd gone down to La Coruna often for the same recurring ailment, actually for several months it had been a weekly occurrence, at least that's what we'd been told. According to what I know now, he'd been lying to me and the clan for years; I guess there was absolutely nothing wrong with him physically, this was apparently just a ruse to get away from me and Carino.

That day when we spoke, Billy was on the boardwalk with his bicycle watching everything we did.

Fortunately, after a half day of searching, I was able to contact the Captain of the "Elso", the freighter that brought Billy to Carino several years previous. The "Elso" is the same freighter that originates from the city of Turku on the Aurajoki River in Finland, it's very well known in northern and western Spain, in Sweden, and also along the western Portuguese coastline. The vessel originates in Bergen Norway and for the last thirty years they've successfully transported electrical machinery, electronic surveillance, computers, and maintenance parts to the fisheries four times yearly. Their main ports of commerce are Malmo, Gijon, Concello de Carino, La Coruna, and Vigo, several of the same places you've visited in your journey thus far.

The Captain said he remembered the boy well; he said they'd picked him up in Bergen while they were loading for their quarterly passage. He was extremely helpful on the voyage, and was immediately liked by everyone; he truly had a way about him. The Captain recalled him saying, at dinner one evening, that his mother, an American woman divorced from a Westray Island clansman, had abandoned him when he was nine years old. After the mother abandoned him he'd been forced to live on the streets of Kirkwall in the Orkney's for several years until some vacationing family took him under their wing, booked passage for him back to Bergen, and gave him work in their food processing plant. The Captain distinctly remembered an odd talisman he always wore under his shirt; according to what the young man had told him, he'd stolen it from the Westray Island clansman his mother had married just before he'd left her. It was a square blue and yellow medallion with black points on all four corners with an evil face in a helmet inscribed in the middle.

Other than what I've told you, everything else about the child's earlier years is still obscure. I know that he successfully maintained a small studio apartment down on the beachfront by the harbor in Carino, and before I officially introduced him to the Rognvald clan up on the escarpment he'd proven himself worthy as my employee for over two years. Three times a week he would ride his bicycle up to the settlement to help with chores. It was strange . . . the elders embraced him the very first week; many times he even ate with the clan leaders, they discussed many details even I wasn't privy too until now. This is all the information I have at this time dear friends; I'm still shocked that this young man is so utterly two-faced, but praise God we know who he really is now.

Unfortunately I have no idea where Billy is at the present; he apparently disappeared from Carino two days after the freighter left. A dear friend that I correspond with, a barber in the Landoi parish assumes that he boarded the mail flight for La Coruna again. He also recalled Billy briefly mentioning, during his last haircut, that he wanted to explore La Paz and the large islands in the Sea of Cortez, a strange coincidence you know, considering that's where you and the *Heimdall* are right now. I'll keep you informed with anything that I find out about him in the future. Blessings to you all!

In Christ's love,

Regan Pendleton

Twenty-six

Operation "Na Hearadh"

July 15th

Father had promptly responded to my inquiry, about transporting the ancient Viking vessel, and asked me to call him as soon as I'd received his e-mail. When I'd finally gotten him on the phone they both were overjoyed to hear my voice and began crying. It was somewhat wearisome though listening to mother and father blubbering about this and that, but within minutes I too was pulled into their emotion and lugubrious tears began streaming down my cheeks. After the poignant exchange ended, I brought them up to date on what was happening with the voyage and after I had, father expressed their concerns about everyone's welfare and the significance of being parsimonious and cautious in all of our decisions and pursuits. I found myself agreeing with their various annotations today, and afterwards felt surprisingly blessed by the obvious concern they'd expressed towards our wellbeing and the journey. After his verbose lecture on frugality, father laughingly informed me that he'd deposited a quarter million dollars into the *Heimdall's* encrypted account this morning, citing a premonition mother and he both had about the voyage requiring substantial funds in the near future. In utter amazement I marveled at how mysteriously God moves in specific circumstances, and today was not any exception. During the conversation father also informed me that all his mammoth tankers were presently indisposed except one.

The "Sac Doyle" was in the Baltic Sea, heading towards Helsinki, the "Evelyn" was headed towards Nova Scotia towards the city of Halifax, the "JMuir" was unloading at Dakar in Senegal, the "Trelantier" was in the Gulf of Mexico, the "Absinthe" was just leaving Edinburgh for Stockholm Sweden, the "Tanager" was in the Hudson Bay, and the "Belanthian" was a total loss, resting at the bottom of the Aberdeen Harbor. Surprisingly though the "Na Hearadh", father's newest, smallest, and most modern tanker, was leaving La Paz Baja early on the 15th of July and its eventual destination was Valdez Alaska. Miraculously, it would be going right past us in the Sea of Cortez.

Father was unusually animated about the discovery of the Viking vessel and told me it could easily be winched out of the water with the enormous cargo crane aboard the Na Hearadh, secured safely on the deck, and then transported non-stop to Alaska. His tankers destination was the city of Valdez in the exquisite Prince William Sound. The Na Hearadh would be entering the sound between Hinchinbrook and Montague Island; there the tanker could anchor for half a day while the Viking vessel was offloaded. From that point on though, we had another challenge . . . the vessel would have to be towed seventy-five miles south, on the eastern side of the island, or a hundred plus miles on the western side of the island, depending on the weather conditions in the Gulf of Alaska, all the way down to the mysterious Cape Cleare on the southern tip of Montague Island.

Father also reminded me that after the tanker “Exxon Valdez” fetched up hard aground on Bligh Island reef in 1989, and had spilled eleven million gallons of crude oil into the pristine waters of the sound, that the Navy had established an outpost with a small contingent of vessels in the Aleut town of Tatitlek to help out with any ecological problems the area might encounter over the next several decades. There was a powerful tugboat in the small fleet there, and father mentioned he was still owed a favor from the surly Commander Abernathy for giving him ten thousand gallons of diesel fuel free in the dreadful winter of 1998. If he could arrange it, and the cantankerous commander agreed to maintain the strictest of confidence, about our mission, we might be employing his tug to pull the ancient Viking vessel down to Cape Cleare.

Captain Olaf was high-spirited and almost childlike with father’s timely news and graciously thanked him for the unexpected increase in funds. For forty-five minutes they laughed heartily together and shared many stories. It was evident that my father and Captain Olaf were forming a solid bond of friendship, their respect for one another was clearly growing and I found great solace in this. After receiving the details, and also up-dating father about our plans, Olaf officially authorized operation "Na Hearadh" and quickly instructed Helga to call Anders to ascertain his arrival time.

After the conversation ended, the Captain started dancing the same sailor's jig I remember him and Rorek performing during the Maelstrom. Caught up in the Captain's exuberance, Rolf the wolfhound began bounded in circles around him and nipping at his shoes. A huge problem had just been resolved and we were all jubilant and humbled, once again God had proven faithful and timely. The "Na Hearadh" would be anchoring at 3:30pm today, a quarter mile due east of Los Barriles. Father had given the Captain of the "Na Hearadh" one of the *Heimdall's* cell phone numbers and informed us that as soon as they'd arrived, Captain Janssen would be personally contacting us. Anders flight would be arriving 9:37am at Los Cabos International, and since his truck had earlier been relocated to the parking lot there, he confirmed he would rendezvous with us somewhere around 10:45am to help get the vessel into the water.

After checking out of the Hotel Punta Pescadero, Captain Olaf moved the Heimdall down to Anders home and anchored fifty yards from his pier. The area still felt creepy and the low rumbling in Rolf's chest, while he crept around sniffing everything, clearly reminded me of the drama and sheer dreadfulness of what we'd seen and experienced that night. Once again I thanked God that we'd made it through unscathed. Blood stains and bits of innards, from the three murdered Mortiken, were still very visible on the ground in several areas. Repulsed by the swarms of flies and horrid stench, I grimly kicked sand and dirt over everything I found that even remotely looked suspect, all the while realizing the evening of July 3rd had been an encounter that I would never forget. Since I'd departed Aberdeen, the list of brutal encounters and unforgettable experiences was getting longer, thankfully though I was getting tougher and my ability to deal with stressful situations was greater than ever.

Anders cottage had been devastated and it seemed everything (except what he and Angelina had taken to San Diego on the Raptor) now lay haphazardly strewn about outside as it had been the night we'd left. While the crew dispassionately rummaged through the mess, Rolf began barking excitedly and ran towards the dirt road. Several moments later a truck horn ripped through the air in a series of staccato blasts, Anders had finally arrived.

Twenty-seven

Anders shares information about the early voyage

"How's it going guys, anybody miss me?" Anders shouted through the window as the truck skid to a halt in the gravel.

"Nobody missed yur sorry Viking butt dude," Garrett shouted, running over and shaking hands with Anders. "Bout time you got back, missed ya man. Hey, you ever thought about gettin a haircut homey, you could sail the *Heimdall* with that freak flag."

"Naw . . ." Anders eyes flared fiercely for a moment, and then he shook his head with a chuckle, "not till you get a lawnmower and cut those nasty spikes off your head dude."

Laughing throatily, and punching each other on the shoulders, Garrett and Anders faced off, flexed their muscles, and then wildly roared at each other while stomping the ground. Afterwards, for several moments, they both stood motionless like clouds, staring at one another, deeply entranced in mysterious contemplations.

What was this strange ritual Anders and Garrett shared in such passionate abandon, and why did I see it being so ludicrous and arcane. It certainly wasn't some sluggish or lifeless performance, because I always found myself in awe watching them. I wondered if this was some vanity of maleness they were compelled to impart to one another, or perhaps they were dancing to a snarling symphony of trumpets that only they heard. Maybe it was the way that they, as warriors, enraptured their souls briefly with an ecstasy of battles not yet won. I could also interpret their behavior philosophically as a fleeting solace from the cold boney fingers and fearfully insensitive indifference of impending death, but of course what did I know, I hated philosophy. Personally I found this flailing of limbs, flexing of muscles, contorted faces, and wild roaring, both perfunctory and disconcerting. At best, I accepted this ritual only as a fleeting cathartic helping to dispel the niggling vapors of life's uncertainties; then of course, I clearly saw that this ritual could also be used quite effectively to put fear into the hearts of one's enemies. Yes of course! When I'd mustered the courage, I would offer them both an apt admonishment about their thoughtlessness in using one of our best defenses so inconsequentially. In less than subtle shades, it did appear though that their troubles and melancholy ceased briefly during these seemingly abstruse rituals. After several moments of deliberation though I found myself still somewhat mystified, I wondered . . . could this ritual simply be the way they acknowledged friendship and respect for one another? Perhaps next time I would just join them and stop trying to analyze everything!

"Hey Ms Lizzy . . . how you doin," Anders asked, turning as she approached with a plate of freshly baked cookies.

"It's so good to see you again Anders honey. You know if I had a son, I'd want one just like you, intelligent, strong and handsome. For some reason though, I was never blessed enough to have my own children. Oh goodness me, I've never been able to figure that one out, and for the longest time I thought it might be some sort of a curse that had afflicted my family, people I unfortunately never really got to know. I hoped someday that it would be lifted and I'd wake from the nightmare blissfully married and there would be a beautiful . . ."

"LIZZY . . . ," Rorek snapped, "get to the point!"

Lizzy looked horrified for a moment and then with an indignant snort stuck her nose up in the air at Rorek. Taking several moments to compose herself she then turned back towards Anders with a deep sigh, and once again became the *Heimdall's* gifted and loving medical practitioner.

"Honey, are you feeling OK physically, no aches or pains anywhere?"

"I feel great, thanks for asking mother." Anders blushed, then chuckled nervously and kissed her on the cheek. "Thanks for the cookie Liz, they're really good."

"Welcome back son, I trust the trip was successful?" Captain Olaf moved over and shook Anders hand.

"It's good to be home Captain and the trip was successful thanks. Angelina sends her love to all and told me to tell all of you that she fell in love with their guest home. The terrain is really beautiful there; it's so unlike Baja. Jonah and Roxanne send their love, Jonah's feelin good, and he's getting his head screwed back on straight. I think he'll be ready to rock in a coupla weeks. Roxanne said he's been having a lot of revelations about his life from things he wrote a long time ago, and he's positive about what God wants him to continue doing now. He also said he's lookin forward to reuniting with the *Heimdall* once again after we arrive in San Diego."

"That's really good to hear my friend; glad you're back warrior," John smiled sincerely as he extended his hand, "it's good to see you again."

"Thanks John, I feel the same way too brother. Guess we got a lotta work ahead of us now huh? I understand you've discovered a way to transport my father's vessel?"

"We have my friend . . . we surely have. Another miracle happened for the *Heimdall* crew, and we have Gabriel's father to thank."

"Anders," Rorek interjected, "would you tell us a little bit about your friends in Guerrero Negro?"

"Uhhhh . . . ," Anders looked quizzically at Rorek, startled by the change of subject, "well Rorek they're my cousins, and they're brothers also, Gudrun and Ulrik Bjornson.

"Goodness me," Captain Olaf exclaimed with a look of amazement, "weren't the Bjornson's one of the families that decided to remain on Isla Socorro?"

"Yes sir they were! They were one of the four families that left the original Rognvald voyage, the Bjornson's, the Undset's, the Amundsen's, and my family the Vildarsen's. Anyway, years ago, ummm, you remember when I told you about my family leaving San Lucas for Sinaloa . . . well my two cousins left with them also. However, a year later they returned to San Lucas because they hated the culture in Sinaloa and they also couldn't stand the way the other part of the family ran their lives and business."

"What was the problem dude?" Garrett asked.

"They were just too bloody religious and legalistic about everything little brother and it drove then nuts."

"Whoaaa dude, I can totally relate to that!" Garrett said shaking his head with a disdainful look.

"My cousins are a bit different with their beliefs than I am," Anders continued. "Anyway, they worked with me in Norse Diving and Fishing for another two years before they decided to head north to Guerrero Negro. They'd been talking for months about starting a whale watching business, you know the gray whales come through there and mate every year, usually from January to March. They also wanted to take people out diving and fishing all year round in

Scammons Lagoon, Sebastian Vizcaino Bay, and around Cedros & Natividad Island, very cool places. There was also a group of marine biologists from the east coast of America we'd met once in San Lucas, they really liked my cousins and were eager to do business with them. They did extensive research on the Northern Elephant Seals, and used to fly down once a year and pay bloody fantastic money for three weeks of exploring the rookeries around Cedros, San Martin, San Benitos, and Guadalupe Island. Most of the money they earned from those expeditions was used for flying lessons, and purchasing their two bi-planes. After they got their licenses, they were able to expand the business to include flying people into remote locations around Baja and across the Sea of Cortez into Mexico. They even went over to visit the family once, and you already know what we experienced flying over Angel de la Guarda Island. My cousins became genuinely interested in our family's lineage, just like I had, especially after they'd returned from Sinaloa. They became really curious about the cave paintings that'd been discovered around Guerrero Negro and out in the Vizcaino Biosphere Reserve and they wanted to research their origins."

"Whoa sailor . . . I can understand wanting to start a business like theirs, especially in that area, but why in the world would they be interested in something as obscure as those old cave paintings? Aren't those places just tourist traps?" Rorek smirked.

"Well . . . yes they are to a certain degree Rorek, but in his research Gudrun found out about an archaeologist named Clement Meighan, I guess this fellow also started out really curious like they'd become.

Anyway, in 1962 this dude accompanied an expedition funded by some famous mystery writer, I think he created that Perry Mason TV character, I can't remember his name though."

"Honey . . . that would have been Earle Stanley Gardner," Lizzy interjected with a nervous titter, "he was the creator of that endearing character, and yes, he was a very wealthy entrepreneur that funded those kinds of archaeological projects, and he also published several comprehensive books on the topic."

"Lizzy, you're the bomb of the galaxy," Garrett laughed with a toothy grin. "You're just like a walkin encyclopedia of trivia, that's so way cool you knew that." Anders smiled at Garrett's comment, nodded at Lizzy, and then continued.

"Anyway, this archaeologist, and a photographer named Howard Crosby went on to record and photograph many of the newly discovered caves throughout the whole area. This fascinated my cousins because we'd all discovered some incontestable evidence that the Rognvald expedition had stopped on Cedros Island and possibly somewhere around Puerto Venustiano Carranza for an extended period. I discovered this from researching some stuff published by a group of unpopular archaeologists about a group of outlying caves that had been neglected on the northwestern shores of Cedros Island, and also along the northern coastline in the Sebastian Vizcaino Bay. Apparently none of those caves had ever been touched by Clement Meighan, or photographed by Howard Crosby.

"Dude, did your cousins ever get to explore the outlying caves?" Garrett inquired.

"Yeah dude, just once. For three days they were able to get over to the northeastern shores of Cedros Island where those two unexplored caves were located. They never got to the one on the northwestern shore though, but they did discover that the caves on the northern coastline of the Vizcaino peninsula had been totally destroyed in that freak storm down here about two years ago, and also the ones on Natividad Island were devastated in the same storm."

"What did they discover on Cedros?" Helga asked.

"They discovered a huge Rognvald symbol inside the larger of the two caves, also runic writings on tablets left in several chests, and over three hundred paintings. Something really cool too, according to the records left in those caves, they found out that the Rognvald's were the ones that had planted all the date palms in the northeastern corner of the island. It's been kind of an on-going whodunit, because nobody in all of Baja knew where those palms had come from, or who'd planted them, but I guess we know now."

"We also discovered something similar along the rivers in the Pontevedra Province," Captain Olaf reminisced, "and also along the entire length of the valley and up on the plateau. Many non-indigenous varieties of trees and fruits had been imported and planted there also."

"That's correct Captain," I added, "everywhere the Rognvald's colonized it appeared that they incorporated different flora into those regions to contribute to their own personal needs, and cultural uniqueness."

"There was a perfectly preserved wooden sculpture of a Viking figure we'd never seen associated with the Rognvald's before. Ulrik found it several hundred yards up from the ocean where the cliffs are. It was found in a smaller satellite cave that they'd christened "Skull Rock" because of the peculiar rock configuration outside the entrance. Gudrun and Ulrik thought the cave might be the outside chamber of a tomb because of the weird markings on the walls. There were never able to thoroughly explore any of the caves so whether this is true is still unknown. All the artifacts they discovered in Skull Rock definitely proved that the First Tribe had stopped for an indefinite period and set up a settlement somewhere in that area. I also remember them saying there was a large round rock in the back of the cave, apparently over a tunnel adjoined to that cave.

Unfortunately they were never able to move it, and never found out for sure if it was a passageway or not.

Just then a distant air horn blared repeatedly through the still air and seconds later the cell phone rang, the "Na Hearadh" had just arrived.

"Let's continue this conversation later Anders," Captain Olaf suggested, "You know something, maybe we'll just have to go over to Cedros Island and find out more about what your cousins discovered in those caves."

Twenty-eight

Loading the Viking vessel

Years ago, Anders father Utgard had come up with the notion that restoring the wooden vessel on a trailer, basically a very large frame equipped with truck tires, would help facilitate moving it from one location to another should the circumstances ever warrant it. Consequently, because of Utgards ingenious insight, removing the vessel from the enormous shed proved a great deal easier than any of us could have ever imagined.

Years before they'd been able to successfully move the semi-restored vessel up from the gulf into the structure with only a winch and wooden rollers, now with Anders truck, we would be reversing that procedure to transfer it down to the beach on the enormous trailer, float it, and then transfer it out to the "Na Hearadh".

The ancient Viking vessel was truly an exquisite expression of ancient craftsmanship. It was completely restored, in perfect condition, and set for it's re-christening into the salty waters of the Sea of Cortez. I realized that Anders and his father had accomplished something beyond belief, and I found myself, as well as the rest of the crew, gaping speechless at a beautifully preserved piece of Viking history. Anders diffidently accepted the gush of compliments; it appeared he possessed a refreshing humility about his abilities and what he and his father had accomplished. At no time during the crew's complimentary exchange did his sincerity seem contrived, or agenda driven, he never once puffed up with pride or bragged about himself, but continually gave all the credit to God and to his father Utgard.

Anders father started the restoration process many decades previous on San Benedicto Island, and according to Anders, he'd taught him everything he knew about boat building, restoration, and sailing. I came to the realization that Anders father had continually held a place of high esteem in his son's life, and despite Anders headiness, and the conflicts Utgard and he had both endured together in years past, they'd always communicated and openly apologized to each other if one had unwittingly offended the other. Always being in touch with how you affected others and quickly dealing with the demoralizing improprieties, we could often inflict on one another, was very important to any relationship continuing to grow and prosper. It was now profoundly obvious to me, by listening to Anders talk about him, that he had considered his father, Utgard Vildarsen, his best friend and hero.

To keep the vessel from shrinking or cracking, during the wearisome extended years spent restoring it in dry dock; Anders had kept the vessel continually wet with an ingenious device he'd invented. This invention quietly circulated sediment filtered saltwater, in a continual state of flow, from the gulf up into the interior of the vessel and then back out into the gulf through copper piping hidden in trenches. With its own internalized generator the invention was self perpetuating, which meant that after the pump had started and achieved its desired momentum, it required no electricity at all to keep it running, it would continually produce its own power until the pump was shut down. I was fascinated with the engineering acumen this device exhibited, but I had no time to discuss the details of its design and assembly with Anders. From what I'd seen of his wonderfully engineered rustic home though, I knew that he and Rorek would certainly be finding their common ground in conversations about their own individual inventions and engineering.

I quickly discovered that the dimensions of this vessel were almost exactly the same as the information Roxanne had recovered from the caves on the Island of Flores. This vessel was also ninety-five feet in length, and twenty feet in the beam, with an enormous carved prow looming sixteen feet higher than the keel amidships. The vessel was clinker built with two inch thick oak planks, and the overall construction was reinforced, for strenuous ocean travel, with thirty-five heavy oaken ribs. The bow of this vessel looked exactly the same as the partial remains we'd seen underwater at the "Shallows of three Rocks".

After floating the vessel just offshore and removing it from the wooden frame, John attached a hemp rope to its bow ring and pulled the vessel out to the tanker behind the raft. The loading process was uncomplicated, and took only forty-five minutes to accomplish. With assistance from one of the scuba divers aboard the "Na Hearadh", John, Garrett and Anders began the process. Four straps were situated under the prow and stern of the vessel, and a steel cable from the tankers powerful deck crane was attached to a firmly secured steel ring between all the ropes. Lifting the ancient vessel from the water to the deck was then accomplished quite effortlessly. Once aboard, the crew lashed it down and covered it with several waterproof tarpaulins for protection, and also to keep it from being seen. Captain Janssen, and Captain Olaf, exchanged e-mail address's and cell phone numbers, afterwhich the "Na Hearadh" slowly pulled away with three long blasts of its air horn, and Captain Janssen's promise that he'd see us up in Alaska somewhere around the third week of August.

Twenty-nine

The *Heimdall* sails north

July 16th 7am

The *Heimdall* weighed anchor and departed Los Barilles with our newest crew member and friend aboard, Anders (the Norse) Vildarsen. Our next destination would be the city of Guerrero Negro and the celebrated surrounding lagoons. We'd also be meeting Anders cousins and hopefully finding out more about the mysterious caves, and why the Rognvald expedition had stopped there for an indefinite period, many centuries previous.

Guerrero Negro was the point of entry into the southern state of Baja California Sur and its location of the 28th parallel made it an ideal mid-way point for north/south travelers using the trans-peninsular highway. Because Guerrero Negro was the only substantial town, for hundreds of miles in either direction, travelers would have to use the resources here to re-supply and refuel both vehicles and aircraft to continue on. Along the Zapata Blvd travelers could find pharmacies, bakeries, markets, tire repair shops, liquor stores, bars, and the almighty Pemex fueling stations. There was not a lack of places for one to spend their money or entertain themselves for several days in the small township here. The township also maintained a very good paved airport with an unusually long runway, seven thousand two hundred and sixteen feet in length, and was often used by the military during their bi-yearly maneuvers.

The origin of the name Guerrero Negro began in the shipyards of Duxbury Massachusetts in 1825. There the whaleboat "Black Warrior" was built. When it was commissioned for service the vessel sailed the Indian Ocean until 1845, and then the North Pacific until 1851. After being sold in Honolulu Hawaii, the vessel sailed to the coasts of Baja California and arrived at the Vizcaino Bay November 28th in 1858. There, the ruthlessly ambitious crew of the Black Warrior waited for the annual arrival of the migrating grey whales. On December 10th, after trying to sail across the bar to enter the lagoon, robust waves bated the vessel against sand bars and broke its keel, forever dooming it to the erratic currents and whims of the oceans bottom. The "Black Warrior" sunk, and in remembrance of that terrible incident the place was christened Black Warrior. Later it was translated Guerrero Negro and became the actual name of the lagoon and the city. Developed originally by English merchants, but now curiously managed by a Japanese conglomerate, Guerrero Negro was also built around what has now become the worlds largest sea salt extraction mines, these being areas where ocean water is evaporated in great ponds and then the salt left behind is quarried for shipment abroad on enormous ocean going vessels.

Our voyage to Guerrero Negro would cover approximately seven hundred nautical miles and take us over the Tropic of Cancer twice. The wind was blowing north on our southern heading, so Captain Olaf and Rorek decided to keep us on diesel power instead of trying to maintain the complicated tack it would take to keep us moving forward with the wind against us. When we'd passed by Lands End and our bow was facing north again, Anders walked to the stern of the vessel. In the direction of San Benedicto Island he snapped to attention and held a rigid salute for more than a minute. It was difficult trying to understand what was going through his mind, but I took it for granted that he was saluting the memory of his father, saying farewell to the mantas for a season, and remembering the Undset family who had all died in that terrible tragedy on the boiler centuries before. Making his way towards the wheelhouse afterwards, Anders suddenly spun back around and ran towards the starboard rails shouting and waving his hands wildly.

"Look everybody, look out there," he pointed, "we've got dolphins swimming along with us."

The crew was immediately overjoyed, and all ran starboard, it was wonderful to finally see them again. Rolf started acting crazy though, and began running lickety split up and down the entire length of the deck, barking excitedly. In his perfunctory eagerness, Rolfy veered towards us on the starboard rails and ended up approaching so fast that he lost his footing and began sliding towards us. Desperately trying to stop, his claws slid hopelessly over the wooden deck, quickly the disenchanted creature began howling pitifully. Because of the velocity he was moving at, he spun around several times and ended up sliding butt first towards the edge. Garrett thankfully averted a likely tragedy by diving through the air and deftly grabbing Rolf by his collar, his quick reflexes kept the mutt from sliding off the schooner and ending up in the Pacific Ocean. Rolf's momentum dragged Garrett so far though that he had to grab the bottom railing with his free hand to keep himself from being dragged overboard himself. It was a pitiful sight, Rolf hanging over the side of the vessel, dangling by the collar around his neck, gasping for breath, and Garrett dangling by one arm from the bottom railing. Thankfully though, our Garrett was a tenacious teenager, and with one muscular arm he was successful in pulling the one hundred and ten pound wolfhound back aboard, and when he had, everyone began applauding. Back aboard Rolf immediately began whimpering with one of his pitiful hangdog expressions, unfortunately there was no sympathy for him today; Rolf had been a bad dog.

Eventually maneuvering towards the bow and sides of the *Heimdall,* the dolphins were now jumping and clacking playfully. Rolf now had his paws on the top rail and was barking franticly at our new friends. He was once again safe, and thankfully his heavily muscled neck hadn't been damaged in the mishap. Considering Rolf's impulsive behavior though; Garrett decided to keep him firmly attached to a leash to avoid any possibility of the wolfhound ending up in the Pacific Ocean.

It had been far too long since we'd seen our playfully clever friends, and I considered their sudden arrival, with the *Heimdall's* bow pointed north, a well-timed sign from God. It appeared that some new challenge was about to present itself in the very near future. It was now a shared understanding that the dolphins were always sent to help us accomplish something we couldn't do without them; I wondered what God had sent them for this time.

As we came parallel to the city of Pozo de Cota, another European schooner was off our starboard. After we spent several minutes waving back and forth, Captain Olaf's order; *"prepare to raise*

sails" reverberated throughout the vessel over the radios. The crew was back on deck in minutes dressed in windbreakers and everyone had either tied their hair back or had put on snug caps. Scurrying about under Rorek's preliminary orders, everyone was focused on the task of engaging the electric motors, raising and trimming all the sails, and tying down all the lines.

"Prepare to fly ya lackey swabs," the Captain roared heartily from the wheelhouse door. The crew paused momentarily, laughing at the Captains order and waving, and then everyone jumped back to their individual tasks. It was exhilarating being focused in one accord like this and my heart began pounding with excitement. Within moments each sail began to accept the ample wind and snapped tight with a loud pop. Several minutes later, after the sails had all finally billowed open, the vessel began leaning larboard and within no time at all, we were flying in vigorous southern winds at thirty-five plus knots.

The smell of salt air intensified sharply, and everyone began shouting or whistling; it was a thrill like no other. Nothing I'd ever accomplished, in my twenty-six years of living, had ever produced such a quixotic mindset, or compelled me to such heights of exhilaration, like sailing this fast over the oceans surface did. Mysteriously . . . off the starboard bow, I began to see the ghost of Moby Dick taunting us to harpoon him, and poor Captain Ahab, bound tightly in a tangled mass of harpoon tethers, was still waving for everyone to follow him down to Davey Jones locker. I quickly rubbed my eyes and shook my head in disbelief, this couldn't be happening. Off the port stern, without warning, I began seeing pirate ships swiftly emerging from a ghostly thick fog, and all were overrun with bloodthirsty, depraved, and iniquitous men. I just knew they were pursuing us in order board and plunder the Rognvald's vast fortune of rubies and steal the Tempest. Would we be defeated and carried off to their God forsaken island and put in chains? Would we be forced to eat raw snails and drink mind numbing grog, swirling with human eyeballs? I was beside myself. With a sudden foreboding I turned to warn Captain Olaf that our lives might soon be forfeit and quickly realized that there was no danger at all. Succumbing to a strange euphoria, I had cunningly been deceived by an open daydream.

Once again, the wake from the *Heimdall's* bow was increasing dramatically in relationship to our speed, and while the brisk wind stung my face and everyone's emotions bubbled with joyfulness, I looked up and thanked God that I was alive and still working with these wonderfully gallant people. I was hopelessly elated and began singing an old song from my homeland, in the loudest voice I could muster, and within seconds the whole crew joined in.

"Oh ye'll take the high road and I'll take the low road
And I'll be in Scotland afore ye.
But me and my true love will never meet again,
On the bonnie, bonnie banks o' Loch Lomond

Twas there that we parted in yon shady glen,
On the steep, steep side o' Ben Lomond.
Where in deep purple hue, the hieland hills we view,
And the moon comin out in the gloamin

The wee birdies sing and the wild flowers spring,
And in sunshine the waters are sleeping:
But the broken heart, it kens nae second spring again,
Tho' the waeful may cease from their greeting

When the Captain and Rorek were satisfied with the trim of the vessel, the rest of us gathered round the bowsprit and let the stout wind bite at our faces for awhile. The dolphins were swimming along effortlessly with us, jumping and criss-crossing in front of the vessel, and riding the ample wake it was generating. It appeared, as the hours passed, that our friends would be staying with us for the duration, and in the quiet of my heart I gave thanks for their companionship.

The powerful southern winds didn't let up at all, but remained constant; consequently we were able to fly, consistently and smoothly, for close to ten hours. Rorek had discovered, listening to the navtex earlier, that a storm blowing west of the Galapagos was responsible for generating these ample winds. Apparently though, the weather bureau was predicting the storm making a landfall somewhere around Guatemala City, so our powerful impetus would unfortunately be dissipating before we'd arrived at the 28th parallel.

Thirty

Scammons Lagoon

July 18

Something had been irritating us since the dolphins reappeared; and like a blinking red light, an irksome premonition had been doggedly nagging the Captains thoughts. After we'd finished with group prayer he issued an unusually cryptic order, Olaf informed us that we'd be entering Scammons Lagoon cloaked in the CSAT. Without any substantial facts to back his decision, the Captain had quite effectively swayed all the misgivings we could invent, and assured us that his reasoning was more than just a whimsical notion.

For many decades the migrating gray whales had been a worldwide draw for the township of Guerrero Negro. The huge mammals endured a six thousand mile round trip yearly from the Arctic to spend several weeks basking and mating in the warm waters of Scammons Lagoon, Magdalena Bay, and San Ignacio Lagoon. Anders told us that his cousin's whale watching business had been one of the most profitable endeavors they'd ever embarked upon. In a three month period of time, it wasn't uncommon for them to generate eighty-five thousand dollars in revenue for just taking people out for two hour excursions to get up close and personal with the enormous creatures, ten to fifteen times per week. There was an enduring curiosity about the whales all along the western coasts, and millions of people would watch the gentle giant's annual migration from numerous locales.

Anders cell phone rang just before lunch; it was his cousin Ulrik. While he was talking I watched Anders face drain of color and his eyes occasionally open wide in astonishment. Responding very little during the call, he sat fairly stone faced until very near the end when he began speaking to Ulrik in the old Orknean dialect.

"Ulrik . . . we'll take care of it," he said quite sternly, "this crew knows how to deal with that scum. You and Gudrun get the bi-planes ready, I'll discuss everything with Captain Olaf and Rorek. I love you man, regards to Gudrun. We're on our way cousin, be very careful, I'll call you, keep your cell phone charged this time dude, and bring the extra batteries cheese ball!"

With a disgruntled look, Anders snapped the cover of the phone shut and shoved it into his shirt pocket. Shaking his head he suddenly looked up and stared at the ceiling fiercely. Pulling the Captain aside, I quietly interpreted what I'd heard Anders say. The Captain became visibly agitated as I talked and his breathing became calculated sighs. After several moments of contemplation Captain Olaf moved over next to Anders.

"What is it son, what's wrong now, what did Ulrik say?"

I could see Ander's beginning to shake after the Captain finished with his questions; it was obvious he was struggling to keep his feelings under control.

"It's about the Mortiken isn't it?" I asked, sitting down next to the Captain. With some disinclination I had considered this a possibility, based on the melancholic frame of mind Anders was in after the call. Captain Olaf radioed John to bring the *Heimdall* to a halt and instructed him to come below decks. Betsy was preparing lunch, so everyone in the galley sat down and waited patiently until Anders was able to gather his wits and talk to us.

"That was Ulrik, my cousin," Anders began softly, "You're right Gabriel; it was about the Mortiken."

"I had a feeling it was brother," I nodded.

"Captain . . ." Anders continued with a sudden resolve, "they've captured the airport at Bahia de Los Angeles, a place we call Baytown, and it looks like they might be moving overland towards Guerrero Negro. Gudrun flew some mechanical parts from Rosarito over to El

Toro for one of his friends who repairs airplanes there; when he was done he decided to fly towards Angel Island to check out the progress of that military installation there, you know, the one that the Morons are building. Well . . . unfortunately he never made it that far. While he was over the gulf he accidentally intercepted a radio transmission about the attack on Baytown and the movement of vehicles. Using the coordinates he heard, he flew back around and discovered a fleet of twenty vehicles full of the Baaldur scum, two miles north of El Toro, heading southwest. He said they're using the old fire road through the mountains to reach Punta Prieta. Based on their route, Ulrik believes they're going to try and intersect Highway One and then drive the one hundred and thirty miles to Guerrero Negro. Captain there's hundreds dead in Baytown; they were attacked early this morning and butchered, the poor people never knew what was coming, they weren't even armed. It's horrible, it's just horrible! It's not right; I can't believe they'd murder civilians like that, and for what? They don't have much time to prepare in town; my cousins have already warned the city council about what Gudrun saw from the air, and heard on the radio. The mayor said seventy-five soldiers from the Mexican Army are in town this month for maneuvers, they're bivouacked around the airport as usual. Those guys are just about half worthless though, most of them are drunken womanizers, and their bi-yearly maneuvers are just a big party. One good thing for sure though, they have a small tank they practice with regularly; I sure hope they can use it wisely."

I quickly looked around the room at the others faces. Everyone looked inflamed with Anders report, this story was horrifying news.

“How much time before they reach the town?” John asked.

“The distance between El Toro and Punta Prieta is twenty-eight miles John. The roads are terrible though, they haven’t been graded for many years, and the last rain whacked them out even worse. I figure it might take them a couple days to cover that distance if they’re really lucky.”

“Anders, considering the condition the road is in, do you think they could travel at night?” Rorek inquired.

“Doubtful . . . like I said, the roads are very rough, potholed, and covered with brush and rocks, there’s no way anyone could travel any faster than five miles an hour during the day in the condition they’re in, so at night, I think it would be impossible Rorek.”

“What are your cousins planning to do son?” Captain Olaf asked.

“They’re planning on leaving Guerrero Negro permanently Captain. They think the whole area is going to erupt into warfare and there’s not a whole lot they can do to stop it. They both figure the Mortiken are after the salt works, there’s nothing else of any value there except the Pemex stations. If they decided to commandeer the fuel stations they could very well control all the traffic up and down the Trans-peninsular highway, and if they can do that, then Cabo San Lucas could soon become another target. Captain . . .” Anders hesitated for several moments.

"What is it son?" The Captain finally asked.

"I think I need to contact Angelina's mother in San Lucas about this and have her inform all our friends."

"I agree that would be wise. Is there something else son?"

"Ummm yeah Captain," Anders answered sheepishly, "my cousins asked if they could join up with the *Heimdall.*"

A hush fell; Anders last statement took everyone by surprise. Could it be that we might have three new members join forces with the *Heimdall* team in less than a month? It seemed fantastic that these men were all blood descendants from the original Rognvald voyage and that our paths had somehow converged. What seemed even more bizarre was the recently discovered fact that Captain Olaf and Rorek were Amundsens, and also blood descendants from the original Rognvald voyage. After several quiet moments were spent considering what Anders had suggested the Captain answered.

"Let's pray before we make that decision Anders."

"Captain Olaf!" Garrett's radio transmission cut noisily through the murmuring.

Garrett hadn't been in the galley while Anders was sharing his phone conversation with us; under Rorek's orders he'd been on the VEW viewing the large bay we were just about to enter, the Bahia Sebastian Vizcaino.

"Garrett, what is it?"

"Boss, the bay is way cool, and it's totally empty. Yur not gonna believe what's anchored in Scammons Lagoon though . . . it's the bloody Red Dragon, one of those stinkin vessels that tried to whack us in the Bay of Biscay."

"WHAT! Garrett, engage the CSAT immediately son," Captain Olaf barked, "I want the exact coordinates of that vessel on a piece of paper in my hands ASAP!"

"Copy that Cap, I'm seriously on it. By the way boss, the CSAT's workin splendidly, Rorek had me check that sucker out too, thought you should know!"

"Thanks son, thanks for a great job. Helga when Garrett has determined the coordinates I want you both to get on the VEW again and pull down on that fleet of vehicles, and I don't want ANY arguing between the two of you, is that understood?"

"Aye sir, I won't," Helga muttered, slightly embarrassed.

"I've got a hunch; let's see whether or not Amalek Baaldur is traveling with the convoy lass."

"I'm on my way! If something does happen between us Captain, it'll be Garrett's fault . . . NOT MINE!" Helga snapped defensively as she ran out the galley door. The Captain chuckled faintly; he knew that stopping the sun, or pouring the entire ocean into a thimble would be easier than what he'd asked of Helga. There was no way anyone could ever change the irrepressible chemistry between Helga and Garrett.

"You know Captain, if Baaldur is headed towards Guerrero Negro, it might explain why the Red Dragon is anchored in the lagoon," John surmised. "I can't think of any other reason why that vessel would be this far from Europe."

"I wonder if the Red Dragon is here to pick him up." Lizzy pondered.

"Do you think Baaldur might be on his way to Alaska to stand against that Rognvald reunion Captain?" Anders asked, standing up and pushing away from the table.

"Let's determine if he's with the vehicles first son, especially before we jump to any conclusions." With an air of finality the Captain also pushed away from the table and stood up with Anders.

"Helga . . ." the Captain blurted.

"Aye sir," Helga responded immediately.

"Lass try and contact the professor in Rabat, maybe he has some information we could use. Go ahead and e-mail him about our situation here, also send the same message to Jonah, remember to encrypt it lass, I want his opinion about what's going on too."

"Copy that Captain; I'll get on it right away!"

"Boss, we're cloaked now," Garrett shouted down the hallway. "The Ghost Vessel just ain't heeah no mo country fans!"

"Thanks son," the Captain shouted back laughing. "Alright people, let's get busy! Stay as quiet as possible from here on out, also make sure we put the earpieces in all the radios, does everyone understand?"

"10/4 Captain," everyone chorused enthusiastically and quickly dispersed.

Within a period of thirty minutes we'd found out that the Red Dragon was anchored in Scammons Lagoon, and the Captains hunch about using the CSAT had been warranted. A fleet of Mortiken vehicles were apparently enroute to Guerrero Negro, the airport at Bay Town had been taken over and hundreds of civilians were dead from a Mortiken sneak attack early this morning, the salt works were in jeopardy of being taken over, and Gudrun and Ulrik were leaving home and had expressed an interest in joining up with the *Heimdall,* all this in combination with our plans to explore the caves on Cedros Island. Dangerous circumstances were now converging on Scammons Lagoon and Guerrero Negro, and it appeared that once again we were headed into harms way. The Mortiken were leaving another trail of bloodshed, destruction, and misery in their wake, and we had arrived here at precisely the time it was happening.

Thirty-one

Considering our state of affairs

"CAPTAIN . . . we've got a clear view of the vehicles on the fire road," Helga shouted excitedly. "They're eight miles outside of El Toro now."

"Copy that lass, good job, I'm on my way down. By the way, what else can you and Garrett see?"

The Captain gave the schooners wheel to Rorek and then bolted out the wheelhouse door, motioning for Anders, John, and me to follow him. We'd traveled thirty minutes on the diesel since our last conversation with Helga, and were now quickly approaching the southern entrance of Scammons Lagoon. The heavily armed Red Dragon was anchored in a small bay on the southern side of

Heart Island, a name we'd decided to give it because of its heart-like configuration. The coordinates, Garrett had established earlier, put the vessel anchored at Latitude 27 degrees 44' north, Longitude 114 degrees 13' west.

"Sir, the vehicles are at a standstill," Helga informed the Captain on the radio. "There appears to be a lot of growth and rocks blocking the road. It also looks like they're in the process of removing it, there's a lot of commotion around the convoy."

"Is Amalek or Krystal Blackeyes with them lass?" the Captain asked as the four of us entered the communications room.

"Sir, right here," Helga pointed at the computer screen as the Captain sat down next to her. "Most of the vehicles are two and a half ton, definitely old military vehicles. There's four newer Humvees, and one is pulling a large gun, Garrett said it's shaped like an old howitzer, the kind they used in Vietnam, and right here sir, there's a ten ton tractor with a covered trailer. I don't see the witch though, I don't believe she's traveling with them, but look right here on the other side of these boulders." The Captain leaned over Helga's shoulder squinting at the twenty-four inch computer screen.

"Oh man . . . its Amalek isn't it?" the Captain groaned, sitting back down heavily and rubbing his forehead with a sigh.

"I believe it is Olaf," Helga agreed with a sullen expression, "it looks like he's in a bad frame of mind too. Considering his size, Garrett and I believe he's being transported in the trailer of the ten ton, it's the only vehicle that can accommodate his bulk."

"I agree with you guys," John concurred. "Little brother how many Mortiken do you count around the other vehicles?"

"Big bro John . . . five minutes ago the VEW counted two hundred and thirty." Garrett answered matter of factly, "If everyone's outside of the twenty vehicles, then I would consider that an accurate count, but if there's still some inside the vehicles, then it's not! It looks like Amalek is surrounded by a minimum of thirty guards at all times, stinkin coward, and it appears that there's at least fifty of the lumpy grey skinned cheesewads guarding the perimeter with weapons at all times, STINKIN PARANOID FREAKS!" Suddenly disgruntled, Garrett stood up hastily, knocking the chair over as he stormed out of the control room.

"I hate those stinkin slime bag freaks Captain!" He shouted several times, each time becoming less discernible as he ran up onto the deck. "We need to whack them permanently!"

While we were discussing the possibilities Helga's cell phone rang; it was the professor in Rabat Morocco, he'd responded to Helga's e-mail. After brief acknowledgments, Helga handed the phone to Captain Olaf and for the next fifteen minutes the professor and Olaf conversed about everything happening around our location. After the exchange the Captain called everyone together and shared what the professor had disclosed.

"First, the professor and his entire staff send their love and well wishes," the Captain began. "Since we sunk those three vessels on July 4th, they've been monitoring the Mortiken movement worldwide daily. He informed me that the fighting and movement of personnel has intensified, especially in Porto Portugal, Edinburgh Scotland, and all along the Sea of Cortez. The Azores are completely under Mortiken control now. The military installation, outside the Panama Canal, is fully operational and the whole country of Panama is autocratic and under Mortiken rule. They say that it's becoming a nightmare for the indigenous citizens. The Mortiken also control all the tanker and freighter traffic through the Panama Canal; the professor conjectured that this will eventually prove catastrophic for world trade. The Mortiken have also begun a takeover of western Costa Rica, this is amazing news. He said that six of their European vessels made passage through the canal a week ago and began assaulting the country through the Golf of Nicoya. He said that after two days of intense fighting, that they were able to take over the city of Puntarenas, and get this; one of the smaller vessels there is the Dolphin."

"Is it the same Dolphin Helga photographed in Carino harbor?" Lizzy asked, her face getting pale.

"Yes dear, regrettably it is." The Captain shook his head solemnly.

"What do those scumbags want with Costa Rica Captain?" Garrett grunted.

Walking back into the room after cooling down from his tirade, he scratched his head with an indignant snort and sat down heavily. I could still see though, that his mind was churning with a strange anger.

"Because the city of Puntarenas is the countries major seaport, and there's a key railroad and well kept highway systems between there and San Jose, the professor feels that this would be a perfect place for the Mortiken to set up a base of operations for controlling both sides of the countries. Apparently San Jose is the capital and seat of all the countries governments and a constant flow of foreign politicians and dignitaries routinely visit there. The professor is convinced that if the Mortiken capture the country of Costa Rica, then along with Panama, they would be able to control six hundred and fifty miles of coastline on the north, and over eleven hundred miles of coastline on the south.

"Whew . . . that's a lotta shoreline boss," Garrett interjected softly, while everyone murmured in agreement.

"It surely is son," the Captain continued, "the economy and flow of all goods in and out of both countries could be brought entirely under Mortiken control. Also, get this, the Pan American Highway goes through the city of David all the way down into Panama City, and considering that this particular highway is a major trucking route, and it's one straight shot all the way up to Laredo Texas, the Mortiken could very well have another point of entry into the USA besides the Colorado River. "

"Captain . . ." Anders interrupted, "does the professor have any idea how many Baaldurians there really are? It seems like they're spreading themselves out kinda thin with all these takeovers."

"Interesting you should ask, the professor also mentioned that they estimate the Baaldurian Viking nation around one hundred and fifty thousand strong. His office estimates a minimum of seventy-five thousand Mortiken are now stationed in Panama and Costa Rica. As far as Edinburgh and Porto is concerned though, they're not quite sure about what their ultimate intentions are concerning those areas yet; they're still waiting to see what develops. Apparently the local and military resistance against them there is fierce. If they happen to be successful in their assault on Costa Rica, he believes their priorities could very well be shifting northwards towards Alaska and the Yukon Territories."

"This could be in conjunction with the day of many collisions we've read about Captain." John surmised. Captain why do you think Amalek is in Baja and not in Panama along with his major forces?"

"There's still a lot unclear John, but according to everyone on the professor's team, they believe that Amalek is making his way up to Alaska now. If that's accurate, then the Red Dragon is here to transport him."

"His move from Angel Island to Scammons Lagoon was supposed to be secretive wasn't it Captain?"

"Yes it was Anders! No one was supposed to know about the repositioning of Mortiken troops in Guerrero Negro. Your cousin Gudrun saw something that was never supposed to be witnessed son. This was certainly not accidental either, I see Gods hand moving very clearly on this situation to help prepare us for something in the very near future. It certainly gives us an edge, and also some time to develop a strategy to stop him, or at least slow him down."

"This is so cool boss . . . dig this," Garrett laughed. "The Ghost Vessel is here just at the right time to upset that pukes plans again, and the wanker doesn't even know it! Yah baby! Looks like we might have another opportunity to really mess with that poop brained, Viking wannabe skid mark."

"That might be true son," the Captain laughed lightheartedly.

"Does the professor know where Krystal Blackeyes may have headed Olaf?"

"All they know now Lizzy is that there was a confirmation from one of their underground field operatives in Miami Florida; she was positively photographed boarding a small jet at an airfield there. He said they hacked into the private air services computers and found out that her ticket was paid for by a Middle Eastern chemical company located in the Mediterranean. There was only one female passenger aboard the small jet when it took off and according to the registered flight plan; the jet was bound for Ponta Delgado in the Azores."

"Boss what are we going to do?" Garrett asked, standing up and stretching. "Should we take the opportunity and whack that stinkin Dragon, or just move north and forget about it?"

"Garrett, I really don't know yet, but . . ."

"Sir sorry to interrupt," John interjected, "but lets be pragmatic, this whole situation could get complicated really quickly, especially if we let ourselves get involved in the wrong way. I really do believe that the elimination of the Red Dragon could seriously jam up Amalek's plans Captain, but we're still very seriously outnumbered, and if we do have to face the Mortiken hand to hand, we might encounter a whole boatload of insurmountable problems. Sir, I don't know about you, but I certainly don't want anyone getting seriously hurt or killed here. The way I see it, we have limited weaponry at our disposal, and also limited man power. We do however still have four magnetic mines left if we need to do something covert, but still . . ."

"Right John, we still have to establish our priorities in this situation, don't we?" Betsy interjected, having obviously understood the gist of John's thoughts.

"We could spread ourselves out to thin otherwise Captain, I agree, besides; we still have those caves on Cedros to explore. Captain I believe our priority is finding clues and information in the caves that we can use to locate the First Tribe up in Alaska, if that's were they really are." John nodded in agreement with Betsy's assessment.

"Yah boss, I agree with Bets. We do need to get into that big cave to see what's in there, that's a fact! But still, I'd sure like another chance to kick some scummy Mortiken butt. I'm really sick and tired of what those pukes are doing to everyone."

"So am I son, all of us are for that matter, but I don't . . ."

Before the Captain could finish, Helga's cell phone rang again, it was Jonah this time, and then several seconds later Anders cell phone rang, Gudrun had called. After a short conversation Captain Olaf snapped the cover shut on the cell phone, and with a huge smile handed it back to Helga. Anders conversation lasted several minutes longer though, and after he'd finished, he was also beaming from ear to ear.

"My cousins are ready to go Captain; the bi-planes are loaded and fueled. They also said that the city is preparing for the Mortiken convoy, and the military is preparing for all out war. According to what Gudrun said, they don't seem very concerned about the invasion, apparently there are more troops in town this time than there's ever been before, almost three hundred, and they have a lot of big equipment with them, enough to possibly turn the tide in their favor. They confirmed again that they're ready to join up sir, if it's all right with you. They also reminded me that there's a dirt airstrip on Cedros they've used several times in the past, a hundred yards from a small cove were we could anchor the *Heimdall* and easily access the beach. They'd be willing to meet us over there to discuss all the details."

"Crew . . ." the Captain looked around at everyone and shrugged his shoulders, "how does everybody feel about this?"

Everyone shook their heads affirmative and gave a thumb up to the plan. I suddenly realized that the possibility of having a Vildarsen, and two Bjornsons part of our journey now was somewhat miraculous.

"OK then," the Captain concluded, "Tell your cousins that we'll rendezvous with them on Cedros to discuss all the details." After the Captain finished, there was patchy applause for a moment and then the Captain held up his hand for silence, and continued.

"Jonah sounds great crew; he sends his love to all. He seems very anxious to get back to work, and personally, I'm very happy about that, I really miss him." The whole crew nodded in agreement, and muttered soft amen's.

"Apparently Jonah has been communicating with the professor regularly and he also strongly believes that Amalek and his contingent are on their way up to Alaska. He also agrees there's nothing we can do to help Guerrero Negro with their current dilemma and suggested that we go ahead and let Ulrik and Gudrun join up and sort out all the details later, Jonah sees Gods hand moving to our benefit in their forced departure. They can certainly help us with our explorations of the caves, knowing the area the way they do. Jonah also reminded me that the *Heimdall's* mission is locating the First Tribe, not engaging the Mortiken every chance we get, and I certainly agree with him. Betsy, John, you were absolutely right in your assessments. As of now we're due up in Alaska the third week of August to unload the old vessel and get it down to Cape Cleare, and any clues we can discover about the First Tribe during that time is our first priority. Remember we still have to deliver the . . .

Thirty-two

Captain Olaf reveals the Tempest to Anders

The Captain hesitated for a moment, cleared his throat, and looked at Anders somewhat benignly. When he had something in Anders demeanor bristled, without hesitation he sat straight and glowered indiscriminately as the Captain continued.

"If the circumstance warrants no other course of action except physical contact with the Mortiken, then we'll take the necessary precautions and accomplish whatever needs to be done to protect the crew and complete our mission."

Now overwhelmingly annoyed, Anders jumped up with a resentful scowl and hit the table with both hands. Everyone was stunned.

“WHAT”S GOING ON HERE?” Anders screamed. “You guys haven’t told me everything yet have you? Did I do something to offend you dweebs? I don’t like what I’m feeling right now, I don’t like it one bit! I’m part of this team too, you’re the ones that invited me to join, remember; we’re on the same mission together. I lost my home, I shut down my business, my father’s vessel is aboard one of Proudmores tankers heading up to Alaska, I won’t be swimming with my Manta’s for who knows how long, the wife that I dearly miss is in Pine Valley and my boat is berthed in San Diego harbor with Jonah’s, you have the rubies my father found locked up on your vessel, I gave um to you in good faith ya know! Do you know how much money they’re worth? What’s wrong with you damn people, WHY DON’T YOU TRUST ME?”

Everyone glanced furtively at each other and began clearing their throats and fidgeting, Anders repugnant outburst had caused the warm vibe in the room to rapidly deteriorate. It was obvious to me that no one was comfortable with how Anders had just expressed himself and I hoped that a fight would not be subsequent in the tense aftermath. Cautiously, with questioning expressions, John and Garrett stood up. Standing at arms length from one another, they stood quietly and fixed their gazes on Anders every movement; they reminded me of two eagles watching their prey. His behavior had become unruly, and the possibility of more verbal hostility seemed forthcoming. Visibly puzzled at Garrett and John's sudden defensive posturing, Anders recoiled considerably when he caught a glimpse of Captain Olaf's face.

Anders was an intense man, simply put; he appeared to be a warrior out of time. Since the day he'd discovered the *Heimdall,* anchored off San Benedicto Island, cloaked in the CSAT and without any compunction whatsoever began pounding angrily on her hull, he had never once hesitated to open up and share exactly what he was feeling. At times though he would express himself in a deprecating manner unbecoming a man of his intelligence and skills, and although these displays were distressing, somehow I found myself empathizing with his outburst today. In the short time that we'd been working together there was one thing that I understood for sure, you always clearly knew where Anders stood; he was a man that didn't hide anything, and he always spoke his mind. I knew Anders life had changed dramatically since our first encounter, and I understood how he'd sacrificed since joining forces with us, but how he'd figured out that the Captain was not disclosing certain information was a mystery that I had no answer for. Did his abilities communicating with the giant Pacific manta rays also give him a special intuition with people? Anders was a very unique man, and at this point in time we still knew very little about him. Did he know intuitively that we were in possession of the legendary Tempest sword? It was difficult to comprehend how he might construe the Captain's hesitancy in divulging certain facts as a lack of trust on our part. Considering what we'd all been through thus far, and considering what he knew about us and the purpose of our mission, it did seem somewhat ludicrous that he would suddenly question our trust. Captain Olaf was always levelheaded and his reasoning for not making certain things known reflected that Gods timing was involved in all that we were doing.

With a remarkably stern look, the Captain held up his hand to calm Anders disruptive spirit and also to end John and Garrett's defensive posturing. The Captain abruptly motioned for all of us to follow him and walked smartly out of the galley.

"Let's go, everyone follow me, RIGHT NOW!" he ordered tersely over his shoulder upon entering the hallway. I knew the Captain had been seriously rankled by Anders conduct and even though he hadn't said much, the clenched jaw, glaring eyes and reddened face was proof that his anger was boiling. Since I'd joined, I was personally aware that Captain Olaf wanted order and stability aboard the *Heimdall.* He did not tolerate disorder, and he was adamant that people communicate with one another in respect and love, and I'd never known him to waver. He hated jealousy and envy between people, and he also hated unresolved, distrustful attitudes created by petty bickering, especially the kind that affected the way people performed their duties. There was an unwritten law aboard this vessel, people must resolve their differences, and not let their misunderstandings develop into something they shouldn't be. If those involved were incapable of doing so themselves, then the

Captain would assign two or more of the crew to act as adjudicators to establish objectivity and help resolve the differences.

I perceived that Anders outburst might have stirred something deep inside our Captain Olaf this morning. Although I knew he'd been infuriated with Anders reprehensible conduct, was it possible that our leader might have finally deemed the time appropriate to reveal the Tempest? While we all walked towards the mechanical room the Captain slowly maneuvered in beside Anders. Pausing for a moment, he turned and without any expression looked him straight in the eyes.

"You're right Mr. Vildarsen, there is something that I haven't talked to you about yet. But young man, I'm the Captain aboard this vessel, and that was my determination to make, you should never take my decisions aboard this vessel personally, especially in context to the mission of the *Heimdall,* there's something much greater at work here than your personal opinions! "

Anders was immediately pensive, and after a long sigh he hung his head in shame. When we'd all reached the mechanical room the Captain turned and asked everyone to join hands and pray. This was indeed a wise decision and it calmed everyone's frayed emotions and also helped instill a sense of peace and camaraderie between us again. Afterwards he unlocked the hydraulic room door and let John and Garrett in, a few moments later they both carried out the large ancient box and put it on the metal table. Anders was taken back, and his eyes opened wide with curiosity.

"What's this?" he muttered, looking back and forth between the box and the Captain quizzically.

"First . . . before we open it," the Captain continued, "let me continue with what I began a few moments ago, and I'm speaking as the leader of this vessel again Anders, from my heart, and for the whole crew. My unwillingness to tell you about this discovery had nothing at all to do with not trusting you; it had everything to do with crucial timing. You might think that your outburst earlier was the motivation for me to reveal this to you, it wasn't! I believe that God planned it this way so you would clearly see a part of yourself that needs to change. Let me reassure you also son that I have accepted you as an essential part of our mission and we all feel that your presence here was predetermined. It was Gods Holy Spirit that put us together and we all take that seriously. Do you understand what I'm saying here Mr. Vildarsen?"

Anders hung his head again and murmured a downhearted "yes sir", and then the Captain nodded at Garrett to go ahead.

"Check it out dude," Garrett blurted enthusiastically. Anders spun around and stood motionless with a bewildered expression on his face.

"Is it the Tempest?" he muttered incredulously.

"Yah . . . it's the real deal, the bomb of all swords, Gamelin's most excellent work, and my homeys and me found it dude!"

Garrett laughed and quickly began playing a rhythm on the tabletop with his hands. Anders chuckled softly at Garrett's animated comments and then promptly wiped away several large tears that had formed. Looking over at the Captain, he asked for permission to pick it up.

"Go ahead Anders," Captain Olaf said motioning to John.

"What do you think of this beauty?" John chuckled.

The next few moments were as poignant as any I'd ever remembered. When Anders grasped the old Viking sword in both hands something in his demeanor changed dramatically, he appeared more centered and peaceful than I'd ever seen him before. Any doubts he might have entertained about his involvement with us, crumbled in a moment right before our eyes. By the look he had in his eyes and the joyous expression on his face, it was apparent that Anders had just found a key piece of a lifelong puzzle.

"Do you know how long I've dreamt about holding this sword," he murmured turning it over and over in wide-eyed amazement. "About six months before I met up with you guys, I'd given up on this sword ever being found. I'd always hoped it might be buried somewhere at the bottom of the boiler, but that was really foolish. Gosh, it's hard to believe I'm holding it, thankyou Captain Olaf for this honor." Anders looked sheepish for a moment and nervously cleared his throat.

"Captain, I'm really very sorry about the outburst earlier. My father always used to get in my face about expressing myself that way; I promise I'll try my best to keep a handle on it in the future sir, especially with you guys, but not with the Baaldurians." Captain Olaf chuckled lightly and shook Anders free hand.

"I'd like to apologize to you guys as well," he said turning towards us, "you've done everything you could to help me in my transition and I want you to know that I really appreciate it. As long as we work together, I'll always have your backs, I promise!"

Everyone offered their thanks, and after we'd accepted his apology and shaken hands, he handed the Tempest back to John. Unexpectedly, as if a bolt of lightening had struck him, Anders impulsively spun back around and walked over to where I was standing. Good Lord, was he going to hit me? With an excitement in his eyes I'd never seen before he stunned all of us with several questions directed at me.

"You're the chosen one aren't you Gabriel? A Vildarsen confirmed this with you. It was Floki wasn't it?"

Thirty-three

There is wisdom in the counsel of others

July 19th

The dawn began this morning with a glowing orange line demarcating the eastern horizon which, over a period of thirty minutes, became billowing clouds interlaced with serpentine ribbons of golden reddish hues. For more than an hour gusts of wind from the north had been pushing up uneven waves which occasionally crested in frothy whitewater and then diffused on the waters surface. Because of these conditions the Captain and Rorek were on deck zealously discussing the possibility of another storm approaching, and the importance of keeping the Navtex on in order to hear the weather reports for our area.

After anchoring the schooner yesterday, several hundred yards from the rocky northern coastline in Vizcaino Bay, the dolphins had disappeared around dusk and were absent all night, now though; they had reappeared and were waiting for whatever snacks they could wheedle. While Rolf ran up and down the deck, barking exuberantly at their return, I could see once again that he was on the verge of getting out of hand. His impulsiveness with the dolphins was now a source of daily anxiety for us and, based on prior experiences, the possibly of calamity was always forthcoming so we needed to be vigilant. After scanning the deck I saw that Garrett had a leash in hand and was keeping a responsible eye on him. As soon as Betsy had reached the rails, with two buckets of wriggling bait, the affable chemistry between the dolphins and the dog changed immediately. Rolfy was quickly forgotten and now Betsy was their best buddy. Eagerly crowded below her they began splashing water up with their cute bottlenoses in anticipation of all the yummy stuff that was ready to be mete out. After the dolphins quit playing with him, Rolf trotted over to the capstan and sat down indignantly, knowing his buddies had abandoned him for mere food he howled sorrowfully several times, and then curled up and quickly fell asleep.

It was mystifying to me how Anders had suddenly known that I was the chosen one; this unexpected revelation had beleaguered me most of the night, and consequently my sleep had ended up being quite restless. After Captain Olaf confirmed Anders insight his whole deportment had changed abruptly. With eyes blazing he began shaking my hand with the vigorousness of a politician and assured me that I would be protected at all costs, day or night. Quite frankly, coming from a man of Anders reputation and physical prowess, it was an assurance that I was quite thankful for and I quietly thanked God for putting this man in our path, and more importantly, letting him become my friend.

There was still some uncertainty about what stratagem we'd be using during the next few days. Bearing in mind the Captain and Rorek's hesitancy to make a sound judgment based on the unfathomable parameters of our present circumstances, we considered it prudent to pray together for Gods wisdom. When we'd finished Captain Olaf told us he would still postpone any decisions until he'd had more time to cogitate the circumstances, he also wanted to communicate with the professor and Jonah to fortify his own view with their objective judgments. There were so many things that could be done, and the general consensus was that we should be taking care of everything we encountered whenever we encountered it. Because of the experiences we'd had with the Mortiken we found ourselves always struggling with a powerful revulsion for the malevolent tribe, and we also burned with a desire for retribution because of their heinous acts against us, and mankind in general. Jonah's observation yesterday had been correct, first and foremost, we were searching for the First Tribe and our primary objective was investigating every clue God had put in our path to achieve that exclusive goal. Even though disrupting the Mortiken agenda was inclusive to the overall mission, there would certainly be times when it would not be Gods will for us to be involved, no matter how passionately we wished it otherwise. Just like our experiences at Anders cottage, we were closely involved there without being physically confrontational. We knew that the counsel of those we respected and trusted was invaluable to determining the right course of action, and also conferring with those more objective than we were was absolutely imperative for the Captain to make the correct decisions. Learning from our own personal experiences, we'd discovered that the counsel of others, of like faith, was essential for a more complete wisdom. We had discovered, on numerous occasions, that pride and skewed emotional involvement can oftentimes blind you to certain actualities, and also cloud the decision making process about the direction you're supposed to go in.

Thirty-four

Helga and Garrett's irrepressible chemistry

In numerous ways, and without equivocation, Helga was the crew's resident nerd. With a remarkable penchant for preciseness and regimentation; she was a woman that embodied an unwavering loyalty to the *Heimdall's* mission, and would steadfastly scrutinize her own role with a purposeful fortitude. Daily she performed her work with an uncanny sense of duty, and was always as persnickety about what she accomplished as our dear Roxanne was, a trait in both women I found refreshingly admirable. With a conscientious aplomb, Helga's tireless integration of myriad facts, inclusive to daily life aboard the *Heimdall,* was extraordinary. Her abilities permitted everyone else the opportunity to stay focused on their own strengths without anyone having to sweat the many details she would have to deal with daily. Thankfully her ability with a high-powered rifle was also remarkable, and it was an irrefutable fact that most of us were still alive because of Helga's shooting skills.

Concerning selected relationships though, there were certain idiosyncrasies occasionally that might be construed as unfavorable aboard the confines of a schooner. The *Heimdall* employed a rare amalgam of personalities. Each individual incorporated exceptional talents, unique and powerful skills, diverse intelligence, laughable impertinence, quirkiness, strong spiritual conviction, and the desire to be the best they could be everyday. But there was something else; on occasion, two of the crew had the ability to mercilessly torment one another, Garrett and Helga could push every button each other had, and would laughingly do so for the fun of it. In the last six months, on numerous occasions, I'd personally witnessed that they dearly loved one other, and considering they both shared the exact same spiritual convictions, I knew that if push came to shove they would both, without a second thought, die for the other. Unfortunately though along with the bond of love there also came the proclivity to mercilessly torment one another, and they had done so frequently. To those that didn't know them, Garrett appeared to be Helga's absolute antithesis. Every nuance involved in the expression of their individual personalities had the potential for chaos and conflict attached to it, all except the extraordinary skills they each used to further the *Heimdall's* journey. When fanciful creative breezes blew through Helga's mind, she always wanted to be the center of attention, but when they blew through Garrett's mind though, he always preferred working quietly by himself. When Helga would accomplish something worthy of mention, she always wanted some form of recognition, but when Garrett did; he was always somewhat self-deprecating, and would often defer an accolade to someone else.

It was an unquestionable fact that Helga's organizational skills were an integral part of the *Heimdall's* successes, and I would often-times admit to Helga's work being worthy of expressive accolades. When Garrett and Helga worked together it was a different story altogether though, an idiosyncratic tension swelled between them that encouraged mordant verbalizing, sodden with cynical humor. Regrettably, there were signs this morning of another breakdown between these two. When Garrett saw Helga shuffle into the communications room I immediately saw his mouth twist scornfully, his forehead crinkle, and I knew a mischievous spirit had gripped him once again.

After impulsively jumping out of bed at 6am, Helga had shuffled into the communications room yawning and half awake; she would be embarking on yet another quest to accomplish something she couldn't put her finger on. When Garrett had first seen her, his mouth opened wide and he stared in wide-eyed disbelief. Grabbing his head with both hands and shaking all over, he began groaning under his breath. Helga quickly snorted at Garrett's impudence and muttered, *"Grow up butthead!"*

From my perspective also, Helga just didn't seem to be herself this morning. The woman was unsightly and seriously out of character. Her brown hair was very oily and disheveled, and she'd entered the room wearing dirty rumpled pajamas that hung awkwardly from one of her shoulders and she had one slipper missing. Not wanting to openly verbalize what we were seeing, Garrett and I also noticed that something alien was hanging out of one of her nostrils that made a faint buzzing sound. Every time she breathed in it would disappear, and then when she exhaled it would reappear. It reminded me of a gopher, fearful of exiting his burrow, but continually poking his head up and down to find an opportunity to do so. Because of this persistent mental image, I was finding it difficult to suppress my silent rumblings of laughter; Garrett though, was absolutely beside himself. Within moments he exhaled an animated moan, raced down to his berth, and then returned several moments later with a YO-YO. Mercilessly, he began mocking this strange ballet coming from Helga's nostril with the up and down motion of the YO-YO. My ability to suppress laughter was beyond problematical now, so I decided to leave so as not to embarrass her. Before I'd had a chance to exit the room though Garrett snapped, he just could not hold back anymore, and in a sudden burst of youthful exuberance he mercilessly began tormenting her.

"Check it out Helga hooger booger; you look whacked! Did you go through a washing machine this morning girl? I can't believe yur hair is so stinkin nasty, wuz up with that?"

"Garrett . . . shut up; I'm not in the mood!"

"Hey princess, when was the last time you checked yourself out in a mirror? Where's your other slipper girl and why's your shirt all buggered up, you look like you slept in a dumpster."

"Garrett . . . I mean it, if you don't shut up and leave me alone, I'm gonna tell the Captain!"

"Hey dweeboid, what does this YO-YO and your nose have in common?"

"What do you mean by that you little goof? There's nothing wrong with my nose!" Helga protested with eyes glaring.

I couldn't stand it any longer, and I found myself suddenly filled with an unexpected compassion. Helga's face had become bright red and the veins in her neck were beginning to bulge, quickly I handed her a small mirror to try and diffuse the possibility of more conflict. She gazed at me with a puzzled expression as I timorously pointed at my own nose, then with a sheepish smile I nodded for her to go ahead and look at hers. Consenting, she got close to a small light so she could see; a look of horror quickly etched her features with an indescribable intensity. With a frustrated gasp she threw down the mirror, and ran out the door shrieking.

"Garrett, you pukey little rat, I swear I'm gonna get you!"

Garrett and I could not suppress our emotions now, and the humorous twitching erupted into gut-wrenching guffaws. We laughed so hard we almost threw up. The impulsive outburst quickly subsided though, and I knew that the way we'd reacted to Helga had been despicable. Suddenly embarrassed at my immaturity, I felt the overwhelming need to apologize.

Three hours later Helga quietly sat down in the galley for one of Betsy's sumptuous breakfasts. There was something different about her; some inscrutable transformation had occurred that no one had ever seen before. Demure elegance walked into the galley with her, and while an enchanting refinement from deep within her soul oozed out all over the room, I found myself hopelessly mesmerized. It was at once obvious that she'd showered, put on make-up, painted her nails, meticulously combed her freshly washed hair, had two shoes on, and was wearing a dress that accentuated her femininity more dramatically than I'd ever witnessed before.

Who was this goddess?

In the past, she'd always just been Helga, kind of tom- boyish, one of the guys, most always wearing shorts or jeans and sandals, hair disheveled quite frequently and pulled back into a sloppy pony-tail, and often brusque in her expressions towards others. When John sauntered in he was also smitten with how captivating she looked. Quickly commenting on how nice she smelled, he kissed her cheek and whispered something in her ear that had her giggling within seconds. After John's efficacious expressions towards her, Helga's stilted temperament vanished and was rapidly replaced with a light-hearted joy for the duration of the meal. She remained dispassionately aloof towards Garrett and me though, and only conversed with John. Somehow I knew that our impudence earlier had wounded her and I felt terrible about it. I hoped that she wouldn't hold anything against me, I'd been naïve, and had also been manipulated by Garrett's foolishness. Garrett was the wrongdoer here, and I'd found myself hopelessly drawn into his shameful intrigues. He never should have gotten that stupid YO-YO out; I could have simply given Helga my handkerchief!

Haphazardly pulling her hair back and tying a ponytail, Helga smiled with the radiance of a morning sunrise and informed everyone that while viewing the VEW earlier, she'd discovered something distressing about the convoy. While we listened she passed out the pictures she'd printed, and shortly thereafter everyone's frame of mind changed dramatically. The convoy moving towards Guerrero Negro had another surprise; *Billy Quoyburray, Regan Pendleton's ex assistant, was now traveling with Amalek Baaldur.*

An hour after breakfast Captain Olaf gathered everyone together for a logistical meeting. The fact that Billy Quoyburray was sympathetic to the Mortiken agenda had already been established in Regan Pendleton's fax several days earlier. The fact that he was now traveling with Amalek Baaldur's convoy was a surprise though, why was he with them, and in the present circumstances, what role was he playing now? Captain Olaf's phone conversations with Jonah and the professor had given him the confidence and insight to formulate a plan for us.

1. The Red Dragon had to be incapacitated before Amalek Baaldur and Billy Quoyburray could get aboard, this was most imperative!

2. Ulrik and Gudrun Bjornson would be joining the *Heimdall* team, but to what extent they would be involved in the long term was still uncertain, we really didn't know anything about these men other than what Anders had shared with us. I had a strong hunch though that their bi-planes and interpretive skills would be finding a noble role in the days ahead.

3. Before sailing north to San Diego, we'd be visiting Cedros Island to investigate the caves there and search for any new clues concerning the whereabouts of the First Tribe. I silently hoped that the information we'd find in these caves would point us in the right direction.

Thirty-five

John's clever suggestion

During his personal morning prayers John mentioned he' been given some unexpected insights about the remarkable predicament we were facing now, and after breakfast he shared these insights with the Captain and Rorek. Within moments I heard the Norwegian brothers laughing throatily and rowdily dancing about, something special was happening.

After we'd made inquiries about the three vessels, we were informed that the Red Dragon was assuredly one of the three vessels that had been anchored in the Concello de Carino harbor, and also one of the three that had surrounded us in the Bay of Biscay while we were diving on the Shallows of Three Rocks. The professor's staff was also able to establish exactly what the Red Dragon was now and the vessel was not what it appeared to be, it was actually a very high-tech floating weapon. All the ships internals had recently been retro-fitted and modernized. They surmised the whole idea was to create something that appeared one way to the observer, but was in fact something entirely different. This was apparently done to deceive those they'd targeted into believing that they were safe and approachable, so they could be destroyed unawares.

We were unanimous in our opinions that the Red Dragon was one of the most unique vessels we'd seen in years. The Captain and Rorek couldn't remember a ship built in this time period still being active, except perhaps the Star of India stationed in San Diego California. Being an ancient three masted wooden frigate with twelve sails; it resembled a floating museum piece in perfect condition. The ten cannons visible were actually non-functioning facades left for appearance sake, and even though all the sails were still functional they were seldom used, a piece of information I found odd. A powerful diesel engine, specifically geared for slow power, had been installed which allowed the Red Dragon to easily pull anything four times its size, and also do an amazing eighteen knots consistently in rough seas. One powerful modern laser weapon, allegedly possessing complex destructive capabilities, had also been installed on the bow on top of the forward part of the main cabin. According to satellite surveillance; the Dragon had already made several retaliations with this weapon in the Panama Canal, and also along the western shores of Costa Rica. The damage resulting from these attacks had been substantial and required the decommissioning of the debilitated vessels; apparently this laser weapon had several functions that were truly sinister. The Red Dragon had also been mechanically refitted and equipped with modern computer technology late last year somewhere in the Mediterranean during the months of November - December. According to the professor's research, the only part of the Red Dragon that hadn't been retro-fitted was the ungainly wooden rudder that had been installed when the vessel was first built; he discovered that it had been left untouched for authenticity of appearance.

John's plan was simple, and quite brilliant. He suggested we remove the rudder and then after relocating it a safe distance away, destroying it permanently. In so doing, we would be rendering the Red Dragon completely useless for any navigation. The inability to steer the vessel would keep it at its anchorage until the rudder had either been replaced, or the ship could be towed to another location. Given the isolated geographical location of Heart Island, and also the improbability of getting parts anywhere on the Baja peninsula, this could take many months to accomplish. I realized, from a military standpoint, that this plan was inspirational and fully anticipated our mission being quite successful.

"Is it possible John?" the Captain gulped in amazement.

"Yes it is Olaf." John responded proudly. "I'll require three others besides myself to accomplish what needs to be done. Anders, Garrett, and since Rorek is busy with the mechanical repairs, I want Gabriel to go along with us. Rorek and I have studied the jpeg and mechanical files and we both strongly believe the mission is well within our capabilities to accomplish."

"I agree with him Olaf," Rorek said with one of his rare smiles, "the mission is doable, and there's no way I can get away from the transmission repair for at least a day. Helga's on the VEW right now checking the Red Dragon for any activity, let me go check on her progress, I'll be back with you shortly!"

"Alright, sounds like a good idea brother. Gabriel, do you agree with John's suggestion about being the fourth member of the mission?"

"Ummm Captain, I uhhh, well . . ."

Aghast at my sudden lack of verbal skills, I looked away timidly as my heart began pounding. Staring intently at the floor, I started reeling as if I were descending into a vortex and I found myself hopelessly jumbled up in emotions and fears. Within seconds, Garrett's belch echoed throughout the room with a gut wrenching juiciness, and was followed swiftly by a mocking chuckle. Garrett seemed to find ways of jarring me back into reality, and sometimes used the strangest methods doing so. Reluctantly I took a deep breath and answered.

"Well, ummmm . . . I know that I'm nowhere near as qualified as the other guys Captain, but I'll do whatever it takes to make the mission work. As long as John has faith in me, I'd be honored to help out. Thanks for another opportunity John."

"Homey . . . what a pecker head you are," Garrett remonstrated, "I can't believe you! Remember how great you were at the Shallows man, you don't have to worry bout squat dude! Did you also forget that you swam with the mantas and the hammerheads dweeb, what's wrong with you . . . you got brain damage?"

Garrett erupted into guttural laugher for several seconds and then with an encouraging punch on the shoulder he sat down with a thud. He was right, I was being an idiot.

"How long will it take John," the Captain asked, chuckling along with the rest of the crew at Garrett's comments, "and when do you think we should begin?"

"Sir, it might take as long as an hour to remove the rudder, I'm not entirely sure yet. There are several unknowns that I won't be able to answer until we're looking at it. If it's alright with you I'd like to get started immediately. We've already checked out the diving equipment and it's ready to go."

"Olaf . . ." Rorek interrupted on the radio, "the VEW shows no activity aboard the Dragon, it appears deserted. We did notice however that three emergency boats are missing, which leads us both to believe the crew went ashore somewhere. Helga's searching Heart Island for confirmation; I'll get back with you as soon as we know something, Rorek out!"

Noticing Anders disheartened demeanor, Olaf finally walked over and placed a hand on his shoulder with the intention of encouraging his participation.

"Anders, how do you feel about John's plan?" He asked.

Anders shrugged his shoulders and answered. "Captain, I'm ready for this mission, that's a fact. Sorry about the mood Captain, I've just been thinking about my father. I can't wait to get started though; I do look forward to working with the other guys. I also feel hesitant about destroying that vessel; it does kinda look like a piece of art. To bad it belongs to the Mortiken, maybe someday we can change that."

"Dude that sounds like a great idea," Garrett laughed. "Let's whack those grunge bags and take it for ourselves. We could tow it to San Diego behind the raft . . . you drive homeboy!"

"Another thing Captain," Anders chuckled, "I feel inclined to call Gudrun and Ulrik to up-date them about our plans. I think it would be wise before we disembark for the mission?"

"Alright, as long as no one else has an opinion about it, I'm good with that." The Captain looked around and everyone gave a thumb up.

"Contact your cousins then and inform them about our plans. Also tell them that Lord willing; if all goes well today, we'll try and meet up with them over on Cedros Island tomorrow afternoon. We'll confirm by phone in the am. Also Anders, get some coordinates about where we're supposed to rendezvous."

"Oh sure, gotcha Captain, that's a good idea, I'll be back shortly!" Smiling, he bolted out of the room.

"John lets get started!" The Captain ordered, standing up and stretching. "I'll reposition the *Heimdall* over near the Dragon while you and the other fellas get the equipment up on deck. You should probably get suited up and ready to go.

By the way John, thanks for checking everything out, and another thing, thanks a lot for your fantastic ideas, you're an inspired man today!"

"I really can't take credit for the idea Olaf; it came to me while I was praying. About the equipment, I wouldn't have it any other way. When I was in the Seals, the main focus was to be the best you could be and the team always came first. I feel genuinely honored to be part of the *Heimdall* team, we're a great team sir and quite frankly, this is the best employment I've ever had. I have no intention of ever letting anyone down on this journey. It really is amazing how God is using us you know." The Captain shook his head in agreement and smiled.

Nodding politely John walked briskly towards the door, turning momentarily he smiled and said, "I love and respect you Captain Olaf; God has made you a wise man, and also an honorable and excellent leader."

While a small tear formed in the corner of one of eyes, the Captain smiled and shook his head in thanks

As the Captain maneuvered the schooner towards Heart Island I found myself vexed with an unusual foreboding, I realizing that this island was nothing more than a large knoll protruding perhaps fifty feet in elevation above the surface of the lagoon. There were no trees, almost nonexistent vegetation, and several hundred yards inland, the island was heavily scattered with a number of peculiar rock formations that resembled colossal bird droppings all clumped together in irregular shapes. As soon as we'd rounded the southern tip of the atoll the Red Dragon was suddenly there, anchored directly ahead of us fifty yards offshore. Her bow was facing directly away, but even from this unfavorable vantage point I found myself quite impressed by the old school craftsmanship.

In several places along the rear bulkhead and exterior cabin walls, we saw the same beautifully carved wooden dragon; the builders of this vessel had been very artistic.

Thankfully our dolphins were still with us. When I had first noticed them a sudden burst of reassurance surged up inside my heart; I anticipated their presence being crucial to our well-being in the hours ahead. When Captain Olaf finally anchored, we were one hundred and fifty feet from the other vessels stern and in clear view of everything on deck. The odd foreboding was still gnawing at me, and for the first time ever, since the voyage had departed the Aberdeen harbor, I found myself questioning the Captain's reasoning for maneuvering in so close to an enemy vessel. Garrett had also whispered we were getting so close that we'd probably be able to see the rotting pores on their gray faces; this of course disturbed me because I knew he was right.

Why was the Captain getting this close?

The radios squawked noisily, and Helga informed us there was no activity aboard the Red Dragon, and no one was visible on Heart Island. It seemed the crew of the Red Dragon had just vanished!

Thirty-six

Removing the Red Dragon's rudder

As Rorek and Helga were quickly discovering, the surrounding areas here were remarkably desolate; only three townships existed in a thirty mile radius, Guerrero Negro, Aguaje, and Ojo de Liebre. Based on this information, Helga increased the diameter of their satellite search by forty miles just to be safe. Continuing to move out systematically, on the VEW's geographical grid, they discovered there were no other vessels in Scammons Lagoon, however a small irregularity near the community of Ojo de Liebre caught both their attentions; the town appeared to have several conflagrations raging throughout. After focusing the VEW down closer on the coordinates, they discovered that three distinct plumes of smoke were blowing eastward into the Vizcaino Desert. Two hundred yards southwest, on the outskirts of the small township, they also discovered that three sailing smacks were pulled up onto the beach. In all probability these were the emergency vessels Rorek had mentioned were missing from the Red Dragon. The explanation for the smoke became sadly apparent; contingents of Mortiken were violently destroying the small township of Ojo de Liebre, and just like the atrocity they'd carried out against Bay Town, they were involved in yet another take-over and annihilation of innocent people. My heart groaned when I heard this terrifying news, it was heart-rending realizing that the Mortiken were once again ravaging another vulnerable and defenseless community. It was also evident that the *Heimdall's* mission had become dangerous again, and the urgency for success in our present endeavors was paramount to our own survival. Surprisingly though, during the confusing hodgepodge of thoughts clanging about inside my mind, I clearly recognized something about our present situation, while the Mortiken were destroying another defenseless small township twenty miles away; we'd been given a clear window of opportunity to incapacitate the Red Dragon with what appeared to be a minimum of resistance.

The four of us were suited up and ready to disembark within thirty minutes of Rorek and Helga's distressing discovery. We understood that after departing the vessel we'd be visible to anyone, being that the modules didn't work underwater, and the CSAT only camouflaged what was aboard the *Heimdall.* Despite this, the four of us still remained surprisingly calm while standing on the stern diving platform. Spitting into our facemasks, and vigorously rubbing it around the inside of the lens so they wouldn't fog up, we rinsed them out, adjusted the air regulators, cleared our mouthpieces, put on the masks, and prepared to leave the vessel. Today we'd be using the same diving equipment we'd used at the Shallows of Three rocks, plus the small cutting torch that John had used so effectively to sink the Wormwood. Without a word, we all quietly slipped into the grayish/blue water and sank from sight.

The visibility wasn't bad, and once submerged, it became obvious that the water was clean and clear at least sixty feet in all directions; I felt comforted knowing that we'd be able to see our work without any visual hindrance. Within seconds the dolphins quickly interspersed themselves amongst us like patches on a quilt. Playfully nudging our legs and arms, they began imparting an interesting kind of strength. Inexplicably, as if a magical thread had suddenly woven our mission firmly together, I began experiencing a unique thankfulness for the unity that I now shared with my gifted crewmates and these intelligent mammals. The dolphin's presence was encouraging me, and that small voice that I'd come to rely on daily quietly reminded me that in Gods strength and focused together in one loving accord that we would always do well against insurmountable odds. I noticed this group of dolphins was not like the pod that had helped us on the Shallows of Three Rocks in Europe; they were colored differently and had an unusual bottlenose shape. It appeared these clever mammals knew exactly what needed to be accomplished here in Scammons Lagoon though, and without any contrived effort, we'd become an inter-connected team with a mysteriously determined focus.

There was very little noise underwater except the steady pulsing of exhaust bubbles coming from the regulator behind my head and also my erratic breathing. The uncertainties I'd struggled with for months, swimming submerged with these creatures, had utterly vanished today and I was very thankful for my obvious growth. Thankfully the water was undisturbed in this area of the lagoon and while the four of us swam towards the hull of the Red Dragon I found myself postulating the possibilities of what was ahead. At the end of our mission today would we have been successful in our endeavors and still be alive?

As of yet I'd never been entirely comfortable breathing from a scuba tank underwater. Invariably, for several minutes after being submerged, I would suck in an abundance of shallow breaths and then feel muddled from excessive oxygen in my blood. I wanted to put into practice what John had taught me months before, but I always seemed to struggle for several minutes. After my breathing finally stabilized, my heart continued pounding with an increasing cadence, there was something quite sinister here that was, as yet, unseen. Bearing in mind what had happened aboard my father's tanker, the Belanthian, and how the feeling I had now was similar to what I'd experienced then, I found no comfort at all considering the possibility of something foul lurking in this place waiting to seize upon us. Garrett startled me with a tap on my arm. When I glanced over at him; his eyes were also filled with consternation.

"Homey, are you feelin what I'm feelin? Remember that funky evil we felt on Cockburn street in Edinburgh, there's something creepy here too dude. Look over at the dolphin's," Garrett pointed. I shook my head in agreement and glanced in the direction Garrett was pointing.

John's sudden and terse order rang through the radios to keep ourselves focused, so I forced myself to shake off the sinister feelings, and bring my attention back to the task at hand. I noticed however that six dolphins had broken ranks with us; I could see vague outlines swimming in circles around our position in the distant gloom. It seemed as if they were guarding the perimeter, and I questioned whether or not they were aware of something approaching us that we hadn't yet seen.

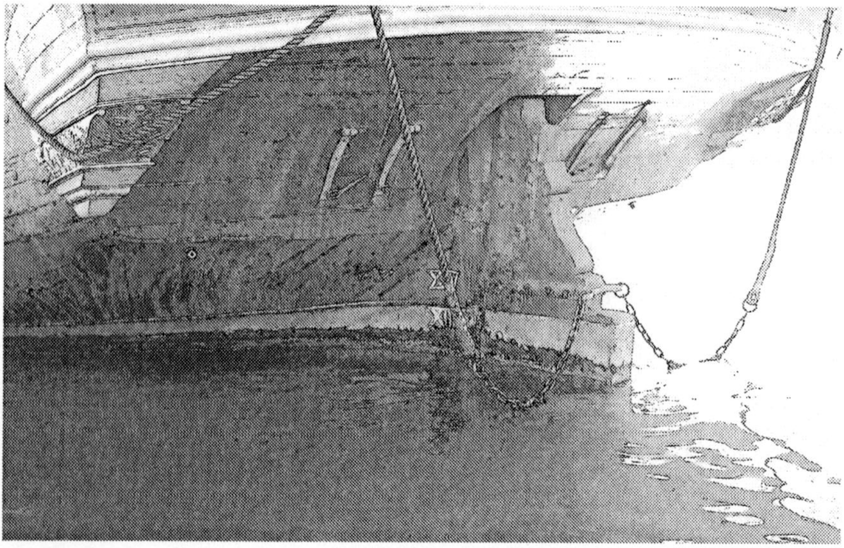

After reaching the rudder and assessing the structure for several moments, John swiftly pointed out the areas that needed to be cut with the hex torch to allow it to break free from the stern of the ship. Anders heartily accepted the job, and began cutting the hardened steel pins while the rest of us kept an eye on the area around us. It took less time than anticipated and twenty minutes later, the archaic rudder arched back off the stern of the vessel and lazily sank thirty feet to the sandy bottom. All but two of the dolphins had departed now and were methodically circling in the distance around our location. I wondered what was happening that we couldn't see.

"Mission accomplished sir," John informed the Captain. "We'll start transporting this thing over towards you. Captain, the dolphins seem agitated about something, is there anything top-side we need to know about?"

"Good job men, lets get that thing outa there. In response to your question John, a short while ago Helga saw one of the three smacks leaving Ojo de Liebre; it appears they might be making their way back to the Red Dragon. If they are, I'm putting their arrival time at sixty minutes; this could be what the dolphins are agitated about. Helga counts ten soldiers aboard the smack, and also fellas, Helga informed me that Amalek's caravan still hasn't reached the highway yet, it appears they've been encountering a lot of problems navigating that dirt road. I find this quite humorous frankly, the scumbags haven't moved any farther than a mile since the last time we checked them out. I've decided to move the *Heimdall* away from this anchorage, so plan on meeting us four hundred yards south, over behind the largest of the southern rock formations. Sorry about the extra swimming men, but we can't take the chance of being discovered, Olaf out."

"Copy that," John replied, "no problem about the swimming, it's a wise precaution, we'll see you there."

Quickly we all dove down and hoisted the large wooden rudder up from the bottom. After we'd reached the surface, and stabilized the ungainly thing between us, we slowly began side-stroking towards the southern shores of Heart Island.

Thirty-seven

Dolphins and Men

For some reason, while we were moving towards the southern tip of the atoll, awkwardly clutching the Red Dragon's rudder between us, and trying to swim at the same time, I began reminiscing about the frightful encounter we'd endured in late April with the Mortiken, just before departing European waters.

It was during the large aftershock, and much to his dismay, that John had helplessly stumbled backwards against the *Heimdall's* deck rails and dropped the RCFM overboard. After all the work the men had accomplished attaching the mines underneath the two enemy vessels hulls, John was forced to watch helplessly as the remote trigger fell from his hand and disappeared into a dark watery abyss. This unfortunate occurrence was certainly shocking, and in one swift moment had caused our hopes for victory to vanish, it had been a dark moment for all of us. It was the one lone dolphin though, clever enough to retrieve the RCFM intact from the oceans bottom, who had saved the day. When the dolphin resurfaced next to the *Heimdall's* stern diving platform, oblivious to the danger, Lizzy's shouts of amazement quickly alerted everyone to what she'd seen in its mouth. During the barrage of bullets, and cannon fire whizzing all around us, it was John who had courageously dropped down and crawled over to investigate. The dolphin truly amazed us, and for all intents and purposes its mystifying behavior had turned the tide of the battle in our favor. Had it not been for Gods hand moving on this mammal, we may very well have been decimated by the Mortiken and this story would have never been written.

The dolphins were very close now, there were twelve in all. Interspersed between us, they'd begun playfully nudging our arms and legs and were gazing directly into our eyes with optimistic smiling faces. I began appreciating the fact that they were sharing love with us on the most primitive of levels, and were compelled to assist us without any agenda whatsoever. Their joyful presence was continuing to impart confidence and fortitude in me, and thankfully this mysterious infusion was off-setting the anxious thoughts about what lay ahead. During this exchange I found myself thankful, in a humorous way, that the dolphins didn't have the same proclivity for sniffing butts that dogs did, this would surely have been awkward in these circumstances. Three of the powerful mammals were suddenly swimming underneath the enormous rudder and holding it up on their backs, how could they have possibly known to do this? I found myself mysteriously enamored with these creatures and their capacity to help without being asked, and now more so than ever, this air breathing, warm-blooded, milk-producing mammal was beginning to captivate my heart and mind with an undeniable respect.

I was born in suckling dependant helplessness, a lone seed from an idealistic father, through an affectionate soft spoken mother, into a cruel self-centered world. I'd been taught by an affable, optimistic father, as I grew, that hard work intelligently executed, coupled together with a persistently regimented diligence, and surrounded by skillful people, would often encourage the creation of something admirable, but would not necessarily guarantee the kind of success that modern society defined itself by. Aside from a strong relationship with Jesus Christ, diligent prayer, and being sensitive to the still small voice of the Holy Spirit, people working daily together in Gods love and unity was the key to success in any endeavor. God used willing people to bless other people in this age of grace, and those He chose always brought glory to the creator in their endeavors before themselves.

Since I'd been accepted into this crew, without any misgiving or mistrust, I understood much better that people who are truly in Christ Jesus must accomplish works and bear fruit that bears witness of Christ Jesus. In other words people must see the attributes of

Christ in what you do and say. Aside from the *Heimdall* crew, Christ centered people seemed few in this modern world. Most people wore very misleading masks; often hiding behind these contrived facades to positively affect those around them to get what they wanted. More often than not, these types of people would never purposely reveal the ugliness of who they really were, and not until they were snared suddenly in unexpected circumstances would you ever know what really dwelt in their hearts. I recalled a passage from "Mere Christianity" by C.S. Lewis that aptly described this.

"Surely what a man does when he is taken off guard is the best evidence for what sort of a man he is. Surely what pops out before the man has time to put on a disguise is the truth. If there are rats in the cellar, you are most likely to see them if you go in very suddenly. But the suddenness does not create the rats: it only prevents them from hiding. In the same way the suddenness of the provocation does not make me an ill-tempered man: it only shows me what an ill-tempered man I am. How true!

No matter how I'd been influenced by my father and mother's substantial character though I still retained innumerable personality quirks that I was continually, and painfully aware of, and they all seemed resistant to transformation. I was a man that had hidden many of his fears and weaknesses over the years, especially all the foolish things that I didn't want others to see and judge me by. Fear and self loathing ended up being the unfortunate consequence of the repugnant cat and mouse game that I played with myself and those around me, and in my middle teens I'd become self deprecating and unsure of my own abilities, especially outside the realm of my own controllable microcosm. This was surely the key though, what I could control I felt safe with! Even though working aboard the *Heimdall* was helping me understand and deal with these problems, often times they would still creep up from my abominable underground fortresses and overwhelm me at the most inopportune times.

As I'd often experienced during my six years of college, quality achievement and success was never an accident or entirely self perpetuated, it relied heavily on unified human interaction and optimistic societal circumstance. Being here in the water and at peace with the dolphins today, I clearly understood how different they were than human beings and how they had circumvented the set of laws man had devised for success and rapport with one another in a corrupt modern world. Dolphins didn't hate, lie, cheat, fornicate, manipulate, consume drugs, worship false gods, or promote wickedness, but they would, with a mystifying regularity, address the impiety that plagued the fallen condition of the human heart with a warrior's passion. It appeared that Gods enemies oftentimes became the Dolphins enemies. They lived in symbiotic harmony together and in their watery environment, unlike man who used anyone he deemed necessary, and destroyed anything he wanted, in pursuit of his ungodly ambitions.

Curiously though, the dolphins lived in harmony with the same needs that paralleled ours. They lived outside the rules that governed our existence but still needed what we needed to survive, food, air, love, community, and communion with God. They weren't dependant on us inside the framework of their own environment, we were dependant on them. All the manipulating and conniving we could conjure to try and intellectually establish a functioning relationship with these mysterious mammals would be futile. It was God that used these magnificent creatures to aid man, when he was out of his natural world and in theirs, not the other way around. It was the dolphins that innocently loved and helped man, and it was man who appeared to love the dolphins but would use them for their own selfish purposes, sometimes even killing them in their loathsome pursuits.

I felt an emotional dependency on these creatures now, especially in context to the line of work we were doing aboard the *Heimdall.* In my mind the Dolphins were quite similar to human beings on many levels, but still wholly different. Breathing air and living underwater was like attempting to mix oil and water, but because of Gods design, they had mastered it so well. I had learned, in one of Rorek's books that whales and dolphins actually breathed more efficiently than most land dwellers did. When most humans breathe they only clear twenty percent of the air in their lungs upon exhaling, but when whales and dolphins breathe, they rid themselves of ninety percent in their roaring, spouting exhalations. Dolphins and whales also have a very high concentration of a substance called myoglobin in their muscles, humans don't; this substance enables Dolphins and Whales to store large amounts of oxygen, thus the ability to stay underwater for long periods of time, humans needed air tanks.

The morning Helga and I were descending the center mast, after discussing the weather station and satellite dish we were about to purchase in Edinburgh, I remembered being amused and besieged by a captivating joy the first time I saw the dolphins swimming vigorously along with us. I still can't determine though if what I was feeling was an honest response to what I was experiencing, or if I was just caught up in the exuberance from Helga and the crew's reaction to the dolphin's unexpected arrival. I find myself still likening that first encounter, with the dolphins, to a hoity toity buxom bleached blonde woman strutting down the street with a fluffy neurotic poodle on a diamond studded leash. I was certainly amused, and superficially charmed with what I saw, but still no real connection had been established in my heart. It was entirely different now with the dolphins though, over the months and the many adventures they'd become a fundamental part of our journey and shared a curious responsibility to the success or failure of any given circumstance. Ostensibly coming and going at will it had been proven, and was now an undeniable fact, that the dolphins were always with us when we needed them and when they were no longer needed, they quietly departed. I categorically saw Gods loving hand moving to our benefit in their timely appearances and remarkable help.

Thirty-eight

An evil mist approaches

The *Heimdall*'s diesel purred softly like a contented cat, the sound becoming less and less discernible as the schooner slowly moved away. Even though I was swimming with Garrett, John, and Anders, and we were surrounded by dolphins, there was still a powerful feeling of isolation in this place, and it made me shudder in the deepest parts of my being. I could see the wake, from the almost imperceptible movement of the cloaked schooner, was leaving two faint lines of foam slowly trailing behind it. While Captain Olaf expeditiously maneuvered the *Heimdall,* and we continued our frustrating struggle with the rudder, the radio earpieces suddenly crackled and Helga startled the four of us with an ominous report.

"Mission . . . three Mortiken are on the Dragon now, they've just come up from below decks." Helga whispered tensely. "They're all smoking cigarettes; from here it looks like they're all hung over by the way they're stumbling about. Oh yuck . . . one just vomited over the railings!"

A chill quivered up my spine when I heard Helga's warning, and I felt abruptly nauseous anticipating the possibility of swimming through vomit. Johns' terse order to stay focused snapped me back to the work at hand, and when I'd realized that the tide was carrying the disgusting mess away from us, I praised God.

We were now probably one hundred yards distant from the stern of the Red Dragon and had all begun breathing deeply from the powerful exertion required to keep this ungainly rudder balanced and afloat, thank God the dolphins were helping, this would have been a task we could never have accomplished by ourselves. After fifteen more minutes of struggling John suggested we take a short break from our intense exertions. Fortunately we'd reached an area where the water was only chest high, so while we rested, and the dolphin's milled around splashing water in our faces, I began analyzing the topography surrounding us. I pointed out to the others that the suns azimuth was now beginning to cause a glare in the eyes of the Mortiken aboard the Red Dragon; thankfully, because of this, no one would be able to see our surreptitious movement. Also right after Helga's radio warning, a mystical zephyr had begun blowing briskly around the southern shores of the atoll and was creating a surface condition that also helped conceal our movement in the water. It was profoundly obvious that God had created these conditions to protect us in our endeavors.

There was an austere magnificence here. I remembered from my studies that deserts were areas on our planet that received less than ten inches of precipitation per year, and from what I was viewing, we were assuredly in vast desert geography. Deeply weathered into the peculiar rock formations was a somber narrative of moisture deprivation abounding in this harsh environment. From what I could see, Heart Island was predominantly a lifeless mound of rock with a smattering of boulders, one to two feet in diameter, strewn about all over the sandy hillsides. These unique forms were called concretions, emerging over decades as the surrounding sedimentary rock had been eroded by wind and what little rain fell here. Only several yards from where we were resting the beach was made up primarily of unassembled constituents of sand, dust, pebbles, and rock. Regrettably it was also littered with manmade junk, probably thrown overboard from the whale watching expeditions. Without enough moisture to bind all these elements together, I knew there would never be any substantial plant or animal life represented here. From this vantage point I saw no plant life whatsoever, the island appeared dead. It was eerie how this forsaken landscape, severely tortured from a lack of rain, exuded such an enigmatic beauty. I construed that only the hardiest varieties of species would have any chance of survival in this God forsaken place.

It was also thought provoking that the ancient Baaldurians had chosen this geography in their bloodthirsty quest for domination; I perceived a sinister resemblance between the surroundings here, and the ancient Viking tribe as a race. This relentlessly hostile environment was similar to what the Mortiken were as people. Endlessly battered by severe heat and desiccating winds, this geography was similar on many levels to the way the Mortiken would carry out their atrocious campaigns and conduct their pitiful lives. In their brutish incursions the Mortiken would debase and brutalize people cities and townships, and then after they'd finished their nefarious deeds only destruction and misery would remain in the aftermath of their wickedness. Yes, this place seemed an appropriate habitat for them; they deserved nothing less, the geography and the Mortiken were a perfect compliment to each other, oppressive, cruel, and lifeless. I personally and sincerely hoped that the Red Dragon and everyone aboard would never leave this place.

"How much farther Captain Olaf," I gasped.

"Another fifty yards Gabriel; we're anchored behind the largest of the three formations. As soon as you come around on the west, dive underwater for a moment and you'll see the anchor chain."

"Copy that sir; it'll be a comfort when we get there."

Back aboard the *Heimdall* we decided to tie the rudder to the stern diving platform and exit the area with all haste. As we had come to understand in the past, our present plans were always subject to change in the light of unfolding circumstance. This was another one of those times when what we wanted to do was changed by what the circumstance was dictating we had to do.

The Mortiken on deck had somehow become mindful of the missing rudder and were now storming about absolutely incensed. One of them was now in the wheelhouse screaming on a radio to someone on the lone smack fast approaching their position. Within moments we began hearing gun fire in the distance.

"They'll be back aboard the Dragon soon sir," we heard Helga informing the Captain. "Also sir, the two smacks near Ojo de Liebre must have heard the radio transmissions, they're moving in the direction of the Red Dragon also. Based on the distance they've traveled from the shoreline, I'm assuming they'll be within proximity of the Red Dragon within two hours. They look fierce Captain; most of them are covered in blood. This group looks possessed Olaf; they don't look like the others we've encountered in the past. There's something horrible on these men that I've never seen before, it doesn't look good sir."

"Thanks lass, I understand your concerns. Listen crew, this is for all of us; remember this people, greater is He that's in us than he that's in them. We are children of the Most High, and Lord willing we will prevail this day. We are small in number, but the One we worship is greater than any of what we are seeing or imagining. He is able to do greater things than we could ever wish for or envision. Our real ability and power is in our mighty God crew; our strength is in God, and we will trust in God and not in our abilities. We will trust in the Holy Spirits working through us this day, and every day from this time forth. If the Lord Jesus Christ chooses to walk with us this day, hallelujah, it's for His glory not ours, praise His name! Remember crew, we can do all things through Christ that strengthens us! Amen and Amen! Watch their progress Helga, and keep all of us informed. By the way, are they carrying any weapons lass?"

"From what I can see, they all have AK47's, several short swords, and various caliber hand pieces sir."

"Do they have anything bigger?"

"No sir, it doesn't look like they do."

"Thank God for that," the Captain sighed. "Helga, when you get a moment please check on the progress of Amalek's convoy."

"10/4 Captain, I'll let you know in five minutes."

Thirty-nine

The Mortiken laser wreaks havoc

Just eighteen miles away Gudrun and Ulrik Bjornson were talking in hushed tones outside a small wooden hangar on the outskirts of the main airfield in Guerrero Negro.

Just twenty yards from where they were huddled, the Steadman bi-planes were fueled and ready to come to our aid. It was evident something had piqued the warrior spirit in both men, unmistakable now in the bristling looks of determination exuding from their faces. After the impassioned call from Anders, the cousins were now aware that the current circumstances were becoming dangerous for the *Heimdall,* and our odds were truly dismal; the crew was outnumbered at least eleven to one.

When Anders came back above decks he immediately began conferring with Captain Olaf, Rorek, and John, and within moments the men's eyes were burning fiercely. When I moved in closer I was stunned at what I overheard Anders saying. Gudrun and Ulrik had shared something disturbing about the workings of the laser weapon aboard the Red Dragon with him, and they had strongly suggested we destroy it before it could be used against us. The insidious weapon was multi-faceted in scope and, depending on how the operator chose to use it, was capable of decimating all opponents, completely, partially, or rendering all electronics useless aboard any vessel. The cousins promised Anders that they would take care of the two long approaching smacks if we could disable the laser and take care of the one smack that was almost back. It appeared that the *Heimdall*

team had just gotten two more players, and surprisingly there was focus and unity from these two men we didn't even know.

After five minutes of heated discussion we all joined hands and prayed fervently for wisdom and understanding. Without any warning, the rock bluff twenty-five yards north of *Heimdall's* anchorage exploded with a deafening intensity.

"Helga, can you see what happened lass?" the Captain shouted over the tumult as we all dove for cover.

"I'm not sure, but I think they might have just discharged the laser sir," Helga screamed!

What was beginning to unfold was making my blood run cold. Dirt and small rocks began showering down all around us and within moments the wooden deck was inundated with a ghastly mess. I realized that the only thing really protecting the *Heimdall* was our safe positioning behind these rock formations. If we had been any closer to that bluff the *Heimdall* might have been seriously damaged, and if the Captain had anchored in open waters we could have been destroyed completely with a direct hit. The CSAT was our most formidable defense, and it had certainly protected us in the most challenging situations in the past, but even this marvelous technology would not diffuse a laser blast. Praise God the Captain was given the insight to anchor in this protected area, the only thing vulnerable now was the last few feet of our three masts, and the chance of these being hit was extremely remote behind these rock formations. We were now as protected as we possibly could be, but still my heart was in my mouth. Another deafening explosion viciously ripped the air and threw sand and rock a hundred feet into the air fifty yards west of us, fortunately though everything fell harmlessly into the water.

"Sir, the laser weapon has definitely been activated and it looks like someone is taking pot shots anywhere they want," Helga screamed again.

"Helga, how close are the last two smacks to the Dragon, and how many are aboard, and also lass, Amalek's caravan, where is it now? Crew, we've got to get prepared . . . Garrett, you and Gabriel fetch the shotguns below son!"

"Copy that boss, we're on it. You want your 357 and bandolier Cap?" Garrett yelled while another deafening explosion collapsed a rock formation one hundred feet from the bow.

"Everything's in my bunk drawer son, yes, bring it along also!"

Captain Olaf had quickly grabbed the reins of command and began issuing orders to everyone. His battle plan seemed to have been formulated from the sudden demands created by the unexpected laser weapon attack, and also from the wisdom he, John, Rorek, and Anders had received earlier in prayer.

"Helga, I want you to get your rifle ready lass, bring plenty of ammo!"

"Aye Captain copy that. Also sir, I've ascertained that the two big smacks are still at least an hour and a half away, I count sixty aboard both, and also, Amalek isn't off the fire road yet."

"Hallelujah, thanks lass! John, you and Anders get over to the Dragon and take care of business NOW?"

"Leaving sir, we'll be in touch as soon as we get there," John shouted over the stern diving platform.

"Captain Olaf, operation Eagle just confirmed they're in the air," Anders shouted, "the bogies are loaded and white-hot, they'll rendezvous with your position within ten minutes and then head north towards the long smacks. Today brothers and sisters, the Bjornson's are gonna cook some filthy Baaldur's."

"Copy that Mr. Vildarsen," the Captain waved, "may God bless our combined efforts this day people. Lizzy, Betsy, I want you both to stay below and monitor the VEW. Helga I need you and your rifle up in the crows nest ASAP."

"On my way sir," Helga groaned.

There was still very limited weaponry at our disposal; thankfully though we had portable CSAT modules, hand grenades, and a great deal of ammunition for the shotguns, rifles, and pistols. We also had the main CSAT hiding the *Heimdall* and the dolphins were once again our allies.

After John and Anders slipped into the water, I watched Anders do something very curious; he swam over to one of the dolphins and stopped right in front of the mammal. John also watched spellbound. Placing both his hands on its head and looking directly into its eyes, Anders spoke to the dolphin for several moments in a strange guttural language. With an exaggerated shake of its head, and animated clacking, the dolphin jumped high into the air and, along with several others, sped off in the direction of Ojo de Liebre.

Saving the Red Dragon was something everyone wanted, but taking the Mortiken hostage, or having any mercy on any of them, was completely out of the question. The Mortiken were ruthless Viking killers, who posed a brutal threat to the survival of anyone who had the misfortune of being caught in their path. The dreadful spiritual allegiances they'd made so many centuries previous had perverted them mentally, physically, and spiritually, and in all honesty, they were beyond any hope and needed to be dealt with appropriately.

I began to see another parallel between the unpredictable drought and the Mortiken; God was giving us many signs to teach us and help guide our steps. We had an enemy that was closer and fiercer than ever. No matter where the drought bands appeared they ended up destroying everything in their path, and so did the Mortiken. The drought was unpredictable; it would randomly emerge anywhere, with no plausible explanation, the Mortiken were also similarly unpredictable and often appeared in the strangest places for seemingly no reason. After the drought devastated the topography the land was never the same; the same thing happened after the Mortiken had finished destroying the hapless townships or cities they'd chosen, they were never the same. We were confronted now with a devastating malevolence that was getting more wicked by the day, and surviving, disabling the Dragon, and eliminating them permanently were the only agendas we cared about now.

The cousins had informed Anders that they'd procured several dozen phosphorous grenades from a one-sided swap with the

Mexican Military, and it was their intention to use these weapons on the unsuspecting Mortiken. Approaching from the west, with the sun blinding the Mortiken's field of vision, the cousin's first pass would have to be successful enough to confuse the Mortiken and preoccupy them with nothing but their own safety. White phosphorous was a devastating weapon and if the cousins could drop only one grenade strategically into each of the smacks, their mission would be successful. If they missed, well, life could get violent and complicated rather quickly for the crew of the *Heimdall.*

Forty

Ulrik and Gudrun Bjornson

Anders cell phone rang unexpectedly and startled us during a lull in the laser attack. I was thankful we were four hundred yards from the Dragon; otherwise the ringing phone might have been heard. Helga answered, it was Gudrun. They inquired about our timetable and where Anders was; Captain Olaf took the phone from Helga and informed the cousins that Anders and John had already departed, he also informed them how long they'd been gone, what Anders had done with the dolphins, and what we were doing aboard the *Heimdall* to prepare for the approaching conflict. After the conversation Captain Olaf hung up with a huge smile and quickly ordered Garrett to uncloak the *Heimdall* momentarily to allow Ulrik and Gudrun to assess our coordinates visually. Within minutes, two bright red bi-planes roared fifty feet over the tops of our masts and rolled their wings. As they passed over, two radiantly smiling faces appeared briefly over the edge of the cockpits and they waved. The cell phone rang again and Ulrik informed the Captain that they had successfully entered our coordinates into their onboard computers and suggested we cloak again. Shortly after the call John radioed in to inform us that they had arrived safely at the Red Dragon.

"Captain Olaf, where is the lone smack now?" John asked. "How long before they reach the Dragon?"

"Give me a minute John, I'll have Helga check," the Captain replied.

"By the way Anders, your cousins just flew over, they have the *Heimdall's* location in their computers, and they're headed towards the two distant smacks."

"Thanks Captain, that's great news," Anders whispered, "those boys are gonna kick some stinkin Baaldur butt today, bank on it!"

"I'll await your reply sir," John continued. "Captain there's a horrible stench coming from this vessel; I've never smelled anything like it before. It smells like death, and the spiritual oppression here is powerful. This is a first for both of us; we need to get our mission completed as soon as possible and get out of here."

"I agree John. The smack is still twenty minutes from your position, can you plant those grenades without . . . wait a minute Rorek just confirmed that the dolphins have surrounded the first smack. Oh Lord, you're not going to believe this; they're ramming the sides of the bloody thing. I'll be back shortly, I'm going down to the computer room; I've got to see this for myself!"

"Copy that Captain, this is incredible news, Anders is beside himself here with Rorek's report. By the way sir, we can get aboard undetected by climbing the bow anchor chain. Once we're aboard it will be easy to destroy the laser encasement. Helga watch where those three Mortiken are please, keep us up-dated, remember honey we're not cloaked, John out."

"Copy that John, I'll keep you posted." Helga affirmed with an uneasy laugh."

There was excitement and tension in the air simultaneously; it appeared that John and Anders timing had been excellent, and the news about what the dolphins were doing was just incredible.

"John, Anders," Rorek shouted excitedly, "all but one of the Mortiken has gone below decks, the other one is in the wheelhouse talking on the radio, so be careful when you board her. From what I'm watching on the VEW, the lone smack is being pummeled by the dolphins, it looks like they're trying to sink the bloody thing. The Mortiken are totally confused. It looks like most of them have lost their weapons overboard; they're being hit simultaneously by the dolphins on both sides, they're scrambling around and holding on for dear life. YAH, go dolphins go! I LOVE IT! Several are floating facedown in the water; it looks like they're dead, PRAISE GOD and HALLELUJAH!"

I'd never heard Rorek so excited; he was absolutely beside himself watching the dolphins working, and had begun dancing a lively jig. Gods Spirit was moving mightily in the preliminary moments of this new confrontation, and the Ghost Vessel was once again moving in mysterious ways. The Mortiken smack was being destroyed by a pod of dolphins God had sent to help us.

"I told the dolphins to whack the bums," Anders admitted in response to Rorek's excitement. "Along with the mantas; I've had abilities with the dolphins since I was a kid. Don't ask me how; we've just always been able to communicate."

"Incredible son, just bloody incredible, praise God in heaven above," the Captain shouted in jubilation. "Gentlemen it's time, obliterate that weapon. You might have to confront the three Mortiken aboard so be careful."

"No problem Captain," Anders growled, "we'll take care of that scum permanently!"

The air was rife with excitement now, and even though Garrett and I weren't physically involved in this stage of the battle, goose pimples were still crawling all over us listening to the radio communication. The phone suddenly rang, cutting through the control rooms edgy excitement like a razor through fabric; it was Gudrun and Ulrik again. The two smacks were visible on their radar and they were preparing to make their preliminary fly by. Garrett quickly prayed with them before the connection was broken and then we slapped high fives in anticipation of victory. I wondered if the cousins were also believers in Christ Jesus.

We were now preparing for a skirmish with the Mortiken on several different fronts. Anders and John were now boarding the Red Dragon to destroy the laser weapon and deal with whoever was still left aboard. Garrett, Captain Olaf and I were monitoring the situation on the VEW and radios. Lizzy and Betsy were preparing all our weapons just in case we needed them. Helga was on her way up to the crows nest with the high powered rifle, and Rorek was lowering the raft into the water in anticipation of any need that might occur with John and Anders mission. The dolphins were destroying the lone smack before it reached the Red Dragon, and in their bi-planes, Gudrun and Ulrik were racing towards the two distant smacks to try and obliterate them with white phosphorous grenades. The adrenaline was high now, and my stomach was in knots.

Forty-one

John and Anders ghastly discovery

John's radio transmission came unexpectedly and shocked us. In a faltering whisper John informed us that while they were climbing up the anchor chain to reach the forward deck, just behind the figurehead on the bow, that they'd felt strongly compelled to stop and investigate; they wanted to ascertain what the dreadful stench was emanating from the vessel.

As inconspicuously as possible, they peered through the forward porthole, propped open with a stick, and discovered something unconscionable. These Mortiken were cannibals!

Recoiling in abomination, at the macabre scene unfolding before their eyes, John and Anders watched in horror while two of the fiends prepared a grisly feast out of the lifeless bodies of young prisoners that they'd captured from Ojo de Liebre.

I was helplessly overwhelmed with John's report and vomited on the floor just outside the control room. Gritting his teeth and groaning, Garrett slumped down against the hall wall and began rocking back and forth. Lizzy and Betsy were at once white as sheets, clutching hands at the table they were whimpering in heaving sobs. The Captain and Rorek sat down heavily; staring down at the floor in dumbfounded silence, they shook their heads in disbelief. Above in the crow's nest Helga collapsed behind the waist high walls; she was weeping in dismay at John's horrible account. What could cause human beings to sink so far into such a depraved condition?

"Captain, Rorek, permission to lob grenades into the ship sir," Anders growled, "this has to be dealt with, we can't allow this to continue, this is despicable."

"John, do you agree with Anders?" The Captain sighed. "Do we have a window?"

"Olaf, the prisoners are dead, they're all in pieces," John responded, his voice cracking emotionally. "It's horrible; I've never seen anything like this. Lord God, give us strength and wisdom."

"John . . . do we have a window to complete our mission?" The Captain reiterated grimly.

"I agree with Anders, yes sir I do agree." John replied, now choking back tears. "Even if it means destroying the Red Dragon Captain, we'll have to take them out permanently. We'll need back-up as soon as possible Olaf, both of us sense more than three aboard."

"Copy that John; give me a moment to discuss this with the others."

"Hurry Olaf, we're beginning to hear moaning all along the sides of the vessel through the other portholes, the demons must be waking up from their drunken stupors."

After John's request, I found myself facing another sobering moment in my life. Sighing in dismay, Garrett and I shook our heads and stared blankly at each other for several moments trying to comprehend this new information.

We could die here today!

At its core, the *Heimdall's* journey was part of a life and death struggle for spiritual dominance on planet Earth and now, all nations were involved in countless and varied wars in pursuit of that end. We'd all read on the internet, over the last several days, about the terrible violence in the Middle East escalating more viciously than ever before, the bloodshed and conflict seemed worse than ever in recorded history, and it seemed now that no country was exempt. Vicious attacks were being perpetrated against the state of Israel and the city of Jerusalem was being demoralized every day by suicide bombers and air strikes.

A tactical nuke had been authorized for use by the British during a battle in Egypt and the repercussions were being heard, and felt, in every major country around the globe in myriad violent demonstrations. Global nuclear conflict was looming closer than ever before in the history of man.

There were tens of thousands of reports yearly now about alien abductions from every corner of the earth, and strangely, everyone had similar stories to convey. What exactly was this? Was this really intergalactic life from distant stars interested in helping Earth with its problems, or was it inter-dimensional angelic activity, demonic in nature, preparing unredeemed mankind for the coming anti-christ, and the great Armageddon, which would eventually culminate in the prophesied Revelation of the Holy Christ?

The Canadian economy had collapsed entirely and they were blaming the United States for manipulating the flow of goods into and out of North America to their benefit. Most of the world was switching over to a cashless system of enterprise; my father had personally e-mailed, two days prior, to inform me that the UK was now on a strict debit/credit system. There was no more currency exchange anywhere in England or Scotland, it had all been recalled.

The Scandinavian countries, Sweden, Norway, Finland, and Denmark, were now jailing anyone, anywhere, who spoke out against homosexuality, lesbianism, or any other form of sexual perversion. Even in the widely scattered Christian churches preachers were being secretly recorded, then turned into the authorities, and incarcerated if they preached against these perversions. There was nothing sacred anymore; the heart of man had become rotten, and the fabric of society was quickly unraveling. Just like it had been in the days of Noah, before the great flood came, the earth was on a collision course with Gods judgment.

The European Community was being heavily swayed by a very persuasive man speaking fluently about global peace and the importance of world unity, and millions were listening. Everything was shaking in the world now, on every level, and in every country, and the drug use, witchcraft, murders and thefts were worse than ever before. Healthy people were dropping dead on the streets and in their homes for no apparent reason. Powerfully influential people and huge mega businesses were folding for no apparent reason too, seemingly overnight. What was once understandable and controllable was now beyond anyone's ability to comprehend or predict.

The magnetic drought was striking everywhere like a merciless phantom, appearing and disappearing at will with no logical explanation, and the experts knew nothing more about why or where, than someone working at a fast food restaurant did.

Having lost their fear of man, animals were coming into the cities and suburban neighborhoods, attacking and killing senselessly, now both man and animal had a vengeance against each other.

There was an epidemic of lawlessness, homelessness, prostitution, suicide, depression and Godlessness, and no one seemed to care. The middle class was disappearing everywhere, and was being replaced with growing pockets of the pitifully poor and the exorbitantly rich; they both hated each other with a passion, and many were finding their ends with guns and knives.

The mega Christian church was spiritually powerless, in shambles, and filled with demons masquerading as light preaching felonious gospels. They were doing anything to keep the cash flowing and their diminishing numbers interested and feeling good about their lukewarm lives. The mainstream gospel of Jesus Christ had become an accepted means to defraud people out of their money, so the real Bride of Christ who worshipped in Spirit and in Truth had gone underground. They were meeting in parks and homes and in caves, and on mountaintops and schooners to worship their Savior and spread the good news. Millions were listening and being changed.

These circumstances, now with the Red Dragon, felt entirely different than the encounter we'd had on the barges off Roscoff

France in March. Even though the enemy here was still the Mortiken, they felt more demented than the other situations we'd faced them in. The other encounters had certainly been vicious, but this group had a vulgar sickness attached to them that was quite disturbing. It was certainly clear now why Rorek had lowered the raft into the water and the ladies had loaded the weapons and stored them aboard. Garrett and I knew we'd be going to help John and Anders fight on the Dragon and what I was beginning to visualize was making me uncomfortable.

Garrett came back to his senses before I did and began stretching, praying out loud, and wildly thrashing his invisible drums in anticipation of another melee; this odd ritual was something that I frequently admired and wanted to emulate. Garrett was an eclectic, headstrong, opinionated youth, that oftentimes became quite perplexing, but at his core he was a gifted Christ-centered warrior with a stubborn faith like no other young person I'd ever known. Setting aside his quirkiness he was a shrewdly gifted teenager, way beyond his eighteen years of age, and his involvement in our journey was always imaginative and would continually, even in the most dangerous situations, encourage everyone to press forward.

Captain Olaf began discussing our options and asked for opinions from everyone present. After several minutes of debate and prayer he got back on the radio and issued his orders.

"John, Anders, as soon as you have a window, take um out! Don't show them any mercy whatsoever! We'll be there shortly men, keep a watch out for us."

"Copy that Captain," John and Anders both said simultaneously.

"And don't worry Olaf, this will be their last day on earth," John growled with a viciousness that I'd never heard before.

"Lizzy, get on the phone to Anders cousins and tell them what we're confronted with here." The Captain continued. "Betsy, stay on the VEW lass. Find out what's happening with the smack and also give me an up-date on the other two. Helga, get yourself ready girl, we're gonna need you now more than ever to watch our backs."

"Copy that sir; I'll be ready when you need me. I can see the whole deck clearly through my scope and I've got the yardage calculated. I'll need two shots to dial in accuracy, and then Helga will be deadly again!"

I could hear courageous determination mixed with anxiety in Helga's voice and I was truly thankful for her skills today. Up in the crow's nest, hidden behind these rock formations, Helga would be totally safe, and her view of the Red Dragon could not have been better. The top rails surrounding the crow's nest just cleared the top of the spiraling rock formation, so her sniping position was as awesome and safe as one could hope for. God had truly given Captain Olaf wisdom about anchoring here; the *Heimdall,* the ladies and Rolf, were absolutely safe.

"Excellent lass, we'll be in touch, Olaf out. Garrett, Gabriel, Rorek, lets go, Anders and John need our assistance. Betsy, Lizzy, you're in charge while we're gone, and Rolf . . . you take care of the ladies, and keep the Mortiken off the deck, do you understand?"

After Rolf's energetic wuff, and a vigorous shake, we all had a short group prayer, afterwhich the Captain assured the women that God would bring us all back together again safely, After quick hugs and an unexpected flood of tears, the four of us piled into the raft and slowly made our way over to the Red Dragon to take care of business.

The sun was sparkling brilliantly on the water now and the mysterious zephyr that had helped conceal us, while we were moving the rudder earlier, had grown in swirling intensity. Off in the distance we heard several concurrent razor-sharp thuds, and knew that John and Anders had just lobbed grenades into the Red Dragon and delivered an unexpected nightmare to the Mortiken degenerates. Within minutes we were alongside the enormous wooden vessel and began our preparations to board her. John had been precise in his observations; the evil here was substantial, and the nauseating stench of death accosted our nostrils with a burning sweet pungency. Garrett and I both shuddered deeply and I suddenly felt like vomiting again; the feeling here was familiar to both of us, but the smell that accompanied the feeling wasn't. Two of the forward portholes had blackish smoke wafting out and I surmised that John and Anders had been successful in eradicating at least two of the wretched scum. My loathing for the Mortiken was at an all time high now, and I found myself daydreaming about ending their existence permanently. In the distance we could see Anders watching our surreptitious approach on the raft, and when we'd gotten near enough he silently gestured towards an area underneath the stern where we could safely tie off. Surprisingly, ten minutes after the grenade attack, there was still no one above decks on the Red Dragon, I wondered if the Mortiken even knew that they'd been attacked. John threw a rope ladder down over the stern and Garrett was the first to grab a hold and scramble up. He had that fierceness in his eyes again, and from what I could see, Anders and John did also. Knowing that God always prepared us for the mission that needed to be accomplished, I wondered if the others struggled with fears the way I did during the process. After we'd boarded over the stern rails we belted the CSAT modules, loaded the weapons, and quickly maneuvered into several protected areas in clear view of each other. Within seconds we were all cloaked and watched breathlessly.

Minutes later the Mortiken began pouring out on deck; the stairwell they were using was up towards the bow of the vessel and appeared to be the only access from below. Eleven enormous beings had roughly crowded through the doorway and were now standing on deck, disheveled, angry, startled, and clearly confused. Three of them had AK47's, and several had short swords, but most were unarmed and half naked. They were dressed in something that looked like baggy burlap diapers. They were at once comical and horrifying, a droll amalgamation that I found perplexing and awkward. In the afternoon sun the Baaldurian physical deformities were striking, their skin was grayish and mottled with subdued reddish splotches. Most had no hair anywhere we could see, except around the very bottom on the backs of their skulls. Their heads appeared lumpy like unevenly stuffed beanbag chairs, and they were grotesque in the most imaginative ways. Most seemed to weigh more than four hundred pounds and were heavily muscled, but not in any symmetrical way. With their grunting, lumbering, idiotic mannerisms, they resembled trolls and did not appear healthy at all. It was hard to believe that centuries previous these creatures had once been proud Viking warriors with normal bodies. After several moments they began belching and looking around at each other with befuddled expressions; it was easy to see that they were very bewildered and unsure about what to do next. I deduced there was no leader aboard and the others unanimously agreed with my deduction.

"Boss," Garrett whispered in the earpieces, "the ugly scuz buckets don't know what to do, let's take um now while we have an advantage!"

Anders and John shook their heads in agreement, but just as the Captain was about to verbalize his decision, Betsy radioed in to joyously confirm that the closer smack had been sunk and there were no survivors, the dolphins had been triumphant. She also told us Gudrun had called and he'd informed her that they'd been successful in destroying only one of the larger smacks. They'd come under such an intense barrage of fire that they had to depart the area or be shot down. Unfortunately there were still thirty infuriated Mortiken headed in our direction.

The dolphins were back congregated around the stern of the *Heimdall* and somewhat unmanageable. Lizzy had tried everything to stop their noisy clacking, but she just couldn't quiet them, they were very agitated and excited. Even after they'd been given snacks they were still highly restless.

"Captain, there," Anders whispered pointing at the Mortiken maneuvering towards our direction. "One of them is talking on a radio now and giving orders to the others, they're spreading themselves out all over the deck. He must be communicating with a leader aboard the approaching smack."

"Garrett, you and Gabriel take four grenades and blow the laser," The Captain whispered, "remember men they can't see us, we're cloaked, but still be very cautious and quiet!

"Aye Captain," I gulped.

Garrett bounced up lithely and we moved away like two cats to accomplish the job; slowly we inched past the foul smelling Mortiken and made our way towards the bow of the vessel to position ourselves. For some unknown reason, while we were moving towards the bow, someone started the vessel's enormous diesel; quite unexpectedly the deck of the vessel began vibrating from the deep throated rumbling below decks. Quickly looking back, the Captain gave us the go ahead sign to continue on. The Mortiken seemed more organized and focused now, and the order to start the diesel seemed in conjunction with the radio conversation the one Mortiken was feverishly involved in. We could use the noise of the diesel to our advantage though; it would help cover up our movement and radio transmissions. When I pointed at my ear and shook my head, Garrett nodded at me in silent acknowledgement, he was also aware of this unforeseen blessing.

Two Mortiken had climbed up on the roof of the forward cabin, slightly behind the laser. One was still talking on the radio and issuing orders, and within moments the other had uncovered something that looked like the bell of a big flugelhorn. This bell was surrounded by a six foot satellite dish; outside the unit was interwoven with numerous clear thin tubes and directly inside the bell was a large protrusion. While the diesels rpm's slowly grew in intensity, Garrett and I watched one Mortiken flick up several switches and begin adjusting a number of knobs on a sizeable control panel adjacent the dish. The tubes began glowing and, accompanied with a strange humming sound, a brilliant glow surrounded the whole unit and began emanating out of the flugelhorn in an intense beam. This surely must be some kind of a weapon, but what was it?

Garrett and I were several yards from the laser now waiting for final confirmation from the Captain to destroy it. Suddenly alert, we both watched Anders move over to the starboard rails behind one of the deck structures and radio Lizzy, he asked her to put the radio up close to one of the dolphins.

"Alright honey it's next to one," She called back moments later. Anders began talking again in that strange guttural language he'd used earlier when he and John had first departed the *Heimdall.* Within seconds Lizzy confirmed that six dolphins had swiftly left the stern and were racing towards our position.

Forty-two

The CSAT fails momentarily

We had no way of knowing that the small satellite dish was a device that negated the CSAT. Unfortunately though, as the translucent beam spread out over the deck, our modules shut down and we all abruptly became visible. I was gripped with a dreadful jolt realizing how vulnerable we were now but at the very moment that I was entertaining my vulnerability, I was inexplicably filled with a stronger faith in what God was going to accomplish with us today.

The Mortiken stood frozen for several moments, staring at us with incredulous expressions. Like ghosts emerging from another dimension we had suddenly materialized right before their eyes, and they appeared petrified. John, Anders, and Rorek roared when we'd been made and drew their weapons in preparation, a second later Captain Olaf gave the order to blow the laser.

When Garrett and I jumped out from our place of concealment the Mortiken spun around disoriented; in one smooth movement we pulled the four pins on the grenades, deftly threw them into the laser housing, and then ran back to where the others were huddled. Seconds later the forward housing exploded in a deafening fireball. It was an awesome sight; hundreds of pieces of the structure flew all around the prow of the ship and instantly killed several of the Mortiken standing in close proximity. The one standing nearest, where Gabriel and Garrett had been hidden, was blown completely over the deck rails and disappeared into the water below. Afterwards the rest stood bewildered with strange expressions, rubbing their ears and grunting.

Anders, John, and Garrett used this moment of shock and confusion to their advantage though and were immediately aggressive. In an instant they buttonholed two brutes at least two hundred pounds heavier than they were, easily knocking them flat, immediately Rorek moved in with his revolver and pumped a number of shots into each of their traumatized grey faces. The other Mortiken stood grunting like cattle, they seemed even more confused and unable to focus after we'd launched our assault and killed two of their own so easily. As soon as they'd realizing we weren't going to be intimidated, they began stomping the deck violently, roaring gutturally, shaking their hands, and spinning in circles. It was the strangest thing I'd ever seen, gawky, half naked Mortiken, dancing in their underwear.

"Look at those idiots dancing," Garrett roared with amusement, "all they need now is some rock and roll and they could be on the hit parade!"

We'd never seen Anders in battle before today, but now we knew, without doubt, that the incredible stories we'd heard from Captain Janus were absolutely true. Anders was genuinely frightening.

With an outlandish war cry he dislocated the knee of one brute with a well placed kick, and Captain Olaf followed up with a deadly shot from his 357 magnum. Quickly we all maneuvered into strategic positions while Anders effortlessly snatched up another four hundred pounder, and in a powerful arching circle brought the ogre down directly on his head and broke his neck, I watched in horror while the huge mass of flesh twitched uncontrollably and blood began flowing out of the mouth. The strength it had taken to accomplish this feat stunned me; even John was momentarily bewildered at Anders strength and saluted him in admiration. When the Mortiken saw what Anders the Norse had accomplished, their posturing and dancing intensified and blasphemies began rocketing through the air.

"Dude that was bloody awesome," Garrett shouted as he ran past and slapped Anders outstretched hand, "but watch this Viking homeboy."

Like a cat, Garrett bounded to the top of the wheelhouse roof and in one unbelievably smooth movement jumped high into the air and drop kicked the Mortiken, still feverishly talking on the radio, down to where John was eagerly waiting with a knife. Spinning around and diving off the starboard side of the roof, Garrett then violently clothes lined another monster behind the neck and knocked him cold. Anders roared his approval and with an upraised fist began laughing throatily. Garrett quickly flexed his muscles smiling. Crouched behind a crate, several yards from where Garrett had landed, another one of Rorek's discerning revolver shots put an end to the enormous foe Garrett had knocked flat, "ROREK YOU'RE THE BOMB!" he screamed.

Immediately after Garrett had acknowledged Rorek's marksmanship, the dancing stopped abruptly and the Mortiken suddenly and viciously went on the offensive. Garrett was grabbed roughly from behind and began flailing valiantly to get loose; the monster was enormous and made the 6'2" muscular Garrett look as if he were an insignificant child in comparison. I quickly realized that the encounter was desperate; this Mortiken was hideous and had large amounts of saliva dripping from his bulbous lips, he was at least nine feet in height and easily six hundred pounds. Garrett appeared shocked as he was being shaken around like a rag doll, and began screaming out for help. Maneuvering towards Garrett's position to help him; I heard all the men crying out for God's help and mercy, and in in-between choking gasps I began doing the same. I tried aiming my revolver, but just couldn't find a safe opening that wouldn't jeopardize my little brother's life. John was the only one close enough to help now, and as I watched him maneuvering towards Garrett I began sobbing, there was no way my little brother was going to die here today; I would rather it be me.

I heard a bullet rip into the wall just left of the Mortikens shoulder and then three more in quick succession splintered the wood around his head. Familiar with the sound, I knew that Helga was trying to hit him from the crows nest. Several more bullets ripped through the wood around his position and two more Mortiken, laughing in close proximity, dropped lifeless.

"CAPTAIN, I CAN'T HIT HIM," I heard Helga shrieking over the radios.

"JOHN . . ., PLEASE HELP HIM!" Captain Olaf screamed with an intensity I'd never heard before.

The scene had become frenetic; Garrett seemed to be loosing consciousness, and I had failed in all my attempts to effectively place a shot because of the continual interchange of bodies. Anders was viciously pummeling another beast twenty-five feet from Garrett, and Rorek and Olaf were also crawling around the deck trying to place shots. While the other Mortiken were screaming their approval, at what was being done to Garrett, we began hearing bullets from the AK47's ripping into the deck around us. I was fearful that the fiend would throw Garrett into the line of fire to finish him off, but thank God, the brute never let go of our little brother. Garrett was clearly unconscious now, but still the gargantuan ogre kept shaking him like an insignificant rag doll and laughing in booming paroxysms.

Without any warning Ulrik and Gudrun flew by on both sides of the Red Dragon and startled the Mortiken firing the AK47's. Quickly refocusing their attention towards the two bi-planes, they opened up as they circled back around. With this fortuitous distraction John was given an opportunity to get behind Garrett's antagonist and in the blink of an eye, one of his long knives sunk up to the hilt in the scum's liver. Immediately, and thankfully dropping Garrett; he stumbled backwards clutching at his back and screaming in pain, within moments he fell back over the rails and disappeared. I heard the crew praising Jesus after Garrett hit the deck, but for what seemed an eternity though, he lay motionless and my heart began breaking imagining the worst. When he'd seen one incensed Mortiken approaching to stomp him, Rorek was quickly beside Garrett. Aiming directly at the brute's knee, Rorek brought him down with one shot and then finished him off with the second. Garrett sat up abruptly and began swearing, grabbing both his temples he began shaking his head in an effort to clear the cobwebs. I watched Rorek bend down and ask him something; Garrett quickly gave a thumb up and smiled feebly.

"You fat slobs stink," Garrett bellowed in rage several moments later after he'd regained his composure. "We're gonna kick your ugly butts today you scum suckers! You skidmarks wanna mess with me, come on over and take your best shot!"

All the Mortiken stopped and roared at young Garrett's brash threat and began stomping the deck violently, there was something about Garrett that infuriated them. Spinning in circles with clenched teeth and closed fists, they resumed their bizarre dance with an even fiercer intensity and began screaming in rage. During this tirade Garrett was able to stumble back up on the roof of the wheelhouse and began taunting someone to follow him.

"I'm up here huckleberry," Garrett growled.

With a wicked sneer one Mortiken stopped dancing and obliged him. When he'd finally reached the roof, Garrett scrambled to brace himself against the massive onslaught. Regrettably though, as he did, he stumbled backwards over a chunk of wood left from the explosion and almost fell off the roof. Impulsively grabbing a vent pipe, Garrett quickly regained his balance and then spun back around just in time to see the Mortikens heavy club fall harmlessly on the roof next to his feet. With a moan and a dreadful curse directed at Garrett, the ogre collapsed in a heap at his feet, Helga's marksmanship had found another victim. After a quick acknowledgement of thanks to Helga, Garrett sat down heavily on the roof; he was visibly exasperated and quite suddenly exhausted. Completely oblivious to what was transpiring around him; Garrett impulsively raised his hands towards heaven and began praying loudly and praising God.

Caught up in Garrett's incredible passion, John and Anders quickly joined hands together and ran screaming towards two Mortiken who were trying to reposition themselves next to the stairwell leading below decks. Knocking both against the wooden wall, and forcing a third down the stairs, all four began scuffling violently while the two bi-planes roared over a second time. The brutes were huge and quickly gained an advantage by sheer size and weight. John quickly ran around the other side of the wheelhouse and Anders began viciously pummeling one with his fists in long powerful blows to the ribs. It didn't seem to faze the heavily muscled giant though, and in a fit of frustration the Mortiken raised both hands above his head and brought them crashing down on Anders shoulders. Instantly knocked flat, Anders wasn't moving at all. Just as the giant was lifting his leg to stomp him, Rorek's revolver shot found the knee still planted on the deck and the brute collapsed backwards screaming. Quickly Rorek ran over and with one well placed shot, he finished the grisly job just as he'd done with Garrett's antagonist.

Having thankfully defeated his enormous foe, John had now run back around the wheelhouse and was kneeling down and slapping Anders face sharply to awaken him. With a start he sat up and began rubbing the back of his neck and moaning. After his head cleared, and Anders had located the brute that knocked him down, he drew his knife and with a roar dove on top of him. I had to turn away; it was gruesome, Anders was assuredly a warrior that showed no mercy to his enemy.

Within seconds of helping Anders, John was sucker punched from behind again and fell to his knees groaning, quickly recovering though he spun back around swinging his knife, but it was knocked out of his hands before it found its mark. Hitting John in the chest and snatching him up, the Mortiken was just about ready to throw him overboard when Captain Olaf's 357 roared and quickly changed the ogre's intentions. Screaming and clutching his left thigh the

Mortiken dropped John, in the blink of an eye John snatched his knife from the deck and buried it deeply into his neck. With a fierce roar John then hoisted the beast up and threw him overboard.

The three Mortiken, with the AK47's, had been firing steadily at the two bi-planes but seemed to be getting frustrated with their inability to hit them. Unfortunately our physical movement and capacity to continue fighting was seriously impaired so we all had to dive for cover. When the remaining Mortiken saw this they began laughing and taunting us. While they were reloading their weapons though we were able to turn the tide to our advantage and take out two more before they began firing again. After they'd emptied their magazines we were able to move about freely, at that point Anders and John exploded into action, this time more viciously than ever. The scene was now a chaotic jumble of guttural sounds; I'd never seen anything like this before. Anders and John were methodically cutting a swathe through one Mortiken after another. Anders would attack the legs, and then when he would stumble John would simultaneously pummel the evil face and neck for several seconds in vicious blows, then when the beast was momentarily helpless either Rorek or Olaf would end its life with their revolvers. The Mortiken now looked stunned and very much disorganized; it appeared that they'd lost their edge after the AK47's had run out of ammo.

One lone Mortiken, who up to this point in time had been out of sight, came up from below decks with an old Browning automatic rifle and quite suddenly turned the tide of battle in favor of the enemy again. A vicious torrent of bullets ripped noisily and indiscriminately into the wood all around us, forcing all of us to dive for cover behind anything substantial we could find. While we were pinned down we watched Ulrik and Gudrun land their bi-planes on the island, one hundred and fifty yards inland, and begin running towards us, both with rifles. Seconds later the Browning ran out of ammo.

"Captain," I screamed, "can Helga hit that dish with her rifle?" The Captain understood and was on the radio in a heartbeat.

"Captain Olaf," she responded immediately, "I'm having trouble seeing it in the scope. Can you give me something larger to zero in on that's near it?"

The Captain didn't answer; he was unexpectedly locked in physical combat with one of the half naked monsters that had snuck up behind him.

"GABRIEL," Rorek screamed over the din while he, John, and Anders began running back to help Olaf, "take this shotgun and destroy that satellite dish!"

After Rorek had screamed my name I barely heard the rest of his order, I only saw his mouth move, the Browning was reloaded and active again and the blasting was very close and deafening. Pointing at my ears and shaking my head Rorek understood and threw the shotgun towards me. For several moments it seemed suspended motionless in space; somehow though it landed in my hands unharmed, and only then did I understand intuitively what he wanted me to do. My nerves had begun fraying now, the noise was disconcerting, and the multitude of butterflies in my stomach had begun exiting my ears and nostrils like swarms of bats from a cave. Out of nowhere it was Helga's voice in my radio earpiece that brought me an unexpected reassurance.

"Gabriel . . . I see you clearly in my scope, I've got your back honey, don't worry, I'll take care of anything that gets near you. Get the job done sweetie, you can do it!"

Within seconds of her encouragement, and as I was maneuvering into a more advantageous position, I heard a sharp splat followed by an intense groan several feet behind me. Spinning around, I watched in horror as one of the largest of the remaining brutes collapsed back against a water barrel with a large hole in his forehead. I had been completely unaware of this monsters presence and shuddered at what might have happened if Helga hadn't been watching me. In the next heartbeat the Mortiken ravaging the area with the Browning automatic rifle also dropped dead, Helga's eye was just unbelievable. Screaming my thanks on the radio, it took only seconds for me to run to the wheelhouse and position myself.

"DO IT SON!" Rorek screamed impatiently, while they were pulling the obstinate Mortiken off the Captain. Without hesitation I began pumping one shot after another into the large dish until the strange humming stopped. Within moments, all that remained was an innocuous white mist hovering around the wreckage of shattered tubes and plastic. It took only seconds for the others to eliminate the few remaining Mortiken after we were cloaked again, and quite abruptly, aside from the deep throated rumbling of the diesel below decks, a blessed silence prevailed aboard the Red Dragon.

Forty-three

A supernatural victory

The aftermath was distressing; the deck was pooled with blood, strewn with corpses, and covered with hundreds of pieces of wood, metal, and plastic from the grenade explosions near the forward part of the bow. Where the laser housing had once been several small fires were burning, but there appeared to be no forthcoming danger to an overwhelming destruction of the vessel. Somehow we'd prevailed against a superior force this afternoon, and had done so mostly without the aid of the Chameleon Surface Adapting Technology, or fancy weaponry. The Red Dragon's laser and the CSAT negating weapon had been completely destroyed; the vessel's enormous rudder had been removed and was now in several pieces four hundred yards away at the oceans bottom. This day, working together in unity with two new people we'd never personally met, and all of us dealing with every fear and doubt imaginable, we had clearly overcome an abominable evil, much more perverse than our previous encounters, and I enthusiastically thanked God for the wisdom and fortitude He'd imparted to us to accomplish this seemingly impossible feat. I again clearly realized that without Helga's sharp shooting skills, this day would have undoubtedly ended in tragedy for the *Heimdall* crew. I stood in awe at how this crew operated together; even I had been instrumental in the success we'd been given this afternoon and because of it, I felt a new strength and significance flowing through my veins.

While continuing my assessment, I noticed that Garrett was still up on the wheelhouse roof, hunkered down in the same corner that I'd last seen him in earlier, and he was praying energetically and oblivious to his surroundings.

"GARRETT," I shouted, "It's over little brother IT'S OVER DUDE!"

Garrett stopped praying and looked at me quizzically for a moment, as if in a trance and then, slowly as his senses cleared, he stood up and climbed down from the roof and hugged me with a genuineness I'd never felt from him before.

When we were all together, the Captain joined hands with everyone and thanked God for our victory, he warned everyone not to come into contact with any of the enemy's blood because it could be diseased. As we stood quietly together in grateful introspections,

Anders agitated radio conversation reminded all of us that the battle was not yet over. We all noticed that Ulrik and Gudrun were now on the beach next to the water about thirty yards from the Dragons anchorage, and Anders was leaning over the port rails talking quite animatedly in the ancient language.

"Where are they now?" was the first thing I heard Anders ask.

"About five hundred yards off the starboard bow cousin," they answered.

"The dolphins are also on your starboard," they informed Anders pointing.

"Send them out again Vildarsen; we'll meet you over there." Anders nodded and waved while the cousins took off running. Turning towards Captain Olaf and Rorek, he began elucidating on Ulrik and Gudrun's plan.

"Sir, the other smack is almost upon us and we have to stay focused! There's no way that we can battle thirty of those scumbags hand to hand, look at the trouble we had with this last group, they're unpredictable and vicious. I can send in the dolphins again sir while you position yourselves here on the bow with your rifles. With the dolphins, grenades, and rifle fire, we might be able to keep them off the Dragon completely Captain. "

The Captain nodded in agreement and pulled everyone together to pray for Gods guidance and wisdom. As soon as we'd finished he motioned for Anders to send the dolphins out again. Without any hesitation Anders put down his pistol and removed his radio earpiece. Also removing his shoes and shirt, he sprinted towards the starboard rails and dove headlong into the water below. Running over, we watched him surface in the midst of the dolphins and begin talking to them again. Within seconds they all noisily scattered in the direction of the approaching smack.

"John . . . ," Anders bellowed from the water below.

"Yo . . ." John shouted back, looking over.

"Brother I'm gonna need your long knife for awhile." John obliged, leaned over the rails, and threw his twelve inch titanium combat knife down into his waiting hand.

"Captain, I'm going ashore with my cousins," Anders reaffirmed, "we're going to intercept the smack when it rounds that neck of land. My cousins brought along more phosphorus grenades, they're gonna try again. I'm gonna be with the dolphins. Pray for me, see ya soon!"

Anders swam ashore and began running towards his cousins, already down at the peninsula waiting for him. Having retrieving the Browning automatic rifle from the fallen Mortiken, John nestled the weapon in his arms and sauntered up next to the Captain.

"Olaf," he began pensively, "if I can find some more ammo for this weapon, this bloody thing could be the deciding factor for us today."

"Go ahead John, but be quick, we don't have much time." John nodded and scrambled below to find the munitions store.

John was successful within minutes, being that the munitions storeroom was right at the bottom of the staircase, and he began carrying the crates back up on deck. When the smack finally rounded the peninsula, we heard the cousins open up with rifle fire from behind the rocks where they'd positioned themselves, and through the binoculars we watched the dolphins begin pummeling the sides of the smack. Once again the Mortiken appeared confused and they were holding on for dear life, this afternoon though none of us had any pity whatsoever for this bloodthirsty scum. These murderous cannibals and destroyers of townships and innocent people were the enemies of the Most High God, the Rognvald's, the *Heimdall* crew, and now all of humanity. We watched several fall overboard and never come back to the surface again. Occasionally I saw a muscular arm, clutching a knife, coming out of the water twenty yards behind the smack, stabbing up and down, and I knew that Anders was underwater permanently taking care of those that had fallen overboard. Within ten minutes two thirds of the Mortiken had been killed either by Anders knife, his cousin's rifles, or the dolphins ramming the sides of the doomed smack. After Anders loud verbal command we watched the dolphins and him move away. When they were a sufficient distance removed, Ulrik and Gudrun lobbed several phosphorous grenades towards the smack. Unfortunately they missed and the weapons exploded harmlessly underwater, savagely boiling on the surface for several moments. Ten more enraged Mortiken were now fifty yards from the Red Dragons bow, out of range from the cousin's rifles, and rapidly closing in.

With a belt of ammo draped over his shoulder, and the old perfectly functioning Browning automatic rifle clutched tightly in both hands, John climbed up on the roof of the wheelhouse exactly where Garrett had been praying earlier, and he positioned himself like a character in a movie. The Mortiken began screaming viciously and swinging their clubs when they spotted John standing above them on their own vessel. John was completely unfazed though and as soon as the Mortiken realized what was going to happen, they all became very silent; with taunting twisted sneers they stared defiantly. John's countenance was overflowing, and with a look of fierce determination he put his finger on the trigger. After looking back at the Captain and getting a nod to proceed, he took a deep breath and opened fire. I was filled with a strange compassion realizing that this scum had all reached their ends, their wretched existence was over; there were no more chances for them to choose life, it was over, and they had all lost their places in God's eternal kingdom. For John it was like shooting fish in a barrel, within seconds the ten remaining Mortiken had all been killed and the smack, thoroughly inundated with bullet holes, quickly sank from view. Afterwards John dropped the weapon and sat down heavily, with head in hands he wept severely. It was over.

God had clearly given us a supernatural victory against ferocious odds, and this time we had been in enemy territory. For several moments I stood in overwhelming gratitude for what God had chosen us to accomplish today, it was a sobering moment for all of us and within moments we all began weeping along with John. The Captain radioed the ladies and told them everyone was alive and well, and shortly afterwards, off in the distance, we faintly heard

Rolfy barking frantically and I had a strong hunch that everyone aboard the *Heimdall* was dancing and rejoicing at the Captains blessed news.

Forty-four

The hidden passageway beneath Cedros Island

July 21st 6:00am

This morning my soul was sullen and motionless. Hopelessly fixed in the aftermath of yesterday's battle; my mind was still reliving the harrowing scenes. Upon awakening an hour before, as the very first glowing line had begun delineating the distant horizon; I observed the environment around us profuse with a vaporously clinging fog. In those first moments of another day, I'd reluctantly resigned myself to the possibility of our explorations being influenced by foul weather. Staring intently at the sea from my berth window,

I was finding some relief from the memories of yesterday's battle reciting verse, and pondering diffused splotches of light reflected on the wet deck. Out around the periphery the sky was beginning to develop a luminous cerulean transparency, and the possibilities of another glorious day began lifting my despondent spirit. When finally the early morning sun pierced the horizon, the radiant sliver of light burst upon the white sides of the *Heimdall's* hull and across my face with a warm resplendency. I felt as if I might launch myself through the porthole and fly, but alas, my wings never unfurled and I remained stationary in pathetic expectancy. Anchored near the northwestern shores of Cedros Island, several hundred yards from the tip of the isthmus, the schooner floated motionlessly on the oceans unperturbed glassy surface. In-between dispersing clouds and slowly dissipating tufts of feathery surface mist, warm yellow fingers of sunlight began illuminating another day.

After the battle, Gudrun and Ulrik flew back to Guerrero Negro to pack up the last of their belongings, with the intention of meeting us the morning of the 23rd, around 11:00am by the cave entrance. Our brief introductions the day before had been pleasant; they were both overjoyed to be associated with the crew of the *Heimdall* and reunited once again with their beloved cousin Anders. They'd reiterated several times being very eager to carry on, and assured us that they were willing to leave behind everything they'd established in Guerrero Negro to make the journey with us. In this offer I not only found something honorable, but also something puzzling that I just couldn't put my finger on. I knew this joining together of distinct personalities was more than just a family reunion, God had evidently chosen these two men, with their wisdom, skills, and aircraft, to help us complete our journey.

From where we were, the entrance to the cave appeared as a small black speck, situated near a verdant knoll, nestled back into an outcropping of craggy rocks, and surrounded by a thick stand of Cedros Island Oak trees, endemic to this particular island. Slightly southeast of our anchorage we could see the islands two main peaks poking up through early morning ground fog, "Pico Gill" at 3,488 ft, and "Cerro de Cedros" at 3,950 ft. Spreading out from the bottom of these two peaks, a series of alluvial fans had joined together in a broad continuous slope, resulting in a landform known as a "bajada," and on this fertile soil, stands of scrub juniper and pine trees grew together in dense asymmetrical clumps. Cedros Island, like Isla Socorro, had been evacuated for an indefinite period because of exposure to the magnetic/drought last year. It appeared that God had given us an opportunity once again to accomplish our work without the interference of foreign politics.

In celebration of our being back together safely, and of course never being fond of half measures, the ladies prepared a sumptuous breakfast buffet, abounding with eggs and fried ham, biscuits with Betsy's special to die for gravy, fruit, sweet rolls, orange juice and coffee, it was truly fit for a king. They had also deemed it appropriate to break free from the customary routine of always eating in the galley below, and decided that we should all join for fellowship in the warm morning sun, an idea I found intriguing and thoroughly acceptable. At Betsy's behest, we all gathered above decks and ate together, all lost in quiet introspections. Obviously sensing the glum spirit of the moment, Rolfy wisely remained detached, and quietly wrestled with his stick near the capstan.

Again . . . yesterday we'd endured a battle that none of us would ever forget. It seemed a feat quite impossible while we were on the Dragon, and I had truly feared for all our lives, especially Garrett's. Somehow we'd managed, between the dolphins, the Bjornsons, and the crew of the *Heimdall,* to incapacitate the Red Dragon and destroy almost seventy-five Mortiken in one afternoon, and not one of us had sustained any debilitating physical injuries. Garrett and Anders were very sore in the shoulders and neck, from their ordeals with the wicked ogres, but after conferring with Lizzy, and graciously ingesting copious amounts of her herbal remedies, both anticipated feeling good as new again in two days. Rorek and Captain Olaf had decided to further incapacitate the Red Dragon by sabotaging its enormous diesel. Within thirty minutes Rorek had rigged the giant motor to blow all the head seals the next time it was started. Without the rudder, or the diesel, or the laser weapon, or the CSAT eradicator, this vessel would be worthless for a very long time, and in this we gave thanks to God.

At Captain Olaf's request, Helga e-mailed Jonah and Roxanne, and forwarded the same letter to the professor in Rabat, to provide them with an up-date about the victory God had given us against the Red Dragon, the progress of Amalek's caravan, and our present intentions here on Cedros Island. We were awaiting their replies. We would have two days now to rest and recuperate, and we all were looking forward to the healing it would bring.

July 23rd 10:30 am

Gudrun and Ulrik landed their red bi-planes seventy five yards from the entrance of the cave on a flat area of the bajada with no flora. Everyone was excited to be back together and after two days of rest, all were eagerly anticipating another exciting day of productive exploration. After group prayer we all loaded our backpacks with food and cave gear and got started.

The cave entrance was somewhat smaller than any of us had anticipated; it was a slit like opening that allowed only one person to go through at a time. Just to the left of the opening was a strange symbol, unlike anything we'd ever seen associated with the Rognvalds. It resembled a football on its end, and had a crude sketch drawn within the white boundaries that seemed to project a concerned figure wearing a sad face. Just inside the entrance, the cave opened up dramatically and at first I saw nothing except what was being haphazardly illuminated through the small entrance. Slowly though, as my eyes adjusted, I began viewing a vast expanse of fairly smooth rock surfaces, and a ceiling that vaulted up dramatically, at least fifty feet. Squinting into the darkness, I could barely distinguish what seemed to be a tumultuous cavalcade of human and animal figures painted, much larger than life size, all along the walls on both sides.

As we stood quietly contemplating our next move, I started realizing what a solemn stillness permeated this place, most perceptible sounds being strange, uncertain, and incomprehensible. Off in the distance, a faint reverberation of water was the only thing that I could distinguish besides the beating of my own heart and quite unexpectedly I was gripped with a different uneasiness than I'd ever known. There was something vague and shapeless in this vast labyrinth, a mesmerizing feeling that I was unfamiliar with, and I felt my blood running cold. Suddenly squeezing my hand, Betsy startled me.

"This place is creepy sweetie," she complained in a soft whisper.

"Dude . . . this place IS creepy!" Garrett agreed.

Anders and his cousins began jabbering excitedly in the ancient language, which in turn began stimulating discussions between all of us.

"John, I think you and Garrett should get all the lanterns fueled," Rorek suggested. "Olaf, why don't we split up and walk the perimeter, this could take days to explore and we might have to come back several times."

"We're on it," Garrett shouted over his shoulder. Immediately he and John exited the cave.

"A good idea brother and you're probably right," the Captain agreed. "John, you, Helga, Garrett, Gabriel, Betsy, and Lizzy make your way around to the left. Anders, you and your cousins go with Rorek and me around to the right."

"Alright Captain," Anders agreed, stopping momentarily during the heated discussion with his cousins.

"Does everyone have their radios on?" the Captain inquired.

"Aye sir," everyone murmured.

"Alright Rolfy, go on boy, find us something," the Captain instructed. Rolf responded with a short wuff and slowly trotted off, fervently sniffing the ground; gradually he disappeared into the consuming darkness. The five lanterns Captain Olaf had decided to take from the cave on Isla Socorro would certainly come in handy today; it had been a good call on the Captains part to procure them for our use.

The inside of the cave was stunning; everywhere we looked there were human figures with black face patches, deer, mountain lions, all surrounded by an abundance of life. Many fire rings were scattered throughout the area, seeming to suggest that all these paintings had been done by firelight. The animals were depicted life size or bigger, but the human figures varied much greater in size, from a few inches to over ten feet. All the animals were shown in profile, with the heads in three-quarter or front view to accentuate horns, or any distinguishing facial features. The humans were shown frontally, but lacked facial features or any distinguishing sexual characteristics. The few birds that were depicted were all painted with out stretched wings and were always near human figures. After several hours of exploring, Lizzy interrupted our contemplations crying out that she'd discovered a whole section of words under one of the giant murals. It became evident, when we'd all congregated around her, that the language was one none of us could understand or even decipher, that is all except Gudrun and Ulrik. After discussing the unfamiliar passages with Anders, Gudrun finally spoke to us in the old language, while Anders and I interpreted.

It appeared that the ancients, who had painted these walls, were very cryptic and superstitious and had purposely obscured their explanations of how they'd lived. The animals depicted were not simply creatures represented in nature, there was an esoteric cultural meaning associated with hunting magic, especially if they'd been hit by a hunter's arrow. Less clear was their preferences for witchcraft or black magic rather than warfare as an explanation for the multiple arrows sometimes found stuck in the human figures. It appeared that humans were painted over the top of animals three times more than the converse, which Gudrun and Ulrik faithfully interpreted as an expression of human dominance over the animal kingdom here. The most intriguing of all the writings was the one towards the bottom though. The cousins clearly established, in their interpretations of these phrases, that these pictures hadn't been painted by the savage and brutalized nations which inhabited Baja California when the Spanish first arrived; these words asserted that this art belonged to another nation, an ancient realm of giants who had migrated from faraway northern lands.

It quickly became clear that none of this art had anything to do with the early Rognvald voyage; there was nothing Viking in nature illustrated on any of these walls. Could the ancient Baaldurians somehow have been involved, or influential, with whoever did paint these baffling masterpieces? Could it be that the Mortiken were the giants written about here?

After a frustrated debate, the Captain halfhearted decided to end our explorations in this cave and head back to the *Heimdall.* It was tentatively agreed upon that we would commence our voyage towards San Diego in the morning, but of course, something happened unexpected that changed our plans. Rolf's impassioned yapping in the distance thoroughly intrigued us, so we all decided to press on. He wouldn't stop barking. Rolf's excitement was now at an all time high, he was even more agitated than he'd been in the old burial grounds on Isla Socorro. With great determination we crept farther into the cave, always straining to hear more distinctly the direction

Rolf's voice was coming from. The sound remained ambiguous though, and no matter what angle we listened from, it continued to reverberate around us like a mystifying phantom. It was indeed difficult to pinpoint where Rolf was, still though; our persistent hopefulness that Rolf had discovered something extraordinary kept all of us eagerly pressing forward.

It had become obvious, the farther we moved back into the cave, that we were on a steady and steep descent into the bowels of the earth. The inky blackness, just beyond the rings of illumination around our lanterns, seemed impenetrable and kept us all huddled close. People working together, unified in one accord, light dispelling the darkness, pressing forward towards a goal that had not yet revealed itself, this certainly sounded like faith in action to me. An overwhelming expectation began flowing through me from this intriguing revelation, and in the newly aroused ardor in my soul I began avidly expressing my thoughts with the rest of the crew as we walked.

Still advancing thirty minutes later, I had begun experiencing a deep respect for the awful grandeur of this vast cavern. Nevertheless, aside from the fact that we still hadn't found the reason for Rolf's high spirits or Rolf for that matter; we were still drawn forward by an all-absorbing and impatient curiosity to do so. At this moment my achievements in college seemed extraneous to me, I felt woefully inadequate and feared that mere human language would fail miserably in describing the savage sublimity that had captured my imagination in this vast and prodigious place. The sound of crashing water was much fiercer now, and had begun gripping my imagination with the dreadfulness of being trapped in turbulent disembogues and washed down into the bowels of the earth. While I was pondering this perplexing fear, Rolf was unexpectedly there in our midst, barking excitedly, he began vigorously pulling on my pant leg to follow him. Without hesitation, Captain Olaf gave the order to continue on and the eleven of us turned to follow our trusty canine companion back even farther.

Ten minutes later, the cave came to a sudden end and my frame of mind plummeted, had we walked all this way for naught?

The reason for my unusual foreboding earlier became apparent at this juncture; a powerful thick spout of water, roaring down with an awful fury from high above, was being swallowed greedily into a huge rock strewn rift in the floor. The reverberation of the water was overwhelming and conversing in any normal way was being diminished considerably. While we stopped to contemplate our surroundings Rolf became agitated and impatient and raced ahead of us, within seconds we all watched in horror as he disappeared into the rock floor. It was awful, our dog was suddenly gone. "Rolfy!" everyone screamed. Had the fears I'd conjured for myself earlier swept our inquisitive Rolf down into a watery grave? What were we going to do without our courageous and trusty companion? A sudden and excited barking pierced through the waters thunderous din though and we all breathed a sigh of relief. There, in the peripheral gloom of our lanterns, we clearly saw Rolf's head poke up and down several times from what appeared to be a sizeable fissure in the floor. What had he found?

Forty-five

An ancient sarcophagus

On roughly chiseled steps, the hidden passageway descended gradually one hundred yards into a large subterranean chamber. Considering the excessive amount of moisture inundating the chamber above, it was surprisingly dry here, and the waters thunderous noise had been substantially lessened. There was an eerie calm in this place and I quickly found myself beleaguered by a profound and sudden melancholy, as if the tears of an entire nation had fallen suddenly in this one room. It seemed I was not alone in these insights either; the entire crew expressed the same feelings and all agreed that something devastating had happened here.

Flowing from one of the walls, a bubbling stream of sweet water was pooling up in a large rock basin near one of the far corners and we all refreshed ourselves in it. There was also a vague but substantial luminosity radiating from several larger rifts in the ceiling, towards the far left corner, that allowed us to extinguish all but one of our lanterns, and after our eyes adjusted to the gloom we were able to extinguish that one also. There were two other openings towards the rear of the chamber and we quickly ascertained them being passageways leading to adjoining chambers. Considering our continuous descent getting here, both the Captain and John quickly calculated that we were well beneath the oceans surface now, perhaps as much as two thousand feet. Looking around we all sighed in thankfulness, clearly etched over the inside of the entrance was a sword and helmet over a shield, the Rognvald's had clearly been here. Rolf had once again made an astounding discovery.

The walls were covered with paintings and everywhere along the walls Viking artifacts were stacked up in heaps. Several chests and many stone tablets covered with runic symbols, intact and broken, lay scattered about. In one area, around the fresh water basin, there were five large copper tubes still sealed. Helga and I immediately began taking photographs in carefully marked quadrants and while the rest slowly dispersed out to admire this treasure of Viking history, I quietly thanked God for the privilege He'd given us of finding this astonishing place. Shouting from one of the adjoining chambers, Garrett's animated voice quickly relocated everyone to where he was. In wonderment, we all stood marveling at what lay before us.

Situated at the center of the room, raised on a beautifully carved pedestal, was an ancient Viking sarcophagus.

Encircled around the outside edge of the room, separated from one another by twelve feet, the tarnished body armor of seven Viking warriors stood in ghostly repose.

"Dudes . . ., can you believe all this?" Garrett gasped. "What the heck is this place? Look at all this stuff on the walls and all the junk everywhere, sheesh, I bet Roxy would love this bloody place!"

We all hastily agreed that this was the most impressive cave find yet, but there was much more.

"It feels sacrosanct here," John shuddered.

"Kinda spooky too," Betsy said shivering and gripping my hand harder.

"Yah guys, it does have a weird vibe," Anders added.

"You know," John continued, "I bet this place has a wealth of information, I have no idea though how we're going to sort through all of this in a few days. I can't imagine what it must have been like for this guy, sailing thousands of miles from the Orkneys and getting so close to the goal and then having to die here."

"Captain Olaf," Gudrun interjected softly, "we cannot disturb or take anything from this tomb."

"Why is that son?" the Captain asked with a puzzled expression.

"Someone holy is buried here," he said nodding at, and pointing towards the suits of armor, "these seven warriors are protecting him;

to disturb the remains would displease the gods, and surely bring us bad luck. It would be . . ."

"What's up with this displeasing the god's junk dude?" Garrett snorted scornfully at Gudrun. "Who gives a rat's patoot what the gods think? We serve one God, the only God, and the Most High God, and He'll squash your puny gods just like He squashed those scumbag Mortiken the other day!"

Gudrun visually bristled at Garrett's comments. Provoked by his pagan remark Garrett then turned towards him scowling with clenched fists. Rolf was barking now and the sound in the small chamber was deafening, it appeared that Rolf had also been provoked by Gudrun's startling remarks. Being familiar with Garrett's tendency to speak his mind, and never ever backing down, John reached out and put his hand on Garrett's shoulder to help diffuse his anger. I knew that Gudrun didn't have a chance against Garrett physically, there was no doubt in my mind and John also knew this, I could see real concern clouding his countenance. Gudrun would be pummeled within seconds, in fact we would surely have to come to his aid to protect him and this would assuredly jeopardize the relationship between both parties. No matter how I considered this impending debacle, I saw disaster, foolishness, and failure sneering back at me. Our whole journey thus far had been a continual infilling of esteem for our resident warriors, but it wasn't until I'd witnessed their intrepid skills on the Red Dragon that I'd gained an unquestionable respect for Garrett, John, and Anders. They were giant slayers, and all fearless in the matters of physical combat, but using these skills against each other was clearly out of the question.

"My cousin and I understand that you are followers of the Holy Christ," Ulrik interposed, trying to end the tension, "there is no disrespect meant to you Garrett or to the crew by Gudrun's suggestion Captain. There are many things to consider here, many things indeed."

"I agree Ulrik, there are many things to consider," the Captain said wryly, "but understand this, both of you, we have made no determination as to what we will do yet, we still need to pray for Gods wisdom in our pursuits and when we do you're both welcome to join us." Both cousins nodded quietly.

"Let's open all those copper tubes and check them out," Betsy suggested cheerfully.

"I agree with Betsy Olaf," Helga exclaimed, "remember the information Rolf found in the copper tube in the graveyard? Gosh, remember how much of it was about Anders, and now he's here working with us."

"Oh goodness me, you're so right Helga," Lizzy agreed eagerly. "Everywhere we've stopped Olaf there have been many clues about where we should go, and what comes next for us. I'm sure this time will be no different."

"I also agree with that brother!" Rorek grunted. "Lizzy you old broad, you're gettin smarter as you age."

For several seconds there was light laughter, but within moments Garrett unfortunately began remonstrating again.

"Hey . . . you know, a few hours ago we were all gonna give up and go back to the *Heimdall* remember? Rolf found this place and he found it for a reason dudes; our God wants to show us somethin here and I'll be a piss ant if I'm gonna stress about what their stinkin gods think," Garrett argued, pointing disdainfully at the cousins.

Gudrun and Ulrik were fidgeting restlessly now, and after Garrett's newest remarks they'd both begun scowling. Reflected in their body language, it was now evident that both were contemplating thoughts about retaliating against my little brother, and this provoked Garrett even further. Offended by their posturing and facial expressions, he forcefully broke free from John's grip and moved close to both of them; he began glaring back into their faces with unblinking eyes. Rolf was again standing next to Garrett, also staring and growling softly.

"I'm right here huckleberries," Garrett taunted, motioning for them to make the first move. It looked as if a confrontation was forthcoming, and it also appeared that my little brother was going to take them both on. Oddly, his challenging remark was exactly what I remembered him saying to the Mortiken when he was up on the wheelhouse roof and I wondered if this was somehow significant in understanding Garrett's present behavior.

Quickly reacting to the mounting frustration Anders gently grabbed Rolf's collar and firmly clutched Garrett's shoulder, he then spoke sternly to his cousins in the ancient language for several minutes. He made quite a strong argument because when he'd finished their spirits had calmed dramatically and they both appeared humbled, afterwards even bowing slightly towards Garrett and Captain Olaf before backing away.

"I agree with what Lizzy said Captain Olaf," Betsy quickly began with a nervous giggle, "God might want us to know something, or show us someplace we need to go."

"Captain what are we gonna do now?" Helga asked, pointing towards the sarcophagus. "Should we open that thing up?"

"Let's look around some more before we make any decisions," the Captain suggested, "perhaps we'll find clues to help us, we certainly don't want to make a foolish decision about anything in this place. Anders, since you and your cousins seem to understand the ancient language in detail; please scrutinize all the symbols on the outside of this sarcophagus. See if there is anything that might be useful. Go ahead and use the flashlights, they might be helpful in seeing details in this gloom."

"Aye sir," Anders responded politely and motioned towards his cousins to get the flashlights.

"Lizzy, you, Helga, and Betsy look closely at all this body armor, see if we can find anything useful, and Helga lass, take pictures of everything."

"No problem Captain, we have spare batteries and plenty of memory left," she confirmed.

"Rorek let's you, John, Gabriel and I go check out that other chamber. Garrett, I want you with me son. Does everyone feel comfortable with staying down here the night?" Everyone shook their heads yes.

"Alright, it's settled then," the Captain shook his head approvingly, "let's get busy and do our jobs!"

As we walked from the chamber I had a hunch that the Captain was going to chew Garrett's butt, but instead he moved in next to me.

"Gabriel, what did Anders tell his cousins that changed them so dramatically?"

"He asked them; no . . . he demanded that they back off Captain. He told them that Garrett had almost been killed on the Red Dragon and he was still certainly upset about the ordeal and not quite himself. He also reminded them that you were in charge sir and that challenging your authority was not going to work, they would loose their standing with us. He also told them that you were an honorable and Godly man and that your decisions were always made after prayer and discussion. He used very strong language making this point sir, it sounded to me like Anders has been talking to both of them for a long while about their flawed spiritual beliefs. Personally, I suppose the incident with the Tempest, a few days ago, changed Anders Captain. I'm quite certain he respects you and the *Heimdall's* endeavors now."

After I'd finished, Olaf nodded with a thoughtful expression, shook my hand vigorously, and then motioned for all of us to move forward.

Forty-six

Skull Rock cave

When we'd all congregated back in the main burial chamber, six hours later, the crew was glowing with excitement. The confrontation between Garrett and the cousins was thankfully just a memory and everyone, including the now humbled cousins, had exciting stories to share about their individual discoveries.

The adjoining chamber we'd entered into was the terminus of another passageway leading to the surface. After forty-five minutes, and at least half a mile in steep ascent, we finally reached the top of the ancient staircase tired but expectant. In the bright light of our two Coleman lanterns we'd discovered another shallow chamber, and a large heavy round stone covering a roughly hewn six foot opening, this stone needed to be rolled aside in order for us to pass through. In all honesty this seemed an impossible task, but after prayer we decided to thoroughly scrutinize the area to see if there were any fulcrums or devices set in place to help roll away the stone. Sadly though, we found none. We did however find deep depressions in the walls very near the top of the staircase, and in these depressions we found several peculiar artifacts we'd never seen associated with the Rognvalds before. There was also numerous hand held weapons and, along with the typical Rognvald icons, there were six pictographic symbols that made me shudder when I saw them, they were completely unfamiliar to me.

I immediately recognized three boldly sketched runes, next to the entrance, taken from the Norwegian Futhark alphabet, so I hurriedly sketched everything I saw for future reference. The first rune was Eithwaz, the rune for yew, a sacred tree used to make runic magic wands. The second in succession was Ansuz, a rune that could be used to refer to any deity, but was most often associated with Odin, the Viking equivalent of Zeus. The third in succession was Gebo, a rune used to signify a sacrifice to the gods. I knew an important message had been left here, and there was also something disturbing about this place we'd found.

What could a magic wand, Odin the Viking war god, and a sacrifice to the gods mean?

On each side of the entrance, in two deep and elongated cracks, John and Rorek discovered two six foot iron spears, and quite suddenly God imparted to them how we were going to move the stone. The spears were wedged in deeply so John and Rorek had to use their titanium long knifes to remove them. It was a tedious process, sticking the knife in and scratching back to slowly move the spears into a position where we could grab a hold of them. They were successful though, and fifteen minutes later we were in possession of two Viking spears. Moving the stone required using them as fulcrums and slowly inching the stone open. The process was quite effective though and took ten minutes to accomplish. Once the stone had been rolled aside, we exited the oppressive passageway and emerged into a shallow dank cave. Haphazardly strewn about the entire perimeter was a surfeit of stone tablets, broken and intact, and several old wooden chests with the Rognvald insignia.

The abrupt abundance of oxygen was like a rejuvenating elixir to our bodies and quickly lifted our spirits. Making our way outside the cave, and into the invigorating dusk air, we breathed in copious amounts. After being thoroughly refreshed we began studying our surroundings and realized that we'd emerged on the northeastern side of Cedros Island. The likelihood of this happening seemed quite remarkable though, I remembered this as being the very cave Ulrik and Gudrun Bjornson had accidentally discovered two years prior and christened Skull Rock. The very stone they hadn't been able to move then, had now been set aside by five men emerging from a recently discovered tomb in the bowels of the earth. I instantly saw a spiritual picture in what we'd accomplished here but as yet, I couldn't comprehend its significance.

Thousands of date palm trees were proliferating all around us and most were filled with tons of unclaimed ripe fruit. I could see at once they were of the Phonexix dactylifera genus and not indigenous to this part of the world at all; they grew primarily in the Middle East. If the Rognvald expedition had relocated these trees here, then were had they taken them from? The area was congested with thousands of these hundred foot evergreen palms. The trunks were covered in fibers, and at the end of all the leaf fronds were needle sharp protrusions. I'd remembered from my studies that nothing was wasted on these trees. When they were used properly, the wood and leaves provided timber and fabric for house building, and from the abundant leaves, ropes, baskets and furniture were fashioned for everyday use. Even the leaf bases and fruit stalks were used for fuel, absolutely nothing was wasted. It was unanimously agreed upon to pick a bagful of the squishy morsels and bring them back for the others, they were quite delicious and we were sure the ladies would be overjoyed. The flesh was sweet and soft as butter, and for several minutes I sighed in delight while gorging myself on the ripe drupes. While we satisfied ourselves Captain Olaf suddenly realized how much closer Skull Rock cave was to the burial chamber than the long cave we'd trekked through earlier in the day. He decided that several of us would go back tomorrow, after a good night of sleep, and move the *Heimdall* back around to this side of the island for easier access, and we all agreed that it was an excellent idea.

As we'd made our way back down the staircase Garrett had opened up with us about what was churning about inside him. He was especially disgruntled that we'd aligned ourselves with non-believers now in our journey, and he didn't like the fact that they had blatantly made mention of their belief in gods other than Jesus Christ. Garrett also confessed that he clearly understood now that he could have died in the grips of that demon possessed raging ogre, and aside from all the skills God had given him, he had been totally powerless to prevent it.

"I am mortal, and I can die at anytime or anywhere," He admitted in choking sobs. "I've never thought about that before dudes, I just never thought about dying before man. Our time on earth is temporary, and what we accomplish for Gods kingdom, while we're here, is really important. We gotta do the jobs God gave us to do man!"

In those terrifying moments of helplessness and introspection, God had revealed something to him about his own faith and where he needed to let go and grow. He also said that while he'd been unconscious that he'd been visited by an angel who told him about the consequences of compromising his faith in Christ Jesus and the dangers in not finding the gift God had given to each person and ministering to it in His power.

"Dudes, no wonder my dad never made it in the world system with his music, God didn't want his gift corrupted. Gosh . . . Jesus is the bomb dudes, He loves us so much!"

Admitting that he'd snapped when Gudrun mentioned other gods, Garrett assured us that he wasn't at all regretful about what he'd done, or how he'd done it. He believed that a strong statement had been made to both cousins about the *Heimdall* crew's unwillingness to compromise spiritually and he also believed, with Anders helpful and timely intervention, that this point had been clearly acknowledged and understood. Garrett also stressed that we needed to judge ourselves daily according to Gods word and not what we thought or felt was right, and we also needed to pray together in unity more often to get the continuing wisdom to do this. Garrett was adamant in his declarations and outspoken like a fiery young evangelist. As we continued our descent back to the burial chamber he fervently expressed the revelations he'd been given in context to a daily spiritual discipline and how this must be applied to our individual lives. I was amazed at how powerfully these words witnessed to me, and Captain Olaf had also been stunned during the extent of Garrett's passionate homily. I could plainly see that Garrett was touching some part of him that long needed shaking so he himself could grow spiritually; afterwards Olaf gave him a great hug and expressed his love and thankfulness for him. Something inscrutable had happened to Garrett during the confrontation with the massive Mortiken, and I clearly saw now that whatever Garrett had gone through was already changing him quite dramatically. One way or another I anticipated that Garrett's ordeal, and the spiritual revelations he'd been given, would also be changing the rest of the crew in the days ahead.

Anders, his cousins, and the ladies had discovered something quite amazing, the runic inscriptions on the sides of the sarcophagus, and most of the tablets they'd scrutinized, appeared to also be derivatives from the early Futhark alphabet. When they'd mentioned this I realized that the majority of the runes around the sides of the sarcophagus were exactly the same as the ones we'd discovered earlier, and the three main runic symbols on the lid of the sarcophagus, Eithwaz, Ansuz, and Gebo were inscribed in exactly the same order that I'd found them at the entrance above. Now my curiosity to solve this puzzle was at an all time high, still though, I wished that Roxanne had been with us here to help out.

Forty-seven

Resolving a Runic mystery

"Anders, how would you interpret these three runes here, and also the line of smaller ones right underneath them?" I inquired.

"Well . . . let's see," Anders pondered. After several minutes of discussion with his cousins he began elucidating.

"OK guys, here goes. The line of small runes below these three larger ones can be interpreted as: *He who lies herein, Magnus, his own self brave and called, lived many hardships in pursuit of father Agar's vision.*

"Wait a bloody minute," Rorek interrupted, "do you mean to tell me that the person in this tomb is Magnus Rognvald, the son of King Agar?"

No one spoke or moved. Could the King of the Rognvald First Tribe be lying before us? We all knew that King Agar had died shortly before the original voyage began, and that this fact had been absolutely corroborated on the seventh and eighth tablets we'd discovered at the Shallows of Three Rocks. The words on the tablets flooded back into my mind as we all stood dumbfounded.

"Christ before all else" inscribed on warriors helmets, swords, and shields, the symbol of great King Agar the beloved, taken yet a fortnight ago in deaths inexhaustible repose."

"There's something else though guys," Anders continued, "these three large runes here, and what's around them, tell a different story about Magnus Rognvald. It appears that he was different spiritually than his father. I don't understand this very well though Captain Olaf, can you help me with this interpretation Gabriel."

After Anders request I was filled momentarily with a flood of memories from my advanced language studies the last year at the university in Aberdeen. It had been a very difficult time in my life, I was only months away from being awarded my doctorate and I was stressed out all the time in pursuit of that grand goal. I remembered learning, in Dr. Jim Young's class, that there were close to thirty-five hundred stone monuments scattered around Europe, mostly in Sweden and Norway, claiming to have been inscribed with the Futhark alphabet, the three most comprehensive stones being the Kylver stone from Stanga Sweden, the Mojbro stone from Upland Sweden, and the Istaby stone from Blekinge Sweden. It had been established that the Northern European Germanic peoples, the Danish, the Swedish, and the Norwegians used this alphabet extensively during the 3rd through 17th centuries, and from these scattered monuments, the runic symbols had derived a lot of their meaning. I also remembered that the word rune meant mystery or secret in the old Germanic languages and that the runes had always been given an important role in rituals and magic . . . .

"Gabriel," Captain Olaf tapped my arm, "can you help Anders with this interpretation son . . . please?"

"Oh goodness sir, I'm sorry, yes of course I can. I sure wish Roxanne was here to help us though Captain." The Captain nodded in agreement.

"Gabriel would you start please," Anders asked politely, "There are just too many semantic compounds surrounding these symbols, those things have always confused me."

Anders was correct, the symbols were surrounded by many intricately woven semantic compounds and also puzzling ideograms, and since these symbols quite graphically represented abstract ideas, I was forced not only to literally interpret the runic phrases, but also to think emotionally like the scribes had when this information had been written, to understand their personal feelings.

"Captain, remember we saw these exact symbols in this precise order up at the top of the staircase inside the second entrance to Skull Rock. I also found this peculiar symbol on the opposite side of the doorway sir; I have no idea what it means . . . do you Anders?"

Anders and his cousins moved next to the Captain when I had handed the paper to him. Within seconds the cousins both laughed uproariously and began speaking sarcastically to Anders in the ancient language.

"Captain Olaf," Anders resumed with a sigh after several minutes of banter, "this is one of the earliest symbols depicting the ancient Troth belief system, a golden circle with four golden apples and four black ravens. Unfortunately sir, my cousins are of this faith. They worship Odin; they think he's a real god."

The crew moaned after Anders shared this and the cousins and he began arguing again in the old language. Garrett bristled, spit on the floor, and turned away, but said nothing. The Captain was perplexed and looked at me for help.

"Gabriel, please . . ."

"Captain, I'll do the best I can! The three runic symbols on top here seem to indicate that Magnus Rognvald secretly worshipped Odin also sir, not Christ Jesus like his father Agar, and all those that followed this pagan belief system were given wooden magic wands as symbols of their faith in Odin. Kind of like a secret club sir, they appeared one way to the rest of the voyage but they were actually something entirely different behind the scenes. A group of people on the original voyage were imposters from the beginning Captain, they believed that Odin was the head of the gods and of all that lived."

"Do you mean to tell me that the original voyage was spiritually compromised from the onset Gabriel?" Rorek barked disdainfully.

"Yes sir, that appears to be true by what this information is telling us."

"Good Lord Olaf, can you bloody believe this crap?" Rorek moaned.

"Captain Olaf, isn't *Heimdall* a mythological character?" Ulrik asked with a mordant chuckle.

"Yes it is son, Rorek and I decided to give the schooner that name while she was being constructed in Stavanger."

"Why did you choose that name and not a Christian one?" Gudrun asked.

"Well son . . . my brother and I both related to what the mythological *Heimdall* represented, him being the god of light. Our God, Christ Jesus, is light and in Him there is no darkness. The name *Heimdall* was intriguing to us and we embraced it only in terms of what we wanted to accomplish with the schooner, a romantic notion of sorts. In Nordic mythology *Heimdall* was the watchman for the gods and guarded Bifrost the rainbow bridge that led into Asgard, the realm of the gods. My brother and I wanted to make a difference in this world with the missions we embarked upon; we wanted to bring glory to Jesus Christ with what we did with this vessel, and be instrumental in keeping evil from proliferating. *Heimdall's* mythological job was to keep evil giants and interlopers from getting into Asgard, which is simply a picture of heaven and the body of Christ becoming polluted by insidious outside forces. We wanted to affect the body of Christ and His eternal kingdom in the same fashion; we wanted to overcome evil with good. The mythological

Heimdall required less sleep than a bird and could see a hundred miles around him, night or day. His hearing was so accurate that no sound escaped him; he basically heard everything, he could even hear the grass grow. We wanted to have a crew of uniquely skilled individuals that could accomplish seemingly impossible things in Christ's power and make a difference that would positively impact the present, and eternity, for the Kingdom of God."

"Boss . . . that was an awesome answer," Garrett said softly with tears in his eyes.

The cousins were also taken back with Captain Olaf's answer, they both stood speechless, and I saw a diminutive smile of satisfaction forming on Anders face. I knew that their questions had been baited and could have easily become a trap, but the Captain had been wise. Eloquently choosing his words, he had quite effectively disarmed their cynicism and I quietly thanked God for this victory.

"I hope that helped you understand our intentions in choosing the name *Heimdall*," the Captain said to both the cousins. Now Gabriel, why don't you continue with this mystery son?"

"Well sir, apparently Magnus, and those that chose his way, really worshipped Odin. Nowadays Odin is most readily depicted as a gray bearded man, tall and thin, and wearing a blue/black cloak. Sometimes he has an eye patch on but most often he's seen wearing a wide brimmed hat that's tilted down to hide his missing eye."

Quite suddenly Anders barked at his cousins and they both reluctantly opened their shirts. Prominently tattooed across the upper part of both their chests was the image I had just described to the crew. Garrett was absolutely beside himself now and kicked a small piece of broken tablet across the room, but still he kept quiet.

"Go ahead Gabriel, please continue," the Captain said motioning at me with a growing look of concern.

"Odin has always been related with war and death in his many manifestations. As a war god, Odin was most often depicted on his gray eight legged horse Sleipner, armed with the spear Gungner, and always followed by his two ravens, Huginn, the thoughtful or the bold, and Munin, the mindful or the desirous. Odin also was accompanied by the two wolves Geri and Freki; both names mean the greedy ones. Captain Olaf, it seems that Magnus deceived his father King Agar into believing that he was a follower of Christ Jesus, but he was in fact a follower of Odin. Unfortunately because of this deceit sir, Agar granted him lordship over the original voyage. If I interpret these ideograms correctly sir, shortly before the original voyage began; King Agar became aware of his son's spiritual deception and before he could make any changes that could impact the voyage, he died mysteriously in his sleep."

"Do you mean that King Agar could have been murdered Gabriel?" Betsy asked with a horrified look.

"I don't know sweetie, but it sure seems possible now. Captain, here on the top of the sarcophagus I see the Algiz rune, I haven't seen this rune anywhere else on this sarcophagus, anywhere in this tomb, or anywhere above in Skull Rock. Have you or your cousins Anders?" Anders shook his head no.

"This rune appears only once Captain, it denotes defense, protection, or self preservation. This is strange guys, from what I feel in these ideograms, I believe that Magnus Rognvald was murdered when the rest of the voyage found out he was Troth and worshipped Odin. I firmly believe that they left him buried under this island, guarded by these seven warriors, so his wretched heresy wouldn't pollute the rest of the voyage. Apparently, during the voyage he was revered like a god for awhile, a spiritual leader of sorts, and the whole crew respected him and the visions he was given. When his deception was found out though, everything changed Captain. One of the strange symbols I found up above had these three lines of runes etched underneath it; it seems to indicate that the voyage split here on Cedros after Magnus was murdered, eight vessels continued north and two went up into the Sea of Cortez. Unfortunately I can't decipher the rest of this, do you know what these last few lines mean Anders?"

Anders took the paper and stared at it for a long while; finally he sighed and shook his head. After discussing the lines with his cousins, Ulrik reluctantly interpreted the phrase in the ancient language and I spoke it out in English.

"There are two separate messages here Captain; the first one seems to be an epitaph that contradicts Magnus Rognvald's spiritual choice.

"The Light of wisdom arrived/descended, the words He uttered/ spoke through His own mouth brought life/ salvation" Captain, this is obviously a reference to Jesus Christ and was meant to refute what

these people had chosen to believe. Also the second part says that the Rognvald's who chose to worship Odin were banished permanently from the voyage. The year before discovering Cedros Island all the vessels had mistakenly traveled up into the northernmost parts of the gulf. Apparently they fought amongst themselves for several weeks about a mysterious discovery they'd made, I guess some wanted to explore it and some didn't. Captain Olaf, these runic symbols seem to indicate that Magnus Rognvald and the entire voyage found the hidden entrance to a massive Underground River."

Forty-eight

North

We departed Cedros Island and sailed north on the 29th of July. The last few hours we'd spent in Magnus Rognvalds tomb, Captain Olaf decided to authorize the removal of the five large copper tubes found near the fresh water basin, all else in the tomb would remain intact. A very thorough photographic record had been made of everything, above and below, and all the discs would be hand delivered to Roxanne when we reached San Diego, afterwhich she would be forwarding them to the University of Porto and the University of Southern California so they could make a decision about what was required for methodical analysis. The copper tubes belonged to the *Heimdall* crew now though, and we were all excited to ascertain what mysteries these containers held. There was something remarkable about copper tubes in our journey and considering what Rolf had dug up in the graveyard, we anticipated discovering something extraordinary that would impact our lives, and our journey, in a very positive way.

Before we set sail and headed north, Ulrik and Gudrun confirmed that they'd be flying to San Diego and meeting us at a small airport outside the logging settlement in the Laguna Mountains around the second week of August and promised that they'd call a day before leaving. We bid them farewell, all wondering what this new association might have in store for us in the future.

I was earnestly awaiting the reunion with Jonah and Roxanne; I missed them dearly and found myself yearning for Jonahs intelligent and insightful camaraderie. Roxanne also held an esteemed place in my heart, and although I had personally grown while she'd been away, I still missed her wit, wisdom, and knowledge about Viking archaeology and runic interpretation. Apparently Jonah had new information about our friend Regan Pendleton and the Rognvald relocation, and I was anxious to hear what he had to say.

The Captain and Rorek would be dry docking the *Heimdall* in San Diego harbor to repair damages incurred during the recent laser attack near Heart Island. While that was being done, the whole crew, and the newly reunited Anders and Angelina, would be fellowshipping and eating in the mountains at Jonah's property in Pine Valley, after which we all would be driving to Southern Utah for two weeks of holiday.

A call from Captain Janssen, on the Na Hearadh, informed us that he had unfortunately been experiencing mechanical problems and would have to dock in Seattle Washington to undergo repair. The estimates for completion were tentatively set at three weeks, but could possibly take as long as seven weeks depending on the availability of parts needed. Captain Janssen assured us that Anders ancient wooden vessel was perfectly safe and no one, other than his officers, was aware of its existence. He promised he would be in touch every few days to keep us all up-dated on the progress. Captain Janssen also informed us that my father was being flown over from Aberdeen Scotland to supervise some of the Na Hearadh's more difficult problems; afterwards Elwin was planning on meeting us in Southern Utah on August 20th for several days at the Rustic Lodge on Panguitch Lake. Jonah also told us the professor from Rabat Morocco had confirmed that he and several of his staff were also going to rendezvous with us at the lodge the very same days my father was going to be there. This was incredible news, it looked like we would be having our first ever summit meeting. The professor was presently on Montague Island in Alaska helping the newly arrived tribes work out some of the more elemental engineering problems in the first few weeks of operation. When he had concluded this work, he would be flying down to Utah to discuss details about the upcoming phase of our journey. Curiously he also mentioned having more information about the mysterious Underground River and would be sharing this with everyone present at the summit meeting. Apparently there were rumors that he had an unusual appeal for the crew, something that required the purchasing of brand new technology, and the training to operate it.

Four times now, on this voyage, we'd heard stories about the discovery of an Underground River in the northern Sea of Cortez. Garrett, Betsy, John, and I were all intrigued with the bits and pieces of information the professor had shared along with the others; we all had an odd premonition that this Underground River, Montague Island in Alaska, new technology, and Anders weird cousins, were going to become an integral and challenging part of our lives very soon.

The spiritual problems revealed to the original voyage, on Cedros Island, were now also plaguing us. Both voyages had been made aware of the same controversy, in the same location, five hundred and forty-two years separated, how bloody paradoxical this seemed. The early voyage had been deceived by the beliefs of an ancient sect known as the Troth and this pollution had been secretly deposited into their midst unawares. Like leaven in bread, it had festered to the point that the journey split apart because of Magnus and those who followed his deceptive spiritual choices. Someone in the original voyage, ostensibly had murdered Magnus Rognvald, possibly in retaliation for this insidious spiritual deception, or perhaps for something else. Could it be that the great and beloved King Agar could have been murdered by his own son and when he had been found out, Magnus Rognvald had been murdered on Cedros Island because of it? Ulrik and Gudrun Bjornson were also of the Elder Assembly of Troth and worshipped Odin, just as Magnus and his followers had. This rankled us deeply, especially Garrett. Now even Anders was unsure about what to do, and saw the possibility of inflammatory spiritual confrontation between parties forthcoming.

In mythology Odin was married to Frigga, and they had two sons, Balder or Baaldur, (which was my middle name and the name of the ancient tribe of Mortiken) and Hod. In the ancient Prose Edda, Balder/Baaldur was often revealed as a rather pallid, heathen imitation of Christ. The younger brother Hod was blind, so Loki, often seen as a Nordic satan, decided to use Hod's affliction to his advantage. Loki was jealous of Baaldurs status and formed an arrow dart from mistletoe. After being deceived by Loki, Hod unknowingly took this mistletoe arrow, (not Loki as some modern legends would have you believe), and killed his older brother Balder by mistake.

What was the significance here? I couldn't get this story out of my head and for days, in my waking hours, it had distressed me. Each night my dreams were progressively getting worse and I found myself awakening in pools of sweat and fearful of everything around me, none of it made any sense. What wisdom did I need to glean from these recurring dreams that would give us understanding about our present and upcoming circumstances? We were a Christian crew that followed Christ's teachings. Mythology wasn't a religion; mythology was creative stories filled with intriguing characters and rife with morals and lessons that were fun to read and learn from. For the most part, in my experiences, most people misunderstood the posture of mythology in modern literature and where mythology had started. This was what most intrigued me; the roots of mythology were apparently spiritual in nature and had something to do with fallen angels.

Now, for some unknown reason, God had given us two new players that didn't believe at all the way we did, they literally worshipped Odin, a mythological Nordic god. I wondered . . . was Odin simply an evil spirit bent on deceiving people into thinking Christ Jesus wasn't really the Most High God? Perhaps in our prayers and studies God would reveal to us how this new state of affairs might impact the journey ahead.

There was tension between the cousins and Anders now that hadn't existed before we'd found Magnus Rognvald's tomb underneath Cedros Island. Now the cousins knew, without any doubt, that Anders "the Norse" Vildarsen's loyalties were with us, and by his volition he'd become a member, and a fellow warrior, on the *Heimdall's* monumental journey. Aside from the insuperable spiritual differences between the cousins and Anders and the crew now, we all still had two keenly shared objectives, dealing ruthlessly with an ancient enemy known as the Mortiken, and the ongoing search for the Rognvald First Tribe.

Coming soon . . . ***A Monumental Journey 3, the Underground River***

Printed in the United States
27803LVS00002B/307-312